THE ESCAPE

Matthew Slater

PROLOGUE

The Wattson Estate. Vestige Island, Sovereign City. 11:35pm.

Bryan Wattson sat in his ornate armchair, lost in thought. The glass of scotch sat untouched on the desk next to him. His elbow had long since left an indent in the crushed leather, a closed fist sure to leave a red mark on his jawline as he leaned on it. His seating was slouched, having long since fallen into its usual position. It had been several minutes since a coherent thought had materialised in his mind, a factor perhaps accounted for by the time, though it was not uncommon for him to struggle with too many thoughts at once, each one fighting for supremacy. His mind, it seemed, was in perfect unison with the weather outside. There was a storm in full swing, the rain striking the windows with a sound like a whiplash. It assuaged the only other noise in the room: two harshly ticking clocks out of sync. The mobile phone on the desk nearby began to ring, interrupting the numbing ticks, and he picked it up. Rising from his chair into a stretch, he heard a familiar voice, its tone saturated with diffidence. His business partner, Tony.

'Midnight calls usually mean something very bad has happened.'

His business partner's voice sounded rushed, as though he didn't want to say what followed. Bryan sensed the apprehension. Thunder rocked somewhere outside, voicing its opinion on the cellular interruption.

'You got a minute? Is this line safe?' Tony asked reluctantly.

'What are you talking about? Of course it's safe.'

'It's just, I don't wanna say nothing without any prying ears, you know?'

'Spit it out, Tone.'

A throat clear and blast of static followed, sounding like lips too close to the mouthpiece.

'I've organised a deal, are you in?'

'What type of deal?'

A cough came down the line. 'The big D, man.'

Damn.

Bryan and Tony were the undisputed criminal kingpins of Sovereign City. Starting small, they had risen through the ranks doing all they could to gain valuable power, and it had worked. They owned the vast majority of the city's major companies and assets. Money makers and service providers. They occasionally undertook deals like this. Personally, Bryan didn't like drugs: he'd seen first-hand what they could do to people, and as such never touched them himself. To him, they were just business, and big business at that. Although all types of deals were possible: stolen cars; imported weaponry; you name it, 'the big D', as Tony had not so subtly put it, always gave Bryan chills. This sense of paranoia manifested strongly, and was perhaps why Bryan always oversaw these deals personally. Tony had explained the situation using small words and clumsy code, predicting correctly the personal involvement by Bryan. He and two small-time members of the organisation (for security, Tony had said, and their cuts would be less), would hand over the drugs in exchange for the money. At least his cut was sizeable.

'Textbook.' Tony said.

'What is it with you and suddenly doing backyard deals? I thought we were all about transparency in these things. Fifty-fifty.'

'I got a call the other day about some possible interest. They didn't say much, and weren't happy about talking on a traceable phone. They told me to head to a payphone in Sovereign Square. So we chatted. I ate a hotdog while we spoke from that vendor that does nice onions. Just trust me on this one. If all goes well, we get a few bucks each and clear out the garage a bit. No problem.'

Over the course of this exchange, Tony's voice grew somewhat in confidence, though Bryan knew that they wouldn't have gotten where they were without at least some measured caution.

2

'I hope not, 'cos you know if you mess this up, we'll have to have strong words.'

'Like you always say you will. Well, I mean, I've never led you astray before, right?' The question had a rhetorical twinge to it. Bryan let it slide. 'We'll come pick you up at 10am tomorrow. Get some sleep, it's *way* past your bedtime.'

'Screw you, Tone,' Bryan said through a smirk.

A click, and the line went dead.

Changing from his tailored business suit into a more comfortable T-shirt and jogging bottoms, Bryan stepped onto the landing, hanging the suit up in a wardrobe as he left. He really must fix that squeaking door. His mansion was located on an island adjoining the two main peninsulas which constituted Sovereign City. Obtaining it had taken some work, but he was proud of it. All the mementos of the mansion's previous owners were long gone. Yawning and rubbing his chin, he walked into his bedroom. Staring into the mirror in the ensuite, he splashed some water onto his face. The face looking back at him was... *tired.* It had bags under its bloodshot eyes; looking drawn out from excess work, stress and not enough sleep, exacerbated further by the red smear on his jaw from where he had been leaning on it earlier.

He wondered what age allowed him to state that he was getting too old for this shit.

The night passed uneasily, as was so often the case. However hard he tried not to; his thoughts tonight could not escape those of the deal. In a few hours he would be making it. Tony hadn't given him all that many details. All he knew was that he and two men whose existence he'd probably never considered would sell a large amount of heroin to someone else whose existence he'd definitely never considered. It sounded so watertight Bryan didn't understand where the hell his paranoia could *possibly* arise from. So typical of Tony to drop a deal on him mere hours before it was due to take place, shaky on the details with an

3

overall sense of 'too good to be true'. They weren't kids anymore. They couldn't afford to be brash in their way of doing things.

Still, he thought, *cash is cash.*

He glanced at his watch, the illuminated hands shining clearly in the dimly lit room. It was 8.21am, and in a little under two hours, the show would begin. Bryan wandered downstairs into the kitchen. After deciding against toast, he simply got dressed and sat down to wait for 10 o'clock.

It rolled around quicker than Bryan hoped it would, and a knock at the door and glance through the peephole confirmed that Tony wasn't making the whole thing up as one of his stupid jokes. Bryan opened it and saw the two men Tony had told him about. One of whom was Bryan's best friend, Phil. The two had known each other since they were both children and classed each other as brothers in all but name.

Bryan was astounded to see him. Not only had he made it plain he didn't want to live the criminal lifestyle anymore, he didn't normally wake up until much later than this. His strange sleep patterns amused Bryan. Something about his internal body clock working on a twenty-eight hour day. Nevertheless, they exchanged pleasantries and a friendly handshake as they met.

'And just what the fucking hell are you doing here?'
'Something about you being so damn useless that I need to come and bail your ass out. His Lordship...' – Phil's nickname for Tony – '...insisted I come along for this one. Cited your tendency to shit yourself on these sorts of deals.'
'Did he really?' Bryan said. 'Well, God damn. I asked for security and got a piss artist.'

The second lackey cleared his throat loudly, interrupting what surely sounded like two men who hated each other. His face Bryan vaguely recognised, but he couldn't quite put his finger on it.

4

'Mr. Wattson? We are here to pick you up and take you to the meeting.' Lackey number two said. Thick as pig shit. Fantastic.

'Well, there's a novelty. And who are you?'

'Mr. Tony sent us.' The man looked like he had muscles instead of brains.

'Fine, okay, whatever. Didn't want your damn name anyway. Let's get this over with.'

Tony was waiting in the car. The scheduled meeting place, Bryan was told, would be the airport, in a secluded spot behind a privately-owned aircraft hangar. The buyers wanted a straight-up exchange on open grounds, with minimal disturbance.

One suitcase for another. Simple.

The whole thing sounded so easy that the paranoia seemed unnecessary. Still, the airport was a big place, and with all the cargo and freight containers, and many dark corners, trouble could be anywhere.

Tony spoke, 'So, you still shitting yourself about this whole thing?' Bryan noticed Phil grin in the back seat.

'I tend to shit myself quite a lot when drugs are involved. You know that. And judging by the size of that suitcase, I'd say there's half of Columbia in there.'

'No, that's at the warehouse, getting rid of THAT comes next week.'

'Let's just get there and leave the sass at home, shall we?'

'The dudes who are buying it are arriving in a fancy helicopter. They're from South America or somewhere.'

'South America? What, like Brazil?'

'Not sure, couldn't really tell from their voices on the phone. And forgive me if I haven't got a degree in accents and dialect. Now, remember, you all know your cuts. We should make a fair few bucks out of this deal, but don't be stupid and start splashing cash left and right. Spread out. Spend little and often, not a shit load all at once. I'm saying this purely for the benefit of everyone, of course.' Tony finished, and Bryan noticed him look in the rear-view mirror at the anonymous associate, who was staring disinterestedly into the footwell.

Kid must be a rookie, Bryan thought. *He doesn't have the brains to be a veteran.*

He spun around in his seat to look at Phil.

'So, what're you doing on this deal, mate? What happened to working at Pratt and Sons?'

'Yeah, I went for the job, but it didn't pan out. I dunno if I told you, but one of the guys hassled me because I was new. Had to come up with a fake job history to cover up my past acts; and the other drones working there were less than impressed. They were all like,' - he changed to a dull voice, which spiked its pitch with each intonation - '*"This is a telephone. If you want to speak to the loading bay, press the button that says loading bay. You might need to wait a few seconds for it to patch through, though.'* Needless to say, I ended up exchanging heated works with the bloke in charge and telling him to stick it. I guess I handed my notice in shortly afterwards. So, this is the last ride, I guess. Unless it goes well, in which case sign me back into the crew again.'

Bryan laughed. It was good to see Phil again. He'd announced a while ago that he was quitting 'the business'. Bryan was saddened at the time, but in the end realised it was for the best. Phil had a wife and newborn daughter to look after, and if the worst should happen under his orders, Bryan would never live it down. They'd been through too much together. He really must make sure this was the last job Phil did, even if it meant pulling some strings so he could see his way forward into a less dangerous lifestyle. It wouldn't be too hard, and it wouldn't be as if Phil quitting would cause them to cut all ties. Most weeks they went and got smashed together.

Fun times, he thought, remembering their last session at their local watering hole, even if Phil didn't.

The airport loomed. The car drove round the back, and sure enough, a helicopter with two Dominican-looking men was waiting where the meet was to take place. A red stripe ran across its length, identification numbers tellingly absent. Bryan was armed as always, just in case. A .45 caliber, its sole function to tear through any trouble with chilling efficiency. Bryan, Phil and the lackey got out of the car. Tony spun the car around before getting out too. The buyers also exited, closing the door behind them with a metallic click. One of them spoke, his accent thick and unplaceable, but for the fact it was distinctly South American.

'Hello, my friends. I believe we are to do a deal? Did you bring the stuff?'
'You got the money?'
'Twenties and fifties, untraceable, as best we can.'
'The stuff is in this suitcase.'
'Okay, good. I will fetch the money from the chopper.'

He began to wander towards the helicopter. It was more of a swagger, as if he was on the wrong end of a bottle of scotch. Either that or he was the type of man to saunter everywhere without a care in the world. In this line of work, it was almost certainly the former. The other buyer's eyes were firmly fixed on Bryan. They were hard, unemotional. They widened slightly and Bryan thought he'd beat him in the staring contest they'd been having. He opened his mouth to speak, but simply gawked like a fish.

A gunshot rang out. Bryan's lackey fell forward like a rock, shot in the back of the head. The spray of brain matter coned out as he hit the dirt hard, not alive long enough to formulate a sound. Phil darted to the left and dove behind a freight container as a second round followed him. He didn't seem quick enough, as there was a loud thud, followed by silence and no other movement. Bryan tried to scream out, the death of his best friend hitting him harder than any bullet would. His heart and stomach exploded within his body, time slowing as the realisation caught up with him. The buyers and been hit as well. They were on the floor, blood smearing the suitcases and the chopper windscreen. The drug suitcase spilled open, white flakes scattering out of a pierced ziplock bag. The whole thing happened so fast, there was barely time to process it all.

What the fuck...? was just about all Bryan had time to think. With almost everyone dead, and his pistol firmly in its shoulder holster, it only left one shooter...

Bryan was shot in the back. His muddled thoughts were halted instantly as the bullet slammed into him. Pain stabbed at him and dull colours clouded his vision. He fell forwards, slamming onto the hard ground; his attempts to grab his sidearm were futile. He looked up, a jolt of pain running up and down his neck, and stared into the barrel of a gun, an evil smile and gloved hand located behind it.

Tony, and his best friend, Mr .44 Magnum. They had been partners in crime for years. And Bryan had been shot with it. How the hell was he still alive? He wondered what would happen next. Would he be shot? Left for dead? No, this was worse.

A fucking monologue.

It hit Bryan like a slap. Tony had taken care where to shoot him so he could gloat. It hurt almost as much as the bullet. Blood was spreading around him, touching his fingertips. It wasn't all his, some belonged to the dead lackey and the buyers. However, Bryan neglected to think about this. It just looked like an ocean of red, smearing the previously grey concrete without care. The pain was unbearable. His body seemed to have gone on strike about releasing adrenaline: he'd heard that could numb a surprising amount of pain.

'What's the matter, Bryan? You don't look so good. Are you feeling okay? Oh, wait. No. You've been shot, haven't you?'

'Bastard,' was all Bryan managed. Talking was agony.

'Naughty naughty, Bryan. It's not nice to talk to others like that. Did you really think that in this day and age, you would just be able to live like you do? Seriously, you must be stupider than you look.'

Bryan tried to reach up and grasp the barrel of the gun, but found his arms mysteriously refusing to obey him.

'You know I've been thinking about this takeover for ages. Months, really. Maybe even years. It feels better than I thought it would. Can't you taste it?'

'I'll kill you. I swear I'll kill you.' The words were as venomous as they were painful.

Tony ignored him. 'Yep. Tastes like victory.'

Bryan saw Phil peek out of cover. He was alive! He felt happy despite the pain, a sense of finality that at least his friend was okay. Tony was looking the other way, and Phil started to creep to the edge of the freight container. He had dropped his gun in the initial spray of lead and the shock which followed. What was he planning? Was he going to try and jump Tony? Bryan looked at him. Their eyes met as Tony glanced into the chopper, regarding the bullet holes in the windscreen and the corpse within. Bryan slowly shook his head, and Phil realised the futility of his actions. But he couldn't just leave his best friend, could he? Maybe he could come back after Tony had left?

Leave me. Save yourself.

Phil slowly nodded. Bryan tried to change his face to one of understanding, but simply coughed violently. Tony began to laugh at the pathetic excuse of a man on the floor next to him. Phil bolted for the fence, which was about ten metres away. He reached it and began to climb. As he reached the top, Tony spun round, not laughing anymore. He noticed Phil and levelled his gun. Before he could fire a shot, Phil dove off the fence behind an aircraft hangar. He landed street-side.

'Shit,' Tony said aloud, 'I'll have to get that prick later. Oh, I'm gonna have fun taking him, and his little family apart, piece by piece. Think I'll start with that daughter of his.'

Anger surged through Bryan and he longed for nothing more than to rip Tony's heart out, which he would have gladly done were it not for his arms not working and the rather large chunk of metal lodged in his spine. Phil had the sense to lay low for a bit, at least Bryan could be sure of that.

What was that? Sirens? If Bryan could stall Tony for a few minutes, they might *both* get arrested.

'Why did you do it?' Bryan asked, pain spiking at every word, the word 'do' turning into a liquefied cough.

'Are you joking? When you own most of Sovereign City, who wouldn't kill for that prize?'

'WE own Sovereign! Together!' Bryan groaned. It was true. They *were* business partners. Any sincerity that came through his words was genuine.

'No. YOU own Sovereign. You know you do.' Tony said, crouching next to Bryan. 'You've never considered me any more than a means to an end. Someone who gets shit done. I'm frankly baffled that you were too stupid, or *arrogant*, to consider doing the same to me. From Raegan to this fucking airport, here we are. Kinda beautiful, ain't it?'

So much for friendship. Bryan had never thought about putting Tony out of the picture. Clearly, it was the biggest mistake of his life. Bryan really thought he and Tony were friends. Hell, they'd been through enough together. But no, it was all about the power. Tony turned towards the helicopter, grabbed the suitcase full of money, shook off the excess blood and began to walk away. Sirens were getting louder, as if the police were only a couple of streets away.

'Wait...'

Tony turned. He had another, somehow different, yet still completely evil smile on his face. He kneeled in front of Bryan, their faces inches apart.

'What, Bryan? You gonna try and stall some more? Hope the cops turn up and arrest the both of us? Ha. I'll see you on the other side.' He began to laugh evilly, and the cold sound chilled Bryan through to his bones.

They weren't chilled for long, however.

The butt of the Magnum smashed into Bryan's face. It felt like a grenade had exploded next to him, and the pain like searing shrapnel. Blood streamed down his face, from his nose. He couldn't raise his arms to cover his face, he couldn't retaliate, all he could do was lie there in a cocoon of agony, trying desperately not to pass out. Tony entered the chopper and it left the ground, pushing the body of the second buyer onto the cold concrete. He had left the drugs, probably to further elongate Bryan's stretch. The police would pin everything on him. Everyone else it seemed was dead, after all.

Some minutes later, as Bryan's vision was starting to darken, a dozen armoured vans pulled up, followed by an army of officers in various amounts of body armour and carrying a dangerous array of weapons. Some had DEA stamped onto their armour, others simply SWAT. They all aimed at the bodies on the floor. The first out of the van to Bryan's nearest left slammed a gloved hand onto the side a few times as he stepped forward. He had apparently been nominated to reconnoitre. Drawn the short straw, maybe. He walked cautiously towards the bodies, assault rifle unflinching, lest any of them be playing a trick.

'What the hell happened here?'
'A bloodbath. Watch your back.'
'Holy crap! We got a live one here! Someone get a paramedic down here, now!'
'Anyone see where that chopper went?'
'Get the air force on it, we need to sort out this mess! Now shut up and *move*!'

The other officers lowered their weapons and moved towards him.

The officer who called for the ambulance knelt beside him, resting his assault rifle on the ground nearby as he fumbled with a pouch on his belt. He flipped up the visor on his helmet as he did so. In the course of his career, he had had to shoot and kill policemen like him. It was strange. In another reality, they could have been friends. Bryan looked at the policeman. His deep set eyes smouldered from underneath the visor, portraying a dark face void of emotion. He was about Bryan's age. No, definitely older.

Two people. Two sides of the same, twisted coin.

'Listen son; just because you've been shot don't mean you're getting off scot-free. You're going away for a long, long time.' He said, shaking his head.

He couldn't talk anymore. His breathing was laboured, and Bryan's last sight as he faded into unconsciousness was three sets of boots around him, their soles splattered with his blood.

CHAPTER ONE: A LONG, LONG TIME

Sirens. A revolver to the face. Morphine. One hell of a combination.

Bryan was carefully lifted into the back of an ambulance. The doctors kept him still as they drove to the hospital. Bryan had been shot before, but it was in the arm. Much less serious, although it hadn't felt like it at the time. He heard the paramedics discussing what would happen if the bullet had found its way into his spine. Chances are he wouldn't be walking again. Two police vans were following closely behind, three in front. They crossed Trestle Bridge. Sovereign City was made up of two main masses of land, separated by two bridges. Trestle Bridge went straight from one landmass to the other. The second – Vestige Bridge – was separated in the centre by a small island. This was where Bryan lived and was populated by around a hundred people. There had been lots of campaigning to get this island separated and given its own governance, but the mayor had regretfully denied it and the island was considered Sovereign's upper-class district. Conveniently, the mayor's second home was located on the same island, and much political controversy surrounded the issue.

As the ambulance crossed the bridge, the police vans amassed around it to create a rolling roadblock. The idea was that if anyone tried to intercept the convoy, everyone would know about it.

They arrived at the prison hospital. Bryan's first opinion would have been that it was an institution for the criminally insane. No colours at all, the walls were painted various shades of grey. The doctors didn't help either. They were dressed in green coveralls with face masks on. They looked like zombies. Each one looked as if they despised the day they'd received their medical degrees and been shipped to the hospital. The pain was all but nonexistent and had been replaced with a feeling of light-headedness. The amount of morphine pumped into him was close to overdose, but it was keeping him alive.

At least that's one thing. I'm not gonna die here. As unappetising as prison sounds, it's better than kicking the bucket on some operating table.

I hope.

Bryan was wheeled into the operating theatre. White tiles this time, the employees were probably sick of all the grey. The orderlies moved him from the cart to the table. Doctors fondled masks and instruments before crowding around Bryan. One of them introduced himself as Doctor Townsend and fitted Bryan with a mask. There was nothing positive in his voice. It took a few seconds for the mask to work, though in his opium-induced state Bryan could barely tell. It finally began to work, pumped gas through and Bryan felt a bitter taste in his mouth before the room blackened.

The operation to find and dislodge the bullet, remove it and to patch Bryan up took eight hours. It left Bryan feeling rough afterwards. He felt like a spear was lodged in his back, and any movement pushed it deeper. Nevertheless, he would be alright. It was a miracle the bullet missed his spine, but it had entered at an angle which meant it was slowed down somewhat before hitting anything important. Every day for what felt like forever the doctors would come in, look at the wound for about a good while, and then leave. None of them would answer any of his questions, like how long he would be here or whether there was permanent damage. It was always 'We can't be sure', or 'We just don't know.'

One nurse called Naomi regularly spoke to Bryan. She was roughly ten years younger than he was, but Bryan got the feeling the things he'd seen were nothing compared to her experiences. She seemed to fill the room with positive energy.

'So, Bryan, how are we feeling today?' They were on first-name terms. It always seemed strange to Bryan that a nurse would get so friendly with someone like him.

I'm a criminal, for Christ's sake! She should be scared, if anything.

But she wasn't. Maybe she was the sort of optimist that saw the best in everyone. She reminded him of Phil, in a way. Bryan wondered where he was now. He could be miles away from Sovereign by now. Or he could be in a box in the ground.

'Well, considering the fact that I'm likely to go to prison for a long time, not bad I guess.'

'Well, your injury's healing nicely, so at least you'll be replacing these four, grey walls with....'

'Four grey walls?' Bryan cut in.

'Well, yes.' She said flatly. 'However, you're likely to get a shortened sentence because of this injury. And you might even get a window.'

Bryan actually laughed at the joke. *'Fantastic.'* Then he remembered. 'That's if I don't get the chair.'

She looked at him in a funny way. *Buzzkill.* She walked over to the various drips and instruments monitoring Bryan. She scribbled some things down onto a clipboard she was carrying.

'Well, Bryan, you're still alive. That's a good thing, and there's nothing else to report that's bad, so that's good as well. If that's all, then I guess I'll be seeing you for another day.'

'Thanks, Naomi. And I'll be sure to lodge a letter of complaint if I don't get a window.'

She went to leave. As she neared the door, she stopped and turned.

'Listen, it's none of my business or anything, but don't you want to let people know you're okay? Family or something? It's just, you've been here a while and not mentioned anyone.'

Bryan sighed. It was true, he did want to let people know he was okay, but it wasn't really worth it. Despite being successful, he didn't have a family to speak of. An only child, and he hadn't spoken to his parents for years. Not that it was *their* fault. That left only Phil and his brother Michael, and he wouldn't call either of them even if he had a contact number, should it put their wellbeing in danger for whatever reason.

'I'm not sure it's worth it. I don't quite think you'd understand if I told you. Or maybe you would. But thanks for asking.'

He hoped he wasn't too abrupt in his answer. She seemed to get the message.

'Oh, okay then. Never mind. I'll see you tomorrow.'

'Goodbye, Naomi.'

She left. Bryan wondered how long these little conversations would continue. He had been in hospital for two months. Over that time, he worked out the full extent of what happened at the airport. He realised people weren't as good as he thought. His sense of humour had all but dried up, replaced by anger at himself and his fellow man.

He wished the gunshot would take as long as possible to heal. Anything to prolong being a free man.

Well, free-ish.

Weeks of physiotherapy passed before the inevitable happened. Bryan got up and began to walk unaided. He'd initially thought the people he'd seen on TV and read about were faking it, or over emphasising for the sake of the cameras. But no, they were right. It was as difficult as it was painful. The doctor had described it as muscular atrophy: when a muscle wastes away due to lack of use. He nearly fell over two or three times, but still refused the stick offered to him by Naomi. She beamed at him, and he managed a smile back. It felt hollow, though.

This is it, then.

That night, Bryan slept uneasily. His dreams kept returning to thoughts of that day, two months back. The day he had sworn an oath to himself to exact revenge. He would not forget. Ever.

People will creep up on you and stab you in the back. The only person I can trust anymore is Phil, and I don't even know where the hell he is.

Three armed police officers arrived in his room the next day. They walked with him out of the hospital cell and into what appeared to be a hastily-assembled interview room. This became a sort of home-away-from-home for the next few days, with a total of twenty-one interviews asking him various probing questions. At an hour long each; Bryan thought it was a bit much.

But he didn't complain. Not that it would have made a difference if he did.

After the interviews had been completed and the word of Bryan's full recovery had passed around the hospital, two different policemen came into his room. They seemed spiteful as they spoke.

'Hello, Mr. Wattson. Let's get you to prison. You have the right to remain silent, and all that shit.'

Bryan was tempted to revoke that right and scream like a madman, but decided against it. They didn't need more of a reason to hate him. Simply being alive was reason enough.

They hauled him out of bed, handcuffed him, and escorted him outside. Bryan didn't resist. He had however many years to figure out to get revenge. There was no point struggling now. He passed Naomi in the corridor. She looked saddened at the fact that he was leaving. He smiled at her as they left; she smiled back.

Maybe I was wrong. Not all people are bad...

He got into the police cruiser. He didn't speak to either policeman on the journey. They kept making jokes at his expense, turning the radio up whenever it mentioned the trial. It wasn't far. He would have his trial at a court close to the prison grounds. There was no question of 'innocent'. It was simply how long his sentence would be. The police car pulled up; the courthouse loomed. Bryan entered. He wasn't even allowed to change from his hospital attire.

Great. Now I'll look like a mental patient in front of everyone...

They entered the courtroom. He didn't get a lawyer. This whole thing was just a sham to humiliate him in front of everybody. Or for the paperwork. Serious criminal trials usually take weeks to complete, but not his. Bryan remembered a case in a nearby city taking three months to come to a close. The man in the smart suit at the front of the courtroom began to speak.

'Court is now in session. The case of Bryan Wattson against Sovereign City is now underway. All rise for Judge Hartmann in the chair.'

Time passed. The allegations made against him were never ending, supposed witnesses and insiders throwing in their two cents to help the process along. Bryan lost count of the allegations. It was at least twenty-five, he reckoned. His career seemed to span longer than he could remember. Half of the things mentioned Bryan had even forgotten about doing.

'And so, Mr. Wattson. We have now noted all the allegations. Do you have anything to say for yourself?'

Bryan was silent. There was simply no point.

'Very well. The judge will now take a few minutes to consider his decision.'

The judge left, and everyone sat down. Bryan wondered exactly he was doing while 'considering his decision'. Probably putting his feet up, spiking a cup of coffee with his spirit of choice and laughing to himself about how open-and-shut this case was.

He was gone for ten minutes. Bryan imagined a Roman emperor gesturing thumbs-down at a coliseum. His life was almost certainly over. He cringed as he waited for the judge to read it out. Then again, he had been expecting it. He was being judged for all his actions in the past. Today, he would find out just how much the gods despised him.

Judgment Day.

'Yes, he's leaving the courthouse now.' The journalist exclaimed, a flick of the hair as she turned to look back at the camera. 'Bryan Wattson, one of Sovereign City's greatest and most powerful criminals, has been found guilty. Convicted of his crimes, he will serve 30 years imprisonment, although it has already caused some controversy that he did not receive the death sentence.

'It has been said that Mr. Wattson received over thirty-five allegations, and was convicted for possession with intent to supply a Class A drug, amongst other things. However, not all is as it seems, because he was found and arrested at the scene of a botched drug deal with a severe gunshot wound to the back.

Clearly, his allies were not as trusted as first thought. We have received information that he spent at least two months in hospital recovering before he was brought before the court earlier, and it was that very gunshot wound which influenced the decision made. More on this news story as we find out more.

'In other news, a mountain of foreign and domestic immigrants has rocked the nearby town of Ridgewater. Although it isn't clear why at this time, the recent uncovering of illegal gambling dens and illicit brewing of alcohol are thought to be the source of blame. Details of this story can be found on our website, the link to which is on your screens now.

'That's all for now, I'm here live, at Sovereign City courthouse, for Channel 1 Action News. Back to the studio.'

The journalist packed her things away into the back of her van. The cameraman wanted to get away as soon as possible, but she refused, so he occupied himself by filming the courthouse. She watched Bryan as he was escorted. She noted the lack of emotion, and thanked the stars that this was her case. The pay would be enormous.

Bryan did not notice the woman staring at him as he was led into a car and taken to the prison. He went through a full body search, an icy cold shower, photos were taken, fingerprints stamped and he changed into the filthiest prison jumpsuit ever seen, making the hospital attire look steam-cleaned by comparison. It smelt like its previous occupant. A prison tag was strapped onto his wrist, identifying both himself and the prison. He was told that there would be severe consequences were he to remove it. He was given an I.D. number, R3-T4-L5, freshly sewn onto the back and breast pocket. It was the cleanest thing about his new clothing, and would be his name for the next thirty years. He wasn't looking forward to it. He couldn't help but feel a gnawing emptiness at having his freedom suddenly taken away. His cell was located on Cell Block D. Nicknamed 'The Pit', it had long, metallic spiral staircases at each end leading up to a walkway which housed more cells. Bryan was located at the far end on the ground floor, right next to the walls of the prison. It was both good and bad. Good because the prison officers could never be bothered to reach the end, hammering on the cell bars with their truncheons as they walked up and down. The *BAD* news was that Bryan had to listen to shouts from other cells as he walked to his own, which ranged from jeers and torrents of abuse, to irritating, starry-eyed awe from a couple of the younger kids who knew about his exploits.

Bastards. It's bad enough that I'm here in the first place, without having to listen to the crap coming from everyone else as well.

So, this was it. It could have been worse. Bryan could have gotten the chair. But what annoyed him more than anything was that Tony was still running free, governing Bryan's empire, making use of *his* assets, raking in *his* money. Hatred flared up again, and he slowly exhaled to calm himself down.

It took a few months before people began to understand that Bryan just wanted to be left alone. He was walking along the cell block, when a fellow inmate who was leaning against the bars of his cell spat at him.

He laughed as Bryan glared at him, rubbing the spittle from his cheek. 'Sorry about that, big-shot. I'm sure you don't like mixing with us common folk, but spittin's what we do.'

Just because Bryan had money he was hated by a lot of people. They weren't bothered about the things he had to do to obtain the money at all. The inmate was called McCarthy, and was in for life for murder. He was surprisingly small. Most murderers Bryan had encountered were built like brick shithouses. McCarthy continued insulting him and pulling faces until Bryan walked up to the cell. The other inmate stepped away slightly.

'What're you gonna do, Bryan? Throw one of your tax forms at me?' He sneered.

Bryan had had enough. He reached through the bars, grabbed McCarthy's jumpsuit and slammed his face forward against the bars. Bone snapped in McCarthy's nose and blood seeped from it. He swore very loudly and fell against the bars, grasping at his face. He was making rather a lot of noise.

'Say stuff about me again, McCarthy, and I'll break more than just your nose.' Bryan said calmly.

He walked off, footsteps echoing down the empty corridor. Bryan had no time for people like that. One of the prison guards wandered over to see what the fuss was about. He saw the state of McCarthy's face and radioed for the infirmary. He didn't, however, go after Bryan. He was new, and didn't particularly want to make an enemy of Bryan Wattson. But fights were nothing new. Just part of prison life. Chances were Bryan would suffer the same or even worse at some point. Bryan returned to his cell. He was against beating people unnecessarily, but he also wasn't a man to be mocked. He just wanted to be left alone, so he could think of a decent revenge strategy. Other inmates had rushed to their cell bars to see what happened when McCarthy swore, but stepped well away when Bryan walked past. No-one else said anything like that to Bryan again. Everyone just addressed him as various shortened versions of his identification number, or even more simply, Wattson.

Daily life in prison was always the same. Rise at 8.00am, exercise, work and eating, then lights out at 8.30pm. Bryan had heard of people who were so used to the routine that once released they had tried to get themselves imprisoned again, or worse. Bryan only hoped he would be better than that. The only bonus he had was that he'd be too busy killing Tony to think about ending it all.

Thirty years.

Prisoner Identification Number R3-T4-L5 settled down for a long shift in prison.

CHAPTER TWO: TEN YEARS IN THE MAKING

Ten years later, 21:57pm.

Bryan lay in his cot, staring out of the window. The moonlight spilt in through the barred windows, dying the cell an off-white hue. It added a sort of tranquillity to the harsh brick.

Bryan heard the background *swishing* sound of a nightstick spinning on a string. A prison officer poked his head around the side of the bars, glancing instinctively into each corner of the cell. It was Officer Brandon. He had begun working at the prison two months into Bryan's stint. Over the years, they had become friends, which Bryan found to be mildly ironic. Not many inmates associated themselves with the screws. Bad blood. Bryan wasn't bothered. He'd made associates in the other inmates, and at first assumed that having an officer on his side might be beneficial. But over the years, he realised that they were more like friends than someone he could simply use to help him get by. He worked night shifts and spoke to Bryan whenever possible. He made the effort to walk all the way along the cell block's considerable length to Bryan's cell, just to make conversation. Bryan had considered that maybe they had been in the same situation, no other people to interact with in their respective newfound social groups.

'E'ning, Bryan.'
'What's up, Malc?'
'Not much, really. Just checking how you were.'
'A third of the way through this thing. Pretty momentous, is this year.'
Bryan turned and sat up. He looked at Brandon. There was something friendly in those eyes. They were the same colour as the moonlight.
'How are Barbara and the kids?' Bryan continued, genuinely wanting to know.
'Not bad. Really difficult to believe it's almost ten years since I started to work here. Barb still wants me to be a lawyer.'

Bryan smiled. 'Somehow I don't see that happening.'

'Me neither, to be honest. She thinks it's too dangerous in this job... blah blah blah. I have it worked out, by the way, how long I've been here.' He slipped the truncheon into his belt and replaced it with a small notebook, proceeding to flip it open and announce, 'Every day I add another line to the tally chart. Years, months, weeks and days. As of right now, it's nine years, nine months, three weeks, one day. Oh, and about twenty-seven minutes.'

'Ha. Not a perfectionist at all then? And besides, I'm sure being a lawyer is *way* more cut-throat than this job.'

This talk of Brandon wanting to change career cast his mind back to Naomi. During one of their friendly chats she hinted that she wanted to move on with her life.

'I don't like having to see people like you day in, day out.' She was saying. 'It starts to grate after a while.'

'I can imagine that. People like me?'

'Yeah. Criminals, I guess. Hurt people. We see all types of injuries and wounds here, and not one person shows any signs of regret. Not one. They all just think 'Well, if I'm not dead now I can carry on tomorrow with some other terrible crime.''

'I regret what happened.' Bryan said.

'You do?'

'Yeah. Think about it. If I hadn't been shot, then I'd still be making tons of money with no problems.'

'You know that's not what I meant.'

Silence.

'So, you want to... move on?'

'Yep. I don't like this job. It's horrible. It upsets me a little. I want to get out. Make use of this doctorate I've got.'

'But you're a doctor. Wherever you go there'll be blood, and death. You can't escape it. Everyone needs stitching up, or to be pumped full of God knows what.'

'I don't mind that. What I do mind is the lack of hope in this place. There's nothing. I want to move somewhere where there is hope. Where I can make people feel better, rather than physically being in top health.'

'You should be a shrink.'

But there was that positive energy again. It followed her like a pleasant aroma. It was from that point that Bryan decided he liked Naomi. He wanted her to get out, even if he couldn't...

'Well, I think you should leave. Get the hell out before you go crazy. I think you're the kind of person to make people feel better. I mean, look at me. I've never been able to express myself easily. Until we started to chat. And even starting the chats was your doing.'

'Anything to stop you being such a miserable bastard.' She said, before smiling.

'Oh, thanks...' Bryan paused. He looked at her with a slight smile.

'What?'

'No, it's nothing. You did a swear. You never swear.'

'I... did a swear?' She sniggered.

'You sure did!' Bryan laughed. It felt good to be around her. She laughed too, then her face changed. For the better.

'But you know what? I think I will consider a little change of career. Thank you, Bryan Wattson.'

She left, and at that moment Bryan realised he'd miss her when he eventually left. He'd miss her a lot.

Back in the prison, a strange *boom* came from down the corridor. It was distant, like someone had set a giant firework off outside. Nevertheless, it rocked the cell doors, shaking Bryan out of his nostalgia.

'What the hell was that?' Brandon asked.

'Hell if I know. There some kind of party going on down there? Sounded like it came from the security room. I'll bet it's that idiot Officer Treston again. If a monkey falls out of a tree in Papua New Guinea he'll have a party to celebrate gravity being there. I've told him he'll get fired for it, one day...'

'I didn't know there were monkeys in Papua New Guinea, Malc.'

'Don't they have zoos over there?' Brandon wasn't really looking at him.

A gunshot rang out. The noise was chillingly obvious in the quiet. Another. A third.

'Holy shit.' Brandon reached for his radio. Bryan got up and walked to the bars. He looked around the corner, trying to fit his head through the bars. A silhouetted figure was striding towards them.

'Control? This is Brandon. What was that, over?' He thought the silhouette was a guard. It quickened its pace, before breaking into a sprint. It was heading straight for Brandon. He reached for his gun. He fumbled with the holster and desperately tried to bring his weapon to bear.

'Freeze!' he yelled. The silhouette was about five metres away. Brandon levelled his weapon.

A sharp *thwack* as the butt of a gun slammed into the bridge of Brandon's nose. The impact made Bryan jump back. Brandon fell backwards, blood covering his face. The pistol in his hand flew away, scattering into the middle of the walkway. The attacker levelled his gun and aimed at Brandon's head. It was a pump-action shotgun, strong enough to blow his face off. Bryan lunged forward and shouted, attempting to grab the attacker through the bars.

'Wait! Don't kill him, you crazy bastard!'

The attacker hesitated, sidestepping Bryan's flailing hand. Rather than pulling the trigger, he forcefully battered Brandon with his weapon butt, knocking him unconscious and silencing the nasally gurgles of pain. He lowered his weapon and turned. Bryan could see he was wearing a gasmask, like those worn by insertion troops. Probably to negate the dust caused by the explosion. A thin layer of it appeared to cover his shoulders and hair. The shadowed figure carried a pistol in a chest holster and a third weapon slung over his back. A submachine gun. He wore body armour and to Bryan seemed like Special Forces, sent to eliminate everyone in the prison in a twisted act of pest control. There was a small army recruitment office with barracks and all the trimmings on the island. The Sovereign City Unified Military. Maybe he had been sent by them, which also probably meant there were more elsewhere.

25

The attacker faced Bryan. He pumped his shotgun. An empty shell fell onto the ground, rolled and touched Bryan's shoe. So it was him who fired one of the shots earlier.

Great. I'm going to be shot by a man who looks like a shadow. So much for getting out of here alive. Bryan's thoughts ended with a cascade not of fear, but disappointment.

The attacker lifted his gasmask, exposing a flushed face with intense eyes.

'You?' Bryan said, amazed at what he saw.

It was Phil. Bryan could not believe what he was seeing. He just stood there, gawping. His mind blanked, unable to process that his best friend was standing in front of him. His feet felt leaden, his mouth dried up. He didn't feel happiness per se, perhaps because he couldn't comprehend that he was being rescued. Bryan found himself leaning his weight against his back foot and reaching forwards for the cell bars to stop himself from falling over. Relief washed over him, pushing out thoughts that he was going to be executed. Phil only regarded him for a moment before getting straight back to business.

'Might want to step back.' Phil said.

Bryan did so. Phil shot the cell door where the lock was and heaved, but it didn't actually move. It was quite useless to try. They were made for tougher punishment than a single shotgun shell. Phil grunted.

'What the hell are you doing here?' Bryan asked, suddenly breathless.

'What does it look like? Saving your arse. Listen, I'll have time to explain later.'

Phil handed him the submachine gun and two spare magazines through the bars. Bryan's jumpsuit didn't have pockets, so he had to hold onto them awkwardly instead. He dropped the mask down again and tapped it with the side of his palm, nudging it into position.

Phil grabbed the radio from his belt. He spoke into it.

'Team B, this is the gaffer. I have the package. Ready the distraction, over.'

Distraction? What fucking distraction?

Bryan soon found out. A loud alarm blared and the room was filled with the sounds of scraping metal. All the cells were being unlocked! The air filled with the sounds of prisoners leaping and running, shouting with delight at their sudden freedom. Bryan was still dumbfounded. His thoughts were fuzzy, a television with static.

'Hey, that guy opened all the doors!' One of the convicts yelled.

'Hey nice one, man! I owe you a drink!'

'Shut the fuck up and get moving, Crispy, we're all home free now, boys!' A third bellowed, barely distinguishable over the din of the other inmates.

Bryan thought he heard another inmate scream his name, but it was indiscernible amongst the cacophony and colliding bodies.

'Oi! Numpty!' Phil shouted, 'What are you playing at? Move it!'

Phil had made his way down the cell block. Bryan followed suit. They left Brandon slumped meekly on the floor. The hole made in the wall was large, and it looked like a lot of explosives were used. Bryan and Phil stepped outside. There were several other men, dressed like Phil, clearly part of the same operation. A stray inmate passed through the hole, not looking where he was going and ran into Phil, staggering backwards in terror as he saw all of the automatic weapons.

'Err, hi.' Bryan said awkwardly to Phil's associates. He got a couple of nods in return. He was thrown a ballistic vest and awkwardly struggled into it. It wasn't his size.

'Alright lads, we've got the target, time to disperse. If you make it, lay low for a bit and then meet me at the rendezvous in a few days. Good luck.' Phil explained.

Bryan was anxious. *If you make it.*

The police could be everywhere. As it turned out, he was right.

Sovereign City State Penitentiary is located on a small island off the mainland. The builders had seen documentaries about Alcatraz and liked what they saw. There was only one bridge on and off the island, and it was thirty metres long. The rest of the island was surrounded by sea. Easy to see and even easier to guard, the prison reminded Bryan of a cartoon haunted house or castle, perched precariously on a hill. There was also a pier for boats and a helipad just below the bridge. It was secure, to say the least.

The hole in the wall led to a concrete square, where several cars were parked. Bryan and Phil could see the bridge over the ledge. They had to go all the way around the side of the island to reach it. However, two prison security cars screeched to a halt in front of them, handbrake-turning 90 degrees to form cover. The members of Phil's team levelled their weapons and begun to fire. Bryan dove behind a car and hit the floor painfully as the windscreen exploded, his gun flying from his grip and landing out of cover as he prioritised his own survival over that of his gun. He decided to risk it. His hand darted out of cover and gripped the snout of the gun, reeling it towards him in a move that he was convinced would get his fingers shot off.

Not what you'd call dignified, but at least I've got my gun back.

Phil dropped into cover next to him. A loud bang and a spray of light erupted near the policemen. It was a flashbang, designed for soldiers to use when breaching doors or entering unknown spaces to disorient occupants. The sounds of gunfire seemed to get louder and louder. Added to this was the sound of a malfunctioning siren as bullets slammed into the parked cars. The officers went down, but managed to take one of Phil's men with them. He screamed, which quickly turned into a watery gurgle.

'Shit! They got Murphy!' one of Phil's team shouted.

'Leave him! We've got to move! We can't stay here!'

Phil smashed the butt of his weapon into the window of the car and pulled open the door. The other members did the same. A frantic minute of hotwiring later, two cars pulled away, one contained Bryan, Phil and two of the team. The other contained the remaining four members, and followed closely behind. The journey around the island seemed to take forever. A police officer leaned out the passenger seat window of a tailing car and fired his pistol repeatedly. A loud bang made Bryan look backwards as the rear car rocketed over the ledge, flecks of shot-out tyre floating down the mountainside. Bryan looked out of the window to see it hit the water.

'Somebody get that car off our arse!' Phil shouted; too busy driving to do it himself. A bullet smashed into the driver's side wing mirror, tearing it off its hinges.

The two men in the back seat kicked out the rear window and fired at the police car as they turned. One shot found its mark, and the police car ground to a halt, horn blaring as the hit driver slammed forwards into the steering wheel.

As the car neared the wide open space before the bridge connecting the prison island and the mainland, a police car appeared out of nowhere, its occupants firing wildly, and Phil had to swerve to avoid a collision. In the chaos the car ran off the road, and came to a stop on a small patch of grass, although it was actually more mud than turf. The car spluttered, and failed to start. Phil cursed, and smacked the steering wheel with his gloved palm. Bryan looked out the window. There were two police cars between them and freedom. The car had spun round at an angle so if they got behind it, they would be in a good point of cover. Gunfire erupted once more. Bryan opened the door and dropped out. Phil slid into Bryan's seat and out the open door. A bullet slammed into the head of the man sitting behind Bryan, spraying blood onto the headrest. The final occupant then had to clamber over the lifeless body to reach the outside.

'Okay,' this was Phil, 'Tamzen, flashbangs up. When I throw mine at that car, you throw yours at the other one. Bryan, when they go off, put some fire on those cops in that car. Then...' he turned to Bryan, 'We'll run and gun on the other car. The car's knackered, so we'll have to foot it. Ready?'

Phil pulled the pin of the flashbang. He hurled it at the police car. Tamzen did the same with his. A loud bang and bright light erupted next to both cars. Bryan calmly inhaled, before standing up. He emptied a clip into the car, tagging one of the policemen, before reloading and doing the same with the other. His aim was far from perfect, a solid mixture of a lack of practice and awkwardly holding both his gun and ammunition at the same time. Meanwhile, Phil and Tamzen sprinted around the car, only getting a few parting shots as they were focusing more on running. Bryan finished firing and decided to make a run for it. It was his last magazine anyway, so what the hell. He slid across the bonnet and sprinted for the bridge. Phil and Tamzen made it across and were beckoning to him. Bryan began to cross the bridge, his desire to escape driving him on.

A helicopter slowly began to rise from beneath the bridge. It was a military-grade assault chopper, equipped with quality ordinance. Racks of missiles, and two machine guns, not to mention a spotlight, infra-red and thermal sensors. Bryan wasn't aware of the chopper until its machine guns spoke, tearing apart the car Bryan had been using for cover mere moments before. The sound of firing bullets and exploding tyres coincided with flying glass and tearing metal.

Bryan made it two thirds of the way across the bridge before the helicopter turned its attention onto him. It launched a concussive shell, which impacted with a low percussive boom at the start of the bridge, catching Bryan in the blast. The force hurled him through the air, wind whistling in his ears and stinging his eyes as he flew. He landed at the other side of the bridge, rolled twice before coming to a painful halt.

Bryan's vision was blurred. The world seemed to slow down as he turned over to face the chopper. He dragged himself to his feet. He could hear his heartbeat. It seemed irregular. The chopper hovered in front of him, over the bridge. The two objects: man and machine faced each other off. Bryan could just see the shadowed head of the pilot in the helicopter and was sure he would be laughing as he reached to fire the helicopter's machine guns.

Clear of the bridge on the other side, Tamzen turned to Phil.

'Are we just gonna let that happen to him?' He shouted over the sound of the rotors.

'Well, to be honest, I was gonna let him squirm for a bit longer, but we should probably do something. Let Michael know we've pulled the pin.'

Tamzen reached for a radio. Phil smirked as Bryan braced himself, before lifting up a small remote, and pressing it melodramatically.

The helicopter disappeared as the bridge beneath it exploded. Phil had a detonator, as did Michael back at the garage, just in case something happened to Phil. The resulting fireball engulfed the helicopter and Bryan heard the sound of it smashing into the water beneath the bridge and the rotors breaking as they struck rock. He was thrown roughly onto his backside, ears ringing to the point it blocked out all other thought.

Bryan was dumbstruck. What had just happened? It took several seconds of open-mouthed musing for him to figure it out. He turned to Phil, who was clapping and laughing. Tamzen looked over the side of the bridge. From his high vantage point, Tamzen saw a small speedboat containing a single man cruising away to the east. At least someone else had survived.

'What the hell was that?' Bryan shouted at the top of his lungs, to overcome the ringing.

'Detonator. What else?'

'You bastard!' Bryan tried to sound angry, but ended up smiling. It was good to see Phil. Then he suddenly asked, 'What the hell are you doing here?'

'You really think I was gonna let your arse rot for thirty years? You clearly don't know me, Bryan.'

'Yeah, I'm touched. But why wait ten bloody years to spring me?'

31

'Because of your former business associate. Decided he didn't like me being alive anymore. I had to escape. I legged it to England for a bit. Settled down. Cornwall. You'd like it. Very tranquil.'

'Tony? Jesus...'

The sound of sirens in the distance broke the calm reunion. There was a car a short way away.

Perfect. I could probably hotwire that model.

'Listen, we've gotta get out of here.' It was still Bryan talking. 'Get in that car. And ditch those damn masks. You look like Halloween rejects.'

The three men clambered into the car. Bryan tore open the panel under the steering wheel and began to fumble with various wires.

'Get the guns hidden. Heads down.' Bryan mumbled, a red wire in his mouth while he spoke. Phil and Tamzen hid the guns under a tartan blanket on the back seats. The car coughed into life, and Bryan reversed, spinning a 180 as he drove on. Police cars began to encircle the area around the bridge, and Bryan's slightly erratic driving style (although not driving for ten years probably had something to do with it) made them look like prison officers fleeing the scene. They drove in silence. The car fumbled and spluttered occasionally as Bryan misjudged the clutch.

'Jesus. Like riding a bike my ass.'

'Whoa a minute, Bryan. Slow down. Do you even know where you're going?'

'Erm... no, not really.' Bryan slowed.

'Right, so there's no point driving around at a million miles an hour, is there? Now listen, first of all, the pleasantries. Bryan, this is Tamzen. Tamzen, Bryan. And I'm Phil. I'm not an alcoholic; I just like to give little speeches. We're going to Michael's garage. It isn't too far from here.'

'Did that really just happen? I mean, we *are* sitting in a car, driving away from a scene of carnage at a prison, right? I didn't just dream the whole thing?'

'Not on your nelly. Face it, B, you're a free man.'

Bryan's head was still spinning as they turned a corner, stopping outside an autoshop. It was locked up, with a small amount of light coming from a window which presumably housed an office.

'Well, here we are.' said Phil.

The auto shop was called Mickey's Motors. The outside had a vague smell of gasoline. Phil got out of the car. Tamzen clambered into the driver's seat when Bryan left it.

'Alright, that went better than expected. You know the drill, T. Ditch the car, lay low. We'll contact you soon.' Phil explained.

Tamzen tuned the radio until a song he apparently liked chimed out. He began to drum the steering wheel with his fingers in tune with it. He nodded at Phil, glanced at Bryan, and said 'Maybe I might have some work for you at some point, eh Bryan? Bye, Phil.'

It was the first time Bryan had heard him speak. He sounded somewhat hoarse and gruff, as if he used to be a heavy smoker, but had stopped recently. He didn't say anything, just nodded slowly as Tamzen drove off. Phil stood a few metres away, gesturing at the now open door with a smug expression on his face.

'What? Is this still a game to you?' Bryan fumed.

'Jeez, B, mellow out. You've always been like this: blow your stack at the slightest thing. Remember how crazy you went when I pushed your bike into the road when we were kids?' Phil recalled.

'Wait, you told me it was stolen!'

'Yeah, it was. But I stole it back, and *then* decided to push it into the road anyway, for giggles.'

Bryan waved him away, refusing to let his choler rise further. 'Nice place. Different to what I remember. Mainly the location.'

'Yep. Lots changed. We figured the best plan was to move away from Tony and his surprisingly large reach. Luckily, Michael almost never had anything to do with him, so Tony left him alone. Never did get why.'

'And all the time you were sunning in Cornwall?'

'Freezing my arse off more like. So... are you gonna stand there all night or are we gonna go inside?'

'Lead on.'

The garage was pokey, to say the least. There was room for maybe one and a half cars and stacks of tyres, boxes and disinfectant lined the rear wall. The pit for looking at the underside didn't look like it had been accessed for years. Phil led Bryan to a small room at the back, containing a bed, clock and not much else.

'Well, here she is. Your home for the next few weeks.'

'Not exactly what I had in mind. But I suppose it's better than a cell.'

'That sounded suspiciously like you were moaning, despite the fact that I've just ran the risk to save you, and I've got half a dozen dead guys back up at the prison. We're just lucky I said no identifying tags or marks. Not that it would make a difference, considering the waterlogged state of half of them...'

'Look, we'll discuss this tomorrow. It's...' Bryan glanced at his wrist, before realising he wasn't wearing a watch. The clock on the wall would have provided a solution, were it working. He simply decided to say 'late.'

'Ten to midnight.'

It had been the best part of two hours since his conversation with Brandon, but it felt to Bryan like two minutes.

'Wow,' he said without realising it.

He regarded his oldest friend properly for the first time since they had escaped.

No, Bryan thought. *For the first time in ten years.*

Ten years had been reasonably kind to Phil. Bryan noticed he wasn't as lean as he used to be, presumably from lack of intense work-related exercise, but he had kept himself together quite well. His face and neck had filled out slightly, and he seemed slightly more doughy than Bryan remembered, but was still the same general shape. His hair had started to spike with the occasional grey, and it looked like Phil didn't care about that in the slightest. Around his temples and the roots of his fringe was the lightest dusting of grey. Bryan was most stunned by his face, though. They had still been relatively young when he went inside, but now age had firmly settled into the creases of Phil's face. It looked more leathery, like it had seen its fair share of cold winters and hot summers. His cheeks had flecks of red and wrinkles around his eyes seemed more pronounced than they had any right to be. They had just spent many minutes running around, high on adrenaline, but nevertheless Phil could no longer be called a young man.

Bryan was marginally terrified about what he himself looked like.

'You got old, amigo.' He said to Phil.

Phil raised his eyebrows, the statement seeming to come out of nowhere.

'Oh, thanks.' He responded, sarcasm brushing his words. 'I'd say no shit, but I did happen to think the same thing when I saw your ugly mug. Best not look in any mirrors for a bit, not till you've mentally prepared yourself.'

'Ten years. Seems like ten minutes now I'm here.'

'What did you expect? We weren't going to be exactly the way we were at that airport when we last saw each other, you know?'

'Yeah, but I didn't expect things to be this different. Like I can still tell it's you, but Jesus.'

'Okay, now I know you're just trying to offend me on purpose.'

'No, honestly I'm not.' Bryan couldn't easily explain it. It made him feel hollow that he'd missed out on so much with his friends. With *anyone*.

'And what time would sir like sir's wake-up call tomorrow, uh, sir?' Phil asked, putting on an unnecessarily posh butler voice. He was quite good at voices.

'I won't need one. I'll be ready at nine-thirty. Pick me up.'

Two hours' worth of running, gunfights and erratic driving took its toll on Bryan a lot more than he thought it would. He knew he was slightly past his prime, yet secretly hoped the ten years wasn't catching up to him already.

'You got it. I'm set up at a hotel a few streets away. One of Michael's mates runs it. I suppose Mikey boy will pop round tomorrow as well. He does work here, after all. When he can be arsed.' Phil turned to the door, opened it and was halfway out before turning again. 'I figured you might need these.'

Grabbing it from a nearby worktop, he hurled a plastic bag sideways at Bryan, containing a pair of trainers, grey cargo trousers, white round-necked t-shirt, green jacket and a battered-looking watch. He almost missed the catch, grabbing the bottom of the bag with the tips of his fingers. However, it didn't stop most of the clothes falling out of the bag and landing in a heap on the bed. Unbeknownst to either of the two men, a mobile phone dropped out of the bag and fell down the side of, and subsequently underneath the bed. Bryan immediately put the watch on; though he didn't have the means to remove the prison tag on his wrist. Instead, he pushed it underneath the watch as best as he could. By this point, the tag itself was heavily faded, ten years of being worn constantly having removed much of the detail. The name of the prison was barely legible, the remaining letters spelling S - O - E - P - E - N. His ID Number, R3-T4-L5 was still readable, although the letters had lost their crisp edge.

At least the watch worked.

CHAPTER THREE: SQUARE ONE

Bryan opened his eyes.

Morning. 08:48am.

He thought about what had happened over the past twelve or so hours. Part of him wondered if he'd soon get woken up by an angry prison guard smashing his truncheon against the cell bars, yelling at him to get up, you useless bastard. A quick glance around and a rub of the eyes confirmed it. Either he WAS free, or he'd finally snapped. Bryan covered his face with his hands as he lay on his back, trying to work out the finer details.

Nine-thirty. That was when Bryan had told Phil to pick him up. What would he do with this new freedom?

Bryan laughed. He laughed out loud for the first time in what felt like a lifetime. He opened his fingers, feeling pure joy at his surroundings. He cheered, whooped and screamed in victory at the top of his lungs. No prison guard was going to clatter on the bars to tell him to shut up today. No prison guard was going to do that *ever again*. An enormous smile spread across his face, threatening to crack it. He rubbed his hands across the thin sheets of the bed, feeling that at some point in the last few years, they had been washed and changed. Gone were the chipped bricks, splintered glass windows and missing panels, the lack of privacy and the idiotic guffaws from his fellow inmates. There was nothing but silence. Glorious, liberating silence.

A few more giddy minutes passed, before Bryan finally rolled out of bed. He hadn't bothered to change into his 'new' clothes, and found great delight in tearing off the filthy prison jumpsuit before stuffing it into a metal dustbin.

'Goodbye, Prisoner R3-T4-L5.' Bryan said aloud, a great weight lifting off his shoulders as he did so. It felt to him like he had sealed the deal with his freedom. A sheet of paper in the carrier bag carried a scrawled phone number, Bryan assumed it was Phil's and stuffed it into the inside pocket of his jacket. He didn't know if he'd need it, but was glad Phil had provided it, just in case.

A grubby sink in the main garage area allowed him to have a wash of sorts, but he could only find some handwash, so focussed on cleaning his hands and face before giving himself a generous blast from a can of deodorant salvaged from a cardboard box.

Not exactly pine-fresh, but at this point it was about as good as he was going to get.

Phil arrived five minutes early with his brother Michael. They were clearly related, with the same hairstyle and face shape. The only thing Michael didn't have was a small amount of stubble which had darkened noticeably since the previous night. That, and the three years' worth of age that separated the two of them.

'Morning, poppet!' Phil exclaimed. He was wearing jeans and a jacket, with a white shirt, making him look older than he was. His younger sibling was only slightly less fashionable, with greasy overalls and workman's boots.

'Uh, hi Bryan.' He said, not bothering to look at him.

'What's up Michael?'

'Not much man, same as usual, you know?'

'Not really, but I'm sure I'll pick it up after a while. Still fixing cars then?'

'As and when I can get round to it, yeah. Been doing it a hell of a long time at this point.'

'Oh yeah, maybe ten years of doing it will have finally made you a half-decent mechanic.'

'I go with *half-assed*, not half-decent, Wattson.'

Phil chuckled. The conversation was hit-and-miss, which surprised Bryan. They shook hands. He and Michael had always been good friends, not in the same league as Phil and he, but strong nonetheless. Phil stepped in regardless, 'All right man, time to take a drive. We've got a lot to sort out. There's someone I want you to meet, but we need to see another man about a different breed of dog first.'

38

Michael walked past them, further into the garage. He flipped on a dilapidated radio before wheeling a tool bench next to a car. Music began to tumble out of it.

The car parked outside of the garage was different to the one they stole yesterday.

Ten minutes out of prison and back to committing crime. Bryan smirked to himself.
I'll stop Monday, I swear.

Regardless, the vehicle was still beginning to show its age. It didn't mind Bryan. Phil entered passenger-side and Bryan clambered into the driver's seat.
'Looks like I'm driving again, am I?'
'Sure does. You need the practice. Won't do very well if you stall all the time if you've got the rozzers or a pack of thugs on your arse, will it?'
'What was wrong with my driving last night?'
'Are you serious? All that prison food making you blind? You nearly stalled it more times than I can count. And you need to check your mirrors more. You don't wanna get pulled over, do you? Get a load of shit pinned on you just because you forgot to indicate? What a way to go...'
'Who says that's gonna happen? There might not be any more shit. I might go straight.'
Phil burst into laughter as the car took off.

'So are we gonna talk about the past decade?' Bryan asked a few streets over.
'Sure, if you really want to.'

Bryan sighed as they trundled along. 'I don't even know where to begin. Patched up in a hospital with less hygiene standards than this car we're driving, thrown into prison, rot for ten years, then escape? Fairytale. Pure and simple.'
'It was pretty hard out here too. After you were disposed of, I legged it to Michael's, hoping I didn't get shot up the arse by

Tony. The nicest bit of news we had is that you weren't dead. Didn't learn that for a while.'

'Nah, you wouldn't have gotten shot up the ass, Tony was too busy gloating and smashing me in the face with the end of his pistol.'

'Rough. He issued an all-points bulletin, saying I should be shot on sight. Unluckily for him, I was already at the airport buying chocolate at the duty-free before news circulated. We grabbed a last minute flight and were away almost immediately.'

'Then it was over to sunny...'

'Left here.'

'...Cornwall? I suppose I can think of worse places to go.'

'To London, then Newquay. That wasn't the worst bit. Unfortunately, because he betrayed you, he came down with what is known in the medical world as 'extreme paranoia', but to all other people is called 'going batshit bonkers'. Thinking that someone was gonna shiv him when you were inside.'

'I did think about it, once or twice. To be honest, when you guys burst in... Oh, up yours too, mate!'

A car had raced out at a crossroads. Bryan braked sharply, missing it by inches and got a mouthed swear word and an offensive gesture for his troubles.

'...I reckoned it was some sort of military operation or Tony or something.'

'After ten years? Nah. It was that 'nervous twitch' sort of paranoia. He had several of his businesses shut down, the ones run by the people he didn't trust. Retreated to his, sorry, YOUR mansion. Hardly leaves the damn place. Gets his cronies to do errands for him.'

'That's brilliant. I know exactly where he is.'

'Look, shut up with the stupid vengeance ideas. It's getting old. And death wishy. We do this the old-fashioned way. But for now, let's focus on not getting re-arrested.'

'I look forward to it.'

'Me too. Hang a right now. We're here.'

Phil left the car and jogged up to the door. Bryan stayed in the car. According to Phil, it was nothing serious, but in Bryan's experience Phil's 'nothing serious' meant he had just parked up outside a secure bunker where negotiations on World War III were taking place. Nevertheless, Bryan sat in the car and looked around. They must have driven into the industrial area of Sovereign City. The building was a warehouse-type affair with a smaller building at the end, as if it had been glued on. It looked out of place amongst all the large warehouses. Bryan drummed the steering wheel, played with the windows before reaching over and flipping the radio on. It was auto-tuned to Rock Sovereign. It played city-wide and Bryan listened to it quite often before prison. He wondered how much it had changed in a decade. He could hardly believe it was still going after all these years.

Around ten minutes later, Phil returned. He was carrying with extreme caution a small box with duct tape almost completely covering it. He re-entered the passenger seat before carefully placing the box on the floor between his legs.

'Those the keys to the doomsday bunker?' Bryan asked, some sarcasm evident.

'Nope, just directions to get there. I'm told to get the keys from Grey Squirrel when I get there. You still remember where Joliet Street is?'

'Not the sort of the thing you forget is it?'

'Well then, what are you waiting for? Let's go.'

'All right, but I want to know how we're doing for assets as we go.'

'You know you're not gonna like it.'

'Yep, but still...'

The car pulled off, a splutter of the exhaust and a curse from Bryan at his own driving being the only evidence of them ever being there. Bryan was quite afraid of what Phil was about to tell him, not because his life was in danger - hell, he was used to that - but because 'square one' is big enough when you're a small time criminal. To him, it felt a million miles wide.

The situation was this: of the approximate eighty-five percent of the city that Tony owned in the time immediately following

Bryan's imprisonment, he had only kept hold of a small amount. Phil guessed at maybe twenty percent, but didn't know for sure. The biggest earners, of course, but also the businesses least likely to be raided by the police. What they earned was still in excess of hundreds of thousands of dollars, but Tony only ever saw a small amount of it because he constantly paid bribes to the police and lawyers to ensure he stayed a free man. Not that he ever needed to *see* any of it. He had everything he could ever want at Bryan's mansion. What was left went into an offshore account where it would hopefully slip through the net, a nice little nest egg for when he finally called it quits. It made Bryan sick. Phil's short-term plan, like he has said, was to not be killed or re-arrested. For the future, though, he outlined a vague plan of anonymously rebuilding a smaller empire on the side and slowly choking the life out of Tony's assets before moving in for the kill.

Everything should be as legitimate as possible, although one or two laws were bound to be broken in the process. Although Tony owned the big businesses and there was nothing they could do to stop him, Phil insisted on being sneaky and owning assets to give advantages in ways other than money. From off the top of his head, Phil rather optimistically suggested looking into buying a printing press which had recently closed three streets away from the garage, using it in some way to publish bad propaganda about crime in the city and point a subtle finger towards the current occupant of Bryan's mansion. The irony wasn't lost on either of the two men. Or failing that, maybe a newspaper or magazine of some description to increase cash flow. As Phil put it: 'Every little helps.'

Then he explained his mystery contact. Though he didn't tell Bryan his name, he was insistent that he would know him. He was also rather insistent that the man not only needed them as much as likewise, but that he was willing to pay for their services.

Their first port of call was none other than the headquarters of the radio station that they were currently listening to. Rock Sovereign.

CHAPTER FOUR: FRONT PAGE

The car pulled up outside the headquarters of Rock Sovereign. It was a dilapidated ex-office building that had been converted to include studios and all the equipment needed to run a radio station. It was starting to show its age, with broken stonework and cracked brick. And that was just the outside. The inside could be much worse. Bryan didn't particularly want to find out.

Phil led the way into a studio, where a scrawny man with enormous glasses sat with a headset on behind a clear window. The window was there to negate any noise which might otherwise disrupt the show. He was talking as if there was a crowd of people in front of him, even going so far as to make hand gestures as he spoke. He looked in his element, as though nothing could stop him when he got on a roll. Bryan tried to read his lips and was sure he saw the word 'chaos' being mouthed. Phil rapped on the glass. The DJ turned and rolled his eyes while shaking his head when he saw Phil. He tapped a button before pointing to the door situated next to the window. It buzzed and Bryan assumed the button controlled the lock. Phil opened it and the DJ made a 'fingers on lips' gesture with the hand he wasn't already waving to add emphasis to his radio speech.

'Although all reports are as yet unconfirmed, some prisoners are thought to have perished in the explosion. More news updates as and when we get 'em. For now though, we reckon we should go back to givin' you what you pay us to give you: rock music. We'll start with this one: an absolute classic. See you shortly.'

As the song began to play the DJ removed his headset and flipped a switch. A red light switched off. It said 'On Air'.

'All right, Gerrard?' Phil asked the DJ.

'What the hell are you doing here, Phil? I'm trying to do a breakfast show here. Can't this wait until after my show finishes?' Gerrard had switched his radio voice off as well.

'Afraid not.'

Gerrard sighed. He removed his glasses before rubbing his eyes. He stared at Bryan when he had repositioned them.

'Who's this fella? Hired muscle? I didn't think things were like that between us, Phil.'

'No man, this is Bryan Wattson.'

Bryan pretended to tip a hat as the DJ jumped at the mention of the name. He nearly fell backwards off his chair, the simple fact it had wheels being the only saving grace.

'B-Bryan Wattson? That fella you told me was locked up? I thought he was meant to be in prison? Wait... Shit.' The realisation dawned, accompanied by an apprehensive look.

'Yep, you know it. He broke out of prison, with a little help from his friends. Now I figured you could help set him up with some work. He's in the market. As it were.'

'R-Right.'

'Oh, pull yourself together, you big girl's blouse. Bryan's not gonna kill you or string you up. He just wants some cash in the bank. Bryan, this is Gerrard. He works the breakfast show here, as you may have guessed, as well as half the other shows they put on. Come to think of it: when the bloody hell do you sleep, Gerrard?'

'D-During the early hours. We then just rely on the computer playin' songs for us. It just picks out a random selection, depending on the day. I'm not on ALL the time, you know?'

Bryan looked at a poster on the wall and the man smiling back was incredibly different to the bumbling wreck he saw in the flesh. Lots of work must have been done on the poster.

'When he's not making an arse of himself in front of hundreds of listeners, he also runs this place.' Phil added.

Bryan raised his eyebrows at the thought. The place didn't look well-run at all.

'Wait, you run this place, too?'

'I don't need much sleep.' As if that explained everything.

'Yeah, don't we know it.' Phil continued. 'And I always thought he nicked the deed after murdering the old owner while he slept. The place has got problems. Big problems.'

'And you're here to sort them out?' Gerrard asked. 'Tha...that's brilliant! We got so many problems I don't even know where to begin.'

'Hang on though. We aren't doing this just for the money. We need help in other ways.' Bryan clarified.

'I'm sure you do.'

'You're a big radio company, right?'

'Second biggest in Sovereign. Only Chillax can claim to be bigger. They freakin' do as well.'

'Right. So you can influence the public. Plant the seed. Make them think stuff they otherwise wouldn't have thought?'

'I think I understand what you're getting at.'

'Well, I don't.' Phil interrupted.

'Think about it. We can get the public thinking Tony did things that would incriminate him, fancy lawyers or not. Make him public enemy number one. A lot of crap piling down on him in the public eye might stir Sovereign City's finest into action or something, right? It's basically the same as your magazine idea. Or the very least we could do is cover my ass for the prison break.'

'Yeah, that's brilliant. I only thought we could use the money, but now that you mention it; that is a nice perk on the side. That, maybe combined with a newspaper story...? More people will believe if there's more than one source,' Phil agreed, 'You got the morning papers, Gerrard?'

'Right here. Get 'em 4.30 a.m. so we know what to tell the public.'

'Fair enough. Pass me that one. We can see what crap the tabloids are pedalling on this day of all days.'

Bryan and Phil looked at a newspaper each. Not surprisingly, the prison break was featured on the front page of the Sovereign Tribune. A darkened and hastily-taken photograph of the prison was shown, with several smaller shots of the destroyed bridge and empty cells finishing off the imagery. An advertisement for helicopter tours was located in the bottom right of the article, to make the page seem more organised. It featured a cartoon picture of a helicopter behind the text. From the looks of the images, it would make an interesting read. Bryan hoped that no names were mentioned. It concerned him already that Phil hadn't been the least bit subtle in performing the breakout. It seemed to Bryan that it was simply a case of gluing a stick of dynamite to the wall, running like hell and praying for the best. Subtlety was never Phil's strong point. Nevertheless, it wouldn't be long at all before Tony began to suspect something was wrong, and Bryan would not be surprised if he hadn't *heard* the explosion or felt it rattle his windows. It probably ripped that damn squeaky wardrobe door off its hinges.

Bryan read the article. The newspaper journalists worked fast. It had only been a few hours. While he read, Gerrard introduced another song, giving an almost textbook accounting of some of the history surrounding it. While it played, Gerrard himself flicked through several front pages, occasionally stealing a glance at Bryan from beneath his large glasses. Between looks at him and looks at the front pages, Bryan assumed he was trying to piece together exactly what happened. Or, he was trying to decide whether Bryan was actually involved in it at all.

In typical tabloid fashion, many of the gritty details had been omitted from the article. Instead, as writer F. Johnson was quick to point out, the main focus was on the politically tumultuous times and the potentially dire consequences that could arise from the act. Was it an act of terrorism? A shameless act of mindless violence, or something darker? The article was reluctant to point fingers, but nonetheless it had an air about it of distinctly recognised foul play. Bryan read the article to himself.

CHAOS AT SOVEREIGN STATE PENITENTIARY

Mass panic as prison riot/breakout occurs.

Article written in aftermath by F. Johnson.

An enormous explosion occurred last night at Sovereign City State Penitentiary, where over 600 inmates are known to reside. The blast occurred at around eleven o'clock, and tore through the security room, killing one officer and injuring three others. The officer was the first of over thirty casualties, from both sides of the law, but police officers are hesitant to provide specific information and details about those casualties. It is assumed that some prisoners escaped; otherwise the police would be able to provide details of last night's events.

This breakout appears to have happened at the worst possible time, as the mayor of Sovereign City has recently denied rumours of unfair treatment of inmates in the prison. Of the 100 inmates reported to have left their cells, at least twenty were shot and killed as they tried to escape, but once again no specific information about names and/or crimes committed are known. Cell Block D was the primary target, with the explosion occurring in the security room that sits between it and its neighbouring block, Cell Block E.

One thing the police are willing to confirm is that the explosion actually detonated outside the prison walls, so perhaps the inmates were helped by an outside force. Conspiracy theories are springing up already, with some being so wild as to suggest a military 'clean-up' operation.

More on p2-3.

When he had finished reading, a smug smile was on Bryan's face. Gerrard finished reading a new article as Phil flipped to a second page.

'So that was you, huh?' Gerrard said. His hands danced between pages, offering Bryan fleeting glimpses at Cell Block D, the concrete square and the destroyed bridge.

'I was only along for the ride, I swear. I had no idea that any of it was planned.'

'And you killed cops to escape?'

'You're asking if a team of armed gunmen had to shoot and kill similarly armed cops to escape?' Bryan fixed him with a hard stare. Gerrard was, for the moment, unwavering.

'Yeah. H-how did it feel?'

Bryan sighed, somewhat dramatically. 'After the millionth kill, it becomes like putting your socks on. Crime is crime. It becomes second nature when you've been doing it as long as we have.'

'Although your aim was garbage.' Phil interjected.

'Yeah, I was rusty. But it was what needed to be done. We all commit crimes in our daily lives. Some just *seem* more drastic than others. You ever crossed the road before the green man flicks on, Gerrard? Same thing.'

Now, Gerrard had cracked. The callous dismissal of human life being likened to jaywalking had turned his stomach. He was more afraid of Bryan than when he'd initially learned his identity when they walked in.

An awkward silence smothered the room.

'It's not, though, is it?' Phil said.

Bryan cracked a smile. 'Of course not. But don't tell *him* that.' He nodded at Gerrard before putting his nose back into the newspaper. Gerrard's face was a sight. It conveyed the dumbstruck confusion of someone who couldn't quite work out if they'd been insulted. Bryan finished reading another column and made a snorting noise in his nose.

'They work fast, these paparazzi. You huffing at the fact they've got no idea what the hell went on up there?' Phil asked.

'Nope. I knew I wasn't crazy. THEY thought it was a military-style cover up too. Ha.'

'Yeah, great priorities there, B.'

'So...' Gerrard began, trying to regain composure and failing miserably, 'What do I tell the public?'

'You tell them exactly what this paper says. But you make it clear you have no idea what the hell went on up there. Do NOT mention Bryan, or anyone else for that matter, by name. Tony's probably listening so go easy on it. Just say 'more on it as it develops' or some other journalist crap.'

'Fine. But now that I'm doin' you a favour, m-maybe I get one in return.'

'Sure thing, if it pays.' Bryan made clear.

'Okay, first things first. I'm not exactly a legitimate businessman.'

'You really think we'd be here if we didn't at least suspect that?'

'Or know it, bang to rights?' Phil added.

'And I admit I've made mistakes in the past. But I'm a man who believes in second chances. Fresh starts. Other people, however, don't quite have the same idea. An old colleague of mine's been threatenin' to go public about certain things that I'd rather he didn't go public about. You understand?'

'Who is he?'

'He's one of the DJs at Chillax FM. We had a slight disagreement about something I forget about now, although it might be something to do with me stealing his girlfriend. Pushed him over the edge.'

Bryan caught Phil's gaze. He smirked back. He could tell what he was thinking. One word. *Bullshit.*

'Anyway. This particular dispute was what caused him to go off and join Chillax, and he's one of the reasons that Rock Sov comes in at second place to Chillax. He's just a damn good DJ. So this gets me to my point. I want Rock Sov to be the undisputed best station in the whole city, but I can't do that unless various problems are made to go away. He's problem number one. He took a lotta shit with him when he left. He's threatenin' to go public and I need you to go and persuade him not to do so. Just don't kill him or anything too serious. I want him to be able to at least crawl to a paper shredder to destroy any evidence he might think he has. You understand?'

'Not in the slightest. But I'm quite good at making problems vanish, so I'll see what I can do. Where can I find him?'

'Right outside. He's expecting me to meet him after the breakfast show. I was gonna ring and ask Phil, but I think it'd make a good induction for you. See if you're any good.'

49

'All right. I'll be right back.' He got up to leave. 'Oh, and Gerrard? Nice prepared speech you cooked up back there, but don't try to salesman pitch me into doing things. I can see through that crap at twenty paces.'

He slammed the door shut just as the second song came to a conclusion.

The weather could be strange in Sovereign City and today was one of those days. The sun was out, but there was a biting wind which whipped at Bryan as he walked around the side of the building. His jacket was zipped up. Not that it made that much of a difference. He wasn't sure what he'd find when he met Gerrard's colleague. He was ready for a suitably large man, and so was pleasantly surprised when he was a good six inches shorter than Bryan. Still, looks could be deceiving, although by the looks of the guy Bryan didn't feel he had anything to fear. He was smoking a cigarette and wearing a sunglasses and hat combo that made him look ridiculous, whilst leaning against a misshapen brick wall. A drainpipe running the full length of the wall stood close by, the brackets holding it in place either missing or on their last legs. The man turned to look at Bryan, stubbed his cigarette against the drainpipe and ground it beneath his boot.

'The hell do you want?' he asked, slight menace in his obviously fine-tuned voice.

'I'm a friend of Gerrard's, although I don't like to admit it.'

'Ha. He always was too spineless to do anything himself. Well, you're too late. I've given him too many chances to give me what I want already. I'm just here to tell him that I've decided to drop this little bundle of joy off at the cop station on my way round. Figured it would be sweeter if he heard it from the horse's mouth.' He held up a battered leather briefcase as he spoke, smiling toothily as he reached the end of his ramble. Toothpaste must have been out of stock when he went shopping. The case reminded Bryan of the suitcases that had the drugs and money in them a decade previously.

'I wouldn't do that if I were you.' Bryan warned. Flashing a snarl, he set his shoulders and took a step towards the man, who held his ground.

'I think you need to back off, pal, before things get out of hand.' His right leg moved to the side, set at a ninety degree angle from his body in a common fighting stance. It would allow him to jab easily should it come to that, corkscrewing his punches to give them more power. Bryan had seen it before, and realised he might have too quickly misjudged the man.

'As much as I hate to admit knowledge of Gerrard's existence, I won't let you extort him. Give me the briefcase.' Bryan demanded.

'Why don't you just make me give it to you?' The man produced a switchblade from somewhere and flicked it open. He held it in his offhand, ready to grab with his main and slash or stab with little effort.

Shit.

The man waved the knife around menacingly at his side. Bryan stood his ground, but glanced around for a weapon of some description. None of the bricks looked loose, nor was there a sizeable enough chunk of mortar to act as an improvised bludgeon. Whilst getting stabbed wasn't currently on his long list of injuries, and although he doubted it would be as bad as getting shot, he was very much aware of the remoteness of the alleyway they were standing in. If he was stabbed badly enough to be unable to shout for help, it would be unlikely that anyone would find him before he bled out.

Think, Wattson, think! Nothing on the floor, no real way to disarm the man without risking serious injury.

The man in the sunglasses was still talking. '...sick and tired of everything that man has piled on top of me in the last six months. It doesn't matter now, though, my new friends will sort everything out even if the cops don't.'

Bryan thought he was done. A terrible showing for his first job out of prison. He sighed heavily, before realising the one thing that might reasonably be classed as a weapon. He would need to change his position before he could properly use it, but it might just work. He moved his feet closer together, and slouched his shoulders.

'Yeah, I thought so.' The man continued again. 'Why don't you fuck off back to Gerrard and tell him to send someone more impressive next time?'

Bryan held his hands in front of him in surrender, taking a step towards the wall.

'Okay buddy, okay. I'm going.'

'Yeah. That's what I...'

Bryan spun round, wrenched part of the drainpipe off its hinges and smashed the man in the side of the head with it, leaving rent sections of plastic where the remaining brackets had been. He hadn't predicted it, and did nothing to attempt to defend himself. The man's head lurched to the side, sunglasses flying off and clinking against the opposite wall. The man managed a cry out, but didn't manage to correct himself in time. It wasn't a lethal or even enormously painful blow, but it startled the man long enough for Bryan to grip the man's wrist, wrench the blade out of his hand and hurl it to one side. He grabbed the briefcase with his free arm and hit the cowboy with it for good measure. The man dropped to the floor.

'Don't ever try to be clever with me.' Bryan spat, straightening up. 'You pull a knife on me and you better be willing to stab me with it. Now why don't you fuck off back to wherever you came from and try to be slightly more impressive next time?' He added extra emphasis to the sarcasm at the end of the sentence.

Bryan left the man in the gutter as he strolled back into the Rock Sovereign building. He heard the man shout something, but dismissed it as an idle threat.

Bryan pushed the door into the staff canteen open with his foot, careful not to attract too much attention to whatever was in the briefcase. He set it down on a table and went to fetch coffee. The machine was out of milk, not that it mattered. Bryan had always liked his coffee black, ever since he was a teenager. He'd run out of milk one day, but already had the coffee and the boiled water in the mug before he noticed. He'd decided just to drink it without and liked what he tasted. A short while later the doors opened and Gerrard walked in, looking nervously around before spotting Bryan.

'You get it?'

'Yeah. Sure.' Bryan passed it across the table. Gerrard extended a hand to take it but Bryan gripped the handle tightly. He fixed the DJ with a hard stare.

'Remember your end of the bargain, Gerrard. I'm not best pleased with that guy pulling a knife on me. I thought there would have been at least a few non-lethal jobs first.'

'He pulled a knife on you?'

'Yes. It wasn't pleasant. Innocuous-looking bastard had tricks under his stetson.'

'I-I'm sorry to hear that. But you're okay, though, right? He didn't stab you or anything. A-and I'm not planning on forgetting. I'll talk to a few of my DJ buddies. We'll see if we can't come to some arrangement.'

'Excellent. It kinda puts a downer on Phil's idea of owning a printing press, though.'

'What?'

'Don't ask. Just something we discussed.'

'Look, did you take care of my ex-colleague as well?'

'I didn't rough him up badly. Smacked him with a drainpipe and then again with the briefcase. He'll be okay.'

'Good. I mainly only wanted his pride to sting anyway. I might offer him his job back as a DJ back at Rock Sov.'

Gerrard's sudden change of plan stunned Bryan.

'Wait a minute, an hour or so ago you considered him sub-human! This is a guy in stupid shades who just pulled a goddamn knife on me! What the hell are you thinking about asking him for a job? Have you gone nuts?'

'Keep your voice down. This is a business, and should be run like one. Don't question logic that doesn't concern you, Bryan. Leave me with my choices. I'll help you. That's as far as you should be concerned.'

Bryan snorted derisively. 'What happened to Phil?'

'He went back to that garage of yours. He took your car, but somehow managed to convince me to let you borrow the keys to one of the company cars. So, uh, here they are. You know, this is turnin' into a good day. I think I'll head over to a casino to celebrate. Maybe a few hands of Blackjack.'

'You a gambling man, Gerrard?'

'Nope. But today, I feel *lucky*.' He tapped the side of his nose with his finger.

Gerrard held a set of keys out on a ring with a plipper. The badge of a muscle car, which pleased Bryan.

Something with a bit more punch than that pile of crap we came here in. Nice.

He took the keys. Gerrard took out an ornate cigarette lighter and began an attempt to set the briefcase alight.

'We'll be in touch.' Bryan said, shaking his head.

The car which responded to the plipper was disappointing. Not the muscle car he was expecting, but a dull saloon with a grille that made it look sad. Reasonably priced, yes, but no real power in a tricky situation. It didn't matter. He got in and started the engine. The drive back to the garage was made marginally less boring by reports on the radio of crazy ideas about the prison break. Bryan's personal favourite somehow involved internationally-sourced soft drinks. Gerrard was sales-pitching his way through the topics, making it sound incredibly real. Bryan was sure he heard the faint sound of a crackling fire in the background, but it could also just as easily be static.

Gotta admit, the man's really good at his job. Grade A bullshit.

Bryan returned to the garage to find Phil and Michael carrying cardboard boxes full of tools inside. He picked one up and followed suit. Phil set his down precariously atop a pile of half a dozen others. It didn't fall down; which Bryan saw as a bit of a let-down.

'Howdy, Bryan. You're back.' Phil beamed.

'Howdy. Do me a favour, and don't set me up with people like Gerrard if you can help it. He's a real dick.'

'Yep. But we take what we can get at this stage. Did you sort out his little problem?'

'Yeah, I did. The funniest little guy I think I've ever seen was meant to meet Gerrard. I got to smack him in the head with a drainpipe. Fun times.'

'Ha. Sounds it.'

'Things took a slight tumble when he pulled a knife on me.'

Phil raised an eyebrow. 'Well, you survived, didn't you?'

'Yeah, but next time I might not be so lucky.'

Bryan trailed off, and neither man said anything for a while, concentrating instead on the pile of boxes.

'Why not try Dempsey?' This was Michael. He was sitting on a pile of tyres, and slapped at the back of his neck to remove an insect of some description.

'What a damn fine idea.' Phil said, suddenly becoming excited. 'You'll like Dempsey, Bryan. The man's bat-shit bonkers, but you'll get along. I personally think he's hilarious. Moans about old wars when I doubt he was even ten when they *ended*. If this was a hundred years ago he'd probably have been set up as a freak show. Hell, *I'd* pay for it.'

'Me too.' Michael sneered.

'So that's our next stop? This... Dempsey?'

'Yep. He's got a line on guns. They're nothing fancy, but they cough lead at people, and that's enough to put the shits in them, if nothing else.'

'Well that seems as good a start as any so far. Let's roll. I'm driving.'

'Of course you are. There was never any doubt.'

'Oh, fine. Leave me with the rest of these boxes, Phil.' Michael moaned.

'Stop your whingeing. Exercise'll do you good.'

He growled, '...lazy bastards.'

'Love you too, bro.'

Bryan and Phil exited the garage as Michael picked up a box. The bottom of the box broke, sending pipes and tools spewing all over the floor. Phil shut the door as it happened, but both men were still sniggering as they got in the car, muffled shouts of anger from Michael echoing from the garage.

CHAPTER FIVE: NOTHING LIKE THE MOVIES

The car pulled up at a set of traffic lights. The radio was on, but neither man was listening to it. Gerrard was interviewing some has-been from a few years back. Phil was concentrating on explaining what they were doing; Bryan didn't know who the has-been was. The sudden realisation that a lot had happened over the last ten years played in his mind. He hadn't initially considered it – although prison was by no means open to the world, it wasn't fundamentally secluded, either. They got the news, and some inmates even insisted on getting newspapers and weeklies ordered in. The inevitable 'men who can get things for you' were rife on the inside. Bryan himself knew at least four, each able to get various items of contraband for a none too insignificant fee. His only problem was that he didn't have access to his wealth. Favours often carried higher worth in prison, which was a way that Bryan was able to shift at least some of the attention away from himself. While he was locked up, he just wanted to be ignored, but he had learned quickly that being ignored was often the priciest convenience to achieve. Still, after around three years he had settled himself into the position he wanted: only seriously bother him under the direst of circumstances. The only item he'd really asked for was a music player, something which would distract him for at least a moment, and allow him to think. Their average lifespan of said music players was six months before they were conveniently removed as 'contraband' for some bullshit reason or another. That left him more or less back at the beginning, and he'd have to once again negotiate the favours for a new one.

'So, just around this corner we'll meet Dempsey. Just watch what you say and you'll be fine. To be honest I'm surprised the cops haven't picked up on what he's got at his place. It's not like he's quiet about it. Oh, and whatever happens, don't tell him you're a communist.'

'I wasn't aware that I was. Prison ain't changed me that much.'

'You might not be, but *he* doesn't know that. Just flat out deny you're a communist.'

'Okay, okay. I'm not a communist.'

'There we go, good attitude. Tell him you're a chauvinist. You'll be fine if you do that.'

'Like hell I will. The system hasn't been kind enough to me.'

The car pulled up outside what could only very loosely be described as a hovel. It was a wooden house that looked as if it had been made drunkenly by hand, with a claw hammer and not enough nails. Most of the windows were boarded up, large pieces of crooked wood hammered over them. The drains and guttering were nonexistent, and a car with no tyres stood sadly in the driveway, its wheels buried a few centimetres into the loose gravel. A low wall encompassed a large portion of the area, splintered and cracked in places, and outright missing in others. One small detail was brand new though, untarnished among a sea of neglect: a small security camera in a wire cage over the front door.

'Well, here we are. Go and knock on the door while I sort out this box.'

Bryan had completely forgotten about the taped package, and hadn't noticed it sitting in the passenger footwell.

Bryan strolled up to the door and pressed the doorbell, ignoring the camera completely. A grunt came from inside and before Bryan could react the door was kicked outwards and a strung-out looking old man wearing a stained tank top aimed a shotgun at him. Bryan flinched as the door missed him by six inches, snapping his head to the side in case it hit him.

'Get on the fucking ground, NOW.' The man demanded. There was no joke in his voice. He was deadly, deadly serious. A single eye pierced him, the second one missing under an eyepatch, surrounded by what looked like faint scar tissue.

'What the fuck?' Bryan cried. He raised his hands in surrender. 'I'm unarmed! ...And I'm not a fucking communist!'

'Yeah?! That's what my squadmate Shifty said in 'Nam. Next thing he's trying to slash me up with the knife he keeps in his boot!'

The man hiccoughed, a bilious exhale following it. He seemed to be distracted for a second and Bryan took it as an opportunity to snatch the shotgun and wrench it sideways. The gun went off, spraying lead to one side, smashing the side windows and denting the bodywork of the car with no wheels.

'What the hell, you crazy old bastard?!' Bryan stormed, pumping the shotgun repeatedly to dump the remaining three shells.

Dempsey burst into drunken laughter. He made no attempt to get the shotgun back, instead turning around and starting to go back inside.

'You're Bryan, right?' His slur caused him to miss the second syllable of the name.

'Yeah... and you're Dempsey.'

'You comin' in, or you gonna stand there lookin' like a streak of piss in a hot flush?'

Bryan didn't calm down. 'The shotgun?'

'Gotta make sure we're all on the same team against communism...' He suddenly darted around, looking in the air for something.

'Jesus Christ, you're completely insane.' Bryan sighed.

'All right, everyone?' Phil confidently walked up to them, apparently unaware of the incident with the shotgun just moments before. Bryan was still holding it.

'Yeah, but your batshit friend just tried to shoot me!'

He threw the empty weapon at Phil, who caught it one-handed.

'How's it going, Dempsey?' Phil asked, throwing the shotgun through the door. It clattered somewhere in the hall.

'You know, usual shit. S.S.D.D.' Dempsey quickly solved the acronym. 'Same shit, different day. I remember the old days, the old problems, everything that happened. I take my pills to help with it and try and forget, but I never can. Folks these days don't give a second thought to the horrors some men have to go through. They just want to catch their latest program on TV or go to the store.' He stared at Bryan, the same determined look from before on his face, the same fire in his one eye. 'But then there are people like me. People who don't forget. People nowadays try to tell you otherwise, that it's all in the past, but you just can't forget.'

Bryan was baffled at the sudden change of mood. He didn't understand what the hell Dempsey had just said, but he was shocked by his delivery nonetheless.

'Listen, D, we need a weapon.' Phil said, steering the conversation back to the reason they were there. 'And I've got that box you wanted...'

'A weapon?! Well, why the hell didn'cha say so?' Dempsey seemed to regain at least seventy percent of his marbles at the mere mention of weapons. He snatched the box off Phil, but paid it little attention.

'Because you never let us try...'

'I got guns like you wouldn't believe! You want assault rifles? I got 'em. Flamethrowers? I might be able to set you up. I think I've got an anti-aircraft battery set up somewhere, for those hard-to-reach targets.'

'Just a pistol, thanks. I don't want anything that's gonna blow up in my face.'

'Fine, fine. But it's never just a pistol. C'mon into the office.'

He gestured into the house. Bryan and Phil entered, both men having to duck to avoid the collapsed doorframe. Dempsey, being a fair amount shorter, didn't have that problem.

Inside, the house was surprisingly tidy. It seemed that Dempsey's experiences in war, if there were any, had gotten to him way more than he let on, even considering his outburst on the doorstep. Bryan could not look anywhere without seeing some piece of army equipment or trinket. He must have been in a war at some point, but Bryan struggled to think of which one. Dempsey seemed either too old or too young for any of them. The room to the left as they walked in was a replica barracks, with a camp bed and uniform neatly pressed on top of it. A glass display case with various medals and another eye patch was positioned above it. A gun case added a sombre atmosphere, with assault rifles fitted neatly inside. They looked like replicas, but Bryan was doubtful. An offshoot room appeared to have dummies stuffed with straw for bayonet practice inside.

'Looks like they wrote the Second Amendment specifically for him.' Bryan found himself muttering.

The level of neatness bordered on obsessive-compulsive. Everything clearly had its place, and was arranged into distinct numbers and tiers. The assault rifles were in sets of three, the medals in twos. Dempsey's footlocker, perfectly placed at the foot of the bed, was opened. The kit inside was arranged to exactly match its dimensions, and there wasn't a square inch of misused or neglected space. The wooden floors were polished to a mirror sheen, the hazy light coming from the windows reflecting off to make the boards seem oily. The walls themselves were similarly clean, with nary a loose nail or speck of dust to be found. Bryan supposed that a thin amount of insulation separated the inner and outer walls of the shack, but the difference between outside and in was staggering.

'Now...' Dempsey said, leading them to another room and setting down the duct-taped box, 'This is a great little number.'

Spinning it around on his forefinger and pulling back the slide, he gingerly passed Bryan a pistol. It was an M1911. A Colt. They were many years old, hence the name, which didn't fill Bryan with much confidence.

'This thing? It's older than you are.'

'Yeah, but it's reliable. You can guarantee that if you pull the trigger a bullet will come out.' He grabbed it back, somewhat reluctant to hand it out. Phil was still grinning.

'Right... You're sure? Normally, I'm used to newer models.'

'And newer models will fail, nearly every time. I've seen weapons straight off the production line fail because dust got in the trigger mechanisms, or open bolts fail because of exposure to water. You know why the AK-47 is the most reliable assault rifle - hell, probably the most reliable weapon period - ever made? Because it has about four working components and was designed to wade across a swamp and still work on the other side. Rookies with their damn fancy newfangled weapons...'

'Alright, matey. Jesus. So, how much would it set me back?'

'We'll sort that out in just a little while. You fancy some target practice?'

'Can't hurt, I guess.'

They walked out of the back door. Once again, it was in disarray. Bryan was hit with a feeling of whiplash. The grass, unkempt and patchy, ranged from off-green to decayed orange. Trees were long since cut down, stumps in various places suggesting they had been butchered for firewood. A brick wall, six feet high and with target roundels painted on it, stood a distance away. A large amount of bottle fragments were strewn about the place.

'Phil, stack those cans up, while I sort this here gun out.' Dempsey said.

The cans were stacked up in rows of three by three, forming a neat square. Bryan smiled when he realised that one of them was a can of the soft drink featured in one of the crazy stories on the radio earlier. Presumably, Dempsey himself never drank any of them, lest they send robots into his brain or something.

The garden was quite long, thirty or forty yards, Bryan would have guessed. Nevertheless, he trained the gunsight on the lower right of his cans, before squeezing the trigger. Click. Nothing happened.

'Safety, dipshit.' Dempsey said, shaking his head. 'Your new pistols still got safeties, right?'

Bryan chuntered under his breath and flicked it off before aiming once again and firing. The bottom-right can exploded before the rest of the stack collapsed.

'Packs a punch, no?' Dempsey said proudly. 'No wonder they used those things for years. Then the Italians muscled in and changed everything.'

They moved along the garden, shooting at almost anything that vaguely resembled a target. Phil produced a similar pistol and joined in. Bryan's personal best shot was when he sent a bullet straight through the entrance hole to a bird house from across the garden. The bullet went clean out the other side. Dempsey didn't seem pleased.

'Yeah, those fancy shots are fine, but when you really want someone to die, there's only one way to go.'

Bryan turned to face him, and stepped back when he saw what Dempsey was holding. It was a light machine gun, belt fed and almost as big as Dempsey himself. An ammunition box sat on the floor next to him. He racked the slide.

'*This*,' he said, 'is what you use when something needs to die.'

He pulled the trigger, and held it down.

The bullets came out of the gun with such ferocity that Bryan was sure the recoil would tear Dempsey's arm off. But it didn't. It barely even flinched. Dempsey kept it level, the gun's foregrip straining ever so slightly under the gun's lethargic chug. Bullets sprayed everywhere, Bryan and Phil had to jump backwards out of the way in case one of them flew to one side. The wall that Dempsey was aiming at became totally perforated extremely quickly. Exploding brickwork combined with smashing glass and tearing bark as everything in the same hemisphere as the wall seemed to get hit. Bryan forced his hands over his ears. The sound was deafening. Dempsey sprayed the gun from left to right.

After about fifteen seconds of continuous firing, the gun came to a juddering halt as the last of the belt-fed ammunition was used. It clicked in defeat. Dempsey had a look of solid determination on his face, which quickly gave way to triumph.

'Well, that settles that.' He said.

Phil removed the light machine gun from Dempsey's grip, straining under its weight. The snout of the gun was still smoking. For a second he looked like a stiff breeze could blow him over. He stuck a finger in one ear and wiggled in around, before sobering up.

'Mental gun. Might get one. But don't do that again, alright mate?' he said.

'So how many'll I put you down for?' Dempsey asked, staring at the amassment of shell casings to his right. They would have made an effective stuffing for a large beanbag, such were the numbers of them.

'Just this pistol, I think.' Bryan said, making both Phil and Dempsey look crushed. 'I'm not in the mood for making everybody *except* the guy I'm aiming at die.'

With his thumb he gestured at the target painted on the wall Dempsey was aiming at. Apart from a few holes in the outer circles, it looked as though Dempsey had completely missed the centre. One of the things he *had* hit, however, was a radio, which lay a good three feet behind the box it was originally sat on. All the electrical tape and superglue in the world couldn't put it back together.

'Fine, fine...' Dempsey said, 'It's just, you never know when you'll be coming up against an army of thugs. Spray and pray, my friend, spray and pray... Unless you're being accurate.'

He turned and went back inside.

Ten minutes later, Bryan and Phil were back in the car they arrived in. It was getting into the afternoon, and both men felt hungry. They were heading somewhere they used to frequent before Bryan's imprisonment, a small pub about two minutes from Trestle Bridge. Phil mentioned that it might not be the best of ideas to cross the bridge, and even going near it might pose a problem. The two bridges were used by Tony to transport his various ill-gotten gains, and there would more than likely be a sentry watching the bridges. Bryan had waved all the advice away, and said that wild horses wouldn't keep him away from this pub. It was called The Forester, and the sign featured a Robin Hood-era man with a bow and arrow taking aim at a deer. It was a traditional English pub, with English owners, and was one of the only places in Sovereign City where they could buy what Phil called 'proper ale'.

The Forester was cosy. Not what you would call large, but it had a friendly atmosphere, and the prices weren't bad either. They settled down for a pint of something ('It doesn't matter what', Bryan made clear) and a meal. The first bite was like heaven. The first sip, less so. It was the first time he'd eaten anything even remotely recognisable as food in the last ten years. All the prison food reminded him of gruel, with no great attempt made to add flavour: that particular institute's thought process when it came to food was as long as it kept the prisoners from dying of starvation, it didn't matter what it tasted like. The ale, on the other hand, tasted bitter. Bryan drank his pint with apprehension, making it last while they ate. Phil, on the other hand, was much more liberal.

'What's the matter? The beer off or something?'

'I don't know. Taste that. Tell me.'

Bryan passed his pint across to his friend.

'No, it's all right. Wondered if the barrel might be ready for a change but it seems alright to me.'

Bryan made a *huh* noise in his throat before continuing to drink.

He'd made sure to leave the gun in the back seat of the car; wrapped up in a package that was similar to the one Phil gave to Dempsey. He was fairly sure he wouldn't need it. Yet.

The landlord of The Forester was on duty as the two men walked in. His name was Simon, and seemed momentarily shocked when Bryan walked through the door, before deciding it was good to see him. Bryan noticed an absence of hair over the past ten years, replaced by an enormous moustache. Simon was a legitimate businessman, and knew better than to mess with anything even remotely crime orientated. So, he resigned himself to pulling pints and serving food with his missus. Bryan, Phil and Simon went way back though, as they had always been loyal patrons of his little pub. He had to thank them for that. At least he remembered their 'usuals' as best he could, though he no longer had the beer that Bryan used to drink.

'So, you enjoying being back in Sovereign City, B?' Phil asked through a mouthful of pie.

'Sort of. It's not exactly what I had in mind.'

Oh yeah, and what did you have in mind?' Phil asked, washing it down with several fingers of ale.

'More money. Not having to hang out with people like Dempsey and Gerrard.'

'Tell me about it. But I still kinda like Dempsey, despite the fact he's a bit of a lost cause. I mean, for example did you know he doesn't even need that eyepatch?'

Bryan stared at him.

'...Right,' he said after a slight pause, not entirely convinced.

'But the good thing is,' Phil went on, 'Is that they're a good source of income and equipment. Gerrard's got so many problems you could make a successful sitcom out of it, and Dempsey's got a line on guns and ammo.'

'And what about Michael? He's still legit?'

'Yeah. I'm glad he kept on the straight and narrow. He keeps face. So we've got a prim and proper supply of cash that way as well. Good for the accounts.'

Bryan flicked his now half-empty glass. He'd worked it out.

'Ten years with no drinking at all. That's what it is.'

'What?'

'I haven't touched a drop in ten years. I'm completely sober. Body isn't used to it.'

'Which is why it tastes bad? Are you sure it isn't just a dud pint?' Phil responded, not convinced.

'I reckon so. I can't have many. I will be on my ass.'

Phil laughed. 'Like you could ever hold your drink before.'

Bryan raised an eyebrow. 'Oh yeah? Did you ever beat thirty-six pints?'

'No I didn't. Point taken, silly bollocks, you don't have to drink it if you don't want.'

They both laughed.

The phone in Phil's pocket vibrated, and he answered it. He listened to the caller for a second, before agreeing with whatever was said. His face then dropped, and he said 'We're on our way.' Bryan responded by finishing his pint, proceeding to put on his jacket as Phil ended the call. Phil stood up, and headed for the door.

'We've got problems. That was Gerrard, said we might be in trouble.'

'What sort of trouble?'

'I'll explain on the way back to Rock Sovereign HQ. Simon, I'm taking this to go!' He yelled at the landlord as they wandered out, gesturing with a near-full pint of beer. Simon didn't have a chance to object as they rushed into the car.

'That person you smacked with the briefcase, he was working for Patrone Alphonso.' Phil said as they weaved in and out of traffic, intermittently drinking his pint. The name Alphonso rang a bell to Bryan. He was an inspiring criminal at some point prior to the imprisonment, and appeared to have escalated in ten years. He was now the head of the Alphonso Crime Family, one of the main gangs within Sovereign City, of Italian origin and not one to mess with. And Bryan had attacked one of his men. No, worse than that, he had *humiliated* him.

That must have been whatever he yelled when I walked off, Bryan thought. It must have been a threat of consequence.

'So, what, we're screwed?' Bryan asked.

'Well, not us *per se*,' Phil responded, 'but there's one or two of Alphonso's scrotes at Rock Sovereign, and Gerrard's in a slightly tough position.'

The car pulled up and both men sprinted into the building. Phil said they should go back to the canteen, as that was where Gerrard and the Alphonso goons were. They rushed in, pushing both of the double doors open at the same time. They were greeted by three armed men in business suits. Gerrard sat on a canteen chair behind them. They swivelled around and aimed at Bryan and Phil. Phil raised his hands to show he was unarmed, but Bryan just stared at them. One of the thugs was in charge, Bryan supposed, purely because of the air of authority that surrounded him. The man Bryan guessed to be leader raised his eyebrows, before speaking to Phil.

'So, you're Bryan and Phil?'

'No, we're Maverick and Ice-Man.' Bryan said flatly.

Phil nodded.

'Sarcasm? Interesting.' The leader said, looking Bryan up and down before continuing to speak. 'Really makes a fuckwit seem more stupid, don't you think?'

Bryan made a derisive laughter noise in his throat, before stuffing his hands into his pockets. He still hadn't put his hands up in surrender to the thugs' firearms. The leader continued to speak.

'Well, that's nice; at least we've got the right people this time. You know, you're the third set of people that have come through those doors and not one was either of you two. Unfortunately we couldn't account for the regular folks that simply *work* at this crappy excuse for a radio station.'

He clamped a hand on to Gerrard's shoulder, gripping it tightly. Bryan noticed Gerrard gritting his teeth. He didn't seem to like his radio station being called 'crappy'.

The leader lowered his weapon, slipping it into a holster at his hip and adjusting his cuffs. The other two kept them trained, one now on Bryan and the other on Gerrard.

'I assume you know who I am?' The leader said.

'Not entirely,' Phil answered. 'We know you're Alphonso's mate?'

'Close enough. I'm a representative of Patrone Alphonso. Yep. Now...' he relaxed his grip, slapping Gerrard's shoulder. '...this man owes us money. Lots of money. Had a bit of a gambling problem, didn't you Gerrard? Come on, now. Speak for the class.'

Gerrard nodded weakly. Although he was looking in Bryan's direction, he wasn't looking directly at him. It was as if he couldn't bring himself to do it. He was staring distractedly at an invisible person over Bryan's right shoulder, nostrils flared.

'My name is Ricardo. Or Ricky, whichever.' The leader said, 'I'm one of the higher ups working for Patrone. A made man, call it what you want. He told me to sort out this fuckwit DJ and get the cash he owes us. We recruited the cowboy from the other station because we became aware of the files he has on Gerrard.

Now, I'll admit, I didn't like having to resort to blackmail and extortion – so often the people you extort are too stupid to figure out what you want and just go to the cops – but in the end I pushed him to go ahead with those files. He was gonna wimp out, originally. Said that maybe things with Gerrard weren't so bad, maybe a simple apology would be fine, blah blah blah.' He chuckled. 'It's funny. People think their lives are so important. And then *you* came along.'

This guy likes the sound of his own voice too much.

'Little did we know Gerrard had his own plans for dealing with the situation. Some high-and-fucking-mighty has-been who he could brainwash into making all his problems go away. He no doubt made up some bullshit story to cover up the gambling?'

Bryan stared hard at Gerrard, angered by his manipulation. He had said something about the argument being caused by the theft of a girlfriend.

'Bingo! Ten points.' Ricky said, gesturing with a finger in the air. 'You beat up the DJ and made off with the files. The files we subsequently reacquired, although they were a little charred. I'm sure you're aware that the mafia don't take kindly to someone attacking their man. So, something needs to be done.'

'Looks that way.' Bryan said.

'Now, if it were up to me we'd just go round the back of the building and shoot you both. And Gerrard too, waste of bullets though he is. But Patrone has other plans. He knows who you are.'

'Oh yeah?' Bryan asked. He turned to Phil, and with slight sarcasm in his voice, added, 'at least people still remember me.'

'Well, you see,' Ricky said smugly scratching at his chest, 'that's where you're wrong. People don't give a shit about you anymore. It's only this recent prison break that's caused a ruckus. Far as they're concerned, 'Bryan Wattson' is just a name, and it's barely even that. You ask someone who you are, and they'll mutter about you being a criminal from about a decade ago in a bored manner. They won't really remember details. Because that's what people are like. But Patrone remembers.'

'Oh, I'm fucking touched.'

'He wants to offer you a job. Although it's not really an offer. More a demand you have to agree to, or we'll break your legs.'

When the word 'job' came from Ricky's lips something clicked in Bryan's mind. Instantly he narrowed down the various thought processes into a single word: *allies.*

'I'm in.' Bryan said, excited about the possibilities of once again having friends in high places.

'Me too.' Phil added determinedly.

'No, Phil.' Ricky said, shaking his head. 'Bryan doesn't have a choice, and Patrone doesn't need you. He told me to let you off with a warning like a kid. You're free to go. Just get out quickly, and take your idiot DJ friend with you. I'm still in two minds about shooting you, so fuck off before it gets made up.'

'You got it, boss. In a bit, Bryan.'

'Yeah, see you later.' Bryan passed Gerrard the car keys as he walked past. Gerrard still wouldn't look at him. The door slammed shut; the thugs lowered their weapons; and Bryan wondered what the hell he'd just gotten himself into.

A short car journey took the four men to a small office building. Inside, Ricky gestured to the others to leave them in peace; and to Bryan to sit down. Bryan nodded, before sitting in a wheeled office chair. The two thugs exited, softly closing the door behind them, an engine noise signifying their departure a few moments later. He leaned back in his chair and looked around. The room was clearly for business, and Bryan guessed some effort had gone into making it look as realistic as possible. A white board with dates and appointments was located on a wall next to a calendar featuring a Sovereign City landmark as its main image. Ricky cleared some paperwork off a desk so he could put his feet up on it. A stereo played quietly to itself from a corner of the room.

'So this is it, the place you're gonna call Job Central for a bit.' Ricky said, smiling to himself as if those two words were an inside joke. 'But first things first, we need to know something. Now, we know you've been in prison for ten years and we know you broke out. But we don't know exactly *why* you were arrested, and what happened after you were. All the radio and TV at the time said was 'things are not as they seem'. So what's the deal, Wattson?'

Bryan proceeded to tell him about the events of ten years ago. He told him about the deal, and of Tony, and of the policeman who found him bleeding on the floor.

'They interviewed me at the hospital. The officer who arrested me was the main interviewer. Another officer I didn't know was with him. Terry something. He didn't say much. They questioned me on various things, seemed quite surprised by some of the answers I gave. But I figured there was no point in lying, I mean why would I? It didn't feel like it was gonna come and bite me in the ass any time soon.'

'So... these questions? What exactly went down?'
'Well... it all happened in those goddamn interviews.'

CHAPTER SIX: THOSE GODDAMN INTERVIEWS

Ten years ago. Interview Seven.

Officer Dwayne Yeasel knew that Bryan Wattson would answer all their questions from the look on his face. It seemed to convey a mixture of defeat and anger at the same time. Yeasel sat on an uncomfortable plastic chair, facing Wattson. His colleague Terry drank coffee whilst the interview took place. The audio recording equipment wasn't in the best of condition, and like the six previous interviews Yeasel fumbled with it for a second before it blinked into life. He hit record and spoke, calmly and clearly. His voice betrayed his years, tarnished by cigarettes in his youth.

'Commencing Interview Seven, one-fourteen p.m. This is Officer Dwayne Yeasel, accompanied by Officer Terrance Norwood. The interviewee, as I'm sure we're all aware now, is Bryan Wattson. Now... Mr. Wattson. We've quizzed you on a lot of things so far: yourself; your job history, if you could call it that. But there are two things we haven't asked you about yet. That is, about your friend and betrayer Mr. Tony Carson; and how it is you two came to be so powerful within Sovereign City in the first place. Perhaps you'd like to enlighten us first of all on Mr. Carson?'

Wattson just smiled. He slouched in his seat, which annoyed Yeasel. He believed he was in control. Yeah, right.

'Anthony James Carson...' Wattson began, 'or 'Tony' to his friends. Ha... guess I won't be calling him Tony for a while, huh?'

Yeasel smirked.

'Born May tenth, a year before me.'

'And how did you two come to meet?'

'Well, when I was starting to forge a career for myself, several years back now, I was working for a local drug pusher called Jeremy Reagan. He introduced me to Tony. At first, we didn't get along. He didn't trust me because of how clinical I was during jobs. Not that I wasn't clinical, I just believe in the old saying: professional, not psychopath. You have your orders, and you carry them out. No questions. There isn't really a place for morality in this line of work, as bad as it makes you feel you have to tell

yourself the guy deserved it. I dunno. I always thought that if morals got in the way, then the people I worked for would take issue with it. But I was always against killing or hurting people unnecessarily.'

'Coulda fooled me,' Norwood interrupted, not changing his vision from the large cup of coffee in his hand.

Yeasel looked at the clock while Wattson spoke. God, he wanted to get home. He'd asked his wife to record the football on TV, and hoped she hadn't forgotten. His favourite team were playing, and he had to shake his head slightly to snap himself out of the thoughts. He needed to focus. He got up and fetched coffee from a thermal flask to regain some semblance of composure. It would be a long afternoon, and a backlog of paperwork meant it would be a long evening as well.

'So, why didn't you and Carson trust each other?' Yeasel asked, taking a sip. Needed sweetener.

'Like I said, he thought I was too clinical. Bordered on obsessive at times. I just told you.'

'And why didn't you like him?'

'To be honest, I always thought he was a bit of a kissass. Three bags full, sir.'

Yeasel wasn't familiar with the term of phrase.

'Anyway... we were on a job together, and I saved his life. We were sitting on a rooftop with a pair of binoculars watching a drug deal with the intention of stealing the stuff. Unfortunately the dealers had other plans. I noticed the lookout on the opposite roof aiming at Tony, and dove at him to knock him behind the low wall we were leaning against. I guess it must have put the shits in him a little bit; man my size leaping at him from across a rooftop.'

He laughed at the memory. But then Wattson's face dropped.

'But that wasn't before I caught a round in the arm. It was a hell of a shot, to be honest. I must've only exposed my arm for about a second, but that was all it seemed he needed.'

He lifted his right sleeve, exposing a four-inch scar. Yeasel couldn't help but wince at the thought.

73

'Tony took the lookout down and basically dragged me off that rooftop. I was bleeding like a bastard, but he got me to one of Reagan's doctors. We started to trust each other slightly more after that.'

'And it just built up from there? This friendship?'

'Yes and no. We weren't what you'd call best buds, but we worked together and started to trust each other's judgement. It all came to a head when we decided that we wanted more. More power. More money. We decided the best way to get those two things was to... shall we say, dispose of Reagan?'

'You killed him?'

Wattson nodded. There was no remorse in his face. No regret. Almost emotionless. Only the barest flicker of determination.

'We drove round to Reagan's office one night and killed him. He had very limited security, didn't think he needed it. Guess he was wrong, huh? Anyway, I was the one to end it, while Tony had taken out several of his thugs. I even used a corny line: 'guess I shot J.R.' which was kinda stupid now that I think about it. It carried weight back then.'

His teeth flashed in the briefest of smiles. Yeasel decided at that point that he'd be glad when this bastard was locked up. He continued with the interview, asking a question that wasn't scripted, but interested him nonetheless.

'And did you ever think it would come to an end? I mean, looking at it, you must have had some inkling or feeling, right? Something was bound to go wrong at some point?'

Wattson shook his head. Flame appeared in his eyes again but for a moment. He seemed good at being able to suppress his emotions.

'Do you have a family, Officer Yeasel?' he asked suddenly.

'Why, yes sir, I do.' Yeasel responded, proud of them all.

'Wife and kids?'

'Two kids, one wife, one dog. As per usual, I believe.'

'Names of the children?' Wattson asked.

'I don't feel like I need to answer that question.'

'Indulge me, Officer Yeasel. You don't need to worry about their privacy. I'm sure your editors are gonna fix this thing to make me seem like Satan anyway. They'll cut this bit.'

'Jackie and Wilson.'

Wattson paused. '...Really? And how would you feel if that was all suddenly taken away from you? As a result of your own actions?'

'Well, I guess I'd feel outraged, upset, and maybe even homicidal.' Yeasel was humouring him. His voice oozed sarcasm.

'My point exactly. You'd want revenge on whichever scumbag took them away from you.'

'I hardly think you could compare what you had to a family, Mr. Wattson.'

'Perhaps not, but I realised a long time ago that it was better not to have a family. I've seen first-hand exactly how losing someone close to you can affect people. Luckily I myself wasn't the person who lost someone, but I felt extremely sorry for the poor guy that did. So I decided not to have a family. Decided not to get settled. Because if anything did happen to me, how would they feel? How would Mrs. Wattson and little Junior feel now if they were at home and I was here? No, I think I made the right choice. Or I certainly hope I did. Or reverse it: what if they were in two different sized boxes in the ground and I was at home all depressed and full of vengeance, drowning myself in scotch and the next thing you know I'm killing everyone in the city to try and track down whoever killed them?'

'Right...' Yeasel began.

'But to answer your previous question, no, I didn't think it would ever end. I never cheated anyone who didn't deserve it, always covered my ass, and always paid my way. What I didn't account for was getting stabbed in the back by someone so close. I thought me and Tony would stick it 'till the end, when we'd go our separate ways in retirement. I guess I don't have to worry about that anymore though, do I?'

'No, I guess not.' Yeasel said, far too smug than he would have liked. He hoped it didn't sound that way on the recording. After a further few questions, they had accomplished their goals for the day. They had learned what they wanted for the time being. Yeasel whispered to Norwood to get him a case file on Reagan. Then he cleared his throat, and spoke towards the tape recorder, clearly and without emotion.

'That's enough for today. Terminating interview; two-twelve p.m. We'll see you tomorrow, Bryan.'

'I look forward to it.'

Yeasel switched off the tape recorder.

******

'So that's how it came to be.' Bryan said when he finished telling his tale.

'Mmm-hmm.' Ricky answered. 'Fair enough. I'll relay the stuff you told me to the boss man.'

'All of it?'

'Well, a cut-down version, yeah. But the basics. Everything he needs to know. Especially the bit about you shooting your former boss.'

'What, you think I'm gonna pay Patrone a visit in the night, too?'

'No, but I think *Mr. Alphonso* needs to know. Just in case you do get any funny ideas.' Ricky made clear. He added extra emphasis to the name.

'But in the meantime, I got a little busywork you could take care of for me. This could be a personal tester. For this particular job you're gonna be calling me boss. I need you to go and pick up a car. One of my associates told me it was parked on Nottingham Road. The fella who owns it tried to take us for a ride, thought it might be a good idea to scrape us out of a lot of cash. Go and show him what it means to mess with us. Steal the car; drop it off at the garage on Mendip Close. There'll be a man waiting. Oh yeah, and if you see the smartass who ripped us off, teach him not to mess with us again.'

Bryan hesitated. He knew he'd be back doing jobs like this eventually, but told himself the man probably had it coming before agreeing.

'Alright, you got it. But I'll want paying.'

'Yeah, I figured as much. Don't worry, we pay our own, and we pay fairly, just no fuckups, okay?'

'It's a deal.'

Bryan stood up, the office chair wheeling back until it gently contacted a filing cabinet, and left the office.

Nottingham Road. It had a certain air to it, that of a road less travelled; a road only travelled when the surrounding means were closed. As such, it was largely deserted, except for four bungalows on one side, and a petrol station with a small shop on the other. The man driving the car had no idea he was being watched, he had simply parked the car close to the petrol pumps and made to fill up. It was an easy drive for him, as he lived in one of the bungalows across the street. Shame his office wasn't as close. Come to think of it, he could see his neighbour's two kids playing some sort of hybrid of football and basketball in the front garden. He dismissed it as the sort of game children play and fumbled with the keys to the fuel filler cap. He briefly clocked a man with a phone before filling up his car. The man was speaking quite angrily into it, as if in an argument with the person on the other end. He stopped about twenty feet away from the car, and waved his free hand as he shouted.

'Listen, Naomi, I don't give a crap about what your mom thinks, we are NOT getting a marriage counsellor... Neither of us could afford it? You really want me to justify why not? What's the damn point? We still love each other! She's insane, you know that? She's always had it in me, that woman! ...No, I'm at the station, now. Just about the fill up and put air in the tyres. Yeah... yeah, I'm on it. Jesus Christ, *women!*'

The man finished putting petrol into his car and went to pay for what he'd put in. He smirked at 'Women!' and paid the man on the phone no more attention, even feeling quite amused that he would probably be asked to leave because of the phone signal and its apparent tendency to blow up petrol stations. As he walked into the little shop he kept his back to his car, and did not notice the man with the phone walk up to it, open the door, fumble with some wires under the steering wheel and drive off.

'That'll be forty-seven dollars and twelve cents, please.' The woman at the till said.

'Thanks, darlin',' the man said, and walked back outside.

The expletive he yelled was heard by two children playing a hybrid of football and basketball across the street.

Bryan adjusted the rear-view mirror as he sped away from the petrol station. He couldn't help laughing inwardly as the station shrank in the mirror.

Like clockwork, he thought.

He'd been watching the man for some time, only minor changes being made to his plans as he realised where the car's former owner lived. It was his plan to begin with to simply steal the car from his home. Witnesses were probable, but ultimately not a major threat. As he pulled his car onto the road opposite the house, the owner had exited and entered the car. Bryan had planned to tail him for a while, in case they passed through a less heavily populated part of town. As luck would have it, the car's former owner was simply crossing the street to fill up with gasoline. Bryan had used the phone trick before, on more than one occasion. It was simple enough, just yell like a bastard and no one was ever any the wiser. The victim had, at best, a short exposure to his raised voice. He was at enough of a distance that a proper description would have been difficult, and he'd made sure to tuck in his arms and slouch his shoulders to conceal his build and height somewhat. The victim simply dismisses you as being in the middle of a domestic crisis and goes on with their day. He was glad that he could use Naomi as a name, and Bryan thanked her silently for being a source of his imagination. He thought about the nurse, and his mind drifted back to ten years ago. He hadn't forgotten what she'd said to him, and what he'd encouraged her to do. He really hoped she'd gotten out of the prison hospital and into somewhere more hospitable. If not, she'd likely be as insane as the people she treated. He'd resigned himself to the fact that he'd never see her again, but was thankful for the little time they did spend together. His creative imagination was never that great; it was always said that Phil was the creative one. Normally he used a simple term such as 'honey' rather than an actual name when attempting to make a fake phone call. Bryan focused his mind on the task in hand as he shifted up to top gear for the long stretch of road leading to Mendip Close. The drop-off point.

The Mendips were a well-off family who lived in Sovereign City many years ago, long before Bryan's imprisonment. During their several generation stay they had amassed themselves a fortune in the business of brewing alcohol, and Mendip Close was the original location of their brewery. The name wasn't a coincidence, of course, they had acquired the rights to rename the road long ago, and it would be a struggle to find someone who could remember what the original name was. The current location of the building - named Supernova Brewery - was on the other main mass of land within Sovereign City's borders, moved on a greater profit motive. However, a slump in the economy meant that the brewery had to close down, and the final remaining Mendip, Steven, had moved out of Sovereign City to the nearby town of Ridgewater to set up a smaller establishment. It had not been a fruitful endeavour, as the pull of potential free alcohol proved too strong in such an anarchic town. Mendip was found three weeks after his arrival to the town. He'd been riding his motorcycle and was involved in a collision, and when police eventually showed up they found his wallet empty and the keys to his new brewery gone. It was obvious that the car had hit him intentionally. The crash helmet he'd been wearing had protected his head brilliantly; the only downside being that the head wasn't attached to his body anymore. The brewery was later found looted and destroyed.

As a result of the large scale movement of Supernova Brewery, the remains of Mendip Close looked miserable. A large portion of the brewery building was gone, either to age or bulldozer. A small garage stood next to the road, looking humble amongst all the broken buildings. Just like Ricky had said. Bryan pulled up outside, and got out. He left the door open as he strolled up to the front door of the garage. It was painted a garish yellow. He knocked on it, and waited. A few seconds later the sound of a chain lock sliding signalled that he had the right place. The door opened inwards, and Bryan was greeted with a red-faced man wearing dungarees and no shoes.

'Yess'um? What'cha want?' The man sounded incredibly tired. Bryan wasn't interested. All he was bothered about was dropping the car off, and getting paid for doing it.

'Erm, I'm one of Ricky's men. Supposed to drop this car off. Just managed to get my hands on one. Tell him he was lucky, it was the last one they had.'

The man didn't move. 'That it there?' He gestured to it. Bryan couldn't help looking around in a condescending manner. There was no other car for a considerable distance.

'Yep.' He left it at that.

'Oh yeah,' the man said, suddenly seeming to remember something. 'He mentioned you'd be coming 'round. It's... Washboard, isn't it? Bryan Washboard?'

'Wattson.'

'Yeah, that's what I said. Wilson.' The man was clearly in no fit state to argue with. He yawned loudly and scratched at his head, blinking slowly. Bryan noticed he was wearing odd socks.

'Rough night, pal?'

'You have no idea, Washton.'

Every time the man got Bryan's surname wrong, it sent a slight twitch through him.

You'll know my name soon enough, you fat fuck.

'Right, well, I'll be off then,' Bryan said, not particularly to the man, but more to anyone who was listening. He turned to leave, but the man held out an envelope.

'This is from Mr. Ricardo. Said to thank you for a good job. I'll get the car where it needs to go.'

'So what do I do?' Bryan said as he pocketed the envelope.

'Walk, I guess. Not too far.'

'Yeah, not far in a car. It's fucking miles on foot.'

'Take your argument up with Mr. Ricardo. I'm just a mechanic,' the man said, holding up his hands.

You're barely that.

Bryan walked away from the garage. The man called back to him.

'Oh... yeah, while I think about it, Mr. Ricardo also said to have a quick look around the car and check it for... 'fuckups'. What he mean by that?'

'I have no idea.' Bryan said as he walked away from the garage.

Cheeky bastard.

CHAPTER SEVEN: SMALL TIME

Five minutes after dropping off the car.

The walk back to Ricky's place was not Bryan's ideal method of getting there, but he couldn't help thinking that the longer he spent away from the man, the better. As he strolled across a good portion of the eastern part of the city, Bryan encountered odd and sometimes stark reminders of the fact he'd been in an isolated grey box for ten years. The majority of the city was very similar, if not the same as it had always been, but it was the little differences that seemed to stick out the most, like differences to buildings and the cosmetics of the streets. As Bryan made to cross a road, he noticed a billboard advertising the latest album for a genre of music that he knew he'd never be able to understand. Cars he'd never seen before drove past him in the street and Bryan was baffled at the style of clothing worn by young kids and teenagers.

Dear God, he really was out of touch with the world.

He felt in his pocket for the envelope. He thought it best to put some distance between him and the garage he dropped the car off at before opening it. He was half expecting it to contain a sarcasm letter from Ricky, and as he turned it over to open it, he wondered why Ricky didn't just wait to give him the envelope when he got back to the office building where Ricky was. He opened it. Inside was a small piece of paper and a very familiar looking bundle. He studied the piece of paper. It contained a short, hand-written note.

Wattson,
    Assuming that a) You can read, and
b) There were no fuckups;
    Get your ass back here as soon as you get this. If you did the job well don't expect any congratulations. I don't get paid for that shit. If you didn't, then why the fuck have you got this letter? Give it back right now and do your fucking job.

Take what else is in the envelope and then eat this note.
Oh, and enjoy the walk.
  Your Boss

Bryan shook his head as he screwed up the note. Ten points on the sarcasm. He was amused by the scrawl handwriting. Was it possible for him to write a sentence without expletives? The mechanic must have written it. Bryan couldn't work out how or why Ricky would have made his way over to the garage to write it himself. Too much effort. So what was the point? To inspire a sense of mild fear? Bryan inwardly chuckled. He'd have to try harder than that: in reality, Ricky was as scary to him as any man trying too hard was. He threw the note nonchalantly into the middle of the road where it was immediately run over by a car. He felt the bundle and – already knowing what it was – opened it. Benjamins. Quite a lot of them. Bryan wondered what the going rate was for a car theft, after tax. Although he wondered when and if he'd get a chance to spend them, what with all the running around for Ricky. Maybe if he played his cards right he'd be able to meet Alphonso. Then it was only a matter of getting Alphonso to trust him. That step would require slightly more effort than stealing a car from a slack-jawed idiot.

As he reached the top of the street where the office building was, the sun was hanging low in the sky. He looked at the battered watch Phil had given him. It was getting late. Bryan stopped for a moment outside the building. He didn't particularly *want* to have anything more to do with Ricky. In the short space of time that Bryan had known him, he had quickly dismissed him as an arrogant prick. But arrogance can get you far in the criminal underworld, especially if you have the guts to back it up. Ricky sure had enough guts. Bryan was happy to tell Ricky where to stick his jobs, and ten years ago he would have probably just taught Ricky a lesson for being so cocky, but not now. These jobs were major sources of income, hell, the stack of notes stuffed into his pocket and zipped up tight were proof of that. He was going to need that money for the plans he had in his head.

With a sigh, he pushed the door of the office building open and stepped inside.

Ricky was waiting for him. There wasn't much reaction as Bryan walked into the room.

'Wattson. How's it going?' he asked.

As if he really wanted to know.

'Fine. A bit tired, but a really long walk'll do that to you.'

'Yeah, especially for guys your age. So I heard you sorted out the problem with the car?'

'I guess your mechanic friend let you know?'

'Sure did. I guess you didn't screw up too badly, *Washboard*...'

He sniggered at the name. Bryan fought off the urge to punch him.

'...but you could have done it faster.'

Well, at least the note was right. Not much in the way of thanks.

'Look, can I go now?' Bryan asked. 'It's getting late, and I'm tired of this room and everyone in it.'

They were the only ones there.

Ricky stared at him flatly. 'Yeah. Get the hell out of here. Report back tomorrow morning. Mr. Alphonso rang earlier and gave me info about a second job. I think you'll be able to handle it. I'll fill you in the details tomorrow.'

'Do I at least get a car home?'

'Yeah, I suppose I owe you that much. Here.'

He held out a single key. Bryan took it.

'Don't keep me waiting tomorrow morning.' Ricky said.

With a slight nod of the head, Bryan left the office. The car was parked outside. Nondescript. Silver. Perfect. He slid into it and began to drive back to Michael's garage. He wasn't particularly looking forward to sleeping there, but realised he had to take what was given to him. However, he made a small pact with himself that the second thing he would buy – after a deliciously greasy takeout meal from a Chinese restaurant three streets from the garage - was an apartment. Somewhere he could sleep without the fear of getting agonising cramp or poisoned from the heavy lead-based fumes emanating from the cans of paint strewn about the place.

Mickey's Motors was empty, save for a few rats, which scurried away from the lights as Bryan flipped them on. The name of the establishment puzzled Bryan, and he yawned loudly whilst considering it. Michael hated being called 'Mickey'. To quote him: 'I don't want to be named after a rodent.' The only nickname he was half okay with was when Phil occasionally called him Mikey, and although he acknowledged the difference between the two was very slight, he still considered it enough to warrant an argument if anyone got them confused. He locked the garage behind him.

Bryan crashed onto the bed, and without bothering to switch the lights in the back room off, fell into an uneasy sleep.

'You just don't fucking get it, do you? I told you how you can leave this all behind, and you said no. Instead, you're risking the lives of all your friends in this stupid thirst for vengeance...'

'The fuck I am. I've been working towards this moment for a long time, and I'll finish it, with or without your help. I'm coming for you, Tony. I want him to know that, and when the time comes, I'll be ready...'

Then cold, heartless laughter rang out, daring defiance in the swirling mists.

Bryan opened his eyes. It was morning. What a weird dream. He couldn't remember all of it. He'd been talking to someone, but he couldn't work out who it was. They were shrouded in darkness, but whoever it was they seemed to not trust him anymore. Bryan hadn't had a dream like that in ages. They used to occur frequently when he was a young man, but not for a long time. He glanced around the room. *The paint fumes*, he told himself. *Ignore it. Get yourself up, gotta go and see Ricky.*

The same car from last night was there. A silver Alfa Romeo. Great. Someone once told Bryan you couldn't be a true petrolhead until you'd driven one, so this was something off his bucket list at least. It almost seemed worth breaking out of prison and doing jobs under the command of an idiot for. Almost. Bryan remembered what Ricky had said yesterday. This job was from the big man himself. Alphonso. That cheered Bryan up a bit, the chance to get into contact with the man. Then it was only a matter of time and effort...

Ricky wasn't at the office, but a telephone was, which conveniently rang a few minutes after Bryan arrived. Just enough time to fetch himself coffee. Maybe caffeine would replace alcohol in his life. Certainly tasted a hell of a lot better than whatever he drank the previous day at The Forester. He glanced around the room as the phone rang. The only other person there was a presumably low-ranking member of the gang who had let him in, who shook his head when Bryan gestured towards the phone. He shrugged, then picked the phone up for himself.

He wasn't in a particularly serious mood.

'Joe's Crematorium: You kill 'em, we grill 'em.'

'It's me, dipshit.' Ricky answered sternly. 'And I wouldn't piss around if I were you. Need I remind you that you owe us? And screwing around like that is likely to get you on my bad side. And trust me, you don't wanna get on my bad side.'

It was meant as a threat. Bryan took it more as a friendly jibe.

'What do you want, Ricky? More work for Mr. Alphonso?'

'Yes. That's better. A bit of respect. Change of plans; we need something done. Except, it's not going to be easy. Compared to driving a car away from a gas station anyway. Some young upstart has been acquiring a lot of money. And we don't know where from. So your job is to go into the place where he works and steal the hard drive to his computer. According to our sources, he's clumsy. Everything we need will be on that drive. Then we can, shall we say *away* with him and use the assets for ourselves.'

Go into an office and steal a computer? Simple. Bryan thought. How is that difficult?

'Your main problem will be getting caught, obviously. This guy has a security detail and they *will* take you down if they see you.'

'Right. You really like the sound of your own voice, don't you Ricky?' Bryan asked. He just wanted to get on with it.

'It's been likened to angels singing hymns. Get to the office, get the computer, and get back. And try not to get caught... the place only operates at night so it should be locked up tight in the day. There'll be a few guards on patrol for thieving scumbags such as yourself. Take 'em down if you need to, but don't leave no trace. And for God's sake, do not do anything which could trace this back to Mr. Alphonso. You may as well write a bounty on a sheet of paper and staple it to your forehead if you do that.' Ricky said the last sentence menacingly; and there was an audible growl as he finished.

'I'll bear that in mind.' Bryan said. He wasn't scared of Ricky, he'd seen too many people like him get their comeuppance in his time. 'Where do you want it?'

'You remember the factory that used to make fireworks?' Bryan did. 'Well, if you get it done right, you can take it there. There'll be a man waiting. Then you can go home while he gives it to the big man himself. Or rather, to me in front of the big man so it looks like I did most of the hard work. You know how it is, chain of command and all. Wouldn't want any of you getting above your place...'

A few minutes later, as the conversation came to a close, Bryan couldn't help thinking two things. He'd need to try and give the hard drive to Patrone himself, or at least be there when it was handed in. He also realised that if that did happen he was going to have to try seriously hard not to headbutt Ricky in front of an influential and powerful crime boss.

The upstart's building was imposing, but Bryan had been given rough instructions on the location of the hard drive. There was a large double front door, which was far too obvious. Parking the car a couple of streets away, Bryan walked around the side of the building. He stopped behind a large dumpster just before he saw the security camera pointing the opposite way down the alley. By the looks of it, he wouldn't be able to slip past it without it catching him. Pressing himself against the wall, he shuffled further along, eyeing a chain link fence around the back of the office. That would make a good place to enter, but what to do about the camera? Bryan considered smashing it, but then had a better idea. One which would not only remove the camera from the equation, but hopefully help him get in at the same time. He lifted himself onto a dustbin and positioned himself underneath the camera. Making sure it didn't catch him; he gripped the camera and flipped it upwards, so it was pointing into the sky. The rotary mechanisms squealed as they rotated. He then jumped off the dustbin and calmly walked through the chain link fence.

The security feed suddenly changed angles, sharply flipping upwards. The security guard tapped the video screen, confused. The cameras could be rotated, sure, but not that fast. He sighed. A bird must have hit it. He'd mentioned that the cameras needed to be changed before, but did anyone ever listen to him? Like hell. He cleared his throat as he lifted himself from the chair, his sizeable bulk making it somewhat awkward. He flipped the TV onto a more sensible channel and exited the room. Maybe he could mess with the joints and fix the camera into place. He considered it as he opened the door to the outside. Or maybe he could just...

The security guard's thoughts abruptly ended as a metal dustbin lid smashed over his head. He slumped to the ground, not conscious for long enough to utter a sound. A dull thud as the body hit the ground, a slightly quieter one as the lid followed suit. Bryan grabbed the guard's leg and proceeded to awkwardly drag him to one side. His size was not helping.
You're a big boy, amigo. Jesus Christ.
Once the guard was out of sight behind the wall, Bryan grabbed his keys, and checked that the security camera was still pointing upwards. It was. It had worked, surprisingly. With one final look around, Bryan slipped into the office.

Inside, the office was dimly lit. And quiet. Open boxes and stacks of paper were strewn everywhere. Bryan flipped a switch to extinguish what little light was coming from a tiny bulb in the ceiling. He found the security room a few moments later. If you could call a single computer with a few video screens and a television playing an antiques program a security room. Bryan unplugged the computer, but left the television on. He didn't want a sudden change in noise levels to risk what he was doing. A noise from outside the door startled him, and he darted around as a knock came on the door, fourfold and fairly forceful.

'Hey man, you okay? Heard something outside...'

Bryan walked towards the door, positioning himself behind it as the noise grew in volume. As the second guard made to enter the room Bryan slammed the door into his face, knocking him back and sending a curse flying into the darkness. Bryan opened the door and dragged the dazed man into the security room. He hit him twice, hard, leaving the man out cold. He suddenly realised that if something did go wrong, he wasn't exactly armed to defend himself. His new pistol was still in the back of Phil's car, which he had driven off in, and the front of a door and a dustbin lid could only get him so far. The two guards he'd taken out were not armed, either. Eventually, he had to settle for a screwdriver lying on the table next to the television.

He forced the unconscious mass awkwardly under the desk, and tucked the chair underneath to hide it somewhat. Not that it would make a massive difference if the lights were switched on, but Bryan reckoned it was the best he could do under the current circumstances. The security room gave no indication as to which direction to go, and it certainly didn't show where the computer was. The rough instructions given to him by Ricky suddenly seemed somewhat meaningless. Bryan decided to move further into the building. He crept along the corridor. It stretched out in front of him, dark and uninviting. As he moved along he became aware of loud voices and laughter coming from a door on the left. It was slightly open. He peeked inside, and saw several security guards around a table, a television on in the background and bottles of alcohol and snacks strewn about the place. They appeared to be part way through a game of cards. Judging by the sound of the voices and laughter it was a staff room of some description, and the guards didn't seem to be doing their jobs very well. Unless, that is, their job descriptions included heavy drinking and the occasional accusation of 'You looked at my cards, you cheating bastard.' These guards were armed. A pistol on the table seemed like it belonged to the unconscious body under the security room's desk.

Moving past the party room, Bryan became aware of a final room at the far end of the corridor. The door looked slightly more professional, and a plaque was on it, which stated 'MANAGER', with a faded name beneath it.

Jackpot.

Inside the room was empty, and Bryan immediately homed in on the laptop on the desk in the centre of the room. He flipped it upside-down and removed the hard drive, cursing inwardly at the heavy-handedness caused by using a screwdriver that was far too large. He thought about simply stealing the entire laptop, but really didn't want to risk an argument with Ricky over it. It was probably too obvious.

The door opened. A small man walked in, fumbling with a set of keys as he entered. He froze as he saw Bryan, Bryan did the same. He opened his mouth to speak, a confused look on his face.

'Who the...' he began loudly.

Bryan didn't have time to do much, and so simply did the first thing that came into his head. He threw the laptop, now without hard drive, at the man and lunged at him. The man caught the laptop, dropping the set of keys. As Bryan flew at him he wildly swung the laptop, catching Bryan in the arm and sending him slightly off-course. The screwdriver flew out of his hand, sticking upright into the soil of a potted plant. Nevertheless, Bryan bundled him against the wall and forced a hand over his mouth, the man flailing in a futile effort to escape. He managed to free one of his arms and threw a wild punch, but Bryan smashed the man's head backwards into the door, sending him crashing to the ground.

Someone would have heard that. Hell, a deaf person with their hands over their ears would have heard that. Bryan grabbed the set of keys from the ground and stuck them in the lock. The third key was correct, and the door clicked in a satisfactory manner. A knock came from the other side. Three different guards asked three different versions of the same question: 'Are you all right, sir?'

Bryan had to get out. But that was the only door. And there were at least three guards. His only weapon was a laptop with a now cracked screen and the only other thing he had was the screwdriver. Bryan looked around desperately. There was no way in hell he could take them on... so what was he going to do?

Think, Bryan, THINK!

He thought he heard the sound of a gun cocking.

'Shit, he might be in trouble in there. Get this door open.'

'You got it. On three.'

Four seconds later the three guards burst in through the door. Two of them had guns drawn, the third noticed the crumpled form of their boss on the floor, blood coming from a large gash on the back of his head. The laptop lay on the desk.

'What the hell happened here?'

'Dunno. Stupid bastard must have hit his head really hard.'

'On the laptop? What, he smash it over his own head?'

'Well there's no-one else here... must have been on the sauce. Fell over again. Least there's no bathtub around like last time. I suspect he'll tell us when he comes to. Get him to the staff room, patch up the back of his head, and then deal me a fresh hand.'

'We should take him to a hospital.'

'Too risky. Besides, he doesn't pay me enough to give that much of a shit. Now, where are those cards? I've got two hundred bucks to win back...'

As the three security guards left the room carrying their boss, not one of them noticed the open window behind the desk.

Like a fucking charm.

Checking to make sure the hard drive was in his pocket; Bryan dusted himself off as he jogged up the street and away from the building. He had to admit, that was pretty good. He was hardly going to stand and attempt to fight three armed guards when there was a perfectly usable window for him to clamber out of. The car was still where he left it, and he climbed in and adjusted the centre mirror. As he drove off, he was sure he heard the sounds of sirens in the far distance. So they had decided to call an ambulance after all.

CHAPTER EIGHT: FOOT IN THE DOOR

The long-derelict fireworks factory had been there for decades. Bryan remembered that his dad had been there to stock up on firecrackers and enormous exploding rockets for the fourth of July when he was younger. That seemed like a lifetime ago now. Well, half of one anyway. Now it was the place he was supposed to drop off the hard drive. He probably should have taken the time to look into the hard drive to see what all the fuss was about. All he could tell from the laptop's desktop was that the upstart sure loved his spreadsheets.

He briefly considered the salary for the job. It would probably be worth a few dollars to Patrone. If it assisted in taking down the upstart, at least Bryan could look forward to a fairly reasonable payout for it. Hopefully Ricky wouldn't attempt to steal all the blame for retrieving it. If he tried, then Bryan was perfectly willing to have an argument with the man to ensure Patrone knew exactly who had risked himself to get the hard drive.

As soon as I get in cahoots with Patrone, Ricky's fucking gone. I'll convince Patrone how much of a tool he is, then he can go and pick a ditch in Ridgewater...

The yard of the factory was empty, which puzzled Bryan somewhat. There was no one around, no pedestrians or anyone who vaguely looked like they wanted to pick up the drive. Bryan stepped out of the car, leaving the door open as he strolled into the yard. There was no one on the security gate either, but the barrier was pre-raised, almost as if it had been expecting visitors. Bryan hadn't noticed the black saloon car tailing him since the office building, and as he pressed his face up against the dirty glass of one of the factory's windows he also didn't notice the same car entering the yard from the other end before disappearing quickly behind the building.

'Where the hell is everyone?' Bryan asked aloud.

The answer to his question came in the form of several gunshots echoing from inside the largest factory building. The glass Bryan had been peering through seconds earlier exploded and he hurled himself behind a low concrete barrier, landing painfully on his side as the thought process that he was being shot at caught up with him.

'Shit! Goddamn it!' Bryan yelled out as he choked on the dust thrown up as he hit the ground. He tucked his legs in, making sure they weren't exposed. The gunfire stopped. Maybe they thought he'd been hit? And just where the hell had it come from?

A smart-looking man in an expensive-looking suit dropped into the cover behind him, pressing the barrel of a pistol into his neck.

'One move, and I'll finally discover if grey matter really is grey.' The man said quietly.

'Oh shit. Who the hell are you?' Bryan asked, raising his hands.

'Shut up. No questions. Keep fucking quiet.' The man said flatly, before 'Wait a minute... green jacket and grey cargos, you're Wattson, right?'

'Yeah, that's me, and that must make you the man I'm meant to give this hard drive to? Well, there's...'

The sentence was interrupted by another torrent of gunfire from within the building, only this time it seemed to come from all sides. Several chunks of concrete were torn out of the barrier the two men were sheltering against.

'Shit!' The sharp-dressed man yelled, followed by a string of Italian. 'Looks like there's four of them. I reckon we can take 'em out if we work together.'

'Yeah, slight problem there mate, I'm unarmed!' Bryan yelled back at him.

'You're what?' The man breathed incredulously. Then he suddenly screamed 'Head down!'

Bryan threw himself onto the ground as the man fired three shots over his head. He could still remember how awful it was to be shot, so he sure as hell wasn't going to ignore the only man with any means of shooting back. A scream came from their left, as the sharp dressed man shot an assailant twice in the chest. He leaned back against the cover, and unloaded the now empty magazine.

'Name's Vini...' The man said, replacing the magazine with a fresh one and tapping the bottom for good luck. 'You said you were unarmed, right? Well, there's your gun. Over there.' He gestured towards the man he'd just shot. Bryan glanced at the body. There was a good thirty feet of open ground between him and the pistol dropped by the assailant. He was never going to make it in a million years. He turned to Vini.

'You've got to be taking the piss! There's no way in hell I'm getting that gun with three of them aiming at us!'

'That's why I'm going to provide covering fire! Then you can run for it while I keep 'em suppressed!' Vini replied.

'I don't like this...' Bryan said, but realised he had no choice.

Just keep running. Head down and run like hell.

He breathed out slowly. He didn't much like the idea of being shot again. His neck was beginning to ache from the awkward angle he was laying at.

'On go.' Vini said. He peered over the top of the concrete barrier. A thug had appeared on a high up gantry. 'Three... Two...'

There was a wet splattering noise as Vini was shot through the head. He collapsed backwards as blood sprayed onto Bryan's shoes, body flailing in spasmodic motion as he hit the floor. The pistol clinked as it hit the dirt next to him.

'Argh! Shit!' Bryan yelled. He coughed and had to fight his gag reflex when he saw Vini's pulverised face. It had been far too long since he'd seen an injury like it, and his stomach wrung itself out as he stared at the lifeless body. He swatted at his sleeves and shoes to remove chunks of meat, reacting as though they were diseased. As Vini's pristine white shirt turned slowly crimson Bryan found himself with the unpleasant task of rifling through the man's pockets for his spare ammunition. That looked like an expensive suit, too. It was perfectly tailored, presumably one of the perks of being a Mafioso. He finally succeeded on the ammunition front: two magazines' worth, plus the one in the gun. At least he didn't have to risk the run to the other pistol, but that still didn't make up for the fact that his only backup was in a smeared mess on the floor next to him. And as it turned out, he couldn't answer Vini's conundrum on whether grey matter really IS grey because of all the gore surrounding it.

The thug was still on the high gantry and was aiming at the barrier to the right of Vini. Bryan was on the opposite side, to the left of Vini's corpse.

Bryan leaned out of the far left of the cover and took aim. The thug didn't have time to react before four bullets, one of which missed, slammed into both him and the adjacent wall. He toppled off the gantry and slammed onto the stone floor. The thug's pistol went off in his death throes when it hit the floor, causing a car alarm to blare from somewhere to Bryan's right. Two more to go. Bryan suddenly realised that he had no idea what the hell he was going to do with the hard drive at this point. It was in the dirt a few inches from his left foot, only lightly splattered with the contents of Vini's head. Bryan stuffed it into his pocket, making a mental note to get his jacket steam cleaned as soon as he was out of here. Or to burn it. He heard the sound of pounding footsteps, and spun to his left to see one of the two remaining thugs aiming at him. He reacted quickly, consciously aware of another set of sprinting footsteps somewhere behind him, and shot the thug three times. The man barely had time to scream in pain as he hit the floor. Bryan exhaled, and then felt a pair of heavy arms grabbing his shoulders as he was hauled over his concrete barrier. As he was being manhandled he emptied the last of his magazine in desperation, firing wildly in all directions. A yelp came from his attacker as one of the bullets tore through his arm, splintering bone and ripping muscle, but he landed a heavy, adrenaline-fuelled punch in Bryan's face. Bryan was thrown to the ground, the dirt and grit exacerbating his battered face. He spluttered in pain and felt blood in his nose. He covered his right nostril with a finger and blew his nose, sending out a spray of viscous red liquid. The pistol had flown out of his hand as he fell, and as he looked up he saw his attacker had fallen to his knees, clutching his bleeding arm. The pistol landed between them.

The thug stood slowly and stumbled towards the pistol, as Bryan got to his hands and knees. His face was on fire, his lungs full of dust. He looked at the thug, his face dropping as he saw the pistol in his hand. Bryan stood up. A good six feet separated them. The thug was pulling a face with a mixture of smug self-satisfaction, with the slightest twinge of pain.

'Goodnight, you bastard.' The thug said.

The pistol clicked. The thug's face dropped, as did Bryan's, although his was more due to shock.

'What the fuck...?' The thug exclaimed.

Bryan charged, wrapping his arms around the man's legs and shoulder barging him to the floor, using his strength and weight to topple his opponent. He forced his foot onto the thug's crippled arm and, sat across him, wrenched the pistol from his grip. He considered executing the thug there and then, but remembered there was no ammo. Instead, he flipped the pistol in his hand and smashed it against the thug's temple. He fell into the dirt next to his unconscious enemy, breathing heavily. His face was killing him. He raised his arms into the air.

'Why is it ALWAYS the FACE?!' Bryan screamed. He wasn't doing very well when it came to facial injuries. He pulled back the slide on the pistol, freezing and feeling a wave of nausea as he noticed the bullet now occupying the chamber. He hurled it through the air, not wanting to be in contact with the round that might have killed him. He lay there for some minutes longer, breathing returning slowly to normal from heavy and laboured.

He became aware of a tinny rendition of *Ride of the Valkyries* coming from the other side of the concrete barrier. He got up and walked around to the other side of it. The source of the instrumental was a mobile phone in Vini's jacket. Miraculously, it was clean. Bryan looked at the display: RICKY CALLING.

He flipped up the phone, answering it with silence.

'Vincenzo? You there? Where's the hard drive?'

'It's me.' Bryan answered, face still hurting.

'Wattson? How the hell did you get this phone? Where's Vincenzo?' Ricky barked angrily. That was the wrong question. It should have been 'Where's Vincenzo's face?' to which the answer would have been 'spread like jam two feet across the dirt next to him'.

'Dead.' Bryan responded, coughing after the word.

'Vini's dead?! You killed him?!'

'No, of course not! I think some of the guys from the office place where I got the hard drive followed me...'

'So it's your damn fault?' Bryan heard Ricky fight off a verbal outburst, instead falling into a sigh on the other end of the phone. 'Do you have the hard drive?'

'Yes.' Bryan answered simply. He turned to face away from Vini. One or two flies had already descended onto him.

'Right. Get it to where I am; you can give it to the big man. Our base of operations is an Italian place called 'Sicilian Hospitality'. On the corner of 22nd.' Ricky told him the address. 'Meantime, we'll get some people to sort out Vini. Give him a proper burial. Ugh, shit, his wife's gonna kill me...'

Bryan ended the call, something in the back of his mind gnawing at him that Vini's death was indeed his fault, and it wasn't Ricky's rather loud accusation. The thugs had followed him, and if he'd been more careful... No. he pushed the thoughts to one side.

Stuff like this happens. With the amount of guns and unfriendly relationships thrown around in this career someone's bound to end up on the receiving end. Besides, Vini would have known what he signed up for. It couldn't be helped.

...or could it?

Bryan stepped into the car, checking one final time that the hard drive was in his pocket. As he sat in the car, he rubbed his forehead with a grimy sleeve, trying not to think about Vini anymore. Who was he kidding? This was all his fault. He only hoped he would never have to meet Vini's wife.

Sicilian Hospitality. Bryan chuckled at the name as he pulled up outside of the place. Although it appeared to be a restaurant, he didn't think that the 'Hospitality' part of the title meant free olives. He assumed it was more of a 'piano wire and concrete shoes' sort of deal. Nevertheless, he was somewhat nervous as he pushed the doors open. Expecting to find half a dozen angry mobsters aiming submachine guns at him for the incident at Rock Sovereign and now with Vini's death being sort of his fault, he was pleasantly surprised to find a friendly-looking man waiting behind a small podium smiling at him.

'Good afternoon, sir.' The man said; an ever-so-slight Italian edge to his voice. 'Table for one is it, or do you have a lady friend waiting in the car?' He grinned wryly at Bryan when he shook his head.

'No thanks, I'm, err, unfortunately here on business.'

'Yes, of course, sir. We hire out for parties and weddings, but request a thirty percent deposit be paid up front.'

'No, not that sort of business. I'm here to see Ricky.'

The waiter's face changed slightly at the mention of the name. It became instantly less customer-focussed.

'Of course. Follow me.'

Bryan hurriedly followed the waiter through the restaurant, not making eye contact with any of the customers eating their meals. He'd left his jacket in the car under the seat; he didn't want the blood on it causing any unwanted attention. He just hoped no-one looked at his shoes. They found Ricky in a secluded alcove at the back of the restaurant, hidden from the regular customers by selectively placed foliage and gilded columns.

He ended a phone call as they approached. He placed his hands on the table and eyed Bryan.

'How you doing, kid?' He asked. 'Still got what I need?'

A solid punch between the eyes?

'Yeah, here it is.' Bryan responded, casually pushing his thoughts aside. The waiter left them. As soon as he was out of earshot, Ricky slammed his palms onto the table.

'So do you mind telling me just what the FUCK went off up there?!' Ricky demanded, quickly dropping to a stage whisper after the initial outburst. 'What the hell happened? How difficult was it to drop a hard drive off and pass it on to someone? Hmm? Or maybe you've forgotten that Vini's dead, and there's the very real situation that this supposed *stealth* mission has gone so far down the shitter it's almost out to sea?!'

'There was nothing I could have done.' Bryan said flatly.

'Nothing you could have done.' Ricky repeated. 'Oh, of course that makes it all alright then. Just give me the damn hard drive. And the keys to your car.'

Bryan placed them on the table. He kept a hand on the hard drive.

'Where's Patrone?'

'He's here. Upstairs. In the VIP area.'

'This place doesn't look like it has a VIP area.'

'It doesn't. But the management has a special arrangement with Mr. Alphonso. So you'll find him upstairs.'

'Shouldn't we go then?'

'We? No. This is your mess. You can sort it out. You can go and tell the big man that you fucked up. I'll keep the hard drive.' He placed a hand over it, as Bryan retracted his own. 'And don't expect this to go well, Wattson. Remember, you're only working for us because of Gerrard's mistakes. And because you don't appreciate the chain of command.'

The waiter appeared behind them.

'Take Wattson up to the VIP area, would you kindly? And get me another gin and tonic.'

'Right you are, Mr. Ricardo.' The waiter responded with a slight bow. 'This way, Mr. Wattson.'

As Bryan moved his hand away from the hard drive to stand, he uncovered the red-spattered corner for Ricky to see. Though he didn't say anything, it was obvious from the way he shifted in his seat that the sight of Vini's blood troubled him deeply. He swallowed, a noise akin to a jet engine in the quietness of the restaurant. Bryan didn't look at him. He almost felt like he couldn't.

They walked up a flight of stairs. And came to a door. It had a small plaque on it with 'VIP AREA' written on it in fancy letters. Bryan thanked the waiter, who walked off to speak to a family sitting around a table nearby. They were apparently unhappy with the quality of the garlic bread. Bryan turned to face the door. He breathed out, cleared his throat and knocked on the door.

Nothing.
It's never easy, is it?
He pushed the door open, and stepped inside.

CHAPTER NINE: ALPHONSO

The so-called 'big man', as Ricky had put it, was leaning against the table and reading from a sheet of paper. He looked up from his reading as Bryan entered. He seemed to be Bryan's age plus five years at least; and while physically imposing his demeanor was friendly as he stepped towards him. He lifted himself up from the desk and spoke to Bryan in a firm, authoritative tone. Hair neatly trimmed and with features sharp enough to cut diamond, his age and the stress of his job was nevertheless shown in his eyes, which were a bloodshot grey.

'Ah, Mr. Wattson,' Patrone Alphonso said warmly, extending a hand for Bryan, who shook it. 'So good to meet you.'

'And you, Mr. Alphonso.' Bryan responded. Still nervous. His face still ached from the blow earlier, and he imagined he looked like he'd been dragged through a hedge backwards. Alphonso's grip was as harsh as his facial features.

'How are you? I must say, I didn't think I'd ever get to speak to you, considering the fact that you're supposed to be incarcerated.'

'I'm sure I haven't the faintest idea what you mean.' Bryan said through a smile. He presented the prison tag on his wrist, its faded lettering and numbers making it look more like an obscure wristband than a prison tag. Patrone looked at it with some interest.

'This is an identification tag? I am surprised you're still wearing it. Surely it makes you feel like you are still in prison?'

'Well, between you and me, I initially didn't have the means to remove it. Now, though, it acts as a reminder to never ever go back there. I didn't really like prison all that much. Felt like I needed a change of scenery.'

Alphonso chuckled through his nose, although he didn't actually smile. 'And why not? Well, I say good for you, you appear to have the authorities stumped, and I must admit I didn't know myself until Ricardo told me. Can I interest you in a drink?'

Alphonso gestured towards a bottle of whisky standing next to two squat tumblers, which appeared to be a vintage of some sort. Considering his privileged position as the head of his crime family, Bryan assumed it was very expensive.

Nevertheless, he shook his head.

'No, I don't anymore. Thank you anyway.'

'Like to keep a clear head? I like that.' Alphonso answered. He poured himself a tumbler's worth. A large one. So large in fact there was barely enough room in the tumbler for the ice he added to it. He took a small sip, eyes not leaving Bryan as his body processed it.

'Now, to business.' He said, lowering himself back onto the desk and crossing his feet. 'As you know, events have recently transpired concerning the radio station Rock Sovereign, fronted by a man who tells everyone to call him Gerrard.'

'Yeah, looks like it.'

'And ultimately the whole debacle culminated in your effort to secure a hard drive, did it not? An effort in which I'm told you succeeded, but at a cost.'

'Mr. Alphonso, listen...'

'Mr. Alphonso? Please, Mr. Wattson, call me Patrone. It is my name, after all.'

'Alright, but only if you call me Bryan.'

'Very well. The cost of said effort was the loss of one Vincenzo Pernigotti. A very respectable man, his death was untimely and unfortunate. He served loyally for many years, and his funeral will be a tragedy at which we will all feel morose. Ricardo has attempted to explain what occurred at that derelict factory, mentioning briefly that there was a shootout and Vincenzo was an unfortunate casualty. If I'm being perfectly honest, the wheres and whyfores do not concern me.'

'There was nothing I could have done. I was unarmed, and he was trying to secure me a weapon. Neither of us saw the thug who killed him.'

'I appreciate that, Bryan. Ultimately though, I understand that nothing can be changed. And despite the loss, you have proven that you can deliver, with both the hard drive and the car Ricardo asked you to pick up.'

'Thanks, Mr. Alphonso.'

'There's something else I wanted to discuss with you though, Bryan. I have not pulled you all the way from your other business to make small talk. It concerns loyalty. As you know, you attacked a DJ at Chillax FM, which happens to be a property under the influence of a dear friend of mine. Personally, I would see it that both establishments formed some sort of co-operative effort. Profit would be greater that way.' He looked like he loathed the word *Chillax*.

Bryan could see where this was going. At best he predicted a serious grilling for attacking the man, and at worse... perhaps he's outlived his usefulness.

'Nevertheless,' Alphonso went on, 'I am not at liberty to tell my associates what to do. Although I've given them advice, they seem somewhat reluctant to follow it. It's a shame. Although I would bet you think I like opera and classical music, I must admit I am quite a fan of progressive rock...'

Bryan gave him a curious smile. He hadn't considered it, but was starting to like the man more and more as he got to know him, regardless of any fate that awaited him.

'But there is still the case of loyalty. As I mentioned, I value it. And we seem to have one or two problems with it at present...' He put a hand into his pocket. Bryan suddenly felt nervous, feeling that he had to intervene.

'Listen, Patrone, I had no idea that the man I attacked was an associate of yours! I just wanted to earn a bit of cash to help me get by! And listen, I don't know what Ricky told you, but there's one or two things I want to say about him...'

Patrone raised his other hand to end Bryan's stammering.

'I would choose your words carefully. I wasn't talking about you, Mr. Wattson.'

Bryan stopped. His mouth hung open for a second while his brain caught up with what Alphonso had just said. He... wasn't talking about him?

The Italian looked at him.

'That changed your tone, did it not? Allow me to ask you something. How much experience have you had with a crime family such as mine?'

Bryan had had minor dealings with Alphonso's ilk in the past, but neither knew nor cared much about them. Aside from their role as buyer or seller, he had no time for the intricacies of their little worlds. Nevertheless, he decided against openly mocking Alphonso in front of him.
'Not enough, I reckon. A few business deals with your sort in the past, but certainly not enough to know how you tick.' Bryan's nerves had not yet subsided.

'Then if you don't mind, allow me to give you a brief insight into how things work. I won't insult your intelligence. Do you know about the concept of the made man?'
Bryan nodded, but said, 'Sort of. Ricky is one. Said so himself.'
'The made man - such an archaic term.' Alphonso placed his tumbler onto the desk behind him, and it was now almost empty. 'There are several terms meaning the same thing. But the concept is the same. Historically speaking, made men were untouchable. In the past, crime families such as mine would go on record with the other families as to which members were made. To threaten or kill a made man required explicit permission from the crime family higher-ups, or in my case, *me*. Anyone who went against this creed, the punishment was death. Now, though, certain rules are more relaxed. Different families in different cities have their own rules regarding this sort of thing, I remember the days when the rules were hard and fast, but now they seem to be changeable as the situation suits.'
'And the DJ was made?'
'Goodness, no.' Alphonso said. 'If he was, you'd be dead.'

That sent a wave of terror through Bryan, followed by a larger wave of relief.

'So I'm not going to get strangled in my sleep?'

'No, the problem was never with you. I appreciate that it wasn't the greatest start to this new career you're trying to forge, but at the same time... I understand that you aren't the man you once were. Trust me; I have the same problems, myself...' He said it with absolutely no trace of sarcasm or irony in his voice.

You cheeky bastard! Not the man I once was...?

'I have discussed the events with my business associate at Rock Sovereign, and the man will live with a bruised ego for a while, but there will be no further conflict.'

Bryan cleared his throat. 'I appreciate the concern, Mr. Alphonso. So why are you telling me?'

'Because I assume that, given your circumstances with being shot, you should come to value loyalty, as do I.'

'You know that. Who is it?'

'Well, that is what you might find humorous.' Alphonso said, although he clearly didn't. 'It's Ricardo.'

Bryan laughed dryly. And brought his hands together in a slow clap. He knew it. He fucking knew it!

'Ha! I called it! I knew there was something not right about that guy.'

'I hardly think that's an appropriate response to what I've just told you, Bryan.' Alphonso said; a stony expression on his face and lips pursed.

'You're right. Of course.' Bryan responded, clearing his throat a second time, trying desperately to fight off the smug smirk that had begun to invade his face. 'So what do you know? Surely if you know you'd be out there right now attacking him with a hammer or something?'

'I know he's wearing a wire, although probably not in the literal sense. Presumably, he's been feeding information to someone. It must be someone who provides a decent source of income, otherwise why would he bother? He is in a rather decent position in the grand scheme of things.'

'And you haven't an idea who it could be at all?'

'Not a clue. There are one or two people I could predict, but hearsay does not necessarily make it true. Unfortunate, I know. Does he have the hard drive?'

'Yeah, I gave it to him as I got here.' Bryan nodded.

'Presumably, he's already looked at the contents of that hard drive. He might even have made copies. But that again does not concern me. What concerns me is his lack of respect for me and for my family as a whole.'

'And you think it'd be better if he stopped it.'

'That's correct, yes.'

'With fucking pleasure.'

Bryan turned to leave. Alphonso cleared his throat obviously and Bryan spun around.

'Something else?' Bryan asked. He was itching to get out of here and remove the biggest pain in his ass from the equation.

'You are forgetting something.'

'Oh, I'm sorry.' Bryan extended a hand to shake, but felt himself cower under the strongest stare he'd ever endured. It felt like it could eclipse the sun.

'I explained it to you not five minutes ago.'

Bryan didn't have a clue what the hell he was talking about. Alphonso drummed his fingers on the desk behind him. His eyes continued to bore into Bryan's very soul. After a few moments, Alphonso drew himself up to his full height and bulk, both of which were far larger than Bryan's own. The way he had leaned on the desk made him seem smaller than he actually was, and the way he appeared to tower over Bryan was disconcerting. Bryan was not a short man, and so there was certainly an element of unease as the seconds dragged by.

'Ask permission to get rid of Ricardo.' Alphonso said, an icy steel to his voice that brimmed with anger at Bryan's forgetfulness.

'Sorry, Mr. Alphonso.' Bryan said, and he genuinely was. 'I want your permission to get rid of Ricky.'

It appeared that the act of asking brought home a crushing reality to Alphonso, as he unconsciously slumped back onto the desk for a second time. Bryan noticed him look away and stare into the corner of the room past Bryan's right elbow.

'Yes.' Alphonso said. 'Do you still have that weapon you spoke of earlier?'

'Well I never needed to risk myself to get it. I borrowed Vini's instead.'

'Hand it over.'

Bryan relinquished it, and a second later Patrone placed a similar pistol in Bryan's hand, albeit with a suppressor attached to the barrel.

'We have been through a lot together, Ricardo and I. It pains me more than I care to explain to grant that permission. You have arrived at the culmination of many years spent working together. Many months of me suspecting that I had a mole in my family, and many unfortunate setbacks with incorrect accusations.' The anger returned to Patrone's face, turning more to disgust the more he inevitably thought about it. Finally, he conceded to whatever he was thinking. 'Make it quick. He was always a good boy, he deserves a man's death.'.

Bryan checked the ammunition in his newest pistol, and left the VIP area of Sicilian Hospitality without another word, nodding his head as a goodbye.

Downstairs, Ricky was eating a plate of carbonara. He dabbed his mouth with a serviette as Bryan approached. Bryan had decided to play it as if he had just received the grilling he had at first predicted. He breathed out heavily as he approached. The pistol was stuffed into the back of his trousers.

Ricky smirked as he approached. 'Wattson! How the hell are you?'

'Shut up Ricky, I don't need your shit on top of everything else...' Bryan said, purposefully trailing off at the end of the sentence. He put his head in his hands and sighed. Ricky seemed to buy it.

'The boss spoke to you then? Hell of a guy, Mr. Alphonso.'

'Yeah, you said it. He mentioned something about another job...' Bryan mumbled.

'Did he now? Well, I...'

The phone on the table next to Ricky began to vibrate.

'... Oh, hang on one sec, I gotta take that.'

Bryan remained silent. He thought it might be a good idea to wait until the end of the conversation before he went further. The voice on the other end of the phone might be Ricky's mysterious benefactor. If he could discern who it was, it would certainly make Alphonso happy. Bryan shifted the way he was sitting, looking disinterested in what Ricky was talking about. Instead, he gestured over to a waiter, who approached after finishing his current order. He asked Bryan what he wanted in a muted tone, not wanting to disturb the made man on the phone. Bryan ordered a glass of water, not once changing his posture or voice from a man who had just been shouted at by Alphonso. The waiter nodded curtly, mildly annoyed that Bryan had only ordered a free drink. He slinked off into the kitchen, pushing open the swinging doors.

The conversation betrayed nothing. Ricky spoke normally, and Bryan couldn't hear the voice on the other end. He was disappointed. Nothing ever went easily in this line of work. He supposed it was fate. Some karmic guide making all the decisions for him. His water arrived and he finished it, using a napkin to wipe his face. By this point the pain in his face had gone away almost completely, though he knew he'd have one hell of a bruise there the following morning. He hoped it didn't turn his entire face purple. As the conversation looked like it was drawing to a close, Bryan leaned an elbow on the table and rested his jaw against his hand. His other retreated under the table, finding comfort in its proximity to his pistol. Ricky ended the call, placing the phone on the table and leaving a hand over it.

'Well, there we are.' He said. He returned to his carbonara. Bryan was sick of waiting.

'Who was that, Ricky? Is it the people you've been on the take to? The people who you've been selling Mr. Alphonso up shit creek to?' Bryan asked him seriously.

Ricky froze, a forkful of pasta halfway between plate and lips. His hand moved away from the phone and towards the edge of the table. Bryan reached closer for the rear waistband of his trousers.

'I don't know what the hell you're talking about...' Ricky began.

'Don't bullshit me, Ricky. All three of us know what you've been doing. So, I reckon it's best to take what's coming to you like a man.'

'Not fucking likely.'

Ricky upended the table at Bryan, sending condiments and pasta flying everywhere. Bryan fell backwards off his chair, garlic breadcrumbs pelting him. Ricky attempted to run, and made it into the middle of the restaurant before Bryan trained the sights on his leg and shot him.

Ricky screamed out, hitting the floor and cursing loudly as he grabbed his leg. A woman screamed in the restaurant, and furious chatter and worried gasps erupted among the customers as they backed away from Ricky. Bryan stuffed the pistol back into his waistband and rushed towards Ricky's still cursing body, and dragged him away. The waiters ushered everyone outside and tried to keep order, discouraging people strongly from dialling 9-1-1.

Bryan hauled Ricky into the kitchen, much to the shock of several of the staff. One of them jumped so much he dropped a tasting spoon into the enormous pot of soup he'd been preparing.

'Everyone out!' Bryan ordered. 'Go home. Nobody saw anything, is that fucking clear?'

The staff agreed quietly, before slipping out of the door.

'Right then you bastard...' Bryan said, turning Ricky onto his back to face him.

Ricky simply spat a curse at him. Bryan responded by hitting him with the pistol, and then with his fist for good measure.

'I fucking knew I should have got Patrone to ice you as soon as I met you...' Ricky said painfully. 'Stupid bastard doesn't know what he's done.'

'Says the guy on the take!' Bryan said, eyeing a walk-in freezer. He walked over to it and heaved it open. It was empty. Not for long. He briefly considered throwing Ricky inside and leaving him to freeze, but then thought better of it. Nevertheless, he dragged Ricky into the freezer, and set him down.

'You thought you were so much better than all of us, didn't you Ricky? Well guess what? You're nothing.'

'Don't you think it's a bit strange that Patrone doesn't know you, and yet he's hired you to kill one of his most trusted capos?' Ricky asked, a sadistic grin on his face despite the pain. 'Killing a made man, you're fucking dead. You and that deadbeat limey you hang around with.'

'The seed of doubt trick won't work, Ricky. You are going to die. Make peace with whatever god you've chosen. And for what it's worth, I am loving every single second of this.'

Bryan placed the suppressor between Ricky's eyes.

He should have put some newspaper down or something. At least Ricky was in the freezer. If they left it a while, hopefully all the blood and fragments would freeze and be easier to scrape away and clean up.

Bryan stepped out of the freezer, flipping the temperature dial to its coldest setting. Out in the restaurant it was empty, except for Alphonso, one of the waiters and a man in a suit, who Bryan presumed was the manager. They were having a one-sided conversation about Ricky, with the manager doing most of the talking.

'Mr. Alphonso, I don't like this!' The manager was saying heatedly, his forehead turning into a sea with sweat. 'I understand that this place is mob-run, but having one of your goons shoot someone in full view of everyone?! It's beyond belief!'

'Calm down, Vito.' Alphonso answered. 'Here is the man now. Bryan! Come over here.'

Bryan did so.

It was the waiter's turn to speak next. 'The customers were all ushered out. No-one saw Bryan's face, and some thought it was the police.'

'Good work, Bryan. You took care of Ricardo, then?' Alphonso asked, sorrow flashing across his face before reverting back to its usual stony facade.

'Yeah, I did. He's in the walk-in freezer. I didn't want to execute him in front of everyone.'

'You see, Vito?' Alphonso said. 'The man is thoughtful.'

'Thoughtful?! Hardly! I will have to remove everything from that kitchen, disinfect the whole place, and the process will be daylight robbery! And it doesn't excuse all the money I've now lost from customers, and from all the staff leaving early! How do you explain that one, *mister executioner*?' The manager fumed, jabbing an accusatory finger in Bryan's direction.

'Vito, please remain calm. Have I ever left you hanging out to dry?' Alphonso said, and Bryan half expected an ounce of rhetoric, but there was none. Alphonso didn't seem like the sort to do that. Sarcasm appeared to be a lost cause with him.

'Remember that incident with the Leone twins? My associates and I look after our clients. We did then, and we will now.' Alphonso continued. 'Now, would you please go and deal with Ricardo? Remove him from the premises and I will endeavour to help with disposal.' He told the waiter.

The Leone twins?

'Certainly, Mr. Patrone.' The waiter bowed. He seemed like no stranger to gunfights and the sight of blood. Bryan held an arm out as he made to walk past, blocking his path.

'I'm sorry about all the red ice.'

As the waiter left and the manager disappeared in a huff, continuing to mutter incessantly under his breath in his native tongue, Bryan and Alphonso were left alone in the now empty restaurant. Bryan turned to face the other man and smirked. He got a raised eyebrow in return.

'Well, boss, I gotta say,' Bryan said, a touch smug, 'That felt good. I think it went well.'

'So it would seem,' was the only response that was deemed necessary.

'You don't smile much, do you?'

'Not unless the situation calls for it. It's very rare that I find the time, and in situations such as these I'd hardly call it fitting, would you?'

'No, I suppose not.' Bryan said; feeling slightly neutered. He felt that now Ricky was out of the picture there was nothing stopping him acting out his plan to start him on his way back to the top. Maybe he should change tack and stop seeming like he owned the place.

'Okay Mr. Alphonso, what else can I do for you? I'm guessing that I'm still somewhat in your debt?'

'I wouldn't say that, exactly. You've proved you can be dependable. You've proved that authority means something to you, so that's a merit.'

Either that or I'm not gonna say 'no' in case I wake up with the better half of a horse in my bed.

'So now, I'm assuming you wish to continue to work for me? As a man out of my debt?' Alphonso asked; a knowing look on his face. Yeah, he already knew the answer.

'Of course I do.'

'Good man. Now, I expect that you'll want payment of some kind for dealing with Ricky, and this is true to an extent. I am a firm believer that in this business, if a man does a job then a man should be paid for it. However, it is not in dollars that you will be paid for this... discrepancy. Rather, I think I can be of some assistance elsewhere. And before your mind soars, don't think you're being 'made'. Goodness no, regardless of my previous rhetoric you've only done well on one job. I wouldn't consider you anyway. For one thing, you aren't Italian, so our personal code forbids it.'

Well, that was deflating.

'I wonder... where exactly are you staying?' The Italian asked him.

'What, as in where do I live?'

Alphonso nodded once.

'Erm...' Bryan didn't particularly want to say. It wasn't the most professional of places to live, and the thought of having to sleep in it again tonight sent a negative tingle through him. 'There's a back room in a garage I'm crashing in. A bed, et cetera... well a mattress more like but it's not ideal. I wonder if I'll wake up and start seeing things because of all the paint fumes and I think I've narrowed it down to six rats.'

'So not the best of locations?'

'No.' Bryan decided to push his luck. He'd already worked out where this was going. 'The rats have names you know. There's Dave, uh, Dee, Dozy, Beaky...' He counted on his fingers.

'That's enough, Bryan.' Alphonso said, holding a hand up for silence. 'I happen to know someone who is an estate agent. I think we might be able to set you up with something more promising.'

'A new place?'

'Something like that, yes. Why don't I get on the phone with him? I'm sure he might be able to set me, and by extension you, up with something more preferable. What do you think?'

'I think that sounds amazing.'

'Good. Now, how about a drink?'

'I think I'll take you up on it this time, Mr. Alphonso.'

Big mistake. The whisky went through him like water. Alphonso's phone conversation had been swift and to-the-point. It seemed like he already knew the answers to all the questions he asked the estate agent, but was asking them anyway for the sake of formalities. Now, a short while later, the two men stepped out of the restaurant. Alphonso led them to a car, and Bryan rubbed his hands as he slipped into it. Alphonso told him the address and instructed him simply to 'drive'. Bryan turned the key in the ignition.

CHAPTER TEN: NEW BEGINNINGS

Sovereign City. More years ago than anyone would prefer to mention when age becomes a defining factor in their lives.

Bryan Wattson, seventeen years old, slung his rucksack into the corner of his bedroom. Another boring day at high school, punctuated by his bitch teacher Mrs. Henderson shouting at him for talking in class. Again. What did she know? For her information, talking to Sian about meeting up at some point next week was WAY more important than learning about vectors. Especially when he'd wimped out of asking her four times already. Although he realised arguing back probably hadn't helped things. Oh, well. As long as his parents didn't find out, he'd be fine. He didn't need to worry about it for a while anyway, he'd get his homework done later but as far as he was concerned, he had an entire weekend to spend messing around with his friends and generally procrastinating. Marvellous.

As he changed into something more comfortable, and less likely to attract his mother's attention if it got dirty, he considered his position in life, as teenagers are wont to do at strange times. He was doing well in his studies, despite the fact he couldn't stand maths. Well, it wasn't that he couldn't stand it *per se*, just that he always found more interesting things happening when he was sat in lessons being droned at. Things were going pretty well with Sian, he'd finally managed to pluck up the courage to ask her if she was busy at all next week, and she'd said no, she wasn't. Weirdly, he'd never considered himself to be 'sheepish' until when he asked her. He had acquaintances and really close friends, and was comfortable with his social standing in the high school environment.

The window was open, and a pleasant breeze was blowing through it. The sun was out, and it had all the makings of a nice evening. This part of Sovereign City was much, much nicer than the area Bryan would eventually find himself in the future. It had a family feel to it, and everyone seemed to know each other.

'Hey, Wattson!' A voice shouted from outside the window. Bryan knew who it was, of course. Who else would it be?

As Bryan crossed to the window, he pulled on a fresh jacket. Phil was waiting for him outside, and continued to yell up as Bryan zipped it up.

'Alright mate? Get your arse down here! We're burning daylight!' Phil shouted. It was strange. Despite living in America for most of his life, Phil had not lost any of his slang, and his accent remained as notable as ever. Maybe he'd never lose it. At fifteen, Bryan certainly doubted he would. Quite the reverse: Bryan had found himself using more and more of the terms Phil did.

Bryan clambered out of the window and onto the branch he had used a thousand times before. Although, this time he wasn't sneaking out without his parent's permission. He yelled back into the bedroom that he was going out, and a retort of some kind came back at him. Bryan didn't really hear it, though. He was too busy dropping down to hold the branch with both hands, and then letting go to free-fall the last ten feet or so. He landed effortlessly, remembering to bend his knees. He wasn't going to make that mistake again.

Phil had his arms folded and gave him a disapproving look as Bryan approached.

'You know, you didn't need to showboat, seeing as how your mum and dad aren't pissed at you. We all know you have an emergency exit, and I would've pissed myself if you'd have fallen on your arse.'

'Oh, I'm sorry. Next time I'll do a forward roll with jazz hands finish. That suit you?'

'Yeah, you wanna try it? We've got all day...' Phil said, raising an eyebrow and gesturing at the window.

'Nah. I don't fancy it. 'Sides, you're just jealous because YOU haven't got an emergency exit.'

'Why do I need one? I just use the stairs like a normal person... I don't ever get in trouble like you do, anyway.'

With a final shrug from Bryan, the two boys set off down the street.

'So what's the plan?' Bryan asked. 'Chill out at the Den, or head further into town...?'

'Den sounds good to me, mate.'

The Den, as it had been known for years, was a place Phil, Bryan and occasionally Michael liked to frequent. When they were younger they had discovered a secluded strip of grassland, known seemingly to very few people, if any at all. At one end was a large tree, and in this tree the three boys had decided to build an equally large and impressive treehouse. It had three levels to it, and they were particularly proud considering they had built it all themselves with no help from adults. They had decided that no-one else should know about its location, and construction had taken the best part of four months and many books about construction borrowed from the local library. Arguably the hardest part was inconspicuously 'borrowing' a hammer from Bryan's dad. They'd saved up their pocket money to pay for nails.

To begin with, it had been little more than a deathtrap. Crudely imagined and even more crudely constructed, it would be a while before they made moves to make it anything resembling safe. The main room had taken the longest, planks of unequal size hammered together with but the merest thought for structural integrity. Nails stuck out at angles where the young boys could not easily reach, and many a sleeve had been snagged on some of the more aggressive ones. But they were proud of it, and it was a place they could relax and unwind. From the top tier you could look over the razorwire-covered fence of a large warehouse located close by and see into the yard, which had been the source of the wood needed to build the Den. Much to the surprise of the workers, who turned up after a weekend to find roughly two hundred planks missing of various shapes and sizes. Over time the treehouse had been repaired, strengthened and expanded to include beanbags, posters and a padlocked crate containing the means to turn the treehouse into a hideaway, rations contained therein being enough to last a weekend, at least. The cold was the largest factor, which they had remedied somewhat by sealing as many of the gaps in the floorboards and walls as possible and by fitting thick, dark blue curtains to the windows. The blankets in another crate dealt with sleeping arrangements. The rope ladder was retractable, and the boys had removed all low-lying branches so the tree couldn't easily be climbed without their permission. After all their hard work, they had turned it from a deathtrap to something they could be proud of.

The two boys clambered up the ladder. They didn't know where Michael was, probably playing baseball with his school friends. Bryan collapsed into his usual seat, before putting his feet onto one of the crates.

'So how was school for you, man?' He asked Phil.

'Usual shit. Got the results on that exam back. Sixty-eight percent. Not too bad. Least I don't need to resit. There were like, four people who got less than thirty percent.'

'I swear the people in your class are all idiots.' Bryan retorted. He knew a couple of them. They really were.

'What about you?' Phil asked, before switching to a condescending tone, 'How's things with Sian?'

'Well, I finally asked her out and she said yes!'

'Aww, cute. Bwyan grew some balls!' Phil smirked.

'Yeah, I did. We arranged to do something at some time. Should be good.'

'Well, I hope it goes well for you, mate. Long as it's better than the last one, it should be amazing...'

'I haven't spoken to *her* in ages. Well, I haven't spoken to her in a civilised way in ages. I mean, she treats me like shit and dumps me, but hell, I'M the bad guy, right?'

'Oh yeah, course. You're a dickhead. We all know it.' Phil laughed. They'd had the discussion about Bryan's ex-girlfriend, and were able to joke about it without causing upset. 'Do you know what you're planning to do with her?'

'No. A movie, maybe...'

A couple of hours of random discussion and messing around passed, before the two boys decided it best to go home and get dinner. They left the area quietly, and were walking down the road parallel to the Den, when a voice called to them. They stopped, and turned.

His name was Ryan Murdoch. He was in Bryan's class, and Bryan could never make his mind up about him. He would go from being friendly one day, then distant the next. While he never had any reason to directly hate the guy, the mood swings really threw him sometimes. Rumours circulated that he'd been through some hard times, and they had left him with a bit of a temper.

He was tall, red-headed and powerfully built. The sort of person you wouldn't mess with. A piggish nose and dull eyes made him appear to lack intelligence, but this was far from the case. Whilst not a genius, Bryan would have said he was possessed of a certain cunning. His flannel shirt emphasised his fiery hair.

'Hey, guys!' Murdoch said cheerfully. At least today was a good one.

'What's going on, Doch?' Bryan asked.

'Nothing all that much, man, I just saw you so I thought I'd ask you what you thought of that homework Henderson set us?'

'Shit, but what can you do? I'll get it done later, I guess.' Bryan shrugged.

'Nice one, yeah, I agree. It's stupid. Still don't change all that much, though.'

'What do you mean?' Phil and Bryan gave him a quizzical look.

'I fucking hate high school, man. Just, school in general I guess. Everything about it. All this work for maybe not even getting a decent job at the end of it all? It's crazy town.'

Bryan shot a glance at Phil. *Just what the hell is this guy going on about?*

He was still talking, 'Don't you think it would be better just to have cash flowing in already?'

'Well, yeah, we all need cash, Murdoch...'

'So you agree with me? You'd rather have instant cashflow, a bit more to help you get by?'

119

'What are you getting at?' Bryan asked, wanting the conversation to be over and done with.

'Well, look, we all need money right? You need it, too? You've got that date with Sian to pay for...' Bryan's eyes widened at the mention. Nosy bastard. Murdoch went on. 'Wouldn't you prefer to be able to take her somewhere nice?'

'You know that none of us are rolling in cash, Doch.' Bryan said flatly. 'We make do, and I'm sure Sian will appreciate whatever we end up doing...'

'What if I could help you out?' Murdoch said, eyes suddenly glinting.

'Help me out?'

'Yeah. I'm glad I ran into you. I've had my eye on you for a while, and I want to offer you a job opportunity.'

'A job?' Bryan glanced at Phil. He seemed as puzzled as Bryan was.

'Yep, a job. You see...' Murdoch put a hand on Bryan's shoulder and led him away from Phil. His voice lowered. 'A friend of mine said to talk to you. Because you seem dependable. So... anyways, how would you like to be a part of a robbery?'

The question came out of nowhere. Bryan had to fight not to laugh in Murdoch's face. He shrugged so Murdoch would take his hand off his shoulder. Murdoch was looking at him earnestly. Which led Bryan to think that this wasn't a joke.

'You can't be serious.'

'Deadly. There's a convenience store a few minutes out of the neighbourhood. Pokey little place, yet the two owners drive really flash cars. Big house, kids in better education than the shithole we have to go to. It doesn't make sense. So this friend of mine worked out that there must be more money around than the guy lets on. We're gonna pay him a visit. And they want to know if you're in.'

'You STILL can't be serious. You're asking me to agree to a robbery? What if the guy shoots me?!' Bryan asked him incredulously.

'Don't worry, you'll have weapons too.'

'So now it's ARMED robbery?!' Bryan breathed, 'We could all go to prison! Remember they still have the death penalty in this state!'

'Bryan, relax. It won't come to that. There's three of us. He tries anything, we make sure he doesn't try it again. We all got masks, gloves, all that good stuff, nothing can go wrong. We go in, tell the guy to stick his hands up, raid the cash register, look in the back for a safe, get him to open it if there is one, knock him out and we're out in two minutes. Lock the doors while we do it. We can even flip the sign around to say sorry, we're closed if you like. It's flawless.'

'Why does everyone always say that?' Bryan's head was spinning, although his generalisation was based on cheating on a test. He'd gone from discussing terrible homework assignments to considering robbery in the space of five minutes. Murdoch didn't seem to be joking. That was the worst thing. There was no way he could agree to this. Was there? Money hadn't exactly been forthcoming in recent months, his parents were working hard, but recent events meant there'd been a slump of sorts. Not their fault, but hard felt nonetheless. And there was always Sian...

'Why me?' He asked.

Murdoch grinned. 'You know how to keep your mouth shut. You always get into trouble, and you hate the thought of working for a living.'

'You what?'

'Am I wrong?' He wasn't. 'And you're a fairly big guy, I bet you could be intimidating if you wanted to.'

What if he got caught? No. He pushed the thoughts aside. There was no way they'd get caught, was there? Of course not. Murdoch had specified what they'd do, and it all seemed straightforward.

'So? What do you think? Remember, we would split the cash evenly three ways with you, but if you even think about saying a word about this to anyone, we'll introduce a bat to your face.'

121

Murdoch smiled. Threats of violence met with a smile. Wonderful.

I have no choice. It hit Bryan with a wave of nausea. Murdoch had literally just said that if he said anything to anyone, they'd murder him. And it didn't take a genius to work out that same threat would extend to him saying no. He felt his legs go weak, and struggled for a moment to remain standing. He looked over at Phil, who was kicking at some gravel, occasionally stealing a glance at the two men. What would he think? What would his family think? He couldn't tell them. He couldn't say anything about this.

'Three guys?' He asked.

'Yes. You don't know the third one. But he's top-notch.'

'And what if I say no?'

Murdoch laughed, placing another hand on Bryan's shoulder. 'You won't. I've already told the other guy how dependable you are.'

'And what would the money be like?'

'Tons. We reckon several thousand dollars each. Probably tens of thousands.' Murdoch had a giddy smile on his face.

That made Bryan's mouth dry up. He *was* sick and tired of always being broke. His parents barely gave him anything, and with ten grand he could buy anything he wanted. He didn't know what Murdoch meant when he said the third guy was 'top-notch'. A top-notch thief? Or killer? Bryan didn't want any of his friends or family - or himself - to come to any harm.

The hand on his shoulder dug in, the forceful grip letting him know that there wasn't really a good outcome for this situation.

Ten. Thousand. Dollars.

Bryan inhaled, and made the decision that would change his life forever.

'I'm in.'

****

Three days later, three mid-to-late-teenagers wearing ski masks clambered out of a car and faced the convenience store. 'GK's Groceries', the sign said. None of them had ever been in it, and they certainly wouldn't again after this.

After a few failed attempts at nicknames, they had all settled on what they would call each other. Murdoch's nickname was Zero, for a reason he hadn't exactly divulged, something to do with a comic he used to read as a kid; Bryan's nickname was Delta, simply because he lived at number four on his street and couldn't think of anything better. The third one went by Shifty. All three men sported brandless black jackets, jeans and shoes, along with thin woollen gloves. Most worryingly, they all sported pistols, supposed 'gifts' from a gun cabinet belonging to Shifty's father. Apparently, he wouldn't miss them for one night. They nodded at each other and looked towards the door.

Showtime.

The three men crashed inside. The shopkeeper stared at them blankly for a brief second before Zero stuffed the barrel of his gun in his face.
'Hands up! Now!' Zero yelled. The shopkeeper obliged, slowly raising his hands.
'Do you have any idea who I am?' The shopkeeper asked.
'Yeah, actually.' Delta said as he flipped the switch to change the automatic doors to exit only. While he spoke, Shifty approached the cash register. 'You're the shopkeeper who's going to open the register and keep his trap shut while doing it.'

A godawful attempt to alter his voice was better than no attempt at all, Delta figured, and simply tried to make it several times huskier.

The shopkeeper spat something at the three of them in his native language. Zero pushed open the back door and stepped into it. Shifty punched the shopkeeper in the face, sending him stumbling backwards and nearly onto the floor.

He's got more money than he needs. Probably committing some major fraud to keep it all under wraps. It's the fastest way to get it out of him. For once, Delta's interior monologue was winning him over.

'Open it! NOW!' Shifty yelled, his voice deep and threatening. 'You've got three seconds before I shoot off one of your fingers.'

The man couldn't hold off the fear in his face much longer, his lip faltering.

'Okay, okay, I've got it.' He removed a key from his pocket and inserted it into the register. A quick turn revealed its contents. Lots of bills. Jackpot.

'Bingo back here, too!' Zero yelled from the other room.

'Just as we thought.' Shifty said, a touch of triumph evident in his voice. 'Get him in the back room. Get it open.'

Delta grabbed the shopkeeper by the lapels and frogmarched him into the back room. Zero had apparently already turned the place upside down looking for the safe, as the presence of several removed framed photographs and a painting indicated. He pointed to the floor next to his feet, next to an overturned armchair.

'A floor safe? Fantastic. This guy ain't as dumb as he looks.' Zero said. Delta shoved the shopkeeper towards the safe, before aiming his pistol at the shopkeeper's waistline.

'You've got five seconds to remember the combination and put it in before I guarantee the bed in your house will be used for nothing but sleeping, and crying.' Delta snarled. The man whimpered at the thought before dejectedly entering the safe combination.

The man had it coming. He had it coming.

The safe sprang open. Serious jackpot. Zero pulled the shopkeeper out of the way, towards Delta, who reluctantly flipped the pistol around in his hand before striking the man hard across the face with it, sending him crashing into a table. Out cold. Shifty stepped into the room with a now full rucksack. He must have grabbed a few things off of the shelves as well, to

124

go with the cash from the register. Zero held up a small sealed bag. It was obvious what was in it.

'No way, man, I ain't touching that shit.' Delta said flatly. 'I don't go anywhere near drugs.'

'How the hell did he even get this? There's about ten bags of the stuff...'

'Leave it there, it's the money we want.' Delta said, eyeing the bundles that were neatly stacked in the safe. He wanted his share, at least.

'No. We take it all.' Shifty said. Zero nodded, and placed the bags into his own rucksack, before tossing the money bundles to Delta, who placed them into his. 'I know somewhere I can offload this stuff. Serious cash.'

'That's if we don't keep it for ourselves!' Zero said happily.

Shifty smiled at him through the ski mask. It was the first time Delta had seen him smile. It wasn't his most attractive feature, in all honesty. Delta shook his head as the three boys left the shop, significantly richer than when they had entered.

The car stopped a few blocks away from anywhere recognisable. It had begun to rain. The three men, ditching their criminal handles, counted the cash and split their shares. Even, three ways. However, Bryan refused any of the sealed packages, along with any of the money that would be made in their sale.

'An absolute natural,' Murdoch said. 'A cold-hearted bastard. Hell, I don't think *I'm* even that calculating now. You were born for this job.'

Bryan's face was emotionless, and he didn't know whether to feel ashamed, relieved or proud. Murdoch continued, asking a question.

'If either of us have any more work that is as foolproof as this one was, can me and Toothy here count on your assistance?'

'Why not? If it's as easy as this job was, then yeah. It's easy money. Just keep me away from drugs.'

'We'll bear that in mind. We know a guy called Jeremy. He'll get rid of it all. See you around, *Delta*.'

The car drove off, any noise drowned by the strengthening rain. Bryan slung his rucksack over his shoulder and walked back to his house, desperate for a shower.

A good social standing at college.

A date with Sian at an expensive restaurant.

Fresh income.

At that point in time, Bryan Wattson was content with his life. It wasn't the most legitimate choice he'd ever made, but in his opinion, the rewards far outweighed the risks.

Yep, this is brilliant.

Just one question remained: Where the hell was he going to keep all this money without anyone finding out?

CHAPTER ELEVEN: FIRST, LAST AND SECURITY

The present.

Bryan shook hands with Patrone in thanks as they stepped into his new apartment, not bothering to hide the enormous grin on his face. It was essentially one large room, on the eleventh floor of the Sovereign Heights apartment complex. Heights, indeed, as the enormous window that covered a large portion of one wall conveyed, giving a spectacular view of the surrounding streets, the prison just barely visible in the far distance. Bryan could see the aurora of the sunset's glittering reflection in the ocean, casting an orange flash across the horizon. Truly, it was beautiful, and Bryan had nothing but thanks for the man that had provided it for him. Otherwise fairly small, the open nature of the apartment gave it a greater sense of volume than the actual measurements would confirm, and all the furniture was positioned in such a way as to maximise space. Although the amount of furniture was somewhat lacking, it had a decent habitable environment to it, with a kitchen, lounge area and several open-plan stairs leading downwards to a bedroom and bathroom immediately to the right as they entered. An ancient-looking computer sat on a desk in the far corner. Compared to his mansion, this was a mere holiday home, but compared to the garage it was a palace. A place he could cement this new career he was forging for himself, and he had to admit, he had started brilliantly, an employer in Patrone and a lovely new abode at this early stage.

'You don't know what this means, Mr. Alphonso.' Bryan explained, still struggling hopelessly to stop grinning.

'Think nothing of it, Bryan.' Patrone said, still not smiling and standing at the enormous window. Despite his face never changing, Bryan was sure he was smiling on the inside, at least he hoped so. Patrone went on, 'You cannot know how much dealing with Ricardo helped this business. I had suspected he had been undercutting us - a small thought in the back of my mind, and yet I pushed it aside, trying to tell myself I was looking at the situation wrongly.'

'I didn't really DO anything, Mr. Alphonso, just pulled the trigger. You said that you thought it was him, you even gave me the pistol I did it with.'

'Perhaps, but to do it any other way would have encouraged more violence, and risked the lives of others. Sending in other people to kill him is way too high profile. No, you did well, Bryan.'

As high profile as scaring the shit out of the customers and ruining a decent Italian meal when the table upturned? Bryan thought, still thinking the whole situation was handled with incompetence on his own part.

Nevertheless, he thanked Patrone again.

'I need to call my friend Phil, he'll be amazed when he sees this place.'

'Your friend?' Patron asked, raising an eyebrow sceptically.

'More like my brother. We've been through it all, and before you look quizzically at me anymore, yes, he's as legitimate as I am.' Bryan said with a slight smile.

'Quite.'

'Well, I'm sure he'd be pleased to make your acquaintance, too. And for what it's worth, if there's ever any more work going, and you were thinking of hiring me, I'd appreciate it if you gave him a thought, too.'

Patrone chuckled. 'I've never met the man, Bryan.'

'I know, but he's as solid as they come. Cast iron. He's the reason I'm here talking to you right now, actually, and not still rotting in prison. We'd even split my share, if that made things easier...'

'Bryan, you're babbling. Why don't you just speak to him before you throw half your pay away unnecessarily? Yes, I suppose I should like to meet him. Besides, I have this apartment's telephone number saved, so I will endeavour to contact you should I have work.'

'You got it.'

Bryan strode over to the landline and picked it up. He hadn't been paid for killing Ricky, and wasn't expecting to be, but Patrone HAD provided this apartment at a fraction of street cost, and Bryan wouldn't have to worry about rent. He searched the inside pocket of his jacket and fished out the now very creased sheet of paper he had placed there when he first escaped and arrived at Michael's garage. He punched in the number, and it rang three times before being answered.

'Hello?' Phil sounded like he had his mouth full.

'Phil, it's me.'

'Bryan!' Phil responded brightly, chewing quickly and swallowing. 'Are you okay? Where are you calling me from? It came up as an unknown number?'

'At my new apartment. You should come and see it. There's somebody I want you to meet.'

'You have a new apartment?! Already?!' Phil responded incredulously.

'Yeah, kinda. Look, we'll explain all when you get here. You know where Sovereign Heights is? Err... Torquemada Avenue I think? I dunno. I'm in 1108 either way.'

'I thought it was off Eakring Avenue. Either way I know the place. I'll be there in ten.'

'Good stuff. See you then.'

Bryan put the phone down, and turned back to Alphonso.

'So, he'll be here soon. What to do in the meantime...' Bryan wondered aloud, scratching awkwardly at the back of his head. He needed to go shopping at some point. Most of the cupboards were bare.

Then a thought clicked into his head. He made downstairs into the bathroom. It was suitably large and contained a washer-dryer, which he stuffed the jacket into. He turned it up high and hoped it would wash out the blood.

Returning upstairs, he realised he'd have to spend most of the money he'd earned earlier on food and clothes, but wasn't really bothered. He wouldn't be parading around in fancy cars and designer suits just yet, but given time...

Phil arrived as Patrone had salvaged a glass in which to pour some whisky from his hip flask. Bryan made the introductions. Phil was initially hesitant of being in the presence of someone who could order a hit on him, but warmed up as soon as Bryan explained the situation.

'So in the first however long of you being here, you managed to off Ricky?' Phil asked.

'Yeah something like that. Apparently he was on the take. Deserved it.'

'Yeah, he was quite the bellend.' Phil said flatly, rubbing his chin before freezing and staring at Patrone.

'Relax, Mr. Kent. I am aware of how much of a... *bellend*... the man was, to put it as bluntly as you do.' Patrone said, showing some disdain at the obscenity. 'I recruited him more out of necessity than desire. The man was good at his job, efficient and a good leader.'

Phil made a discreet snorting noise. Bryan could have sworn it was a lie.

'So, Bryan, you really need to get some more stuff to put in this place, man...' Phil said, steering the topic of conversation.

'I know. Well, you brought your car, right?'

'At this time of night? The only place I'm gonna be bringing my car is back to the hotel I'm staying at. You can walk your merry way down to the shops yourself and get your own shopping. Do it tomorrow, even.'

Bryan grunted. 'Fine. Pizza it is tonight, then. Then I need to change clothes, there are too many pebbles and bullets in these ones.'

'Sorted.'

Patrone cleared his throat. 'Well, gentleman, if you'll excuse me, I need to be going. As Mr. Kent said, it is getting late and I must be getting home. If more work arises, I will certainly consider you. Goodnight.'

'Please don't call me *Mr. Kent*. As tired and clichéd as it sounds, Mr. Kent was my dad. Or it was on those forms all that time ago.' Phil said, somewhat bluntly. Still a slightly sorry subject, and of course why wouldn't it be? Bryan and Phil never spoke of it, but Phil didn't like anyone talking about either of his parents, and come to think of it, neither did Michael, but *he* was slightly more relaxed about the whole situation. Bryan had always wondered if he was too young to understand at the time.

'Understood. It seems neither of you like formalities.'

'Call me Phil. Because that's my name.' Phil turned his face into a grin.

The two men said goodbye to the Italian as he walked out. As the door slammed shut, Phil turned to Bryan, who had himself sported an equal smile. He gestured all around the apartment with outstretched arms.

'Pretty good, eh?' Bryan said.

'Yeah, you certainly scored big on this one. Jammy bastard.' Phil confirmed.

'Patrone seemed like he'd have more work. If he pays as well as he does favours, we'll be richer than Tony in no time.'

'Yeah... this place is alright though. You'll be able to sort all your shit out from here. Get your act together.'

'That's the idea. Get myself established. Make plans. All that good stuff. But for now, I'm gonna focus on getting a few dollars together. I need my own car first. Maybe I'll just steal one to make things easier...'

Phil laughed. 'I guess that would be simpler.' The end of the sentence collapsed into a yawn. 'Well, Alphonso was right. I'm knackered. You really couldn't have waited till tomorrow to invite me to your housewarming shindig?'

'Well, I couldn't have guaranteed that he would have been around again, but it's cool. You met him, and he said he'd consider us both for work. Win-win in my book.'

'Mine too. Now, if you'll excuse me, I've gotta go. There's a bed waiting for me, and I intend to sleep soundly in it. The missus will be getting irate.'

'Wait, you're *all* holed up in a hotel room?' Bryan asked. He hadn't even given a second thought to Phil's wife and daughter. 'How's Sophie?'

'She's okay, thanks. Fast approaching those horrible, horrible teen years. I've told myself I'm booking a flight to the moon when she starts the whole angsty teen cycle. H can take care of it.'

Bryan chuckled. H was Phil's wife, going on twelve years now. Match made in heaven, Bryan always acknowledged, and he was insanely jealous. He'd never made it clear to Phil, but he really was. Not that it seemed like a match made in heaven on the face of it, Phil and Helena were openly horrible to each other, but it was all in jest. In truth, Bryan didn't think he could remember them ever arguing, and they'd been an item for five years even *before* he was imprisoned.

'And the hotel?'

'Well, yeah, we're all *sorta* holed up in one. All three of us went to Cornwall all that time ago, and seeing as we were all sort of fugitives, when we got back we weren't exactly sure about going back to our old place. Doesn't matter though. The hotel is reasonably alright, and since Michael's mate owns it, we get the best room anyway. It's more like an apartment. All good. We'll find our own place soon enough. Right, I'm off anyway. I'll catch you later.'

Phil left the apartment, leaving Bryan alone. He ordered pizza, watched television while he ate, completely baffled at the difference in the sort of programmes being shown, before crashing onto the bed into the best night's sleep he'd had in ten years.

CHAPTER TWELVE: PLAYING WITH FIRE

Bryan stretched as he got out of bed, feeling completely refreshed. A soft mattress and a comfortable night's sleep was exactly what he needed, and exactly what he'd been lacking for a long time. He showered, another luxury, since he wasn't surrounded by several other convicts and angry guards. He made sure to take his sweet time, without fear of the water suddenly being turned off or going cold. Breakfast he'd have to skip, but he wasn't bothered. He had other things on his mind at that particular moment, and scooped up his keys as well as a written list of things he needed before heading out of the door. The lift journey down eleven floors was quiet, and as he stepped out at the ground floor, a friendly receptionist greeted him. She was much younger than him, and very naïve-looking. Nevertheless, Bryan responded to her warmly.

'Hello!' She said. 'Haven't seen you here before, are you new?'

'Yeah, I just moved in here yesterday. It was a real pain moving in, but I like it here so far.' Bryan moved up to the desk and leaned his arms on it. The receptionist stood up to match him, nursing a hot drink..

'I'm glad to hear that. Well, my name's Alice. Let me know if there's anything you need.' She smiled politely at him.

'I will do, thank you. My name's Bryan.'

'Good to meet you!' She sipped her drink. 'What's Soepen?'

'What's open?' Bryan thought he'd misheard her.

'Yeah.' She said, nodding at Bryan's wrist. His prison tag had pushed its way out above his watch, and Alice was looking at it in amusement. 'Your wristband. Soepen.'

'Oh, I uh, I'm sorry, yeah. I was miles away, sorry.' Bryan fumbled over his words as he tried to think of a good explanation. SOEPEN was still visible on it, the rest of the letters had worn away. 'I went to a music festival when I was a little kid. They were selling these wristbands so I picked one up.'

It seemed to wash. Alice didn't comment further on the wristband. It knocked Bryan for six a little bit. His explanation was mediocre at best, and the receptionist probably didn't believe him. She still had a positive expression though. 'You apologise a lot, don't you?'

'Not normally, I don't. I do when I trip over my words when I get asked a simple question though.' Bryan scratched at his temple, hoping he hadn't gone red.

'I'm messing with you.' The receptionist giggled. Damn. That was cute. 'We've only just met, and I'm making things awkward. I'm the one that should apologise.'

'No, you don't. Look, I need to...'

'Get out of this awkward situation with an overly inquisitive receptionist?'

'Yes, exactly that. I've got some bits of shopping to do. Can we raincheck this awkward as fuck conversation?'

The receptionist laughed. 'I'd love to. Nice to meet you again, Bryan.'

Okay, now he was definitely red. Bryan quickly nodded goodbye to her as he pushed open the glass doors to step outside. It was a bright, pleasant morning, with the faintest of breezes polishing off the weather. He ventured down the street to a series of shops, taking the list out of the pocket of his cargos as he walked. They were starting to smell at this point and the blood hadn't washed out properly, so he was grateful for the chance to buy replacement clothing. His first purchase was a wallet, which he bought alongside a slightly less broken-looking watch. He strapped it onto his wrist, and stuck the few notes he'd brought out into the wallet. Other than that, it was empty, and Bryan smiled briefly at the lack of identification he had. They'd taken his driving license, credit cards and the rest of his old wallet's contents when he'd been imprisoned. Safe to say, he wasn't going to be reapplying for any of them any time soon. In the next shop he bought himself an inexpensive but smart-looking navy suit, with a powder blue shirt and some black, hard-wearing shoes. As much as he'd have preferred to buy some expensive dress shoes, they were entirely impractical for all the running around he'd no doubt have to do.

He crossed off *Suit*, *Wallet* and *Watch* from the list as he walked down the street. He'd use the computer in his apartment to fill his fridge when he got back, so hadn't bothered to write *Food* on the list. He still had the pistol Patrone gave him, but it was back at the apartment, safe and sound. A ballistic vest wouldn't have gone amiss, although he wondered where exactly he could obtain one. Before his imprisonment he happened to be friends with someone who owned a gun shop, but he wasn't around anymore, a victim of illness some years ago. Maybe he could ask Dempsey, the man seemed to have everything else after all.

Several shops later, there were a couple of other minor things remaining on the list as he strolled back to his apartment. He studied the most difficult to obtain: *Car*. He had been right, it *would* just be easier to steal one. The question of morality he could easily overcome: he'd done much worse before than steal a car and could guarantee he would do worse afterwards. The question of whether the car could be tracked, less easily overcome. It was easy enough to track a car even before he was imprisoned, so adding ten years to their development and manufacture would offer nothing but problems.

Was it worth the risk? The thought had occurred to him that maybe he could perform a few more jobs for Alphonso and simply use his payment to get himself a car of his own, but that seemed a long time coming. Bryan remembered the first time he had stolen a car: a year or two after his career began, an opportune moment, a screaming woman as he pulled her out of the car, a brief moment of moral composure as he tossed her handbag out of the window to her, and a rev of the engine. At the time, it had been more of an impulse, and he could justify his decisions – he'd threatened, robbed and even killed by that point, and to steal a car felt as sequential as the list he had written before leaving Sovereign Heights this morning.

But now...?

The hedonism had long since vanished, the self-indulgence dried up. Sovereign was a large city, and he needed a means of traversing it. Other factors still turned him towards the theft, however. He wondered how hard it could be to procure new plates for the car, and he always had Michael to look over the car and remove anything which might create a paper trail.

Bryan smirked to himself.
Maybe next time.

He strolled back up the street's length, purchasing a few more oddments of clothing and accessories, piling them into a duffel bag from an athletics branch. Clothes shopping never really was his strongpoint. It bored him, and as he hoped was obvious he preferred function over appearance. A proper haircut tied off the day's purchases, a momentary hiccough as he realised he had no idea what passed for a modern haircut anymore. The images stuck to the interior of the barber's offered no help: their subjects way too young and their hair too long. He simply settled with telling the barber to tidy it up as best he could, agreeing to any executive decisions made by him. It felt good to have a hairdresser who had actually trained in his craft, the prison equivalent attacking the convicts with what was essentially a pair of gardening shears every time they were forced to visit. He thanked the man as he left, his new style nowhere near anything from before his imprisonment, but adequate nonetheless.

Bryan nudged the door to his apartment open with his foot, dumping his new duffel bag onto the kitchen counter and flipping on the coffee machine. A flashing red light on his landline caught his eye as he made his drink, and busied himself with his new clothes while it played.

'Good morning, Mr. Wattson. I hope you are settled in. I have a business proposition for you and your friend. Further information on yesterday's discrepancy has arisen. I believe we might finally be able to draw a line under this whole debacle and move on afterwards. If you wouldn't mind meeting up with him and coming to see me at my office this afternoon, we can discuss this further. How does two-thirty sound? I hope to see you soon.'

Spoken like it were a written letter. Patrone didn't seem like he could tell the difference in levels of register. Bryan sipped his coffee and punched Phil's number back into the phone.

He answered after four rings. 'Bryan?'

'Philip.'

'How do?'

'Not bad. Settling in really well here, but it looks like I don't have time to put my feet up and watch TV. Patrone left a message while I was out buying some things. He's got a job for us. Wants us to meet him at two-thirty back at his restaurant. You busy?'

'Not particularly, just helping H make sandwiches. Meet you there?'

'Err, no, actually. I was rather hoping you could give me a lift. I don't have a car anymore, remember?'

Phil groaned audibly. 'You get through more cars than Michael, and he once told me that he occasionally blowtorches the bloody things apart for shits and giggles.'

'I'm at the apartment, can you be here at, like, two? Thanks.'

'Wait a minute, what did your last slave die of? Ever heard of public transport?'

'I kicked the shit out of him for not giving me a lift. And we both know I'm too good for buses. We both are. Just get over here already.'

Bryan heard Phil snort, before the phone flatlined. That still gave him a couple of hours, so lunch was in order. A simple ordeal, as his food order from the internet still hadn't arrived yet. Bryan still couldn't believe exactly how good food could actually be. Prison food was sub-par to say the least. It felt like a completely different aspect of his life had been reinvigorated, and couldn't wait until he had the money to eat at some of the best restaurants Sovereign had to offer. He wasn't the world's best cook, but wasn't incapable either; yet he usually had better things to do than slave over a hot stove. Bryan's father, by contrast, was a fantastic cook, able to throw any old ingredients together and produce something brilliant. When he was younger Bryan had inquired as to why his father had never written books or opened a restaurant, and the response was simple: there were only a select few Bryan's father ever wanted to cook for.

Phil arrived a little early, buzzing the apartment door from below. A trip down the elevator reunited them, and Phil raised an eyebrow at Bryan's new attire and laughed at the overall style.

'You look like such a twat. What's with the suit?'

'Well, I didn't want to look like a bum forever, did I?'

'A bum...? I picked out those clothes!' Phil grinned.

'I'm sure the effort was substantial. The big man'll be waiting, and it sounds like we could make a few bucks out of this one, so we should get a move on.'

'After you. Any idea what it might be?' Phil asked as he entered the car. He was driving this time.

'Not a clue. Alphonso mentioned that it was something to do with 'business', I think. Although presumably that means something to do with the fact that I shot Ricky yesterday.'

'Right. You said he was on the take, yeah. Patrone doesn't know who?'

'I reckon it'll be bigger than just one guy, but he must know more or he wouldn't have asked, right?'

'I guess, unless we're on recon duty.'

Bryan smiled with an exhale. 'How much are you betting it has something to do with Tony?'

Phil cocked his head to one side and stared absent-mindedly out of the window for a moment as they were stopped at a traffic light. 'It HAD crossed my mind. I mean, why else would Patrone take such an interest in you?'

'When I was at the restaurant yesterday, he mentioned something about me valuing loyalty. Probably had something to do with it, too.'

'He isn't stupid, Bryan. Unless he was off his face on Limoncello there's no way he'd trust a random scrote fresh out of prison. Even someone who'd been around the block as much as you. But for him to trust the great Bryan Wattson?' He flashed a falsified look of awe, 'If anything, that'd surely make him trust you LESS.'

'I'm not losing sleep over it. It brings in the money, and I'm fairly certain he isn't sizing me up for concrete shoes. So we take it at face value, and keep working for him. It gets me the heads-up I need to start retaking this town, and it gets you out of making sandwiches all day.'

'And for now I guess, we can't say fairer than that.'

Sicilian Hospitality. Half an hour later.

'I know who Ricardo was working for,' Patrone Alphonso said heavily, juggling an empty tumbler.

'You do?'

Bryan and Phil were seated in the high-backed, leather-bound chairs in Patrone's office. Paperwork cluttered the desk, Bryan's rudimentary ability to read upside-down telling him they were invoices and earnings sheets, with the occasional handwritten note interspersed. He made out 'Undercutting Profits' and 'Tax Avoidance' on one of the more crumpled-looking sheets. It looked as if it had been thrown away and fished back out again. Phil was staring at the stark emptiness of Patrone's decanter, now two-thirds down. He hadn't immediately pinned him as a serious drinker, but came to the conclusion that either he'd initially misread him, or the events of Ricky's betrayal had gotten to him more than his stony expression and eloquent way of speaking would suggest. Nevertheless, Phil seemed locked in his thoughts, and Bryan knew all too well that this was likely to go on for some time. Phil was usually brilliant at reading people, from the way they talk, dress or interact to their overall demeanour, he was normally able to tell the way they ticked. Whilst incarcerated, Bryan had pondered as to why Phil hadn't sniffed Tony out earlier, although since they'd been through so much together, Bryan did nothing but vouch for his former partner-in-crime. Maybe that had something to do with it.

Patrone seated himself back into his chair. He was sober, that much Bryan was sure of. He hoped he wouldn't have to deal with him drunk. Patrone leaned forward on his elbows and spoke, quietly.

'Do you know Marshall Lucas?' Patrone asked. Bryan didn't, and discreetly nudged Phil out of his entranced state, diverting his attention from the single malt.

'I'm not familiar, no.'

'Well, you shouldn't be. He's a nobody. But he's the one who Ricardo was working for. And can you guess who *Lucas* was working for?'

Bryan heaved out a sigh. 'I can probably make an educated attempt, yeah.'

'Carson.' Patrone clarified. 'Presumably he has been doing it for years.'

'Do you have proof?' Phil asked.

'I'm not particularly sure I want to go rooting around to find some, Mr. Kent.' Patrone said, looking at him.

'So what do we do?' Bryan asked. 'Do you have a plan, or am I gonna take charge on this one?'

'I know Marshall Lucas' place of work, and I want it to stop.' Patrone said, as if it were an ultimatum for Bryan and Phil. Bryan didn't take it as such. Phil went back to the decanter.

'How?'

'I thought I'd leave that up to you. I know you want to kill Tony and get your old life back, and I figured maybe this would be a stepping stone for you.'

'Kill this Lucas guy to get Tony's attention, and then I can kill him when he comes looking for me. I could get behind that.'

Phil slapped a hand onto the table.

'You're both being stupid. You need to think.' He said to two stunned faces. 'As a *stepping stone* to get to Tony?! Are you both mad? The whole thing with Ricky being on the take throws a massive spanner in the works, because if he had even the slightest trace of a braincell, then telling Tony you're actually still alive is the first thing he'd have done, isn't it?'

Bryan hadn't considered it. Phil went on.

'Let's assume that Tony now knows you're alive, because something like that wouldn't have taken long to march its way along the corridors of power, now would it? And considering it

140

was YOU...' – he pointed at Patrone – '...that he was undercutting, then you can be damn sure he knows exactly what you're capable of. So we can't just run in guns blazing. It's suicide. Say what you want about Tony Carson, but he isn't stupid. If he thinks he can get away with undercutting you, then he clearly isn't *afraid* of you, Patrone. He must be able to take you on.'

Bryan looked at Patrone, who spoke. 'This stops. We remove the business that was stealing money from me. I don't care how you do it, you just get it done. Is that okay, Mr. Kent?'

'Fine, if we have to, but no blowing the place to kingdom come with rocket launchers, alright?'

'How else are we going to make it known that you don't fuck with us? And if Tony now knows I'm alive and out, then what's the damn point of being sneaky anymore?' Bryan asked, although it wasn't meant as a question.

'I don't understand why the hell you have this almighty death wish all of a sudden, B.'

'Because that bastard ruined my life. He took it away from me, didn't he? Put yourself in my position, Phil. What would you do?'

'I'd consult the facts.' Phil said, sharply, and abruptly.

'The facts are these. We will get Tony. One day. He's been fucking with all of us, and we need to show him we aren't scared. I say we trash the place.'

'Or deliver to Tony the head of Marshall Lucas.' Patrone said. Phil was slightly shocked at the morbid turn, but supposed Patrone hadn't become a mob boss through selling cookies to old people.

'That's not bad.' Bryan concurred.

Phil was getting increasingly concerned for the reckless nature of his two friends. Not even Bryan was this bad, and they'd known each other for decades. He snorted once again. 'You two are playing with fire.'

Bryan paused.
And looked at Phil.
'What?'

Bryan grinned at him, as Phil clocked the reason why. 'Oh, no...'

Patrone was now in on Bryan's method of thinking, and was sporting an equal look of determination.

'You guys cannot be serious.' Phil continued. Pleading, almost.

'Why not? What's the one thing that will kill both birds with one stone – we torch it.'

'It does make sense, Mr. Kent.' Patrone said.

'We can get in when the place is all quiet, then get to work on it.' Bryan concluded.

Against rocket launchers and suicidal attacks on Tony's mansion, Phil conceded that this was the best option, although it went hand-in-hand with the crushing reality that the whole world was, in fact, mad.

'Alright. When are we going to do this thing?'

'Tonight.' Patrone said. 'I'll supply you with all you need.'

'The only thing we'll need is a car to get us there, and some payment for afterwards.' Bryan said. A grin had spread over his face. He was eager to get started on his way back up to the top. Everything so far had seemed like filler, as if it were not entirely necessary to his end goal. This, however, did matter to him. He rose from his chair, tucking it back in after himself. 'You ready, mate?'

Phil nodded. 'Let's get it over with.'

****

As it turned out, the business was called Impeccable Industries, and Bryan supposed it was being nominated this year for the least legitimate-sounding name in history. The small, but adequately-sized sign wasn't helpful in the slightest, giving exactly no indication of what the business did. On the contrary, if anything it made the business seem shoddy and hastily designed – the logo looked like it was thrown together in minutes, and featured two of the letter I, the larger seemingly giving birth to the smaller.

Bryan realised he really must stop daydreaming in situations like these and focused himself. He sure did that a lot, didn't he? It was night time, the setting of the sun stealing all the heat as well as the light. Bryan had wrapped up in a hooded jacket. Phil was similarly layered, and both men wore gloves. The heater from the car Patrone had provided was doing its best to keep them warm, but the two men appreciated all it had to offer. Phil rubbed his unshaven chin, glancing in the rear-view mirror before speaking.

'Well, autumn's sure as hell on us. Hope it doesn't drop freezing out of nowhere like it did last winter.'

'Believe it or not, being cold was one of the few things I didn't have to worry about in prison.' Bryan said, grinning at his best friend.

'Really?'

'Yep. It was heaven when the radiator I was chained to started to warm up.'

Phil laughed as he shifted in his seat. They'd been watching the place for some thirty minutes now, and it had been ten of those since the final light in the tiny office went out. Both men had figured that they had all night to torch the place, so there was no sense in rushing. All it took was one of the workers to realise they'd forgotten their keys and come back to work, and the whole operation would be blown apart. Phil looked at an imaginary watch melodramatically.

'Can we get this show on the road?'

'Alright, let's move.'

Bryan was first out of the car, and made for the boot, flipping it open. Inside was a small assortment of things the two men would need. A pistol each, which they stuffed into shoulder holsters under their jackets. First and foremost, they needed to get in. They would worry about the arson when they were inside. The pistols were there in case anyone was still present in the building and preferred to work with the lights off. Both men had discussed the fact that there would most definitely be an alarm, but figured it didn't matter – the smoke alarm would blare as soon as the fire started anyway, and who would take the time to distinguish between the two when the building was on fire? As much as possible they wanted to avoid an alarm, true enough, but it was with a sense of resignation on both their parts. Bryan walked the furthest distance with his petrol can, around the outside of the building to a door. Phil was at the front, awaiting his signal. Bryan produced a gasoline-filled glass bottle. It was sealed shut, the rag simply providing a source of flame for when the bottle broke. Arson at its most basic, but necessary for them to accomplish their goal. He didn't light it, and wasn't going to, just yet. The biggest problem for the two men is the fact that if they dumped the gasoline onto the floor and threw a match at it, they would both be incinerated by the vapour emanating from the gasoline. Gasoline itself does not burn, rather the vapour it produces ignites with the air when a flame is introduced. Since the vapour would be omnipresent when the gasoline is dumped around, it would be on their clothes and skin. Introduce a flame and the two men would need more than surgery to save them – they'd need a full-body skin transplant.

Phil poked his head around the corner of the building and looked at Bryan, who responded with a thumbs-up. Phil booted in the door and listened, the room responding with a tiny, almost inaudible beep. An alarm of some sort.

'Alarm! Let's move it!' Phil yelled, quickly unscrewing the lid on his petrol can and dumping it onto the floor. Bryan heard the yell and responded by crashing through his own door. They didn't know how long until the alarm went off, but didn't want to stick around after it did. If they didn't manage to dump all the gasoline, they didn't care. Enough would be enough. The two men met in the centre of the ground floor as an ear-searing alarm ripped through the building. They exchanged a nod before arching their cans into different rooms and running for the front door. Outside, Bryan waved his arms to disperse the last of the vapour, flicked a lighter onto the rag of his Molotov, waiting for it to catch light before hurling it back through the open door and sprinting away. It landed in the hallway, breaking apart and quickly igniting both the contents of the bottle and the rest of the gasoline throughout the building. The fire spread with astounding speed, ripping through all of the rooms in the ground floor and setting its sights on the upstairs. Bryan and Phil were perfectly safe – they were well away from the building before the

144

fire from the rag entered the confined space and the vapour caught light. The two arsonists clambered into the car and sped away before the security alarm gave way to the fire alarm. With the amount of gasoline they'd used, it wouldn't be more than a few minutes before the entire building was engulfed. And needless to say, the members of staff who worked there wouldn't need to go in to work tomorrow.

'Perfect!' Bryan said triumphantly as they drove away. He was in the driver's seat, quickly pulling off his gloves and throwing them onto the back seat. The car he was driving was now essentially his, although he wouldn't have been surprised if Patrone asked for it back. He would have to wait, though. At least until the car had been cleaned – Bryan wanted no trace of gasoline in the thing. He was glad he wasn't a smoker.

Phil was giving him an odd look.

'What?' Bryan asked. He knew Phil had second thoughts about this job, but it had gone swimmingly, and it was over now at least. He proceeded to tell Phil exactly that.

'Aren't we above this sort of thing?' Phil asked, as they moved on from a red light.

'What sort of thing? Criminal shenanigans?' Bryan responded. 'And getting paid for it?'

'Arson. We aren't kids anymore, you know. I'll go ahead and admit it, even if you won't.'

Bryan snorted. 'You speak for yourself. I feel fine. A lot better now that we're gonna get paid for setting one of Tony's businesses on fire.'

'All right, whatever.' Phil said. 'This had better be worth it. I got plans for that money.'

Bryan raised an eyebrow. 'Like what?'

'Plans like never you mind, Wattson. Let's just say I'm not letting you take back ALL of this city. There are one or two things that I have my eye on.' He flashed a knowing grin.

Bryan didn't say anything. He returned it as best he could. It didn't bother him at all that maybe he wouldn't own the ENTIRE city. He hadn't owned the whole thing even before his imprisonment, but what Phil said reminded him exactly how much of the city was, as of right now, not under his control. It would change, he knew that much, but just wasn't aware of how long it would take.

Phil was still talking, and had apparently been doing so while Bryan was zoned out. 'So when are you going to see Patrone and get paid?'

'Later.' Bryan said flatly. 'It's late, and he can probably see the burning building from where he is anyway. It can wait till tomorrow, then I'll give him a call.'

Phil agreed, and the rest of the journey was spent discussing other things.

With some distance now under the tyres, Bryan pulled up outside the hotel Phil was staying at. A suitably classy affair, it did indeed look like the sort of place to have an upmarket suite within which his family could stay. Bryan declined his invitation inside, as it was too late and he didn't want his first meeting with Phil's wife and child in ten years to be a disturbance that reeked of gasoline, however he did wish Phil goodnight, and asked his friend to say hi to Helena and Sophie for him. Phil said of course he would. Bryan had always got on well with Helena, although seeing as how the last time he had seen Sophie she was a baby, he had no idea what the rapport would be like.

As he watched Phil walk into the hotel, he turned the key in the ignition, and set off for his apartment.

CHAPTER THIRTEEN: THE JOURNALIST

Two weeks later. An apartment in downtown Sovereign City.

Reaching into a small pot and withdrawing a pin, the journalist affixed a blurry photograph of Bryan Wattson onto her cork board. Wrapping a length of red string around it, she repeated the process with a copy of the article headed CHAOS AT SOVEREIGN STATE PENITENTIARY. She'd had an inkling for some time now that the man she reported on ten years ago was, in fact, not dead, and now the proof was right in front of her. She couldn't believe how fast the public had forgotten about one of the city's most infamous criminals, and yet here he was: back on the scene. She had been tailing him for some time: a quick photograph here; a little digging there, and now the full picture was simply awaiting the correct method of assembly. Of course, getting a few drinks into the DJ had paid dividends as well, the rewards more than worth the price of admission.

The journalist moved back from her board, studying it. She absent-mindedly brushed her hair behind a gold-studded ear while she thought. What was his next move? What was he planning? To say she was obsessive would be an understatement. It fascinated her that two men could, as near as makes no difference, own a city. She wanted to know how they'd managed it. And more importantly, she wanted to capitalise on it. She had enough information here to get Bryan Wattson back in prison. She probably had enough to get him the death sentence. Perhaps. But she didn't want that. The reason she'd gotten into journalism was to meet new and interesting people. To see how they think, and act. To travel the world and work out what the point of everything was. And naturally... she was stuck working for a tiny newspaper in the middle of Sovereign City. That, she hadn't planned for. Her job at Channel 1 had fallen through a few months after her report on Wattson's imprisonment. It had fallen through before she could complete what she'd started. Bryan Wattson's picture was not at the top of the hierarchy present on her cork board, rather it was roughly centred, alongside an unpredictable-looking man in an eyepatch, a granite-faced Italian, and two Brits. No, the man at the summit of her intricate, triangular work of art was her ultimate goal, similarly linked with red string to smaller photographs of his mansion and some of his known business interests.

Tony Carson was the one man whom no news company could touch. No police officer could arrest, and no journalist could report on. He was frustrating in his quiet, the activity from the mansion on the small island all but dried up. That, and business interests of Carson's ability to always be where the evidence wasn't. She wanted to change that. She knew her name would go down in history if she were to be in front of the camera that captured his incarceration. She had thought the same of his former business associate, however the attitude of ten years ago had quickly dissolved into a simple train of thought: One down, one more to go.

But the one more hadn't gone anywhere, and now the journalist was convinced that she could take him down. And her methods for doing so? Her former partner had said she was crazy, and as it turned out he didn't want to stick around to find out – they'd broken up a fortnight previously, and the journalist had treated the whole situation with complete apathy. He clearly didn't care about what *she* wanted, and if she had to go it alone, so be it.

The intricacy of her art project was bordering on obsessive, born of an occasionally dangerous desire to know absolutely everything about her chosen target. Cut-to-size photographs were pinned underneath statements, accounts and the occasional handwritten post-it note. A printed copy of a map of Sovereign City encompassed the bottom-right corner of her cork board, covered in red circles, crosses and triangulations. Bulletpointed notes that had been written and rewritten listed the pros and cons of everything she was doing. The journalist possessed an outwardly calm demeanour, yet behind closed doors the amount of work she did to find out everything she could was startling. She assumed she knew enough about the subjects of her warped collage to force their hands. It had worked surely enough in the past, her old news office essentially assigning her free reign to report as she pleased so long as it brought in the figures. She found a tangible cork board to be so much easier to wrap her head around than using her computer. Archaic, but effective.

And her crazy plan? As she thought about it, she could feel her nerve faltering somewhat, but before she had time to change her mind she picked up her phone and dialled a number.

****

'You cannot be serious.'
'I am.'
'And she just straight up said it?'
'Like blazing brass.'
'Shit.'

Bryan heaved out a sigh. What the hell had he done to deserve this? Not half an hour ago he'd gotten off the phone with a mysterious woman who'd made him an ultimatum: either he was going to help her, or he'd be on death row by the end of the week. At first, he was dumbstruck; he didn't know who the hell this woman was, and he sure as hell didn't know how she'd gotten so much dirt on him. But… the way she quoted things as fact, the way she had an account – a vague one, admittedly – of some of the events of the past few weeks… it had set alarm bells off in Bryan's head. He thought he'd been relatively careful thus far: no way for any authorities to trace what he'd been up to. And yet here she was, refusing to say what or whom she worked for. It certainly dealt his confidence a blow. She simply stated that they had a 'mutual interest'. Bryan had to admit, confidence aside, he was almost feeling a little flattered. He almost had to commend her for her brazen attitude.

Almost.

'So what the fuck are we going to do?'

'I'm going to go and see her.'

'You what?! Are you mental?'

'She has me by the balls. I have no choice.'

A pause, before a grunt of agreement. 'I don't like this.'

'And you think I do? What the hell could she mean by a mutual interest?'

'I don't know.'

The conversation had ended there. Bryan had made up his mind. He would play her little game. And see just what the hell she wanted. He'd get to the bottom of this.

The following day, Bryan had donned another one of his smart-looking business suits as he stepped out of his car. The past two weeks had been profitable, to say the least. He had helped Patrone out more than once, and his weekly earnings went a long way to explaining why. He fastened the buttons on his jacket and adjusted his lapels as he stepped towards the rendezvous. It was a café, nothing more and nothing less, and yet it still worried him. His was the only car parked for some distance too, something else which exacerbated the whole situation. He heaved out another sigh, something he'd done an awful lot over the past few days, and pushed the door, setting off a welcoming bellchime as it swung inwards.

The journalist was seated in the far corner of the café, in between an overgrown plant and a window adorned with photographs and postcards. Seemingly tucked away from the world, it offered a large distance from the counter. Bryan ordered a coffee, not looking immediately at her, although it was obvious she was his mysterious contact. Apart from an elderly couple nattering away about a television show from the previous evening, she was the only other customer. He paid for his coffee and was informed it would be brought to him. He thanked the waitress and walked over to the table. She was reading from a newspaper as he undid the buttons of his jacket in preparation for sitting down.

Holy shit was she attractive. If a visual impression could produce force, it would have pitched Bryan off his feet. She probably saw it as an asset. Bryan had to remind himself at least twice just why he was here.

'Mr. Wattson.' She said, in a silky-smooth voice. Bryan supposed she'd had a lot of practice.

'You.' Bryan returned.

'I'm glad you decided to come and have this little chat with me.'

'I didn't particularly think I had a choice.'

'Oh, of course you had a choice. I thought I made that clear on the phone.'

Help you, or get fried.

She smiled at him, resting her cigarette on an ashtray. She placed her newspaper onto the table and chuckled slightly when she saw Bryan glance at the 'No Smoking' sign.

'Mr. Wattson... or may I call you Bryan?'

She didn't give him chance to tell her to fuck off.

'I'm truly glad you came to see me, since I'm convinced we can help each other out.'

'How? What the hell have you got to offer me?'

She took a sip of her coffee, stirring it as she spoke. 'You get right on down to the point, don't you Bryan? I like that, yes I do. Obviously, I know you're out of prison, because we're having this little chat. But the police? They don't know jack. And as it turns out, neither do you.'

Bryan shuffled awkwardly in his chair. Where was his damn coffee?

'I've been following you and your little band of merry men for a while now, and let me tell you, you don't exactly make it difficult.'

'Who are you? How do you know me?'

'Hmm... Don't you recognise this face? Even after all this time?'

'You're maybe the fifth female face I've seen in detail in ten years. I think I'd try to hold onto those memories.' Bryan said quietly. It was true. He hadn't exactly been looking for female attention, and there sure as hell wasn't any in prison. All of his business partners were male, too.

She laughed. Shrill, yet dry.

'I'm the journalist who reported on your trial ten years ago.'

The journalist hadn't exactly been expecting the response she got from Wattson. He looked at her for a long moment, his eyes keeping up with her own, and then shrugged.

'Is that it?' He asked.

She hadn't counted on this kind of reaction. She'd expected anger, or something. The waitress brought his coffee and he thanked her, not taking his eyes off the journalist. The young waitress performed a slight curtsey before shuffling off again.

'I'm sorry?' The journalist asked.

'You dragged me all the way over here to tell me you reported on my trial?'

'Well, I...'

'What a damn waste of my time.'

Bryan leaned back in his chair, unsure if he'd successfully wrestled the ball into his own court. He was still somewhat nervous, and he studied the journalist as she thought of what to say next.

He thought he had at least a decade on her, but probably more. She sure looked like a journalist, a photogenic face nestled underneath a prim-looking head of red hair, brushed behind her ears. Whilst initially fiery and full of purpose, her deep blue eyes had momentarily lost their flicker, appearing to cloud somewhat as she thought. Her immaculately kept fingernails drummed on the table without meaning to, slender wrists disappearing into a figure-hugging pinstriped business suit. A simple gold chain hung around her neck, disappearing beneath her collared shirt. Attractive, yes. Appealing, no. Bryan supposed she thought she'd seen it all, the years changing her whether she liked to admit it or not.

In all honesty, he didn't care.

She looked away from him, down at the table, before stroking the side of her face with one of her fingers. Bryan noticed a lack of wedding ring. That explained a lot. She seemed like the type to prefer her own company, probably because she thought everyone else was beneath her.

'Oh, I rather think you still want to listen to what I have to say.'

Bryan smirked. He was fighting off the desire to laugh. Nevertheless, he kept playing.

'Oh yes? And what have you got to offer me? You're a reporter. That's nice. Really.'

'You're a real charmer, aren't you Bryan?'

'No. I'm not trying to impress.'

'I want to help you. Really, I do.' The journalist continued. 'With one of your biggest problems.'

Bryan thought of Gerrard. Did she work for him? Was this some elaborate plan of his?

'And what, pray tell, is my biggest problem?'

She flashed him a smile that might have been considered flirtatious if he wasn't filled with a sense of mild hatred towards her.

'Anthony James Carson.' She produced a photograph of him and threw it across the table. it rotated as it slide across, resting ninety degrees clockwise of where it should have.

Bryan froze, his mouth falling open without his permission. His mind momentarily drew a blank, before promptly exploding into no less than fifteen million questions.

'You...?' Was all he could manage for the moment.

Her face had grown into a smug smile. Yeah, alright, she had him.

'Tony?' Bryan asked, still not past more than single-word sentences.

'The same. The one who's sat in your mansion right now.'

'What the hell could you possibly know about Tony? And what could you possibly offer ME about him?' Bryan was now angry, feeling out of the loop concerning his current goal in life.

'More than you could possibly know. You see...'

The journalist proceeded to tell him about her ambition. She went on for some minutes, and at the end of it Bryan felt no closer to understanding what was going on. He closed his eyes, pinching the bridge of his nose with thumb and forefinger. Her story added up. It made sense that she would want Tony behind bars, as it would, surely, cause her to rocket back to fortune were she to report on it. One thing made him cautious, though. The whole situation was still shaky, and yet he didn't consider anything past his one biggest gripe.

'Why come to me?' He asked, moving his hand away. He couldn't work it out.

'What do you mean? We share a common interest.' The journalist retorted, as if that made everything else agreeable.

'A common interest? No, I don't think we do.' Bryan explained. 'You want him locked up. And I want him *dead*.' He moved a hand towards his coffee, but paused halfway.

'I want to report on him. Whether I report on his imprisonment or his death is irrelevant.'

'You're crazy. Has anyone ever told you that?'

The journalist looked momentarily out of the window.

Yeah, of course someone fucking has.

'Why do you think I'm crazy?' The woman in the pinstripe suit asked him.

'Do you have a death wish? I should shoot you right here, right now.' Bryan said sharply. 'You know too much about me, and if I were to kill you right now, all that would disappear along with you.'

The journalist hoped he didn't see her eyes widen.

'But then you'd have to carry on without my help. And trust me, I could be very helpful to you.'

154

'But YOU were the one who reported on MY trial!' Bryan said, voice raised a little too high. The waitress looked up from her phone for a second, and Bryan dropped his volume to a stage whisper. He jabbed at the journalist's newspaper on the desk with a finger, eliciting several muffled crunching noises. 'You were there when I went down. You probably got off on the whole thing – being present when I was sent to Block D.'

'It was profitable, to say the least.'

'And now you want me to forget that you profited off of my misery, drop the whole thing and help you get your A-game back?'

'You want Tony dead, and your empire back. Simple as that.' The journalist concluded, 'You've been dawdling around with minor jobs and making acquaintances. But now I can help push you a little further to your goal.'

'And how do you plan to do that?' Bryan asked. Were they getting somewhere?

'I've had... shall we say, *run-ins* with your friend at Rock Sovereign.'

'Fucking *Gerrard*!' Bryan breathed incredulously. He was going to kill him!

'That's the one, and he mentioned something about you wanting to control what the public hears.'

Bryan was clenching his teeth so strongly he thought it was audible. 'Yes, I remember saying that. Are you saying you can help that happen?'

'Correct.' She gave him that smile again. He frowned.

Bryan's coffee had long since gone cold, and remained on the table, completely untouched. As both parties left the café it appeared they had reached some semblance of agreement. The journalist wanted the fame and fortune that would come from reporting on Carson's fate. A fate which would indeed be his death, Bryan had made that clear. The journalist was unmoved by this fact, explaining that she would only have to change a few sentences in her report regardless of what fate awaited him. She would act as a firm anchor in the media, using the same guile she had exhibited thus far to keep the public off Bryan's back. Her methods were her own, and Bryan didn't particularly want to get into the world of journalism. It seemed as dirty as his own line of work. At the back of his mind, however, a seed was planted. This woman was in no way trustworthy. He immediately assumed she might try to sell him out as soon as Tony was dealt with. Perhaps before, should it prove an effective means of the journalist garnering this 'rocket back to fame' she so fiercely spoke of. Although he figured that was a long time coming, he was confident that it would be soon, and the concept of being stabbed in the back a second time was not appealing. Yet he would deal with that situation when it reared its ugly head. He made a mental note to keep tabs on her, and to hire someone to keep an eye on her for him. He didn't consider it paranoia as much as common sense.

Regardless, for the time being at least, he could see this being very profitable for him.

The journalist had similar thoughts, knowing the various ways to drop hints and point fingers without it being obvious. She had said that her newspaper was bigger and more efficient than anything Gerrard could accomplish, and had silently thanked the stars that Bryan had chosen not to ask her to back up her claims – she didn't know the audiences of either medium, but would keep in touch with the DJ regardless. If they were both working towards the same common goal, it would make the job easier for her. She knew that Bryan Wattson was dangerous, of course. She had no doubt of it. However, she hoped she would appear as enough of an ally to stay out of his criminal gaze, and at the end of it all, it would be worth it. She had the sense to get out of the country when it was all over, too. She knew that criminals could be paranoid, and she hadn't exactly sold herself in the most trustworthy light. She would save up some money and cross that bridge when she came to it, absconding if necessary.

Regardless, for the time being at least, she could see this being very profitable for her.

CHAPTER FOURTEEN: AMBUSH

'You know, this isn't what I'd call *subtle*.'
'Since when did you give a shit about subtle?'
'Touché.'

Bryan flipped up the sun visor and turned the key in the ignition, pulling his car into a right turn. Phil removed his sunglasses and slid them into the front pocket of his flannel shirt. They were going home, having just spent the last two hours eating fast food, imbibing caffeinated drinks, and chatting while the sun went down.

The two men had been planning a job. No Patrone to help them along this time – this was all their idea, and would be all their profit. They had learned that twice a week a van belonging to Tony crossed Vestige Bridge, once full of drugs, and once full of money. It possessed the outward appearance of an armoured security van, right down to the decals and guards, but inside the contents were far from legitimate. On the same days at around the same time, week in, week out. This was the second consecutive week that the two men had performed this surveillance, in a different car and starkly different outfits both times. They wanted to make sure the rumours they'd heard were consistent. Their sources had sure paid off. The van they had been monitoring was full of money, and they wanted it. Hearsay had turned into fact concerning the vans, and now it was time for ideas to become tangible. Bryan and Phil had discussed to some length the ways that they could hijack Tony's van over the days whilst having a drink, in the same way most other people might discuss sports or politics. For the time being, neither of those two alternatives interested either man in the slightest.

As the car rolled along and the fast food boxes shuffled to themselves on the back seat, Phil cleared his throat, rubbing his chin. He'd let it grow out, a beard which was now rivalling the length of the hair on his head. Not that there was a whole lot of that, but nonetheless he scratched at it as they drove.

'Well, looks like it's on, then.' He stated.

'Sure does look that way, unless anything unfortunate decides to drop itself into our laps.'

'Next week should be all good. I can arrange with the missus to let me go out.' Phil grinned. There still wasn't any contest as to who wore the trousers in his relationship.

'And I'll arrange with the girl who works the desk at the apartments.' Bryan responded with a faint smile.

'So the plan is still the same, right?'

'I don't know. It depends on if we can get everything else we need.'

An armoured van is difficult to get into. Fact. That is the whole point of them. Yet, Bryan was quietly confident, for two reasons. The first was that once it was stolen, they would have Michael rip it to pieces, layer by reinforced layer if he needed to, to get to what was inside. The second was that when it did finally land in Michael's possession, he wouldn't have to worry about anybody tracking him down. Michael was a complete outlier, unknown to virtually everybody in the city. His legitimacy and unknown location were a massive ally, and unless he was crazy Tony wouldn't go public about a stolen armoured car full of illegal cash or drugs. That left Phil's brother with all the time in the world to get to the money stored therein.

So, that left the other massive question: how to get the van off the road. This question was slightly trickier, and had required a great deal of thought. They'd almost immediately ruled out tyre damage – most armoured vehicles are actually designed to function perfectly well with blown-out tyres, and all a frontal attack on the vehicle would do is attract backup, and likely result in a messy shootout.

They had to be quiet, then. And quiet is tricky when you're dealing with reinforced windows and guards with ballistic vests. Fortunately for the two men, there was a small oversight on the part of the guards that they had noticed initially, dismissed, and then reconsidered when they had made their second observation: the guard on the driver's side left his window open whilst he drove. The windows did not roll down in the typical sense, instead using a hinge to open horizontally outwards. Bryan and Phil had surmised that the man was a smoker, and left it open so as not to irritate his colleague. From this, a gap of around six inches, the two men felt they could get inside. And hopefully, in a way which would draw minimal attention. Though Phil had initially been confused as to how they were still employed if they left open the window of an armoured car, Bryan had replied by saying they were almost certainly not legitimate security guards; probably hired guns with more bullets in their magazines than braincells.

Bryan arrived at Phil's place and dropped him off. The stage was set, and they considered that even if they made a tremendous amount of noise, there was barely any chance of them getting caught. Shot, yes. But that came with the job at this point. Guns for themselves were easy: Dempsey asked no questions and took cash, similarly with a getaway car in case things went south: Michael said he had called in a favour to acquire an unassuming vehicle with a tricked-out engine. That would be placed a block away in case the two men needed it. They would be undertaking the job as a pair, any more would likely attract attention. Nothing spooks security guards like half a dozen men approaching.

The plan? Well, now that they had their point of ingress, that was the fun part.

******

Bryan fastened the shoulder holster under his arm and slipped on his jacket. The obvious bulges of his ballistic vest were hidden as best as possible, but he was going for function over form for this endeavour. The ammunition acquired from Dempsey, at least if *his* word was to be believed, should punch through the guard's own vests, and the price tag appeared to suit this claim. They had not been cheap, but Bryan felt that the contents of the van would still present enough profit. Besides, he was sure the rounds would come in handy elsewhere if not today.

He had parked the getaway car in place two days previously, fastening the keys on the underside of the rear bumper. The wheel arch was too clichéd, and Bryan would have been lying if he said he'd never been left stranded by some obnoxious wannabee car thief checking the arches on an expensive-looking parked car. Sure it would still be there, given its generic appearance and rusted alloys, Bryan parked the vehicle he had arrived in some distance away. Walking to the pre-planned spot, Bryan fiddled with the buttons on his shirtsleeves, feeling their security through his gloved fingers. Almost unconsciously, he patted at the rest of his pockets. Empty, save for two things.

He had only brought himself and his few trappings for one reason: he didn't want any trace that could link this crime to anyone he knew, or even himself. It was for this reason that his wallet was back at his apartment, and all the tags had been removed from his clothes. Similarly, he had made sure that his gloves were the first thing he had put on before dressing. Though it sounded ridiculously overcomplicated, and Bryan was sure the plan would work flawlessly, it paid to be neat in this business.

Phil had radioed on ahead and confirmed he was in position. Bryan approached the meeting point and stopped, leaning against a telegraph pole and reaching into his jacket pocket, pulling out a cigarette and pretending to fumble for a light. While he did this, his eyes darted around the chosen point, confirming that he knew the layout of the place where they would commit their crime. A T-junction with a pedestrian crossing lay at the end of the street, the traffic light blinking unceremoniously as vehicles rumbled past. To his left, a chain-link fence surrounding a dilapidated children's park rattled slightly in the wind, a dog cocking up its leg to water the grass. A mother pushing a child's buggy whilst nattering into her phone bustled past, the child itself wailing audibly. Bryan smirked. To his right, across the street a ramen shop was opening for the day, its overweight owner fussing with the sign outside and muttering about its weight. Phil was nowhere to be seen; Bryan assumed he would attempt to keep as low a profile as possible. At the T-junction, a truck barked its horn at several pedestrians who were crossing, clearly eager to continue on its way. Bryan finished pretending to fumble for a lighter, and proceeded to place the cigarette back into his inside pocket. Otherwise, the street was clear, birds chirping quietly, occasionally interrupted by the revving of an engine. Bryan wasn't wearing a watch, but guessed he had been standing there for nearly five minutes. That made it very close to showtime.

As if following stage directions, the van appeared at the end of the street, driving towards him slowly, but surely. Bryan proceeded to implement phase one of the plan: he crossed the road when the van drew nearer. Making sure not to look directly at the driver and to come across as a complete moron, as the traffic lights in the far distance blinked to green, he jogged in a mock hurried fashion into the road and in front of the van, which had been going at a slow speed anyway, causing it to brake and honk its horn at him. He waved a hand at the driver without looking at him, jogging further still down the street towards the pedestrian crossing. Slowing to a brisk walk, he pretended to pull his phone out of his pocket and darted his head back across the road. He rolled his head and looked annoyed.

That side of the road...

If the armoured guards were watching him in annoyance for cutting across them, they would see him, flustered and looking lost.

In addition to pissing them off, Bryan's act of crossing the road had placed enough distance between the armoured van and the car in front that it meant it was the first vehicle to stop when the light flashed red. Grinning inwardly, Bryan slowed and watched the van stop, and glanced at the crowd of around six people that were waiting to cross. A second mother, looking hoarse and wearing a belly-revealing tracksuit was chewing constantly whilst her young daughter fought to free herself from her mother's tight grip. An elderly gentleman appeared to chuckle and mutter something to the child, which caused her to giggle and her mother to cast him a stern glance. He looked away, swaying slightly on his cane. Finally, a squat man in a business suit was tapping at his phone, juggling his briefcase in the other hand.

Across the road, a hooded figure looked Bryan's way, hands in pockets and wearing a body warmer. Under the hood, Bryan could see a wire leading up to his ears and the effects of two or three days without shaving. He bounced on his feet as he waited patiently for the light to turn green. Next to him, a plump, middle-aged woman was staring at the Italian restaurant over Bryan's shoulder, her mitten-covered hands wringing without realising it.

The pedestrian crossing turned to 'Walk', and the crowd of people began to cross.

Setting forth at an elevated pace, Bryan reached the front of the truck first, a hand in his pocket flicking outwards as he passed by. He darted towards the driver's door, unpinning a flashbang and jumping onto the small step as he dumped it squarely into the open gap in the driver's window. He dropped to one side and looked away, covering his ears as the driver registered that they had been breached. The truck lurched backwards, crashing squarely into the car waiting behind it. An indistinct cry came from his lips as the flashbang detonated, causing a spray of white to engulf the cabin along with an ear-splitting crack. The pedestrians screamed in panic, unsure of what had just happened and predicting a car crash. The truck ground to a halt, unable to drive forward as it would surely crush the confused mass of people in front of it. Bryan whipped his pistol out as the driver's door clattered open, the thug gripping an ear with his free hand whilst blindly firing a pistol with his other. Three rounds tore past where Bryan was standing, slamming into the buildings on the opposite side of the road, a tinkling of glass suggesting a panelled shop window was located there. As the thug stumbled down the step of the truck, eyes streaming and pistol aimed outwards, Bryan dropped a gloved hand onto it from the side, thumbing the magazine release. It hit the ground as the thug's head snapped to him, and he jabbed the barrel of his pistol into the man's eye socket.

The fake security guard's pistol dropped out of his hand and he yelped in pain, cursing loudly and gripping his eye. Bryan smashed him over the head with the handle of his pistol, splaying the guard onto the pavement. He kicked the pistol away from them as the passenger's door slammed shut. Taking a few moments to check the man's pockets as he lay in a crumpled heap, Bryan was annoyed to find no trace of a key or means to get into the truck's rear. He shook his head and growled, before hauling himself into the driver's seat; the hooded figure with the headphones nodded from outside before clambering into the seat next to him. The second guard lay unconscious on the pavement on the other side. Bryan slammed the truck into Drive as the lights turned green, the pedestrians having moved swiftly out of the way and the children still screaming as their mothers called 9-1-1. He turned the truck right into the bracket of the T-junction, and was away before any of the pedestrians had finished giving their location to the operator.

Pulling the truck through a series of random turns to throw potential followers off the scent, Bryan slowed down to normal driving speed. Phil had lowered his hood and removed the headphones from his ears. Bryan could hear them playing to themselves as they hung down onto his chest. The two men couldn't actually see what was in the back of the truck, as a darkened sheet of opaque plastic separated the cabin from the back.

'Hope this thing was worth it...' Bryan mumbled as they drove along. He glanced into his mirror, noting that the cars behind him had changed since the last left turn.

'Oh, I should say it will be.' Phil noted, eagerness in his voice. He had let on just how desperate he was to move his family out of the hotel room they occupied, presidential suite or not. 'I mean, we know that it isn't empty back there.' Phil gestured towards the opaque plastic. The back of the vehicle did carry a certain weight, and Bryan could hear the occasional grating sound of something metal resisting its harnesses.

'Yeah, but it could just be the sound of metal boxes banging around.'

'Well, yeah, I suppose it could.' Phil said, 'But I'm being optimistic about this one. It's clearly one of Tony's vans, so therefore the loot in the back must be worth a few quid.'

Bryan could at least agree on that. The interior of the van wasn't anything like an armoured security car. It had a simple dashboard, centre console and gear lever. The decals on the outside were entirely superfluous. Bryan reckoned he could have picked up a truck like this at any used car dealer.

'Makes you wonder, doesn't it?' Phil asked him rhetorically.

'What? Why someone would go through all the trouble of making the vans look good on the outside?'

Phil paused for a moment. 'Well, yeah, I mean I was thinking why someone like Tony simply wouldn't use real vans?'

'I don't know if he needs to.' Bryan responded. 'He's never going to think that someone would actually think about stealing one of them, surely.'

Phil smirked.

'I guess not. But he's not poor. Why not splash out a bit and at least get the right type of van? They can't be that much more.'

'I don't know, Phil. Why not ask him when we see him next?'

'Nah, mate. Not worth it.'

A few seconds of pause. Bryan changed the subject.

'Right, let's play the hypotheticals for a bit. Say there's a million dollars in this van. What are you going to do with your cut?' Bryan asked, his own brain alive with possibilities.

'My cut? Hmm. Is this before or after you inevitably try to short change me for parts and labour?' Came the sarcastic reply.

'Flashbangs count as parts, and since I was the one who dropped it in there-'

'My idea to slow the truck down...'

'-generally do the whole thing myself while you listened to music and looked all suspicious and shit, I'd say you're left with about thirty bucks at the end of it all.'

'THIRTY whole dollars?!' Phil said, like a child with free reign over their Christmas presents. 'Saddest thing about that is you can't get hardly anything for thirty bucks anymore. Before you went away, you'd be able to get a full tank of petrol, snacks from the shop, flowers for the missus and use the change to invest in whatever the latest thing was to sweep the stocks. Can't do that anymore, like.'

'I had completely forgotten what absolute bollocks you could speak sometimes, Phil.' Bryan said, finding it difficult to keep a straight face. 'Oh shit, don't forget ten bucks of that is Michael's too, for helping us with the getaway car and getting into the back.'

'He'll be pissed when we tell him that not only did we not need the getaway car, but we left it parked in a dodgy part of town.'

'Dodgy?' Bryan asked, raising an eyebrow. 'More like on fire.'

Phil laughed.

'No, no, serious time now. Half a million dollars, flat. What do you spend it on? Go.'

Phil twisted his face into his typical 'I'm thinking, leave me alone because this is an arduous process' look. Bryan had seen it many times before. Entirely falsified, there was nonetheless at least a small number of cogs turning in his passenger's mind.

'House, obviously.'

'Can get a hell of a house for half a million, you know.' Bryan said, aware that before he was imprisoned, the housing market was on its backside. He suspected that it hadn't improved much in the last decade, but admittedly it wasn't something he'd kept track of.

'Don't need a hell of a house. I need something that I can live in, with the wife and a bedroom for Sophie until she inevitably fucks off when she's 18. Cosy more than enormous I think, H seems to be all about cosy these days. Think it's her age.'

'See, I'm lucky. I don't *need* a house.' Bryan said with a wry smile.

'I know.' Phil had mock scorn in his voice. He cast a sideways glance at Bryan, his opinions on the 'luck' of the situation expressed multiple times by this point. 'But,' he continued, 'it's not exactly a forever home, is it?'

When they were children, they had discussed their idea of a perfect home, which usually stretched to an enlarged version of their treehouse. They wanted space to do their own thing, and little adult supervision. As they had grown older the vision had not changed so much in the abstract, yet in the concrete they had at least conceded that bricks and mortar are better than wood.

'Not a prison cell.' Phil said, clearly the final product of a thought process.

'Yes. Not that.' Bryan agreed. The truth was that he didn't care where he lived, so long as there were no bars on the windows, plumbing that worked all the time, and no prison guards.

'Cardboard box on the side of the road, then?' Phil grinned. They had often made fun of one of their classmates at school, suggesting he had similar living arrangements. The opposite was, in fact, true – their classmate was incredibly rich, and lived in an enormous house converted from old stabling.

'I'm thinking with the change I could get a proper car.' Bryan said. He was sick of having to borrow cars from Patrone, Michael and Phil at this point. He wanted something of his own. It was an interesting dilemma. City cops, at least in Bryan's experience, were very likely to ask for ID and run the cars of those they pull over through their databases. He couldn't very well complete the paperwork using his Christian name, it had been a while now since the prison breakout, and although details were still being heavily censored by the authorities to prevent public panic, it wouldn't have taken a genius to conclude that he wasn't among the prisoners arrested or found dead at the scene. That left the possibility that he'd fallen off the cliffside into the water along with the carload of Phil's partners. He wasn't bothered by this, though it was possible the authorities had swept the waters

166

surrounding the prison peninsula, water was as good at destroying evidence as any other medium, especially given the time that had elapsed.

'A proper car? Like an eco-thingy?' Phil queried.

'Not exactly.' Bryan responded. 'More like something conspicuous, but fast enough to be able to go like crazy if the need arose.'

'Why not get one and then ask Michael to have a look at it? He's done upgrade jobs before. He put nitrous into a pickup once. Went like the clappers.'

'Perhaps I'll ask him.' Bryan concluded.

The conversation ended there. They were approaching Michael's garage. In the few minutes that it took for them to arrive, Phil called his brother to confirm everything that was going on. Michael said that he was ready, and as the armoured truck pulled into the open garage door, Bryan could not only see that Michael was more than prepared for what awaited him, but appeared to be itching at the chance to tear the truck to pieces.

Phil and Bryan exited the truck, handing the keys to Michael. He studied the truck for a while, occasionally stopping to look at it from a different angle. Opening the bonnet, he reeled off a line of mechanical jargon that Bryan didn't really understand. What he did understand, however, was Michael's explanation of how he was going to get into it.

'Right. Step one.' He said, clutching a cross-peen hammer. Inside the cabin, he slammed the head into the opaque plastic, cracking it in the centre. It was thickly bolted to the sides of the cabin, and Michael said he wasn't going to bother prizing them off. Instead, with a few more sharp hits, the plastic had bowed inwards and dented to the point where he could use his hands to pull it outwards. With a grunt and another sharp cracking noise, he wrenched a large piece of it off, splintering it near the thick bolts. The force of the break sent him backwards, narrowly avoiding hitting his head on the dashboard. A few more strategic hammer strikes and strong tugs later, most of the opaque plastic was removed. Michael cursed, before he collected it together, exiting the vehicle and dumping it into a recycling bin.

'What's up, bro?' Phil asked him, having heard the swear.

'Like I thought there might be, there's two parallel metal bars on the other side of the Perspex.' Michael said. He dropped the hammer onto a nearby workbench, where it clanged against a motley selection of other tools. 'Thick ones.'

Bryan looked inside through the windscreen. Sure enough, two vertical metal bars around four inches thick were stopping anyone from getting so much as an arm into the back of the truck.

'My initial plan had been to clamber in through there, open whatever else is inside and get it back out the same way. But since that's fucked, we'll have to try a different tactic.'

He led the two of them to the back of the truck. Gesturing to the formidable looking mechanism surrounding the rear door, he began to explain the next problem.

'These doors are probably thicker than I am.' He began.

'Fort Knox, then.' His brother retorted, earning him a 'fuck off' for his troubles.

'And I'm guessing that the other drivers didn't have a key?'

'Mine didn't.' Bryan said, remembering his growl of rage.

Phil had gone slightly pale. 'I didn't think to look.' Bryan and Michael snapped their heads to the third man, giving him a pair of looks that were equal parts baffled, annoyed and dumbstruck. Michael shook his head. 'Honest to God, I got the brains and the looks. What the fuck did you get left with?'

Phil actually didn't bother with a snarky retort. Instead, he raised his arms into a shrug, and apologised. 'It didn't even cross my mind. Sorry guys, I hope it didn't actually matter.'

'I doubt it would anyway.' Bryan said, smiling. 'If the driver didn't have any keys, it's unlikely the passenger would, right? It doesn't surprise me.'

'Perhaps Tony has the keys.' Michael pondered. 'Adds to security if the goons don't have access to the trucks.'

'We've spoken about the terrible lack of care on the security side of things.' Bryan said, glancing towards the cab of the truck. 'Piss-poor would be an understatement.'

Michael furrowed his brow, in thought. 'Well, the back door is out. I'd be there for months, and although I have time I suppose, I'd rather not spend every waking second trying to cut through a thick lock.'

'What about cutting through the side?' Phil asked.

'Same problem. The interior of the back will be small. Most trucks like this are. Even more so if the thing is armoured.'

To emphasise his point, Michael grabbed a torch from inside a nearby toolbox. He re-entered the cab and shone it through the gap previously occupied by the plastic. The interior of the back lit up, casting a shadow over the back doors as the torchlight was interrupted by a large, metal box. Michael shone the torch into each corner, checking for any hatches or other easy means to open the back doors. Annoyed that there were none, he nonetheless had a smile on his face as he once again exited via the passenger door.

'Safe.' He said. The single word sent a pleasant wash over Bryan and Phil. The three-way split of its contents pushed all other thoughts aside. Bryan wished he could open it right now, but knew that it could be days or even weeks before any of them had access to it.

'Looks like a big one, too. Four foot, at least.' Michael went on. 'I ain't a safecracker, but it means that there's two giant metal boxes to get through before we get to whatever is inside.' He rapped his knuckles against the side of the truck, eliciting some minor *thunk* sounds. 'I'm gonna look into cutting through those metal bars that were behind the plastic, but I wouldn't hold my breath. Even if I could get through them, I'm not sure any of us would be able to actually fit through the gap. Myself and Bryan are too bulky, and you're too fat.' He said, striding past Phil and back towards the cab. Phil looked crushed. Bryan felt the same way.

'Does that also rule out the roof?' He asked, wondering to what extent Tony had thought of possible theft.

'I think so. Big-ass metal boxes usually have lids.' Michael said.

'So it was a waste of time us even getting it?' Bryan snapped the question at nobody in particular. He spun around, thrusting his hands into his pockets and being overcome with a gnawing urge to boot something across the room.

'Oh, no. I don't think so.' Michael said. He had clambered into the cabin once more with his torch, and was angling it towards the sides of the truck's interior. 'The wheel arches.'

Phil climbed in after him and stuck his face up to the vertical bars. 'Wheel arches.' He repeated.

'Wheel arches.' Michael said, finishing the trifecta. 'Look at them.'

In the interior of the truck's rear compartment, the wheel arches were not visible. Instead, thick, angular metal jutted out where the wheels would have been if not for the armour. Though the inside of most vans had these bumps to accommodate for the location of the wheels, several inches of metal plating had been welded over the top to maintain the security of the truck as a whole. Phil could see the welding lines. On the outside, Bryan ran his still-gloved fingers under the exterior wheel arch. The mud flaps could be easily removed, and he knocked onto the metal above the tyres. Inside the truck, Phil and Michael heard the faint reverberations of Bryan's knock. Large grins spread across the two brothers' faces.

'The armour is weaker there.' Bryan reasoned. 'The wheels are bulletproof, but this thing is a patch job.'

'Exactly.' Michael confirmed. 'I can use the weaker joints and frankly dogshit welding job to get into the car from the underside. The wheels will have to come off first, so I guess that's job number one.'

He still had the keys, and used them to start the engine, reversing out of the garage slightly, before banking right and driving the truck over the pit on the far side of the garage. Bryan heard the grinding of the handbrake before the engine cut out. Michael exited the truck for a final time, leaving the door open but removing the ignition key – a worn, old-fashioned affair stained with a smudged number 11 in marker pen – before placing it onto the top of a nearby toolbox. He rubbed his hands, before turning to Bryan.

'You're not stopping here anymore, are you?' He said, as if he didn't wish to intrude.

'No.' Bryan said, slightly confused. 'I have my own place now, didn't Phil...?'

'Yeah, yeah, it's fine.' Michael responded, staring at the truck. 'I usually stop here if I have a big job to get done, didn't want to step on toes or anything.'

'Nope, I'm out of here now. Be my guest. Oh, and thanks for letting me stay here in the first place, Michael.'

'Sure thing.' Michael was no longer paying either of the other two any attention. He had salvaged some bricks from outside to use as chocks, and slammed one before and after the front wheels, kicking them into place with his foot for good measure.

'I'll let you know when it's done. When I ring you to tell you I'm inside though, you'd best get here as soon as you can. I'd hate to open the safe without you.' A smug smile was on his face, which Bryan wasn't sure he liked.

'Wait, you said you aren't a safecracker.' Bryan said, whilst he and Phil secured chocks of their own to the rear wheels.

'I'm not, but I know a guy.' Michael said suspiciously.

'Of fucking course you do,' Bryan retorted.

Continuing to rub his hands to the point where he looked to grind down to bone, Michael ended the conversation by gesturing to the open door and saying, 'Now, if you wouldn't mind, I've got a job to do, so kindly bugger off.'

'Sound.' His brother replied. 'Catch you later, Mikey.'

Bryan simply nodded at him, aware that the afternoon was growing late. Michael was usually nocturnal, especially when it came to mechanical things that deeply interested him, like this truck. He placed a different toolbox at the steps of the pit before clambering down into it and checking a few things underneath with his torch. Bryan and Phil closed the garage door as they left, hearing the faint scraping of metal as it banged onto the ground.

'Let's hope it doesn't take forever.' Phil said.

'Doubt it will. Michael's a good lad, he knows what he's doing.'

'*He* says that. You don't say that.' Phil grinned.

At the end of the street, both men shook hands and said their goodbyes, walking off in opposite directions, to starkly different living arrangements, and starkly different things waiting for them at home.

****

Despite the good news that Michael was surely well on his way to removing the wheels and getting inside the armoured security van, Bryan was grumbling under his breath as he pushed open the door to his apartment building. The sun was low, the temperature lower, yet the receptionist at Bryan's building – the young woman called Alice – still had her ever-present smile. Though Bryan wasn't in the mood to entertain, he nonetheless managed a small smile in return as he marched past her deck.

'Well, someone doesn't look happy.' She said to him, raising an eyebrow and looking him up and down. He had removed his gloves, and his hands were stuffed into the pockets of his trousers as he walked. He slowed to a halt, and removed them. He tried to return Alice's smile in full, but found himself wanting. Having lived here for some time now, he had spoken to his receptionist almost every time he had left or returned to his apartment, from simple good mornings to reasonably expanded conversations about the weather or what they were up to that day. Bryan had, of course, lied about the true nature of many of his daily events. Even if he wasn't a criminal, he wasn't the sort of person to discuss the finer details of his life. He wasn't self-conscious about his actions; he simply didn't think anyone else needed to know about his doings.

'Shit afternoon, Al.' He said.

'How come?' She asked him, knowing he would give a vague answer.

172

'I got a lift to a place downtown, but couldn't get that same lift back, so I had to walk halfway across the city to get back here.' He felt like it was becoming a running theme.

'Oh dear.' She said, pushing out her bottom lip, a mocking impression of a child looking for pity. Bryan eyed her.

'Indeed.' He replied. He knew she was winding him up, but still felt marginally annoyed that neither him or Phil had thought to leave a car at Michael's. They were smarter than that.

Seemingly not.

He noticed that Alice had her coat on. She had been shuffling papers around as he walked in, and closed a ring binder before placing it to one side. He hadn't noticed the time, but it *was* getting late. Alice worked the day shift, arriving at around eight and leaving at around this time. When she was gone, an older woman named Maude took over her position. Bryan didn't like Maude. She was always looking down her nose at him, her pince-nez threatening to jump off her face. Hardly a word had been spoken between them, unlike between himself and Alice.

He looked at her. She was small. A little over five feet, her hair was incredibly long, usually reaching down to her waist. Silky and dark brown, it made her seem smaller than she was, and in one of their little conversations he had asked her just how the hell it had grown to be so long. She had said she didn't know, and couldn't remember a time where it was short. This evening, though, it was scrunched into a tight bun, the excess hair wrapped around multiple times to stop it going anywhere. It made her look old. Bryan didn't like it. The rest of Alice's features were pretty, her smile friendly without being sickly, her eyes bright and knowing. The slightness of her features were emphasised by a strong vein running down her temple, clearly a point of self-consciousness because it appeared to be the focal point of her makeup. The only real imperfection was her nose, the bridge ever so slightly crooked, from an accident as a child she had said. It didn't matter to Bryan. He had thought himself above crushes at his age, but he thought Alice was so damn cute.

It had broken his heart a little when she said she liked girls. Still, he hadn't held it against her one bit, and she had become the closest thing he had to a new friend since getting out of prison.

'Look, you'd better get out of here before *she* comes.' Bryan said, shivering in false fear.

'She's already here, in the back making green tea. She's always nice to me, you know.' Alice replied, rising from her desk.

'That's because she probably can't see you over her giant nose.' Bryan said.

Alice laughed. 'You know she can probably hear you, right? She's got ears like a bat.'

'More like a whale.' Bryan himself chuckled at the thought of a whale wearing tiny glasses and a wig with hair curlers.

'Alright, I'm off anyway, I guess I'll see you tomorrow?'

'Possibly. I've got no clue what time I'm out and about tomorrow morning.'

'You got it. Night, Watts.'

'Goodnight, Alice.'

She gave him one last infectious smile and strolled out of the door. Fumbling for her keys as she walked, she produced them from her bag and unlocked her car, a simple blue hatchback with smoky rear windows. It looked brand new, and Bryan wondered how she had managed to afford it on the surely pitiful salary that came with working here in this building. He let out a humoured snort as she drove away, making a mental note to ask her car thieving technique. Without another word, he turned and pressed the elevator call button with his middle finger. The elevator doors slid clumsily open as the door behind Bryan began to open. He darted inside and pressed the button for his floor as Maude exited the small kitchen area that accompanied the front desk, reversing out of it and holding a tray of tea and cookies. She didn't look up to see him as the doors closed, and Bryan thanked heaven for small mercies.

CHAPTER FIFTEEN: SPREADING OUT

A celebration of success. A bottle of wine opened and shared between friends. A gravesite unvisited, headstone cracked and letters fading.

Bryan opened his eyes, darting his head upwards before remembering where he was. Last night's dream was as clouded and incomprehensible as they ever were, though unlike usual it was a distinctly positive experience. Bryan looked at the clock on his bedside. Eight-thirty. He turned onto his back, resting an arm under his head as he stared at the ceiling. It seemed like every day he had to wake up and remember where he was. Despite being out of prison for over two weeks at this point, it didn't seem to matter to his brain. It made him feel like he wasn't in control of his own thinking. The sun had been up for a while, yet the blinds and curtains were doing their job of keeping the rays at bay. He ran his free hand across the sheets, brushing them as if covered in crumbs. They were silk, and together with the mattress made his bed one of the most expensive things he now owned, having gone all out in the pursuit of a good night's sleep after over a decade of bad ones. He hadn't been garish enough to go for red silken sheets – off-white was good enough for him – but they complemented the room well enough.

Home décor wasn't at the top of his list of strengths or necessities in his life. Indeed, it was lucky to make the top ten, yet he preferred the simple, uncluttered life, and his apartment showed it. People had made reference to his sporadic decorations in his mansion, entire rooms and corridors bare save for the occasional hanging picture or unassuming shelf. His bedroom was around twenty square feet, separated from the main living space by two doors with a small, cloakroom style affair between them. One mirror hung on the wall of the small cloakroom, and Bryan had initially thought of it as like an airlock. The extra privacy it offered would have been appreciated were he not the only one living in the place, and as such he usually left the outer door open. His bed was at a ninety-degree angle to the door as he walked in, flanked by two bedside cabinets, and a portrait of a mountain hanging above it. It had been there when he arrived, and as such he hadn't bothered to move it. It showed a snow-capped peak, with wooded foothills, an old bridge providing a crossing to the river at the edge of the forest. Bryan liked the picture enough; it was understandable in its simplicity, and not at all over-the-top.

Elsewhere in his bedroom, an oaken wardrobe and chest of drawers provided storage for his clothes while curtains and blinds covered the two windows. The view from his apartment was impressive, yet not without imperfection. Though the bedroom was to the right as one entered the apartment, the windows faced the same direction as the large one in the main living space. The bedroom's ceiling was slightly raised in comparison to the rest of the apartment, to accommodate for the three steps down that a person had to take to reach it. Out of the window, thankfully, the prison was obscured by a distant skyscraper, yet Bryan could see the island where his mansion was located on the other side, and it hadn't taken him long to ascertain which mansion was his. Thus, he refrained from looking out of the window in that direction, yet had realised that whichever window he looked from, the bedroom or the main living space, he could not escape the stark reminders of his past. The mansion from this window, and the prison from the other.

Bryan showered, unconsciously thanking the stars for the consistent warm water. He had found himself doing that for many of the things most people would take for granted. Warm water, delicious food, an appropriate time to wake up. He doubted he would ever stop thanking them. He wouldn't describe himself as institutionalised, yet certain things had become facts of life for him, and now they were gone he was finding it difficult to adjust. He reached for a towel and stepped onto a soft mat – another luxury. As he dried, he glanced into the mirror, chuckling to himself as he did so. He thought he looked old *before* he went into prison. Just what the hell happened to him while he was inside to make him look like *that*? He grabbed the day's clothing from the wardrobe and ate breakfast, wondering what today's plan was. He'd discussed with Phil, and Patrone to a lesser extent, that it was perhaps time to begin forging their new paths on the way back to the top. They had to start small, sure, but every successful business worth a damn started small. As he thought, he unconsciously tidied up the living space, throwing cushions back into place or stacking objects on shelves. Perhaps he would take the day off. He could use the time to surf the internet for properties for sale or investments to capitalise on. Alternatively, he could head back downtown to look at the various estate agents, pressing his nose up to the outside window and trying to read the ridiculously tiny text.

His morning coffee was interrupted by the landline ringing, its display showing that it was Patrone calling. Bryan had replaced the original wired telephone with a wireless one, moving its dockpoint from its original position so as to make it more easily accessible. It now lived on the end of the kitchen countertop, the charging cord hanging in a low arc and touching the table it originally sat on. Bryan lifted the handset, wedging it between his jaw and shoulder so he could still use both his hands. He needed to quickly rinse the crockery he had used for his meal, and turned the tap to heat up as he spoke to the Italian.

'Hello?'
'Good morning, Mr. Wattson.'
'Morning, Patrone. How are you?'
'Very well, thank you. I'm calling because I need to ask you something. Have you seen the news regarding Impeccable Industries?' His tone was as formal as ever, but in their business meetings – if you could call them that – Bryan had learned what to listen or look out for when Patrone was talking. Today, he sounded perfectly fine. That was surprising, especially when he was speaking about the arson that Bryan and Phil had committed recently. As for the news, he hadn't heard anything. He replied in the negative.

177

'Marshall Lucas is dead.' Patrone carried on. 'Found hanged in his apartment. There was no note, and the man appeared to show no previous tendencies. The police are treating the situation with suspicion.'

'Can't imagine why.' Bryan replied. He placed his now-clean coffee mug back into the cupboard, before taking the phone back into his hand to speak into it properly. 'When did they find him?' He asked phatically.

'Yesterday. The police responded to a call made by the landlord. Apparently, he was due to check the electricity and gas meters.'

'And you don't think it was suicide?'

'No. I don't. The situation does not bother me too much. Instead, I was calling to inform you about the proposed plans for the site of Impeccable Industries. Now that the building was razed to the ground, there is a rather large hole in the city. A large hole that I believe could be filled. Officials will go and check the integrity of the building. If anything can be done about it, it will be. If not, it will be demolished and the land put up for sale.' Patrone finished, allowing Bryan a moment to fit the pieces together.

'You want to buy it.' He said.

'Yes. But I suspect you will, too. It is in a prime location, and I imagine the idea of purchasing a business that belonged to Carson is something that would please you greatly.'

Bryan imagined a knife being twisted into Tony's back, and himself sitting in a chair in the office building that Tony had once owned. There was an irony to it that he found both delicious and hilarious in equal parts.

'So, you want to arm wrestle for it or what?' Bryan asked him, remaining jovial despite Patrone's clear interest in the plot.

'No. Yet, I feel like we may be able to enter a joint partnership for it. Mr. Kent may also be interested, but we will have to wait until the authorities finish their investigation and their reports on the building itself. Then we can discuss the possibility of purchasing the property or the land it is on, and discuss afterwards what we intend to do with it.'

'That sounds... profitable.' Bryan said, not entirely sure it would be. 'You do know I'm not that rich though, right?' He asked. 'I would probably have to pay for the property with the money that you pay me for my help.'

More irony. Even Patrone seemed to get it. There was no laughter, yet a pause before he replied suggested his mind had understood the situation.

'Do not worry about it for now, Mr. Wattson. We will discuss this at length closer to the time. By then, I assume you will have more money, and more things to buy.'

The conversation ended shortly thereafter, and Bryan took a notebook out of a drawer and began to scribble. He wrote a checklist of what he needed to do, and some notes on the location and possible cost of buying Impeccable Industries, using the value of surrounding property as a rough estimate. Next, he called Phil, and quickly explained the situation to him, including the details about Marshall Lucas.

'You know it's gonna be horrendously expensive, right?' Phil asked him. He hadn't reacted with as much excitement as Bryan had expected.

'Well, yeah, I mean... It's not gonna be fifty cents, but think about what we could do with it. Great location, great opportunities.'

'Must be if Patrone has such a hard-on for it.' Phil mused.

'Look, it's something to think about, isn't it? He said not to worry about it just yet, but we don't want some randomer picking up the place because we were too slow.'

'And in the meantime?'

'I've been busy.' Bryan told him. 'Been looking at what we can do, and I've got myself a list of things to do before we can start spreading out.'

He heard Phil laugh down the phone. '...Your bloody lists.'

Bryan smiled. He knew exactly what he meant.

Bryan was a list writer. He found himself with a brain that was often difficult to control, and had realised over the years that organising his thoughts into a coherent sequence and writing them onto paper was a great way to focus himself. It gave him a tangible means of working everything out, not allowing for the possibility of his mind running away with things. Among a few scribblings out and the occasional changed or reordered point was a plan of attack. He had done the same thing when they had planned the robbery of the armoured truck, and indeed with a great many of his greatest jobs in the past. It allowed no room for error. At least, in theory.

'Lucas is dead too? Who even was he, anyway?'

'Doesn't matter. I'm guessing nobody. Someone who worked for Tony, and I'm guessing invoked his holy wrath when we torched Impeccable Industries.'

'And then Tony strung him up. Hell of a way to go.' Phil made a *glurck* sound with his throat down the phone, mimicking a man choking to death.

'I can think of worse.'

'I'm wondering about this money, you know.' Phil said. 'We know that there's a few quid on the way from this armoured truck, but Mickey boy did only start yesterday, he's unlikely to have made even a small dent in the thing. But we aren't exactly skint anymore, are we? Why don't we go and look at places to buy?'

'You read my mind.' Bryan said. He flipped on the screen of his computer, waiting for a moment for it to boot up. Phil didn't give him chance to sit down, his next point said with the finality of a decision already made.

'Let's check out that printing press near Rock Sovereign. It's been on its last legs for a while now, or so Gerrard says. The owner might be susceptible to a buyout, if the offer's good.'

'You weren't actually serious about the printing press, were you?' Bryan was sceptical. His first choice for taking the city over wasn't exactly a fortnightly.

'Course. Somewhere to begin, isn't it? We buy it, do it up, bail it out of the shit and start a steady influx of money. Simple.'

'And how the hell do we do that?' Bryan asked. He shifted the phone to the other side. He'd partaken in similar ventures before his imprisonment, but had always found it best to leave the actual day-to-day to the professionals, and sit and cut a quiet slice from above.

'I dunno. Haven't got that far.' Bryan could smell the grin down the phone. He sighed.

'Alright. I'll meet you there in ten minutes.'

'You want to *buy* my business? Are you completely insane?'

The plump owner of the printing press dabbed a filthy handkerchief at his brow, doing very little to alleviate the amount of sweat covering it. His hair had long since given up, sitting in a messy combover that Bryan struggled to classify. It was either the best or worst he had ever seen, depending upon the angle at which he observed it. The man's eyes sat deeply in his face, the swelling of his cheeks and bushiness of his eyebrows threatening to completely cover them.

An ill-fitting tweed jacket covered a shirt threatening to burst at the seams, and even from behind the desk it was obvious that his seat was about to give way. Despite the man's enormous stature, and indeed perhaps because of it, everything else in the room seemed comparably small. His mug of coffee was tiny next to his ham fists, the nameplate on his desk – Oscar Clarke – seeming miniscule. Bryan sat momentarily in silence as he observed the overweight owner. Flecks of red touched his cheeks; it was obvious that they had deeply offended him with the mere mention of giving up his business, irrespective of how downhill the whole thing was going. Bryan had dressed to impress, his suit an appealing maroon. An impulse buy at first, Alice had said it suited him after asking him to do a twirl.

His left leg was resting on his right knee, exposing a pair of black socks with blue clocks on them. He was waiting for the man to unleash a tirade of insults, prepared entirely for a slew of how dare yous and I've never been so insulted in my lifes. Phil was doing the same. He was similarly garbed in a simple charcoal suit and tie, with a mint green shirt and pocket square. They were both sitting in small wingback chairs in the owner's office. As with everything in the room, they felt tiny, yet Bryan could feel the comfort it offered as the man stumbled over his next words.

'Just who the devil do you think you are, waltzing in here and making such an outlandish statement?' The owner breathed. His voice was nasally and laboured, as if his lungs were losing the fight against the flab.

'Mr. Clarke.' Phil said, a goodhearted note in his voice. 'Myself and my partner are businessmen. We have a mutual interest in your property. We think it'll be a fine addition to our business conglomerate, and therefore we feel it only appropriate that we have this meeting with you, to make our intentions clear.'

'A business *conglomerate*?' Clarke snorted, like he'd never heard the word before. 'Is that some fancy, *limey* word that you all use to make people feel stupid?'

'No.' Phil said, a cursory glance up at the owner. 'It means a...'

'I know what it means!' Clarke snapped. They were going to have to be careful. The man hadn't told them to piss off just yet, which meant he wasn't totally against the idea. They just needed to capitalise on that.

'It means that we think we can make more money off your business than you can.' Bryan said. He thought he would try a different tactic. Brazen. No fucks given.

'And how'd'ya reckon that, then, friend?' Clarke asked, a bushy eyebrow raised.

'Ha-ha, that would be telling.' Bryan tilted his head knowingly. 'I can see this place isn't exactly the pinnacle of its kind, is it?'

'Well, I mean...'

'Mr. Clarke, we've been doing this for a long time. We've bought businesses from Calvert to California.'

'From Newton to Newquay.' Phil interjected with a smile.

'Yeah. I think we can cut the bullshit. What are your profits, like ten percent?'

Clarke grumbled. 'Seven.'

'Seven. So for every dollar that you spend, you make a dollar and seven cents.'

'That's how profits work.' Clarke snorted. Bryan thought about how much he was patronising him and slowed down.

182

'We would like to offer you a buyout. We want to purchase this from you, today.'

He gestured around the office with his arms.

'Today? Never gonna happen. No way, no how.' Clarke said, jabbing a pudgy finger onto the wooden tabletop. 'Need lawyers, people to countersign and all the rest of that shit.'

Bryan smiled. Not in his experience they didn't.

'In your head right now you have a figure.' Bryan held up a hand to stem the inevitable response. 'Every man has a price, Mr. Clarke. A means to get them to retire early, if you will. We want to hook that figure and drag it out of you.'

Bryan had realised a while back that he was speaking like Patrone, and Phil had seemed to cotton onto it as well. He was staring at Bryan as he spoke, nodding occasionally to show his ascent. He turned away from Bryan to look into the owner's flabby face.

'We've had our people value the place. Gave it a good once-over from the outside, checked out the nearby business, places of interest, all the rest of it. We've got an offer to make you.'

Phil reached a hand towards his inside pocket. Inside it was a folded piece of paper with an amount of money on it. An amount of money that the two men had agreed was the maximum they would spend on this business. He hesitated as his hand reached for the inside pocket, instead using it to point at a picture behind the owner's desk.

'You like golf, Mr. Clarke?'

'Well, yes, as a matter of fact I do.' Clarke spun in his chair slightly to face the picture, the chair squeaking in protest. 'The wife does, too. That's the two of us last year, playing golf in Florida.'

'Hell of a place. Hell of a sport, too. I could never work on my short game.' Phil admitted, a guilty look on his face.

'It's all in the hips.' Clarke said. 'Gotta get yourself to the point where you can just tap it in. Spin the pelvis, not the whole of you.'

Bryan widened his eyes unconsciously. He couldn't imagine the man sat before him playing any kind of sport at all. He supposed it wasn't the most athletic sport, even if a great amount of skill was required to play it properly.

'So you and the wife play often?' Phil asked him.

'Not as often as I'd like.' Clarke said sadly. 'The plan was for Pamela and I to retire there soon. We could spend the rest of our time baking our bones in the sunshine, a few drinks, some fine food and a round of golf whenever we felt like it.'

Bryan studied the picture more intently. He had initially thought it was two sumo wrestlers at a Hawaiian fancy dress party, but upon closer inspection it was, indeed, the owner and his wife, an equally rotund woman both in Hawaiian shirts and with a bag of golf clubs slung onto their shoulders. The picture looked candid to a degree, the woman seeming more shocked that smiling, but Clarke himself looked absolutely delighted to be there.

'I mean, I'm fifty-seven now, you know.' Clarke was beginning to sound like the printing presses they'd seen downstairs. 'Not getting any younger.'

'Well, we've got property in Miami, haven't we, Bryan?'

Bryan realised he'd been asked a question a split second before it became obvious that it wasn't true. 'Oh, yeah. You heard of La Granada?'

'No, I'm afraid I haven't.' Clarke said, after a moment of very obviously fake thought.

Bryan leaned a little closer to Clarke's desk. 'Gentleman's club. Very classy. You'd like it, I'm sure. Although as for the wife...'

Clarke chuckled.

'We let all out clients in for free, you know.' Bryan waved his hand as if it were an aside. 'Not that that would influence your decision, of course.' He smiled cheekily.

The fat man continued to chuckle, suggesting that they were getting there. Slowly.

'I'm not even sure you'd want the place, you know.'

'Why not? The place ain't got rats, has it?' Phil asked.

'No, nothing like that. It's just, you don't know what it's like to be a small-time company in this climate. Nobody reads anymore.' Clarke said, dismayed.

'Isn't that your job? To make them want to read more?' Bryan asked him.

'Well, yes, I suppose it is. Doesn't make it easy to do though. Profits have been getting smaller and smaller, while our overheads are getting larger and larger. I was going to have to shut up shop eventually, but I wanted to do it on my terms, ya know?' Clarke finished.

'Indeed I do, Mr. Clarke. But, hey, if we get to give you a bit of a push in the right direction, isn't that a good thing? Get the ball rolling that bit quicker, as it were?'

'The golf ball.' Phil added, his attempt at wit both awful and ignored in equal measure.

The owner simply mumbled an agreement, beginning to dab once again at his forehead.

'It's still mildly insulting, you know. Two men who clearly know what they're doing, accosting their fellow man about his business.'

Bryan fought the urge to laugh. They barely had any idea of what they were doing, and yet it was working. They were almost there; he could feel it. He glanced sideways at Phil, who was wearing another of his rictus grins.

'At least you know it will be in good hands.' Bryan said, through a shrug.

'And you would take on everything that comes with the business?' The owner asked, matches lit in his eye sockets.

'I mean, in theory.' Phil answered. 'If the place owes millions to the taxman then we probably wouldn't bother. But a few quid either way doesn't really bother us.'

'And you would pay for me to retire to Florida, no questions asked?'

'Sounds a bit Scarface, but I suppose what we pay for it would go towards that.'

'And the things that I print?'

'Well, there might be a few changes, I mean we plan to try and print some things of our own.' Bryan admitted. It was a fair point. Exactly what did this printing press do? They hadn't been able to dig up any information on the place, other than that the surrounding land and proximity to Rock Sovereign had a relative impact on the worth of the place. Clarke leaned back in his chair, the bottom of his enormous belly erupting from under his shirt. He rubbed his second and third chin with his hand. Bryan continued to speak, pausing to look at Phil, who nodded in agreement, 'We were thinking about using this place to print all the pamphlets and brochures of our other business in the city and surrounding area. Menus, newsletters, headed letters, things like that. If it's possible of course.'

'Yes, yes. No doubt.' The owner smiled devilishly and obviously. 'Fine. Okay. I can see where you are going. I feel like we don't need to talk about it anymore.'

'Yeah? Well that's good.' Bryan said. His inner voice was wondering loudly why the man had changed his mind so quickly. He didn't want to walk straight into a financial trap.

'Yeah, it *is* good,' Clarke responded. 'I guess I'd been thinking about retirement, and this is the push in the right direction I needed. I can have all my stuff cleared out in a few days. I'll probably leave some stuff behind, though. You can get rid of it in any means you see fit.'

'Like we said, we'd probably hold onto anything that benefits the company.'

'Long as the tax man doesn't see it, that's fine by me.' Clarke said ominously.

Bryan wanted to seize this with both hands. Something that might otherwise alter what they said, or indeed what they offered the man for his business. He also wanted to keep it casual, as if it wasn't a giant concern. After all, as big businessmen, what would his and Phil's relationship with the tax man be?

'You and the tax man not on the best terms either?' He said, continuing to aim his interest at the man instead of the business.

'I should say not.' Clarke stifled another chuckle. 'As it turns out, he wants lots of money. And it's always been a point of personal pride of mine to give him as little as I possibly could.'

'And how little is that?'

'Not a damn cent in six years.'

Bingo.

Phil laughed. 'Our issue was with the insurance man. See, we met in London oh, twelve, thirteen years ago. I was a struggling businessman, and this handsome bugger bailed me right out of the gutter, didn't you?' He raised an eyebrow at Bryan, who nodded in reply. 'I used to run pubs in England before I came here, and for insurance purposes I have actually been killed in four separate pub fires.'

The fat man slapped a beefy hand onto the table, guffawing loudly.

'Four separate pub fires!' He said, his voice threatening to choke on itself. 'Ahh, you limeys have the best words for stuff.'

'Thanks very much.'

'So if you haven't declared anything in six years, where do you get all your paper?' Bryan asked, turning businesslike again. 'Do you know a guy, or...?'

'Yeah, I know a guy. Done business with him a long time. Paper and inks. He's probably not going to like it when I retire, though. They tend to be quite... *territorial*.'

'Hmm. A backhander, eh?' Phil said, continuing to be positive.

'Yeah, that's it.' The owner paused, and Bryan could see him swallow because it sent a ripple across his chins. 'That ain't gonna be a problem, is it?'

'A printing press with no access to the materials it needs to print stuff?' Bryan asked. He looked at Phil, as if they were deliberating it. Phil looked somewhat worried, before shaking his head.

'No. I don't think it will be.' Bryan nodded his head at Phil.

'Right. I think it's time to make you an offer, Mr. Clarke.'

Phil reached his hand once again towards his inside pocket. Bryan absent-mindedly scratched at his chin as he did so. So, they had managed to weasel out of the owner that not only was the business on its last legs, but also that the owner had not paid the tax man for a number of years, *and* that they would probably be unable to use his source for paper and inks. In other words, the business was next to useless. It would be financial suicide for any normal businessmen to invest their money into it, unless they were so fabulously wealthy that it didn't matter. Fabulously wealthy, or they knew something that would give them the edge. Bryan and Phil had the latter. With a bit of luck, they would be able to turn this printing press into something loosely resembling a profitable business venture. But given its current state, they would be able to curry an enormous discount.

Phil's hand reached the inside pocket of his jacket while Bryan thought, although it was not the same pocket as he had reached for earlier. It was instead the pocket on the opposite side, which contained a similar piece of paper, albeit with a different, much lower offer on it. The two men had decided before they came out that they would bring multiple sheets with them. Bryan himself had one in each inside pocket, each with varying amounts of money written on it. A trick they had practised over time, the two men had talked Clarke into revealing the business' small profits and many issues, and now they were confident that the sheet of paper Phil was holding as he retracted his hand – a sheet of paper containing their lowest offer – would suffice.

Phil placed it onto the desk, tapping it twice with his fingers for good luck. Clarke slid the paper between his meaty fingers and flipped it open. He studied the paper for a few seconds in silence, before looking at Bryan and Phil and opening his mouth to speak.

The word they had used was 'expedite'. Three days had passed since they took over, and now the printing press was something vaguely like a functioning business. The first thing they had done was clear the place out. It was ridiculous how much clutter had accumulated during Clarke's tenure, and Bryan and Phil took great pleasure in destroying all of it. Faxes, expense reports and anything else that looked somewhat like paperwork was gotten rid of. A fresh start, as it were. Now, the two friends stood in the office where Clarke had once been. Bryan was sitting in the same wingback as before, slouched and sporting the biggest smile. Phil was sitting where the big man had once sat, his feet up on the desk. After years of punishment, the wheeled office chair was finally glad to support someone of the correct body mass index. Well, nearly correct.

'So now what the fuck do we do?' Phil asked. He moved his feet to the side to look Bryan in the face. The office was almost empty; they had managed to keep the furniture, but the bric-a-brac and photographs were gone.

'Simple. We continue with the next part of the plan. Start publishing. Start printing. Boring as it sounds, it will bring in the cash. Make Patrone less of a crutch for us.'

'Oh yeah, we'll be rolling it in by next month,' Phil said dismissively.

'Maybe the month after that,' Bryan retorted.

'How.' It wasn't a question. Just a word, said to emphasise the fact that we're not trained publishers. Bryan had the answer, though.

'We get the right people to help us. Or rather, the right *woman*.'

He picked the phone on the desk up with his left hand, whipped it into his right, and dialled a number.

******

'Oh yes, this will do you very nicely.'

The journalist wiped an elegant finger along the edge of the largest press, unconsciously rubbing it against her thumb despite its relative cleanliness. She was dressed not for a formal meeting, but instead fully prepared for dust and grime. Her jeans were skin-tight, once again emphasising her figure, and the

189

sleeves of her cardigan were rolled up. Her t-shirt looked freshly washed and not ironed, her red hair pulled into an unbrushed ponytail. She rounded on Phil. Both men were similarly dressed for an informal occasion. Bryan was wearing chinos and a green t-shirt, Phil an old and faded hockey jersey and jogging bottoms.

'And who is this one?' She asked, regarding Phil with the same interest that a child demonstrates when looking at an animatronic. Phil looked back at her face, sticking to the old salesman trick of looking between her perfectly kept eyebrows so he didn't need to look at her eyes. When she had arrived she'd walked right past him.

'Associate.' Bryan said. His coat was hung up on the rack outside the office. It had unofficially become Phil's, because he had decided to make Clarke's old desk his own. Bryan didn't mind. It wasn't as if they would actually work there at all.

'Associate? You have associates now?' She gave him the flirtatious look especially reserved for him. 'Before you were all lone wolf and 'me against the world'.' Her last four words were said in a mocking attempt at Bryan's voice, accompanied by a stamping foot like a child denied its favourite toy. Phil laughed.

'I believe he prefers the term solitary eagle. I'm Phil. I bail him out of the shit. And you are?'

'Phil the shit-bailer? You can call me Robin.' She said it through devious eyes.

'Is that your real name?'

'Does it matter?'

'No,' Bryan said, 'To both questions. What do you think, anyway?'

'It looks good. It sure looks like a printing press.'

He gave her momentary stink eye. She looked offended.

'What? Why are you looking at me like that?'

'I know you aren't that stupid. Do you think you can do things with it?'

'Do things? I could probably find an on switch if I looked hard enough.'

'You know that's not what I meant. Could you use it?'

'You're offering me a job?'

'I thought that was obvious. Why else would I call you?'

190

'Perhaps you just wanted me to look at the hardware and compare it to what I'm used to. Selfishly though, I presumed it was because you wanted to see me again. Because you missed me, and because things *sparked* between us last time.' She winked at him. He felt his cheeks redden. Phil was a loud, staged whistle away from it being incredibly awkward.

'Just shut up and answer the question.' Bryan looked at Phil. He was struggling to keep a straight face. It turns out you are never too old for situations like this flirtatious awkwardness. He hadn't experienced it properly in years. The journalist was still looking at the printing presses. She patted one.

'Well, well, nice to know your personality wasn't just for show at the café. Do you know what he said to me before, Phil the shit-bailer? He said the meeting was a waste of his damn time. I don't think I've ever been a waste of time to anyone before.'

Her eyes seemed to cloud with genuine sadness. Phil turned away from her and glared almost unconsciously at Bryan.

'Probably because you gave absolutely zero useful information up until that point. The journalist at my trial? Please.' Bryan responded, not at all in the mood for the same word games from the café.

'And then he leans back, giving me those eyes that bore into your soul. Very enrapturing, I must say.'

'Yeah...' Phil said, trailing off intentionally. 'Do you know what, there's a box of stuff over there that isn't quite straight on the shelf. I'm just going to head over there and sort it.' He shot across the room and out of earshot faster than Bryan had ever seen him move.

'Well, that's a first. You've actually awkwarded Phil to death.' Bryan said, managing to smile despite everything. 'Never thought I'd see the day.'

'I suppose he just cannot handle my charms.' The journalist replied. He couldn't work out if it was her brazen attitude, or the false layer of sweetness that touched her words. 'You, though. You're handling things surprisingly well.'

'I suppose I know how to look past your charms, journalist.'

'Robin, please. I call you Bryan.'

'That's because Bryan is my name. I didn't introduce myself as something like *Nathaniel*.'

'Nathaniel? Now that's a sexy name. I'd be all over you if you told me you were called Nathaniel.' She fanned herself with a hand in an over-the-top manner, blowing air out of her lungs.

'And I'd be all over you if you were in any way different to the way you are.'

'Any way different to the way I am?' She continued to stare dejectedly at him, hands lowering from the fan and resting on hips in mock defiance. The sleeve of her cardigan began to creep down, and she repeatedly shoved it back into place by her elbow as she spoke. 'Well it's nice to know you wear your heart on your sleeve. Honesty is good in any relationship. You've let slip your hand though now, Nathaniel. You've said there's a chance between us.'

She stuck her tongue out at him. He momentarily forgot that both of them were grown adults. For a second - and not the first one since they'd known each other - he was a helpless awkward teenager, fumbling over his words to ask out the girl he had a massive crush on.

'No, I'm not. I'm saying if you were even the slightest bit different, there'd be a chance. But there isn't. You're a business associate, and by the looks of it a liability as well.'

The journalist fought to keep her emotions in check. She wasn't sure how to feel about this man. On one hand it was most fun to toy with him, she'd only known him for a short while but knew exactly which buttons to press to irritate him. But she saw it as playful. He, on the other hand, well... he didn't. That much was obvious. She was going to keep going. She *wanted* to keep going. She wasn't hurt by his comments, perhaps slightly ruffled, but not hurt. She sighed.

'Well, goddamn. I'll remember that one.' She smiled her most flirtatious smile yet at him, and saw him momentarily drop his guard. She couldn't resist. '...Natty.'

That was it. Bryan's patience had run out. He took a step towards her, pointing a finger at her. 'Listen, you...'

'OH, SHUT UP AND GET ON WITH IT!' Phil blared across the room. 'It's bad enough me having to piss about over here without you two getting to the point of killing each other.'

'Fine.' The journalist said flatly. 'I was getting bored of this banter, anyway. I already have a job, you know.' She turned her head, her perfect teeth flashing between her lips.

'At a pokey newspaper company publishing, what, agony columns?'

'Actually,' she snapped, 'I write a column about local businesses.' Sore subject. Great.

'Excellent. That means you can write an ironic last piece about how you're leaving to become a key player in your own local business.'

Her expression became quizzical. 'Key player? Like, the *boss*?'

Bryan glanced at Phil. It was the latter who spoke, returning with a modicum of reservation from his box-straightening enterprise. 'Well, not the top dog, you'll still be working for the two of us.'

'But what do you need me for, Phil?'

'Because we know sod all about being a journalist.' He replied, unconsciously tugging at the fraying hem of his jersey.

'Don't you get it?' Bryan cut in. 'We can start the war against Tony. You get to do exactly what you wanted to do. You can report on the whole thing from the newspaper printing press that you basically run. It's perfect.'

Her eyes burst to life, widening with the realisation of something she hadn't previously worked out. 'What about money? I can't just quit my job. What do I do, apply for an apprenticeship?'

'Obviously not. We know people. They'll sort you out with what you need. Get your affairs together and ditch your old job. When can you start?'

'Immediately. I think so, anyway. Won't take long to leave my old place; it's more or less a zero-hour contract anyway. I guess I can start on Monday?'

'Perfect.'

She stepped towards him, closing the gap. 'I want that office.'

She pointed a slender finger up towards the office that had once been Clarke's. Bryan looked back at her, moving a step closer until they could feel each other's breath.

'It's not mine. You'll have to take it up with the man in charge.'

The journalist looked at Phil, pouting.

'...Please?'

'Fine by me,' Phil replied, 'Anything to cut through this tension.'

'That is *great* news.' The journalist said. She folded her arms under her chest. 'I will start as soon as possible. If I can sweet-talk the suppliers and distributors in the place I'm working at right now to get us the traction and supplies we need, I'll have negative propaganda about crime in this city flooding out in no time.'

'About the right type of criminals, though?'

'All criminals are the wrong type of criminal, Bryan.' She responded. 'But yes, you and your friends will not be mentioned at all. In fact, I heard you were all killed in the breakout riots. Isn't that true?'

'The truth, *Robin*, is whatever you want it to be.'

They were still standing close to each other. The journalist reached out a warm hand and touched Bryan's cheek, resting it on his jaw and rubbing his cheek softly with her thumb. 'You know, if you wanted to see me in action, all you had to do was ask.' She softly slapped his cheek twice, before striding off in the direction of her new office, an overemphasised spring in her step. She called over her shoulder, 'Oh, and before you go, be a pair of dears and clear out the rest of those boxes. I doubt I'll need them.'

When they heard the door close upstairs, Phil pointed after her.

'Dude, you have *got* to get on that.'

'Piss off. I have *got* to shoot her.'

'No, I'm serious. Did you want a chainsaw to cut the sexual tension with, or is a knife alright?'

'Leave it, Phil.' Bryan said sternly. Although the journalist was undoubtedly attractive, something about her bothered him. He'd seen her type before. The wicked queen whose suitors bend over backwards for the chance at her approval. It was her eyes. He'd finally worked it out. Something about her eyes was incredibly inviting. Perfectly free of bloodshot, they were the kind of eyes that could move mountains or take over governments, if they were just given the chance.

'You don't have to actually talk to each other while you do it, you know.' Phil was being annoyingly persistent.

'What, like with you and H?' Bryan snapped back.

'Of course. It's a hell of a lot different when you've been together as long as we have. It all becomes just something to do, ya know? Our telly's broken.'

'Still?'

'Well, yeah. I ain't fixing it while it still gets me my leg over. But this journalist though, man...'

He let out a long whistle.

'I never said she isn't attractive.' Bryan said flatly.

'No, no, presumably it's some preconceived notion about her being all slimy or irritating.'

Bryan smiled weakly. Phil *was* his best friend; it was obvious that he would get the reason why. He did miss female company, sure, but the journalist? The one who called herself Robin? Bryan didn't know if he could get over her personality. She had clearly won Phil over. To him, it was sugary. To Bryan, it was diabetes.

Still, if he ever did find himself getting so incredibly lonely, there was no harm in seeing where things went, was there?

He realised he'd been staring up at the office for some seconds, and cleared his throat to snap his mind to more important factors. They were in business. The journalist had said she could get started by Monday. That left a weekend of little to do but wait. To start with, they spent some time clearing the rest of the boxes that Phil had straightened. Back and forth they went, speaking little except for exchanging suggestions of who should take the boxes and where they should go.

'You'd have thought a journalist would want paper.' Phil said, grunting with a particularly heavy box.

'It's not all paper. That one says...' Bryan angled his head to read the writing stamped on the box. Phil wasn't adhering to 'this way up'.

'...It's full of staplers. Don't they need staples to stick the magazines together?'

'I doubt they'd use a normal office one.' Phil replied. They had decided his car would be the one to take the boxes. They needed to get rid of any evidence, since the building they were in would no longer be used for legitimate purposes.

As well as clearing out most of the evidence of the previous management - except for the things they thought the journalist would need - they had taken the time to remove all signage from the building itself. Previously, it was known as Original Content Printing. Now, it looked like a victim of the times, darkened outlines of letters and screw holes the only reminder of the business' legitimate origins. Bryan would ask the journalist to sort out any new signage and bunting for the place - she could take what she needed from the petty cash when it started to become disposable.

Phil would have to take the boxes to the waste recycling plant. It wasn't a particularly difficult thing to do, the place wasn't far from where he was staying, and Bryan didn't imagine that the boxes would arouse any immediate suspicion because they were being dumped before anything illegal came out of the printing press. The only thing was that it was now too late to take them, so Phil would have to wait until tomorrow to get rid of them.

'Obviously don't draw attention to yourself.' Bryan said.

'Bryan, look.' Phil said, hands on hips. 'I'm a 'fessional. You're not dealing with a mug here, you know. I'll keep the car out of sight and get shut tomorrow, first thing.'

'Excellent. It feels nice to get a foot on the ladder again.' Bryan was pleased, though he still knew it would take time to get up and running. Time, though, was something they had as much or as little of as they wanted. It was a precious commodity for the first time in a while. In theory, they had all the time in the world, and could simply have laid low until money started rolling in from the printing press.

However, Bryan knew that they needed way more money than a few dollars an hour from a printing press. He still had some big plans on what to spend his money on, and was still itching for Michael to get the safe in the back of the armoured truck open.

That left a weekend of nothing to do. Bryan and Phil agreed to spend the weekend doing very little, and although it would probably leave Bryan feeling a little stir-crazy, he reluctantly agreed to bide his time and not draw any attention to himself or the printing press until it was up and running.

If only it were that easy.

CHAPTER SIXTEEN: THE SPOILS

That weekend and the week that followed it passed uneventfully. By the Monday, the journalist had quit her previous job writing about local businesses. She had written her ironic final piece, a passionate and heartfelt farewell to the newspaper she had toiled at for some years and as far as her readers were concerned, a farewell to journalism in general. She had made it seem like it was with heavy regret and a heavier heart that she had finally laid down her quill, instead moving to the less hectic world of managing her own business. A business that was sure to challenge her in new and exciting ways, and allow her to move in a new direction away from an otherwise stagnant career. Her column was normally no more than half a page in length, but for her last hurrah, she had written a full two-page spread. She had said thanks to all her editors; she had said that she was grateful for all the opportunities the newspaper had given her; she had said that she was sure that a new generation of upstart and headstrong journalists would replace and surpass her.

She had said a lot of things.

Bryan never inquired further as to which magazine she had worked for. He showed the outward appearance of apathy, yet deep down he really wanted to see the final article she had written. When he teased her about the article when they next met, her voice had conveyed genuine feeling that this *was* the correct next move for her. She seemed to believe in this printing press, and everything that it could do for the city as a whole.

And why wouldn't she? Who in the journalism field wouldn't want to be in charge of her own press, printing whatever she wanted? To Bryan, it seemed like a dream come true for someone in her position. It went without saying that it would bring in lots of money, the journalist expected to get paid for what she was doing, but that wasn't at the forefront of her mind. Bryan knew that. They were using each other, pure and simple.

He wanted to make money, and she wanted to skyrocket her reputation. So far, it was working a treat. But as long as it was making money, Bryan was secretly happy that he and the journalist were working together.

Ha. He smiled to himself. *The journalist.* He still couldn't bring himself to call her Robin. Aside from the single use at the press which had been said with the utmost sarcasm, he had never used that name. He had been sure since the moment she said it that it wasn't her real name. But she had kept it very close to her chest. She had stuck to Robin, even going so far as to use it on the signage and credentials of the printing press. And now they were over a week into the press being open for business. And true to her word, the journalist had sent something out of the doors every single day. Bryan was baffled at the speed of it all. It never was what you know, it was always who you know, and the journalist seemed to know absolutely everybody needed to get things up and running.

Plans were in motion and were being acted upon, which was now why Bryan found himself in the journalist's office. He was several minutes deep into a conversation about how things were going with the press and what they could do to allow it to progress further. The journalist was as physically captivating as ever, back to a suit similar to the one worn in the cafe. Her jacket and skirt were a deep red rivalling her hair, a plain t-shirt underneath showing the gold chain around her neck. She'd had her nails and hair done to a pristine standard, and Bryan had wondered if the press had paid for it. Her chin rested on her hands, forming an upside-down V on the desk. She was staring into his eyes, seemingly unblinking.

'And where is Philip?' She asked him, a smile creeping into the corners of her lips.
'He's taken his own advice and given himself a break. Wants to sit back and let things over here simmer a while.' Bryan returned. He himself was wearing a shirt and trousers, sleeves

rolled up. The journalist had tried and failed to subtly look him up and down as he walked in.

'Good to know. Though I would have thought he'd want to hear all this himself.'

'The press was his idea, sure, but I doubt he gives a crap about the details of it. If it brings in money, he'll be happy I'm sure.'

'Wow. I could have sworn those roles would have been reversed.' She raised an eyebrow.

'Call it me going stir crazy.' Bryan responded with a shrug. His arms were folded, and he was starting to think he'd been here too long. He thought about calling Patrone and asking if there were any jobs going, and wished the journalist would cut to the chase about the situation here. 'I want to be kept in the loop to a certain extent.'

'Kept in the loop without actually having to *do* anything?' The journalist said sarcastically.

'Yes. I bought the place, I own it. I even cleared some boxes away, but the actual printing bit, that's your job.'

'And a profitable job it is too!' She said, voice rising with excitement. 'It's the first honest day's work I've done in a long time! Isn't it marvellous?' She pulled her hands apart and gestured around the room. Though the press may have paid for her manicure, it hadn't paid for any lavish decoration. Instead, the room was mostly covered in oddments of paper, stationary and several cork boards covered in articles joined with string.

'It is good, yeah.' Bryan admitted, smiling at her. 'I can't honestly believe you've got stuff rolling out this soon. It's only just been a week.' He looked at her accusingly.

'You know when you work for a small newspaper company?' She asked him.

'No. My life isn't that pathetic.'

She screwed her face up, her cheeks flashing red for a moment. *Still* a sore spot.

'Well, I do. And so do most of the other people working there. They know the ceiling is low, and often made of thick glass. It didn't take much convincing to get some of their skills on board.'

Bryan had passed some menials as he walked into the press. Maybe she meant them.

'And what's the next step?'

'Simple. Break into the internet. Get a website going.'

'You want to get a website going already? Isn't it a little early for that?' Bryan asked her, knowing literally nothing about the subject.

'Some publications start with a website and then move onto paper. We're just doing it the other way around. Throw a small amount towards getting the domain for the website set up, and then upload stuff there. Easy.'

'If you're sure.' Bryan said.

'I don't have to be. I know an IT guy. He'll get it all set up.'

'An IT guy?' Bryan was instantly suspicious. The less people that knew about this venture the better.

'Yes. IT like computers.'

'I know what IT means!' Bryan snapped at her, his choler rising. She smiled at him again from behind her hands. Even though her mouth was covered, he could see the smile in her eyes.

'Deaglán!' She called, over Bryan's shoulder and out of the door.

'Yeah?' A twitchy Irish brogue replied.

'Would you come in here please?' The journalist asked. Still looking at Bryan. Still not blinking.

A moment later, the voice's owner entered the room, carrying a laptop under his arm. Tall and skinny, though not as tall as Bryan, he entered with a reluctance exacerbated by his physical appearance. Bespectacled, he wore a simple shirt and trousers, and a smile that would otherwise have powdered marble. He looked at the journalist as though enchanted, and barely paid Bryan a moment of notice. The biggest thing out of place was his hair, which looked greasy and unwashed.

'What can I do you for, Robin?' He asked.

'This is Bryan. Say hello.' She replied. The Irishman turned to Bryan as if noticing him for the first time, and flashed teeth in a crooked smile. Bryan regarded him for a moment as he stretched out a hand. He wondered how he and the journalist knew each other.

'You alright?' Deaglán asked warmly.

'Not the worst, how about you?'

'Well, the weather's been kind to us. Robin mentioned you the other day. Said you were some kinda big shot.' They shook hands.

'She talks a lot of bullshit.' Bryan said flatly. His grip was forced, his voice annoying. *Pff.*

'This handsome man can help us get onto the internet.' The journalist said. Deaglán sat down next to Bryan. Her eyes had left Bryan and were focussed solely on Deaglán. Bryan folded his arms again and sat down himself. Deaglán lifted the lid of the laptop and switched it on.

'And can't you just do it without me being here?' Bryan asked. He took to staring at the stringed notes stuck to a cork board over to the right.

'Well, I might need your input on some things for it.'

'Oh do you?' Bryan said. 'That surprises me, cos I don't know jack about computers.'

'He can do most of it, but he might need to talk to you about some bits and pieces. He's a whiz with computers, Bryan,' the journalist said. Deaglán beamed at her. Bryan wanted to throw up over both of them.

'And how do you two know each other?' Bryan asked, flicking a finger between the two of them.

'Oh, we go *way* back, don't we Robin?' Deaglán said, tapping at the keyboard with a twitching finger.

'Way,' the journalist affirmed, flicking a hand through her hair nonchalantly. 'Talk to each other, see what Deaglán has to say. I need to go and sort some things for tomorrow's publication. Have fun!'

She rose from the desk and walked towards the door. Bryan noticed her run a hand across Deaglán's shoulder as she walked past. He didn't react to it. She flashed a glance at Bryan as she left, leaving the two men sitting next to each other in her office.

Bryan stood almost immediately after she left and made for the door himself. He wasn't entirely sure why, but he needed to leave this room more than he had ever needed to do anything else in his life. It eclipsed absolutely every other feeling in his head.

'Don't go just yet.' Deaglán said. He still hadn't looked up from the computer screen.

'Why not?' Bryan snapped at him. He didn't like the Irishman, though if he was true to himself he didn't know why.

'Because if you wander off, you won't get to see what I'm about to show you.'

Bryan moved his hand back from reaching towards the door. He turned on his heel. Deaglán still hadn't moved, though over his shoulder Bryan could see that some programs were running on the computer. He strode back across the room and sat heavily at the journalist's desk, cursing inwardly at the fact he had to be here. Deaglán placed the laptop onto the desk and looked at Bryan. His prescription must be quite strong, because the eyes behind his glasses looked large comparable to his face. Bryan got a good look at his face, skin leathery but eyes fierce. While they spoke, his foot tapped automatically, a nervous twitch or sign of impatience.

'I was over the moon when Robin got back in touch with me. I didn't realise exactly who I was working for until a little later on, though. The boss lady had a boss herself, as it turned out.' He said.

'What do you mean, exactly who you were working for? You work for her. She runs the place. That's as far as it goes.' Bryan replied.

'Yes, she runs the place, but she answers to you.'

'I think we both know that's a crock. She does whatever the hell she wants. I'm no more in charge of her than I am the weather in this city.'

Deaglán chuckled, almost inaudibly. 'Her strongest feature is her fierce independence, isn't it? It always has been.'

Bryan's hand clenched into a fist without him realising it.

'But *you*.' Deaglán said, pointing a finger at him. 'You're Bryan Wattson. And if I've learned anything from Robin, you like people who can help you out.'

'Help me? I've had nothing but people... *helping* me for a while now. Can't say it ever goes well, to be honest.'

'Trust me, Bryan, I can help you.'

He spun the laptop around and showed it to Bryan. It took a moment for Bryan to realise what it was, but the screen had a map on it. A map of Sovereign City. A map of...

'That's my house!' Bryan said, almost snarling the words.

'It used to be.' Deaglán corrected him. Bryan snapped his head up to look into the Irishman's glasses.

'Is this some kind of joke?' He audibly growled the words this time. Patience was back to wearing very thin. Who the fuck did this guy think he was?

'Not at all. I don't mean any offence by it.' Deaglán clarified, spinning the laptop around again and gesturing at it. 'This is your mansion, and I'm showing you because I can offer you some help regarding it.'

'Help?' He was sick of people he didn't know getting into his business.

'Robin told me that you are thinking about getting at the man living inside it. I can help you get closer.'

'Explain.' Bryan said the single word. He was going to have a serious talk with the journalist about who she told about him.

'Like she said, I'm a real whiz with computers,' Deaglán explained, tapping away. His hands were possessed of a tremor that seemed forgotten about. 'Know the things like the back of my hand. I can help you get a website going for this place, and I can help you get at Tony too.'

'Like how she said *she* could. How come everyone else knows more about my business than I do?' Bryan asked the room, to no answer.

'Maybe you've got more friends than you think.' Deaglán said, a slight shrug punctuating his words.

'What I've *got*,' Bryan said sarcastically, 'Is too many people sticking an oar into a boat that's barely afloat. First her, then you.

That's at least two more people than I initially wanted, and that's assuming that she hasn't told anybody else.'

'I don't think so.' Deaglán looked at him, more irritated now.

'And what's your story anyway?' Bryan continued to be standoffish. 'How do you know so much about Tony?'

A smug smile spread across Deaglán's face, as if the next thing he said was some long-hidden secret that Bryan was out of the loop for not knowing. He melodramatically and unnecessarily pushed his glasses up his nose with his twitching forefinger.

'Because I used to work for him.'

A wave of anger washed over Bryan. On instinct, he drew his pistol from its holster and aimed it at Deaglán, right between his lenses. Deaglán froze, a look of abject terror spreading across his face. The obviousness that he had not expected this was reflected tangibly in the features of his face. Bryan knew he had a reason to distrust this man, and he had just revealed in a moment of attempted arrogance a reason that made him an instant threat to both Bryan and the journalist. Bryan gripped the pistol in his left hand, right hand holding the bottom for supported aiming and reduced weapon sway. his finger rested against the side of the trigger, ready to snap and pull it at a moment's notice. He suddenly felt very exposed, and glanced towards the door, listening for disturbances. The room had dropped silent, and Bryan felt sure that an altercation would have broken out if his pistol hadn't ended it before it started. He felt angry at the journalist for introducing him to Deaglán, and felt angry at himself for allowing the conversation to get to this point. He flicked off the safety with his thumb.

'You used to work for Tony, huh?' Bryan said it through gritted teeth. 'Lemme guess, he hired you to come and take me down. Is that right?'

Deaglán raised his hands, holding them in front of his chest to show he was unarmed.

'No, that's not-'

'And you say you used to work for him like I'm supposed to just laugh at the thought and think, 'Ooh, I bet that will be beneficial to me.' Just who the fuck do you think you are, coming in here and trying to act all high and mighty?' Bryan was shouting now.

'I didn't mean anything by it, I'm sorry!' Deaglán pleaded, an upset to his face now that was probably a mixture of fear and being called out for being cocky. 'I was just an IT guy, I helped move some of Tony's money to an offshore account once, but he got all paranoid and fired me after I worked there for about a month!' Hands trembling, foot still going.

So, now they were getting somewhere. Deaglán was a weasel, a bottom feeder who was trying to use the minor interaction he'd had with Tony in the past to make himself seem better than he was. Bryan almost found it funny, indeed he would have laughed if it weren't for the danger that Deaglán still posed. He knew Tony, he had worked for Tony, and he was allowed near Tony's money. Not even Bryan was allowed near Tony's money when they had been business partners. That was a terrifying prospect to stomach. It meant two things, so far as Bryan could see. One, he *really* should have seen Tony's betrayal coming (which made him mad at Tony and even more so at himself). Two, Tony was slipping, and in his deluded mind he was allowing anyone at his money (which made him very happy indeed).

He did not lower his pistol. Deaglán's arms remained raised, although the slight shake moving through them suggested they were getting tired, regardless of the unconscious movements in his fingers.

'Rest them on the arms of the chair.' Bryan said. His order was followed. Deaglán was sweating, a single bead running down his temple and splashing on the rim of his glasses.

'You moved his money?' Bryan asked. Deaglán nodded, slowly. 'I don't believe you.'

'I did it *once*. Moved about twenty grand from an online account at TTA Savings and General to an offshore account in a bank I'd never heard of before. All above board.'

'Moving twenty grand to another country is *never* above board.'

'Well this was. It all went off without a hitch. I went to report it to some other fella that worked for him, and a day later I got a call back saying I was fired.'

'And then what?'

'Then what? That was about a year and a half ago. I got a job working for the same company that Robin worked for. We met, hit it off, and I became her IT guy.'

'And now you're here telling me that you might be able to do something to get at Tony?'

'No.' Bryan's eyes narrowed as Deaglán replied. 'I'm guaranteeing it. See, I bet you a dime to a dollar that account is still open. I bet you I can get into it, and I bet you I can figure out how to transfer the money that is in there to you.'

Bryan's mind bristled at the thought. If Deaglán had transferred twenty thousand dollars before getting fired, then there might have been others.

'How?'

'Well, that's what I need you for. I need to install a backdoor into Tony's internet. And I thought about doing it for myself, pocketing whatever was in there and making a run for it, but then I thought I should be slightly more clever about it and try and get paid properly for my services.'

'Paid properly?'

'Of course!' Deaglán said. 'Nobody does anything for free in this country.'

Bryan snorted. 'Not even when there's a pistol in their face, it seems.'

'Capitalism wouldn't be a very good system if it was stopped by firearms, now would it?'

'How much do you want?'

'Half.'

Bryan blinked, thinking momentarily. 'You want half of what's in the account?' Deaglán nodded in agreement. 'But what if there's a million dollars?'

Deaglán smiled, a creasing in his cheek that showed teeth. 'Then the two of us will become half a million richer each, I suppose.'

The inherent prospect of stealing that much money from Tony momentarily took over Bryan's senses. Greed is a powerful adversary, and he did not like the idea of giving half of anything to Deaglán.

'Alright, I'll bite. What are you going to do with Tony's backdoor?'

Deaglán burst out into a fit of boyish laughter, the question and its phrasing seeming to take him by surprise.

'Well there's a question and a half.' He said, still chuckling. 'I'm gonna attempt to hack into his bank account, but to do that I need information. When you two worked together did you use the internet for banking at all?'

'I didn't. I don't know about him. I only learned that other people touched his money today when you said it.'

'Alright fine, so I'm guessing you don't use it now either.' Bryan shook his head. 'That doesn't matter, what matters is that Tony's internet accounts and computers in general will be password protected. I need you to think about anything you remember about him that could give us a clue as to what the passwords are.'

'What kinds of hints? Like his mother's maiden name...?' Bryan was sceptical.

'Sort of. My plan is fairly straightforward. The bank Tony used wasn't exactly cutting edge for security. I've seen on their website that there is a *Forgot Your Password* section. When you click it, it asks you to input your email address, and if they match it sends an email to you guiding you through the password changing process.'

'So you need his email?'

'Nah. That bit was easy.' Deaglán smirked again. 'There are email databases everywhere on the internet. How else do you think that random advertising agencies send you stuff? I narrowed his email down based on the location in which it is used, and the frequency in which emails are sent. Took about ten minutes.'

The prospect that it could be that short scared Bryan somewhat. He nodded for Deaglán to continue.

'The tricky bits are the security questions.' He said, looking a little down. 'Passwords are usually easy to crack, but they get exponentially harder to crack the more complicated they are. A single word that has something to do with the person whose password it is can take minutes. Start adding numbers, capitals, symbols and all the rest and it can take years.'

Bryan didn't exactly know the details, but he was following along so far. His own passwords were, admittedly, crap. Luckily, he didn't have an online bank account to worry about anymore, or indeed any account on the internet after the seizure of his assets ten years ago.

'So the password is fine, but what about the security questions? I don't get how I factor into this.'

'Same deal as the password. I just want to pick your brain for information, see if I can get anything out of you that would help me get in there quicker. If I can get a ballpark, it's only a matter of time before the rest falls into place.'

'I mean, I'll do what I can, but I don't know how much info I can give you.'

Deaglán grabbed a notepad from the nearby table, flipped it over, clicked a pen and tapped it onto the top. 'Well, let me make a note of some things, and we'll go from there, alright?'

Bryan nodded, before ficking the safety back on and holstering the pistol.

****

'You'd lose your fucking head!'

Phil had been berating Bryan for some time. He had received a call from Michael saying that he was finally through the safe after some weeks toying with it, but despite Bryan's rush to the garage and an excitement to see what was inside akin to a child on their birthday, it was not the safe that first greeted him when he arrived at Mickey's Motors, but a rather disgruntled-looking Phil.

He was holding a mobile phone in his hand.

'Pardon?' Bryan had initially asked. He had no idea what Phil was saying.

'Mickey boy said he found this while he was looking for some tools earlier.' He held the very dusty phone in his fingers, the screen covered in grime. His brother's eyes were boring into Phil's back like a drill at the use of his most hated nickname.

'Did he lose it?' Bryan asked, still not sure what was going on.

'It's not his phone, it's *yours*!' Phil replied incredulously.

'No it isn't. I don't have a mobile.'

'No, you don't, because...' Phil trailed off. He pinched the bridge of his nose with his fingers, and took a breath. 'I got you this phone so I could keep in touch with you. And it's been sitting under the bed in the garage, dead as dogshit, for how long? Weeks?'

'I've honestly never seen that phone in my life.' Bryan said, plucking it from between Phil's fingers and looking at it. Phil scoffed.

'I wondered why the bloody hell I could never get in touch with you. What if you'd been killed, and you were lying in a ditch somewhere bleeding all over the place and nobody knew about it?'

'And you didn't think to tell me you'd got me a phone? Or ask why I never picked up in person?'

Phil paused a moment. It was a good question. 'I thought I did.' Bryan shook his head.

'Well, after you got your new place, you started to use the landline, so I assumed you preferred that.'

'I do.' Bryan looked at the bottom of the phone. The socket to plug in the charger was scratched around the edges. It looked second-hand, and fairly cheap, but then again he assumed it was only to be used for communication so it didn't exactly need all the bells and whistles. 'Where's the charger for it?'

'I've got one in the garage.' Michael said to him. He offered a hand and Bryan placed the phone into it. 'If you've done bickering for the next ten minutes, maybe we can actually get around to what we're all here for?'

The three of them headed into the garage, where the van was still located, though now it looked a sad sight. It had been moved, parked now next to its original position. Michael had reversed it into the garage whereas Bryan had simply pulled in forwards. The van now rested on four piles of stacked bricks, the wheels removed and lined up neatly against the countervailing wall. The windscreen was gone too, as were both doors to the front. The thick metal bars that had originally blocked their entrance from the interior were still there, and still as firm-looking as ever. Otherwise, the two men couldn't see anything that would suggest they were able to get in. The rear doors were still attached, with seemingly no attempt to remove the thick latches that held them shut. Looking into the front compartment, Bryan saw that many of the panels had been smashed or removed entirely, a buildup of dust and plastic fragments on the dashboard. Dents and scratches were found along the flanks of the van and the wheel arches, and overall it looked like it had been through the wars.

Michael was smiling. Bryan and Phil were not.

'I don't get it.' Phil said.

'You're not going to get it.' Michael said. He had been working - tirelessly, was the word he'd used - for some weeks now, and all it seemed he had done was taken a few extraneous bits and pieces off the van, and then smashed it repeatedly with a hammer.

'Why does it look so shit? And why have you taken the doors off?' Bryan asked him. It was leaning against the wall next to the wheels.

'So I didn't have to keep opening it. I'm lazy, what can I say?' Michael was wiping his hands on a filthy towel, and he draped it

211

over the back of a nearby sack truck. 'And it looks so *shit*, to reduce suspicion. You know how every single garage has a motor in it that looks beyond repair? The sort that it looks like a mechanic tinkers with in his spare time that would take a miracle to actually fix?'

Bryan nodded.

'This is that motor.' Michael said, gesturing at the front quarters of the van. 'It looks like a shit heap - and don't get me wrong, it actually *is* - but I thought nobody would ask questions if they happened to snoop around the garage and looked at it.'

He patted the front headlights on the van's left, and it looked like it had been replaced with a new one. Michael made a gesture that looked like *voila*.

'That's actually really clever.' Bryan said, scratching his jawline and looking at the replaced headlight.

'Well, cheers. There's no flies on me, you know.'

'Even though you can see where they've been.' Phil said. 'But other than replacing a headlight what have you actually done to get into the back of the van?'

The two of them looked at Michael, who moved around to the back of the vehicle, speaking as he went.

'My safe guy said it took him a little while to get into it, and I kept an eye on him while he worked so he didn't pocket whatever's in it.' He still wasn't answering the question.

At the back of the van was the steps down into the pit. Dark and uninviting, Bryan assumed he had used it to work on the underside of the van. What neither of them was expecting was the gaping hole in the floor of the vehicle that awaited them at the bottom. Around three feet across, it stretched across most of the undercarriage. Michael had cut through the welding that attached the armoured shell to the frame of the vehicle, and the soft crunch of metal under their feet suggested that the welding underneath the vehicle was as terrible as Michael had first predicted. When Michael had said he was going to get into the vehicle from the underside Bryan assumed he actually meant from where the wheels are, not slicing a giant, gaping hole in the floor.

'I told you the welding was dogshit.' Michael said. 'Most of it was rusted and half-arsed.'

He stopped and gestured at the wheel arches. 'Careful when you pull yourself up, it's sharp as all hell. Grip the cover.'

He raised his arms into the rear of the van and, using a sheet of thick rubber that covered the sharp edges, disappeared up into the rear compartment. He leaned back down and offered a hand out to Phil, who took it, followed by Bryan shortly afterwards.

The rear compartment of the van was cramped and not high enough, the three men having to stoop over to fit inside it. Michael produced a phone and switched on the torch, its small light blaring across the front of the safe. Bryan could see that the locking mechanism had been removed entirely, the door ajar but the contents not visible.

'So who wants to do the honours?' Michael asked. He sat cross-legged on the cold metal floor, his hands drumming against his knees. A prime viewing position for when the safe door opened, his job was holding the phone torch aloft. Bryan had moved next to the safe and was crouching awkwardly on one knee, the grid pattern of the floor digging into it painfully.

'I'll do it.' Phil said, smiling in the light of the phone.

'Why you?' Bryan asked, looking at him.

'Because I'm in the best position. Look.' Phil gestured at where Bryan was kneeling, and the awkwardness of the rear compartment meant that the safe door would swing open into him, making it hard for him to reach his arm into the safe to remove its contents.

'With this lazy toerag clearly not wanting to do the work-'

'I opened the fucking van.' Michael said, shining the phone's torch in his brother's face.

'And now you're sat about like a lemon. And with you in the wrong place, I'll do it. Everyone okay with that?'

Bryan reluctantly agreed, and Michael looked like he didn't give a shit who opened it so long as it got done.

Phil gripped the door of the safe, making sure his legs were out of the way. He shifted it rapidly back and forth about an inch while making a dramatic *Ooo* noise like a ghost, and when it got him a light clip around the ear from Michael and a 'get the fuck on with it' from Bryan, he opened it to its full extent. The door grated as it swung open, and Bryan awkwardly had to reposition himself so he could see into it. The view he had wasn't good at all, so instead he resigned to looking at Phil's face for an indication of what was inside.

Phil's face portrayed an emotion that Bryan couldn't easily comprehend. It was a strange mixture of happiness and annoyance, the face someone pulls when they pass an examination, but do not receive the score they needed.

'Well? Was it worth it?' Bryan asked. Michael was looking around his brother's side, a look of confusion on his face.

'Sort of.' Phil replied. He reached an arm into the safe and withdrew something. In the dim light, Bryan couldn't see what was in it. Then Phil withdrew something else, and then a third, and so on until a small pile of somethings was placed into the available space on the floor of the van. He closed the door of the safe so that Bryan could manoeuvre around it. They exited the van with a single package so they could take a closer look at it, although as soon as they reached the top of the stairs Bryan knew for certain what was inside. He could see now that it was covered in plastic wrap and sealed with parcel tape. He knew the contents, and it sent a wave of nausea through him that sat directly in his gut and stayed there.

'Well I'll be damned.' Phil said, waving the package at the others. 'You know what this is, don't you?'

'Of course I do!' Bryan said harshly. 'Drugs. Fucking drugs. The one poison I can't seem to shake.'

'Heroin or cocaine, I'd wager.'

Michael took an involuntary step away from the package, the look of disgust apparent on his face. 'I thought it was supposed to be money in the safe. What the hell is all that lot doing in there?'

'I don't know.' Phil responded. 'We scouted the vans for ages, we were certain that the one we pinched had money in it.'

'And we *clearly* need our eyes examined!' Bryan stormed. 'Just what the hell are we gonna do with all of this? I can't believe we fucked up that badly. This is terrible, even for us.'

Phil's eyebrows were raised. Michael picked up the filthy towel and began wiping his hands with it again. 'Calm down, dude. It's not a big deal. So we didn't get the money. But we do have all this stuff, and it's probably worth more than that safe could hold.'

Bryan waved a hand at the package. 'No, no it makes me feel uneasy. I'm getting flashbacks to ten years ago, it was drugs related to that bastard that got me shot and locked away in the first place. I don't want anything to do with them. He probably knows we're here. How hard could it be to trace us?'

'Calm down. He doesn't know we're here. Michael has been tinkering with it for ages now, I doubt he even knows that it was us that stole it.'

Bryan was still anxious. Although he was looking at a pile of powdered money, he didn't know anybody anymore that he could offload it too, nor indeed did he want to set up another deal that could be as ill-fated as the one ten years previously. He gulped.

'And when a crapload of product flushes its way onto the market? What then?'

'Well I assume we get very rich indeed.'

'And do you know any buyers?'

Phil snapped his fingers. 'I bet Patrone does.'

'Bad idea. He doesn't know about the van, he doesn't know about the drugs, and I don't think that's something we want to rope him into either.'

'It's probably worth a try anyway. What's the worst that could happen? He says,' Phil changed his voice to a decent replica of Patrone's, though he wasn't anywhere near deep enough, '*I am afraid I cannot help you, Mr. Wattson. Perhaps you should like to consider your other options.*'

Michael snorted with laughter, even though he had never met Patrone.

'You can ring him on your *new* phone.' Phil continued sarcastically.

'Fine. But I need to let it charge for a bit longer first, it will be damn near dead. Did you count the packages?'

'Erm, I think it was twenty-seven?' Phil didn't sound convincing.

'You think or you know?'

'Think. You should probably get back in there and see for sure. I put some of them on the floor of the van, but there were still some left.'

Bryan clambered back into the interior of the van, and holding Michael's phone in one hand, began to pass the packages around the safe down through the hole to Phil, who placed them neatly in a pile at the end of the pit. When they were all out of the safe and off the floor, Bryan swept the phone torch across the interior of the van one final time. when he was satisfied that there were no longer any remaining, he shouted down at Phil for a final count.

'Turns out I can't count, there are actually twenty-nine packages.'

Bryan heard Michael say 'Christ' under his breath, the thickness of the van's armour muffling it somewhat. Although the sheer amount of product they now had should have made his mind race at the potential profit, he couldn't shake the idea that they were a very bad idea. He had known they were a very bad idea ten years ago, but since his life was going so well at the time he hadn't allowed it to gain a foothold in his mind. Instead, it was all focussed on the money. This time, he had an excellent new perspective with which to view the whole thing: one through a window with thick metal bars.

'All right. I wouldn't mind weighing them so we can work out exactly what's going on, but for now we need to put them back into the van and keep very quiet about them.'

'You're not keeping it here!' Michael's head appeared in the gap between floor and van.

Phil looked at him midway through bending down to pick up the top package.

'Why not?'

'Because they're drugs! I want nothing to do with them.'

Unlike his brother and Bryan, Michael was completely legitimate. He had never committed a crime - so far as Bryan knew, anyway - in his life. Indeed, he was always very conscious of the law in his youth, taking the threat and fear factor associated with going to prison very much to heart. When he had inevitably learned of Bryan's, and then Phil's, criminal activities, he had initially been incredibly eager to distance himself from both of them. Practicality, however, had made that next to impossible, and over the years Michael had softened somewhat, but he was still never going to want anything to do with the packages in a million years. Opening a van that could be seen as a strangely specific task for a mechanic, yes. A pile of drug packages nearly as tall as himself, no.

'Mikey, you've had them in your garage for over a fortnight now. What's a few more days?' Phil asked. He had begun to pass the packages back into the armoured van to Bryan.

'No means no, Phil. Get them out of here.'

He reached an arm through the hole to swat at the package Phil was holding, who pulled it close to his chest protectively.

'Gerroff.' Phil said. 'You'll split the wrapping.'

'Michael, calm down.' Bryan's voice reverberated from inside the van as he grabbed the package from Phil. 'We don't need long, just enough to get rid of it. We *all* want rid of it.'

There was a silence. Bryan wasn't sure Michael had heard him.

'Has he stormed off or something? I can't hear him.'

'No, he's just pacing around, looking like a crazy person.' Phil responded.

A few more moments of silence as the two men passed the final packages to each other, before Michael's voice once again was heard.

'You've got two days. I'm washing my hands of them. Far as I know, I never opened the safe and never knew what was inside. You can pay me for getting the van open but I don't want it to be out of the profit that they make. If they aren't gone in two days, I'm spraying the inside of the safe with a hose. Got it?'

'Jesus, *fine*.' Bryan said. 'We'll get rid of them before then.'

Michael didn't reply, and by the time Bryan lowered himself out of the van for what felt like the tenth time that day, he heard the hum of an engine outside.

'Two days.' Phil said. It was a question without the rising intonation. The two men were now out of the pit, and Bryan regretted his decision not to wear his scruffiest clothes today.

'Yeah, two days. Plenty of time, right?' Bryan had an uneasy smile on his face.

'I'll leave it up to you. But now the nagging question is who we're gonna sell it to. And I guess, for how much.'

'I'll ask Patrone. Like you said, the worst he can do is say no. Then we'll just have to move the product somewhere in the meantime so Michael doesn't shit his pants.'

'Do you reckon he'd actually spray them with a hose?'

'I don't think so. He wouldn't want to physically touch anything that is inside the packages, and the wrappings look waterproof enough. I think he was being metaphorical.'

Phil whistled, long and slowly. Bryan looked at him.

'Motherload, right?'

'Something like that. It puts the shits right in me.'

A chuckle. 'We'll get rid, and we'll make a lot of money from it.'

'And if something goes wrong?'

'Let's cross that bridge when we get to it. We need to find a buyer, first and foremost. Get on the blower with Patrone and see what he says.'

Bryan crossed the room for the final time that day and picked up his phone. In large orange letters it said it was on 41% battery. He smirked at it, before unplugging the charger to take with him as well. He hoped Michael wouldn't mind. He waved the phone at Phil and said 'Wish me luck.'

'Now that you've actually got a phone, Wattson, you don't need luck.'

Phil's impersonation of Patrone wasn't perfect, but it wasn't far off. He wanted nothing to do with the packages in the back of the van. He had refused as eloquently and politely as ever, but through his voice he had made clear that his word was final. He wasn't annoyed with Bryan for hijacking the van, nor for failing to inform him. Instead, Patrone was quick to remind Bryan of the events that led to him getting locked up in the past. Bryan had acknowledged what he was saying, though neglected to mention that he felt patronised.

Bryan sat down in his apartment, thinking. The pen and paper with which he had attempted a list of possible outs now lay discarded on the table, all of the possibilities he could think of messily scribbled out. A blank had initially been drawn. Now it had been painted, signed and sent for framing. While he thought, Bryan had fiddled with his new phone. It now had a full battery, a cup of coffee providing ample distraction while it charged. He had flicked through the settings, changed his ringtone and background, changed the clock to 24-hour instead of twelve, and had a quick look through his contacts. The first thing that had repeatedly bombarded him when the phone was switched on was the first second or two of the notification sound as the phone caught up with the plethora of missed calls and messages from when it was underneath the bed in the garage. Phil had rang and messaged him multiple times, as had Michael. Both of their names had been saved into his contacts when he switched it on (under 'Phil' and 'Mickey', respectively). Bryan had added Patrone and the journalist's numbers to his contacts too. He had fired off a quick message to both of them saying who he was, and they had replied in neat prose and cheeky sarcasm respectively.

Now the coffee mug was empty, and with it so was Bryan's well of ideas. He had thought about what to do with packages for

219

close to an hour now, but had resigned to the idea that nobody he knew was a good enough contact, or reliable enough, for what he wanted. But in the end his thoughts had fizzled out, producing not so much as a vague idea of what to do next. And with that he had retired for the evening, hoping that a good night's sleep would bring with it both refreshment and inspiration in equal measure.

It didn't.

Indeed, nothing more happened for the entirety of the following day. Michael was quick to remind him of the deadline, Bryan woke up to a message that said 'Don't forget about tomorrow', and Phil hadn't come up with anything either. The journalist had been similarly quiet, working away with her new press and not bothering to message or call Bryan with any updates. Bryan figured that meant that everything was going fine, and nothing so catastrophic that would threaten the entire business venture had yet happened.

The evening of the following day was when Bryan finally found an answer to at least one of his problems, although it was an answer that he didn't want to receive. Deaglán called him, an update to his machinations on the internet.

'It's empty.'

'What?'

'The account.' He said, his usual brogue raspy. 'There's nothing in it.'

'Wait, you managed to guess the answers to the security questions?' Bryan paced as he spoke, traversing most of the length and breadth of his apartment.

'They weren't hard, after all the stuff you told me it only took a few days. Tony seems to subscribe to the 'put a 1 on the end of the password for safety' school of thought as well.'

'Are you alright? You sound on edge.' Bryan looked at the screen while Deaglan replied, checking the time.

'Some sleepless nights, you know how it is. Tried taking some sleeping tablets, didn't do anything. Some caffeine, a shower and a decent night's sleep'll do me right as rain in the end. I reckon.'

The combination of caffeine and a decent night's sleep did not compute in Bryan's head.

'And the account is empty?' He asked, quick to move on.

'Not a cent in it.'

'I don't believe you.'

'I'll send you screenshots. And then I'll send you screenshots of my own account so you'll see there isn't a transfer. Jesus.' Deaglán sounded perturbed.

'Shit.'

'Shit indeed. It's alright though. Nothing ventured and all that.'

'Yeah, alright. Thanks for letting me know.'

'No worries. So I can expect my paycheck in the mail sometime soon then, yeah?'

'Your paycheck? There was nothing in the account. You didn't actually do anything.'

'Yeah but, I figured that now we know the password, if anything does get transferred into it, then we can just transfer it out again.'

'But if nothing has been put into it in the last ten years, why would it be there all of a sudden now?'

'I don't know. But that doesn't change the fact that I helped you and should be compensated for it.

Bryan could hear himself grunt down the line.

'You said you wanted half. Half of nothing is still nothing, so be my guest. Help yourself.'

Deaglán made a funny noise in his throat. Bryan continued, asking the question that was now plaguing him.

'What was his password, anyway?'

Deaglán suppressed a laugh. 'I had to change the password, remember?'

'Okay then, what's the new one?'

'I'm not telling you.'

'What?!' Bryan shouted the word, and Deaglán's next words were quieter, suggesting he'd moved the phone away from his face.

'Call it leverage. I feel pissed off that I didn't get paid, so I'll hold on to the valuable bits until a time when I feel properly compensated, how's about that?'

Bryan had had enough with Deaglán for today.

'You feel pissed? Think how I feel, getting screwed around by some streak of piss who knows how to work a word processor. If there's nothing else you can help me with, then you should probably focus on working with the journalist to get the printing press running properly. Seems more your calibre.'

'Thanks for that, you jackass.'

The insult was said in a hushed tone that Bryan only half heard. He snorted an acknowledgement at Deaglan and hung up.

He let the phone slip from his fingers onto the carpeted floor as he slid down the wall. Landing on his backside with a soft thud, the phone stood on end for a brief moment, before falling backwards. A crushing sense of futility threatened to overwhelm Bryan, a sense that was fuelled by what a waste it felt like the last few days had been. True to himself, he did not consider anything short of buying the printing press to be a success in recent times, indeed it often felt like nothing had gone right at all since he had been broken out of prison. The only thing that had followed him so far was a messily conducted series of petty crimes. He placed his hands over his face, allowing them to slide down his chin before they settled in his lap. He snorted what might have been considered a laugh, but instead it felt self-deprecating, the only thing he could manage in reaction to the situation.

Like anything was ever actually going to come of the bank account. Like he was ever actually going to find a giant pile of neatly arranged bills in the safe. Like anything that he wanted to happen was actually going to come to pass. He could see his scribbled list some feet away from him. He had trodden on it during his pacing, and could see the curled up edges of where he'd written 'Try to sell them back to Tony?' It was scribbled through with such ferocity that the point of the pen had torn through the paper. Nothing had come from Deaglán, a conclusion that felt like a complete non sequitur. He had said he would try to hack the account, had fiddled with it for a few days, and ultimately come up flat. And as for the safe? He knew he couldn't blame Michael, he had done his job well, but he hadn't been prepared for the packages that now sat in the opened safe. He hadn't considered for a second that they would get the vans wrong, and now he was still drawing blanks as to what to do with them.

Bryan started to wonder very much exactly when his quest to take back his empire from Tony was going to begin, because at this point he felt like all his plans were doomed to fail.

Across the city, a phone rang on a desk, where it was picked up after a moment's notice. Next to the desk, a comfortable leather armchair with two large windows overlooking the bridge.

'Yeah.'

The voice on the other end was deadpan and lacking in emotion, the speech sounding rehearsed. It conveyed a sense of plans in motion, and warranted a response of some kind.

'Alright, tomorrow then. We'll see what he has to say for himself.'

CHAPTER SEVENTEEN: REVERSE CHARGES

Staying up late in an attempt to think of an answer had proved fruitless, and simply led to a later wakeup and generally foul mood over the next day. Alice had been cheery as Bryan walked across the length of the reception corridor, though he had been less than accommodating. He had meant to say 'I'm feeling in a bad mood, probably best if you just leave me to grumble for a bit.' What he had actually said was 'Do I look like I'm in the mood for fucking chitchat?' She had stared at him blinking, mouth slightly open, before looking down at her computer. Bryan had paid her no further attention as he had walked past, not thinking for a second about anything past the foulness of his mood.

He needed to get out of his apartment for a while. Since the previous evening it had felt like a prison cell, and irony was not lost on Bryan. He should have gone for a walk to clear his head last night, the brisk night air blowing away the cobwebs. Instead he was content to languish in his room, staring at the ceiling without so much as a hint of an idea. Bryan rounded a corner, pushing the door of a cafe open and ignoring the tinkling bell. He thought that a nice cup of coffee might energise him some more for another day of thinking and presumably getting nowhere, so he ordered the biggest cappuccino that they would give him and paid for it quickly, retiring to a table facing the window to people watch while he thought. People watching was a strange guilty pleasure of his, though admittedly he had not had much chance to do it since being released, or indeed the entire decade previously.

His phone rang in his pocket while he blew cold air into his cup. It was the journalist. It had been a few days since they had spoken. He answered it, still focussed mostly on his coffee.
'Yeah.'
'Good morning, Bryan!' She said sparkily. 'How are you?'
'Not bad, I suppose.' Bryan separated his sentences with a slurp of coffee. 'You?'

'Not bad at all.' Her voice was bright and full of energy. 'Listen, I know you don't like getting bothered with the minutiae of the press, but something's come up regarding the shipping and...'

'The shipping of the paper?' She was right, it *did* sound like something he wasn't interested in.

'Sort of. You remember how Clarke told you that he had a line on getting supplies shipped in without questions being asked?'

'Yeah, *tax deductible*.' Bryan said, making sarcastic airquotes with the fingers on his free hand. 'Something like that. Why, do you have a line on them?'

'Well, like I said, I've still got some contacts who might be able to get us some bits, but it looks like it comes in bulk. A friend of mine told me about a wholesale opportunity. Tons of stuff.'

'Alright, sounds good if it's a discount. What do you need me for?' Bryan still thought it wasn't important enough to warrant his attention.

'Because it's got to be delivered by truck, and it has to be delivered to the press.'

'Yeah, and?'

'And it's *tax deductible*.' The journalist said. He felt her shaking her head on the other end of the phone, and then it hit him. The goods were stolen or otherwise obtained on the wrong side of the law. So maybe they needed to be shipped in the small hours. Bryan sighed.

'Alright, journalist, I'll come round in a bit. When are you in?'

'Robin.'

'Journalist.' Bryan had gotten so used to calling her it that her full name might as well have been A. Journalist. He heard her make a groaning noise in her throat.

'I'll be in all day, *Natty*.' Bryan could do nothing but grin. 'Bring the shit-bailer, too, he might want to see what's going on.' And with that, she ended the conversation.

Bryan's focus returned to his coffee. The call had raised his mood somewhat. Despite any of his previous feelings, he had stamped upon most of them and now regarded the journalist as a friend of sorts. He still had an attraction to her above this, but was able to suppress it enough to work with her. And work well she did; she was damn good at her job. Bryan didn't think he'd ever met anyone as devoted to her craft. Admittedly, that could be because he never considered what he did to be a craft, and since his ilk were the kind of people he associated with the most, he guessed that none of his friends had a proper craft at all. Michael had his mechanics, but he was struck with a bout of laziness that could plague his work from time to time. When the money or motivation was good, he was excellent. But otherwise, it could take him days to do the most trivial of tasks.

He snapped off a message to Phil asking if he was free. He replied in the affirmative, and Bryan sent him a vague message asking him to meet at the printing press later on. Phil said to give him an hour.

What exactly did she mean by shipping problems, he wondered. Since the journalist had started working at the press she had taken the lead with almost everything that was within her skillset. She wasn't above asking for help or advice if she needed it, knowing her failings as well as her strengths. But this seemed almost too trivial to warrant Bryan's help. He wondered if it was an excuse for her to see him again. He looked at his phone screen before setting down on the table and moving back to his coffee. The cafe in which he was seated was a suitably-sized affair, populated by a single waiter who was at this moment reading a book on a high chair behind the counter. Bryan couldn't blame him, the cafe was sleepy at this time of morning, and apart from himself there were only three other customers, already deep into their meals, drinks or conversation. The only thing this cafe didn't do was a fried breakfast, something Bryan thought was to its detriment. He had skipped breakfast this morning, and could feel that it wouldn't be too long before his appetite got the better of him. For now at least, he was content with his coffee. He stared at the cup, steam rising from it. He needed to-

His phone began to ring again.

He had it on vibrate, and jumped slightly as it rattled against the tabletop. It was screen-down, and he flipped it over and hit the green phone symbol.

'Hello?'
'Hello, Bryan.'

Bryan's world froze. His heart stopped beating, the breath caught in his throat, and his mouth dried up. No. It couldn't be. He choked a little, squeezing the paper cup until coffee spilled onto his fingers.

'Tony.'

The hatred welled up inside him like a volcano. The shock factor vanished, a momentary blink in his thoughts which was quickly replaced with intense anger and loathing. Instinctively he stood up, the red mist threatening to take over. His fingers burned; his temper burned brighter.

'How the fuck did you get this number, you motherfucking...' He realised where he was. He realised that he was in the middle of a cafe making a very obvious scene. Quick as a flash he stormed out of the cafe, ignoring the waiter and all the other customers, who had forgotten their book and meals to stare at him. Out of the door, he turned right down the street, then right again immediately into an alleyway, where he had to grip onto a wall to stop himself punching it.

'It's nice to hear your voice again, my old friend.' Tony said. His voice was aged beyond his actual years, a sarcasm like a thick crust around it. 'What have you been up to?'
'You know what I've been up to, you bastard.' Voice rising once again, Bryan knew deep down that he should hang up the phone. He knew he should. And yet he did not. Something deep in his mind kept rejecting the thought. Tony chuckled down the phone, the end result sounding more like static than laughter.

'Yes, I suppose I do. What was prison like? Did they feed you well?'

'I'm gonna fucking kill you.'

'Good God man, so aggressive. Yes, I suppose so. I'm not calling you to listen to your little threats though.'

'Fuck. Off.'

Tony laughed again. 'You know, I wondered how you would react. I assumed you'd be pissed. I don't know why, you've had ten years to get over it. How is the back, by the way?'

'It still gets sore from time to time.' The sound of Bryan's teeth grinding could probably be heard physically by Tony, phone connection be damned.

'Shame. And then I've heard all sorts of things. The newspapers say that you were killed in a giant explosion that happened in the prison. They say your prison cell was opened like all the rest, and that you made an attempt to get out but were crushed by debris from the boom.'

'Newspapers always exaggerate.'

'I know right!' Tony almost sounded giddy through the phone. 'It's great! I mean I mourned, don't get me wrong. I thought 'such a sad way for the old man to go'.'

Bryan's anger still had not subsided, though the brick he was gripping was going a long way to help.

'What the fuck do you want? You still haven't told me how you got this number.'

'I have my contacts. People talk. They sing like little birds, and everything winds its way back to me. I'm calling you from the phone inside your office, you know.'

Bryan gripped the phone so tightly it was sure to splinter between his fingers.

'Fuck you. You don't deserve my office. You deserve a blowtorch to the balls and a bullet shortly afterwards.'

'And yet I have it! It's great. And things were going great until I heard that, oh wait, you actually weren't killed in the fiery explosion at the prison. You're out.'

'Yeah. I'm out. And I'm coming for you. I'm gonna rip you apart.'

'Starting with my businesses and vans, it seems! You will pay for both of those.'

'It should be MY business! MY VANS!' Bryan screamed the words down the phone. He moved further into the alleyway, the brick no longer enough to overcome his rage.

'Oh, you can have them. The vans and that stupid place weren't big moneymakers anyway. They're of no concern to me.'

Tony's words were as callous as ever, though Bryan could hear the weight of a decade on them. He remembered for a second the paranoia that Phil had mentioned.

'When people find out I'm back, they will remember what happened. How many friends do you think you'll have when they hear about me?'

'Friends?! What do you know about friends?' Tony almost sang the questions.

'More than you, you backstabbing fuck.'

'Fantastic. Nice to know that you haven't evolved past blind rage.'

Bryan didn't immediately reply. He had placed a hand onto a wall, and was scratching at the mortar separating the bricks.

'No, I haven't.'

'If you want to kill me so badly, why don't you tell me where you are? We can sort this problem we both have very easily, ya know.'

Bryan smirked.

'No, I think I know where you are already. And I'm sure I'll be seeing you very soon.'

Tony's voice turned to fire down the phone.

'Listen to me you jumped-up little fuck, I'm gonna send my men to scour this city one street at a time if they need to. They'll search every dumpster, every dive, every scum-infested square inch of the city to find you so I can finish what I started ten years ago. You and your friends are dead. Do you hear me? DEAD.'

'Fuck you, Carson.'

Tony laughed. The same cold, evil laugh from the airport all that time ago. The same cold, evil laugh that had plagued Bryan's nightmares for the last ten years.

'And then when you and your friends are all dead, I'll keep on living it up with all of your money. And you will die knowing that there was nothing you could have done to stop me.'

Bryan's anger surged a final time as Tony said his final sentence. He had had enough, the thought of muttering another word to the man he hated most in the world becoming physically repulsive. In a flare of red he hammered on the bricks, growling aloud, before he dashed the phone against the opposite wall. The casing exploded into fragments, chunks of plastic scattering across the alleyway. The screen cracked along its length multiple times, rendering it completely useless. Head still full of hatred, Bryan ran out of the alleyway and got into his car, tyres squealing as he pulled off. He left the remains of the phone where they were.

He needed to get out of here.

He needed to speak to Phil, beginning the journey to the printing press with a sense of crushing dread.

CHAPTER EIGHTEEN: YOUR ROUND

Why was the printing press so fucking far away? Bryan's mind was still plagued with the phone call. Alright, yes, he could probably hold his hands up and say that hurling his phone across the world in rage was not the best thing to do. It would prove some time before he would care to admit it to himself, and even longer before he would admit it to those around him. He turned left, anger rising at the tiniest details. Why didn't other road users indicate? Why did they leave it till the last possible second before pulling their cars into a turn? Bryan still fumed as he approached the press, though he had calmed down enough to the point where he could realise the gravity of the situation. How the hell had Tony found him? How had he managed to track down his phone specifically and call him? Perhaps smashing it was for the best. Bryan couldn't be sure.

He pulled up outside the press, pulling the handbrake and switching off the engine. As the handbrake elicited its typical grinding noise he looked out of the rear window, a moment of relief washing over him as he realised he wasn't being followed. Bryan had stopped in the customer parking, but could not see Phil's car. He breathed out a heavy sigh, before opening the car door and stepping out.

Bryan found the journalist in the studio, clearing out a filing cabinet in the back room. She nodded acknowledgement as he walked him, but had a roll of tape in her mouth so was physically unable to speak. She placed a stack of papers into a box before taping it closed. Then she placed the tape onto the now empty filing cabinet.

'Hiya.' She said, sounding professional as ever.

'Is Phil here yet?' Bryan asked, bypassing pleasantries entirely. She looked annoyed.

'Hi Robin, how are you, Robin? I'd let you call me journalist if you said hello.'

'Yeah, hi, is he here yet?' Bryan looked her in the eyes.

'No, he isn't... Why, what have you done now?'

Bryan didn't want prying questions. 'Nothing, nothing, just wanted a word before we get down to your business.' Her hands went onto her hips, but she asked nothing more.

'Well, I haven't seen him for a while. You want coffee while you wait?'

'No, thanks, I just had one.'

'Bet it was awful compared to mine!' She smiled at him, and he couldn't blame her. She didn't know the phone call he had just received. He needed to act amiably.

'Don't flatter yourself.'

She screwed her nose up at him. 'My coffee is amazing, I'll have you know. None of that cheap garbage that you're used to. I always make the effort to buy the best possible coffee when I get groceries.' She was smiling at him.

'I do that with toilet paper.'

This got a strange, confused look, like she wasn't expecting it. She seemed like she didn't know what to say for the first time since he had known her.

'I- I...'

'The stuff we had in prison was like sandpaper.'

She sniggered and lightly punched him on the shoulder.

'I bet you're very glad to be back on the soft stuff.'

'Indeed. Look, I know we're colleagues and stuff but I didn't come here to discuss my ablutions. What is this shipping thing you've been up to? I hope you aren't drawing attention to us.'

'No, I'm not. Honest. Like I said on the phone, Clarke did a lot of backyard business. Managed to get a lot of supplies on the cheap.'

'He said he hadn't paid a cent in tax in a long time, too. I think he said five years.'

'Six.' The journalist said. She looked uneasy as she gently tapped on the table. 'He kept notes of all his expenses *except* his taxes, obviously. Problem was they were all in paper form.'

'I know, Phil got rid of a stack of it the other time we were here.'

'That wasn't expenses. Anyway, I asked Deaglán to computerise it all for us. He agreed, and has been tinkering with that alongside whatever else after your little chat the other day.

This is his new office, actually.' She waved her arms around the room.

'You've given him his own office?'

'Well, yeah. Before he had to perch himself awkwardly on whatever corner he could fit. Now he has a place to do his work properly. It was mostly full of junk, anyway. He's around here somewhere, maybe you should be the one to give it to him.' She extended a hand, a key in it with a blue plastic tag attached. Bryan took it, flicking it between his fingers.

The office was not originally intended to be one, instead it appeared to be a supply room of sorts that had been repurposed to fit. Perfectly measured screw holes in the walls suggested that shelving had been in there until very recently. The journalist had not redecorated, merely emptied. The carpet was dulled, evidence of repeated traffic through the room. The clock on the wall had long since exhausted its batteries, the lighting from the aged bulb not enough to fully extinguish the gloom.

Bryan lowered his voice.

'Look, about Deaglán. Do you trust him?' His mind was still on the bank account.

'Yes. I do.' The journalist said flatly. She returned to her usual hands-on-hips posture, which she only seemed to bring out when she was mildly irked at him.

'Don't you think he's a bit... greasy?'

'Greasy? Bryan, we've all got history. He used to be a junkie. Never got past the look even if he did flush the habit down the toilet.'

'He what?'

'Yeah, duh. Look at him. But he's damn good at his job and I trust him. I've known him for a long time. He gets things done. And I think giving him this office is a nice gesture.'

'No, I...' Bryan's thoughts were halted as Phil walked through the door. The journalist looked out of the door of Deaglán's office and noticed him.

'Ah, the shit-bailer arrives!' Her attention had been totally stolen. Phil waved a hand at them both. As the journalist moved towards the door, Bryan bustled past her, walking with purpose

233

towards him. She stumbled a little, grasping the door frame as he moved past.

'Take it easy, Bryan, jeez. I know I can't ever hope to compete but you don't have to be aggressive.' Bryan ignored her, striding up to Phil, who took a dramatic step backwards as if he was expecting to be punched.

'Can I have a word?' Bryan asked him, not looking at the journalist.

'Err, yeah.' The two of them walked towards the door and out of it, coming to a stop next to a window looking back into the press.

'Fucking hell fire.' Phil rested an arm against the glass of the window, leaning his head against his knuckles. Through the window, the journalist was doing a terrible job of spying on them, even though they were pretty sure she couldn't hear them. Bryan had given him a very quick rundown of the phone call he had received from Tony.

'Yes. Not good.'

'And what did you say?'

'Well... I might not have reacted most favourably.' Bryan replied.

'Yes but you didn't do anything stupid, did you?'

Bryan held his hands up like he was being interrogated. 'I got a bit angry. What the fuck do you expect?'

'How did he find you?!' Phil raised his voice, an uncommon occurrence for him. His hands were stretched out, gesturing at Bryan as if to help him focus his mind.

'I don't know.' Bryan's own voice was level. The magnitude of the situation was beginning to catch up to him. 'I guess he backtracked my phone, or some other bullshit five dollar word that explains it.'

'You should have remained calm.'

'I didn't tell him anything. I think I reacted perfectly normally, given the situation. I didn't do anything stupid.'

Bryan neglected to tell Phil about him smashing the phone. He felt that he didn't want to give Phil the satisfaction.

'And what did *he* say to *you*?'

'Some bullshit about tracking me down, wanting to know where I was so we could settle all our old blood.'

Phil snapped a finger at him.

'So he doesn't know where you are. That's fantastic. Did he sound serious or was he being rhetorical?'

'Serious, I think. I told him *I* would find him sooner or later, and he flipped at me.'

Phil wiped at his brow with the sleeve of his shirt. 'Thank Christ for that.' He had a smile on his face after he had finished. 'We might be alright then. Fucking heck, you've got me shitting myself here.'

Bryan's expression was purely cosmetic. Phil went on.

'We shouldn't worry about him for now. He can be all pissy in his little ivory tower all he wants, long as he doesn't descend from upon high.'

'Yeah.'

'Alright, sound.' He sniffed, then smiled at Bryan. 'So, what does Robin want?'

'Something about shipping. Ten bucks says it's bullshit.'

'You're on.'

Bryan pushed the door into the press open again, with Phil following behind him. He pointed a finger at the journalist, who was now nonchalantly fiddling with some papers.

'Some hotshot investigative reporter *you* are!' Bryan said, his tone not confrontational.

'I've seen machine gun fire less obvious than you.'

The matter of the shipping was a trivial one. Not exactly in the realm of bullshit, as Bryan had predicted. He passed the note across to Phil when the journalist was looking the other way. His friend's victorious face could have boiled mercury. The journalist had managed to track down some of Clarke's old friends, and although they were initially hesitant to do business with three 'young upstarts', they had relented under the journalist's silver tongue. What she had said or promised them she had not divulged, but she explained to Bryan and Phil that their deliveries were to happen towards the end of the day - not exactly rare, but many deliveries in these sorts of establishments happened during the morning or middle of the day. The journalist explained that towards the end of the day the officials tend to get sloppy, their minds more focussed on getting home or to the nearest drink than ensuring that every task is completed to textbook standards. All the journalist wanted their opinion on was which day she should get everything shipped. Bryan had said he didn't care, and Phil had countered by offering up Thursday or Friday evenings, his thought process being that people's attention would be more focussed on the weekend than their business affairs. Bryan had shrugged, and agreed. The journalist had said their decision was a good one, and explained that even though she knew the pair of them didn't care for the business much, she at least wanted to keep them in the loop. She had then eyed Bryan and muttered something about trust issues.

As the three of them prepared to leave - for it was getting to the end of the working day at this point - Bryan finally spotted Deaglán loitering in his office, plugging in a fairly old computer. The journalist and Phil went their separate ways, the former confirming that they would both help with the shipping issues under pain of death. He knocked on the door, feeling that even though he owned this building, he should try to be somewhat cheerful, instead of bullish. Deaglán was under the table, feeding cables through a hole in the desk and fiddling with the casing on the computer.

'Yeah, come in.' Deaglán's mind seemed focussed on the task at hand.

'I wondered if I could speak to you about something.'

'What's up? Nothing else has gone into the account, before you ask.'

'No, something else. Something that might earn me a punch in the face.'

A faint laugh came from under the desk. 'Oh yeah? And what might that be?'

'Well...' Bryan rubbed at his forearm with his opposite hand. 'It's about you. More specifically about your past.'

236

'Nothing happened between me and Robin, honest. She said I wasn't her type.'

Well, that lifted Bryan's mood. Nonetheless.

'No, I didn't mean that. I meant about you. Is it true you used to be a junkie?'

Bryan was sure he heard a record player scratch. Deaglán stopped whatever he was doing with the computer case and leaned out, brushing hair away from his eyes.

'I see what you mean about punching you in the face, now.'

Then he smiled. 'Grab this cable, will ya?' Bryan did so. 'I was never a 'junkie'. Awful term. I was a user. Wouldn't have thought you'd have given a shit though.'

'No, I don't.'

'I mean, you probably supplied me at some point.'

That was an interesting statement. Bryan had never thought of himself as a dealer.

'How long ago was it?'

'A fair while now. Have you been speaking to Robin?'

'It's how I know, yeah.'

Deaglán slid himself out from under the table, grabbing the cable Bryan had been holding on to and standing. He plugged it into the back of the monitor.

'Hell of a woman, isn't she? Doesn't judge at all.'

'I don't know about that. She did report on my trial, after all.'

'I don't mean that. I mean outside of her professional life.' He turned back to the monitor, flipping it on. 'You should hold onto that one, you know. She'll do you right.'

'That's what I'm worried about.'

Deaglán smiled, showing teeth. Then he sighed. 'Yes, Bryan, I used to be a junkie. Damn near took over my life. Fucked me up pretty bad.'

Shit.

'Look, I'm just gonna say it flat. It's just that I have a line on some potential business and I wondered if you were still involved with that crowd and could help me out.'

237

Deaglán put the mouse down, leaving it with the cable still unravelled on the mousemat.

'What the fuck?'

Bryan responded with a shrug.

'I thought you didn't trust me as far as you could throw me.' Deaglán raised an eyebrow.

'I'm still not a hundred percent, but the journalist vouches for you so that must count for something.'

'And you trust her?'

'I guess.'

'I knew there was something going on between the two of you.'

'What?! No, no no no there isn't.'

'Relax, Bryan, I'm busting your balls.' He blinked behind the lenses of his glasses. 'What product have you got?'

'A line on a lot.'

'How much is a lot?'

'Just, a lot. I don't know the street value but that much H was worth a few bucks before I got locked up.'

'Wait, H? H like Heroin?'

Bryan thought it would have been obvious. Nonetheless he nodded his head. Deaglán's face shifted. 'Can't help you, I don't think.'

'Why not?' That was a bit abrupt, Bryan thought.

'I don't do heroin. It's not my thing.'

Bryan looked at him sceptically. Deaglán shrugged.

'I do cocaine. Tried H once, never felt so bad in my life. Won't touch it now. Cocaine gives me a buzz, ya know? Helps me to focus, sets me on a knife edge.'

'So you *DO* still do practise now?'

Deaglán sighed. 'Shit. Got me.'

He moved over to the desk, produced a keyboard from a drawer in it, and plugged it in. For a moment he said nothing, focussing instead on finishing plugging the components into the computer. Bryan could see the cogs turning in his head, multiple conflicting ideas doing battle to decide on whether he was going to help him. After a long minute of thought, in which Bryan had put his hands in his pockets and was staring over Deaglán's shoulder, he finally looked back.

'I don't know. It's a slippery slope. One that could end in a huge pile of shit.'

'Yes, but one that could end in a huge pile of money, too. What was it you wanted? Half a million? I don't think there's quite that much here but there might not be far off.' The prospect of that much money clearly hit the right notes, because the look of greed that swept across Deaglán's face was matched only by the expectation on Bryan's own.

'I might know some people.'

'Yeah? Tell me about them.'

'Like I said, I've only done H once. And I fucking hated it. Some folks say that the logical steps are weed, to cocaine, to heroin. I tried it and regretted it like nothing else before. But two of my friends - who aren't my friends anymore, so that'll be fun to get back in touch - made the logical steps. I fell out with them when I wasn't hitting the same stuff as them. But I never deleted their numbers. I might be able to get in touch. I might be able to get them to buy off you. But it's only a might.'

'Names. Ages. Can you trust them?'

'Not explicitly. Like I said, I fell out of favour with them somewhat when we didn't follow the same paths. Names are John and Rob. Early thirties now.'

Bryan scratched at his chin.

'Hey, you approached me in this one.' Deaglán held his hands up in a shrug. 'It's up to you, but I can call them and see what they say. I can't guarantee it'll be perfect but by the sounds of things, you can't afford to be picky.'

The problem was, he was right.

'Do it.' Bryan confirmed.

'Alright, but it'll take a while.' Deaglán had plugged a desk phone in, and was syncing it up to his mobile. 'I'll give you a call if they're interested.'

'Excellent. When you call, say nothing about the details, in case our phones are being tracked. Just say yay or nay.'

'Yay or nay.'

'Exactly. We will sort out the time and location, all they need to do is turn up with the money.'

And with that, Bryan bid him farewell, wishing in his head that for once something could go without a hitch.

The next day, Bryan and Phil met to discuss the finer details of the deal. Phil turned up with a partner, a man whose face Bryan did not immediately recognise. Tall and powerfully built, his rough features equalled his voice. He and Phil were chatting as they approached, the realisation dawning on Bryan as the two men approached him. Bryan couldn't remember his name, though.

'You remember Tamzen, right Bryan?' Phil said, a look of expectation on his face.

'I do now,' Bryan said, holding a hand out for a shake. Tamzen accepted it, still not talking. 'How have you been?'

'Like shit. Had the cops all over me for weeks. Had to flee and lay low to get the bastards off my back.' Tamzen replied. Bryan found it crazy that a human could sound so much like a rotating saw.

Tamzen had been the only other survivor of the prison break. Bryan had barely said a word to him at the time: he had said something about some work and then said goodbye to Phil. Bryan assumed that said work was delayed or entirely forgotten about due to him having to lie low. It was only now that Bryan could get a solid look at him. Younger than Phil and he, but not by much, he was physically imposing, though it was perhaps due to an abundance of tattoos lacing each arm and a roughness around his eyes and knuckles that suggested a lot of fighting in the past. He had been perfectly capable at wielding automatic weaponry at the prison break and knew his way around a flashbang too. Professional, then. Bryan hoped so. Phil seemed to

240

know him, but the acquaintance must have been made during Bryan's imprisonment.

They were in a bar. Neutral ground to all of them save Phil. He had claimed to have visited the place during Bryan's imprisonment, though based on the decor it seemed fairly certain that he was lying. Phil was a gruff old traditionalist when it came to bars. Shitty wallpaper on the top half, a thick wooden border across the centre of the walls and flimsy wood panelling on the bottom half was about where Phil liked to haunt. This one was actually very contemporary by comparison to a pub like The Forester. It seemed, though, that the decoration was a recent addition, and a banner above the bar advertising the place as 'Brand New!' probably meant that Phil had been here before the redecoration. They were gathered around a standing table, the chairs that had been there pushed unceremoniously to one side. Bryan had, in the many times he had been out drinking before his imprisonment, been a typical barfly, preferring to stand and listen to the idle goings on of the other patrons more than contribute to the conversation himself. He and Phil stood opposite each other, the three beer mats under their drinks not stopping spillage onto the painted black wood of the table. Bryan had ordered a soft drink, as had Phil. It was the early morning, after all. That little fact seemed to mean absolutely nothing to Tamzen, who had gone straight for the hard stuff. A single ice cube was now melting in his empty tumbler. Bryan had watched him tip back the vodka with a feeling of nausea in his stomach, wondering just what the hell had gone wrong in Tamzen's past to make him drink it without a mixer.

'And you managed it? Escaping the cops, I mean.' He asked, shifting his gaze from the melting cube to the man who had stranded it there.
'Easily. The cops 'round here are sticklers for jurisdiction. Leave town and then you have to deal with an entirely different force that knows jack shit about you.'
'Well, that's good to know. Heat gets too much and I can just leave with no problems.'

Tamzen laughed, a raucous, grating sound like sandpaper. 'I knew it was no waste of time to break you out of prison.'

'Well, I'm glad you did. I suppose I should thank you.'

'No need.' Tamzen shook his head slightly. 'It was a favour to Phil.'

Bryan looked at Phil. He gave him a look that said 'I have no idea what he's talking about'. Bryan could almost hear him say it.

'A favour?'

'Yes.' Bryan could tell from Tamzen's demeanour that he wasn't going to expand upon it.

'So where did you go?' Bryan asked, trying to get a little more information from him in a different manner.

'Here and there. To be honest, the best way to get the cops off your back is to not stop running. Trust that they'll eventually find something worse than you to try and take down.'

'And how did they find you?'

'Technically, they didn't. One of the prison workers reported their car stolen a few days after the break. The same car I drove off in after you drove us to the garage. It had completely slipped my mind that I should get rid of it. Weirdly though it had also escaped the minds of the cops to try and track it down. It wasn't until that dumbass reported the damn thing stolen that cops put two and two together.'

'So what, they followed you?'

'Have you ever been going about your business and noticed the same car is parked around near where you are?' Bryan wasn't immediately clued in to what he was saying. He continued nonetheless. 'Just sat there, nearby but not so near as to draw attention.'

'An unmarked police car.' Phil said.

'Exactly. They'd got off their asses and were tailing me but didn't make an immediate move because they were probably hoping I would lead them to the others on the breakout. After I'd seen the same car parked around with the same people in it, I made plans to steal away into the night.'

'Well, it looks like it worked.'

'Oh, yeah. No problem. Not exactly new to the game.'

'So then for the last few weeks you've been...' Tamzen cut him off, moving focus from himself back onto Bryan.

'And for the last few weeks you've been very busy! Nice work on the printing press, by the way, very clever.'

Bryan looked at Phil, lightning in his eyes. 'Is there anyone in this fucking city that thinks the press is legit?' Phil could only respond with laughter.

'Only Robin, by the looks of things. It must be obvious that the place is bent as a nine bob note.'

'But it *isn't*.' Bryan tried to assure them, but mostly himself. Tamzen was looking with confusion at Phil, clearly unfamiliar with the expression. 'Mostly.'

'Yeah, right. It is as legit as you make it.' Tamzen said, managing to ascertain the general idea. 'And now Phil tells me there is work to be done? He said there is a job opportunity that will do us all very nicely.'

Phil's eagerness was mildly concerning. There wasn't actually a job to speak of at all. Deaglán had merely said he would try to get in touch with his former associates, and had been fairly clear that it was unlikely anything would actually come of it. Instead, it was Bryan who had hoped there would be a deal at the end of it all. He felt he needed to clarify things with Tamzen, to avoid any possible confusion, or indeed and negative consequences should he feel like he was being messed around. Bryan wasn't exactly intimidated by him, there were very few people in the world who could actually achieve that, but he had been around enough brick shithouses in this line of work to know that pissing them off needlessly was a very bad idea. He shifted his gaze from Phil, before reaching into his wallet and withdrawing enough for a round of drinks.

'Do you mind getting them? I need to have a word with laughing boy here.'

Tamzen slapped a hand onto the notes, sliding them towards his edge of the table with a soft squeak. 'No problem at all. The same?' He couldn't hide his displeasure at buying soft drinks. The remaining two men nodded.

As he slid off to chat to the barmaid, Bryan leant forward, lowering his voice to a whisper. 'So you want to tell me what the hell you were doing inviting him here when there isn't even a concrete job yet?'

'You made it seem like it was set in stone!' Phil's voice was a stage whisper at best.

'No I didn't! I made specifically clear it was *not* set in stone.' Bryan wasn't lying.

'The words you used were *'definitely gonna try'.'*

'Yeah, exactly! In what world does that mean bring all and sundry to be hired muscle?'

'Tamzen isn't hired muscle.' Phil looked dejected. 'You know he's part of the reason you're here in this pub right now, don't you?'

Bryan could only respond to this with a low noise in his throat, somewhere between a grunt and a snort. In his head he was prepared to say some nonsense about not actually asking to be broken out, and that it wasn't his problem who Phil chose. He decided not to bother, because he knew deep down it would sound ridiculous. Instead, he looked across at Tamzen, whose back was to both of them. He was chatting to the barmaid with a tone treading a very fine line between forcefully confident and downright creepy. Phil tried to smile after him, but found himself wanting. Instead, he simply looked back at Bryan with a grimace.

'Yeah, he's rough as arsehole, but he's dependable and gets shit done.'

At that moment Bryan's phone rattled in his pocket. He removed it faster than light and glanced at the screen. A single message, containing a single word.

'YAY.'

Bryan's exhale was not only audible but tangible. Phil sipped the final dregs of his lemonade.

'You know, you're the luckiest bastard I think I've ever met.' Bryan said to him.

'Moi?' Phil placed a hand on his chest in a dramatic fashion, fanning his eyelashes. 'Does that mean we're in business?'

'It sure does. I hope that Tamzen is up for it.'

'Thanks darling.' Tamzen said. Yes, creepy was the right adjective. It was the way his head bobbed down and then back up again, obviously checking the barmaid out. She gave him a false look like he was a valued customer, apparently used to his sort. Tamzen returned with the drinks, holding all three in his hands. He placed them onto the table with a loud clink, before withdrawing his own tumbler and leaving the others where they were. Bryan and Phil reached out for their drinks.

'So what are we talking about?' Tamzen asked. There was no change, even though Bryan had given him more money than would be necessary. A final uneasy look passed between the other two, before Bryan spoke. He thought it best to be straight down the middle.

'We've just got the nod on our job, if you're interested.'

'That depends on what it is. Phil tells me it's concerning product.'

'He's right, and like you said earlier it will be profitable for all of us.'

'Buying or selling?'

'Selling.'

Tamzen snorted with laughter, before scratching at his chin ceremoniously. 'I can't help but think that the reason you got imprisoned was because of a deal similar to this.'

Bryan had considered that. He'd considered it a lot. But throughout his imprisonment he'd come to the conclusion that the reason that everything went so pear-shaped ten years ago was because the job was set up by Tony. Carson wanted to usurp Bryan and had put together the job with that express intention in mind. He had likely not cared about the money or drugs, simply seeing them as a pleasant side effect. This time, however, things were different. Bryan was organising the deal himself, with people he knew and trusted.

Mostly.

Shit.

'Not this time,' was what he decided on saying. 'Things are different now.'

'You've had ten years to refine your practises, huh?' Tamzen was looking into the bottom of his glass.

'Not exactly.'

'Give me details.' Tamzen said, finishing his second large vodka of the day.

'We choose the time and place. So, we choose somewhere we know and we check the place out before. We wait for them to arrive and make sure there's no funny business before showing ourselves. We do the deal, and then we leave. We get the money, they get the product. Easy.'

'Do you know the buyers?' Tamzen asked. He had lowered his voice to avoid the suspicion of the bar staff.

'Not exactly. I know one of them. He isn't technically a buyer, but he knows the buyers.'

Nothing in that sentence made a whole lot of sense at face value.

'Riiiight.' Tamzen said, not looking convinced. 'So there's three buyers?'

'No. There's two buyers. And a guy who works at the press used to be a user and so he's the one who put us in contact. He'll be there to oversee the thing. So it's more like three against two.'

'Against? You make it sound like a fight.'

'You know what I mean. We'll have numbers.'

'Even though numbers mean fuck all against assault rifles.' Phil interjected.

'Shut up.'

'And how much do you trust this buyer than isn't a buyer?'

'Well enough.'

'I think I get it. And where were you thinking about doing the deal?' Tamzen asked.

'Well, I've got an idea. We should probably go check it out before the deal.'

'That's a good idea.' Tamzen drummed on the table with his fingers, nudging his empty glass back and forth with his fingertips.

'You won't need another one of those. We'll go now.'

'I *always* need another one of those.'

Tamzen turned to leave as Bryan and Phil drained their own glasses. Bryan could share Tamzen's enthusiasm to leave to a certain extent, though he must admit that he was asking all the right questions. All the right questions that Bryan didn't seem to have many answers to. What if Deaglán didn't show up? What if he showed up with more than just his two acquaintances? And - a slightly less important one, but still flaring in his mind - what was going to happen at the press whilst the deal was under way?

It was decided that Phil would not attend the deal. He had protested and cried blue murder at the mere mention of it, but Bryan had managed, sort of, to talk him around. He was needed elsewhere. Specifically, someone needed to help the journalist with the shipping that she'd spoken about, and with Bryan and Deaglán both occupied elsewhere, that only left Phil. There were other reasons that Bryan had not exactly been forthcoming with: he thought that there was little point in putting all of them in danger unnecessarily, and taking that with the fact that the buyers had been given a description of Bryan, it would look suspicious if more than just he and Deaglán were to turn up. They had not said anything to Deaglán about Tamzen, another part of Bryan's plan to ensure everything went as smoothly as possible. He thought that the buyers would be even *less* likely to show if they knew about Tamzen. The hired muscle description from their discreet conversation at the bar was right enough; Tamzen looked physically daunting enough to deter anyone from wanting to conduct business.

Bryan had other plans for Tamzen, though. He already knew he was an excellent shot, so planned to make the most out of his talents. Phil, on the other hand, had chewed Bryan's ear off with his complaints about not attending, but had eventually relented. The final nail was Bryan explaining about how an alibi was good for any of them, and that they would certainly be murdered by the journalist for not helping with the shipping even if they were to survive any funny business at the deal.

All things considered, Bryan would rather have been murdered by gunfire.

CHAPTER NINETEEN: PLAYBACK

'This is a shit place for a drug deal.'

Tamzen's face betrayed his opinions long before he opened his mouth. Now he stood, looking at Bryan with accusatory eyes, his brow furrowed to accommodate. The funny thing was that Bryan couldn't have disagreed more. A point he made clear, resulting in a head shake and wide-armed gesture around the place. The eyes did not leave him.

Throughout the years, the economy had clearly not been kind to Sovereign City. Sure, in the upmarket parts of town it was clean and desirable, but in the slums it was found wanting. Much of the money that should have been spent on maintenance was flitted away elsewhere, and many of the promises to keep the city looking ship-shape by the politicians were largely overlooked or forgotten entirely. The alleyway in which they were standing was a testament to this, evidence that the darker corners of the city were easily neglected. What should have been a perfectly functional passage between buildings was instead a decayed wreck, populated by cracked walls and the fragments of tiles long dislodged from roofs. In size long and thin, in shape a rough, backwards L surrounded by tall buildings. Built behind a series of warehouses away from any main streets, Bryan had chosen it because he had used it before, though not for anything of this nature. He had remembered the location with a strange feeling of familiarity and nostalgia. Well, he thought, as nostalgic as one can get over a damp backstreet.

He stood now with Tamzen at the point where the alleyway turned, a near ninety degree angle forming the corner of the L shape. Their car was parked at the opening some metres away, where Bryan had reversed in to make their exit easier. Ahead of them, a cobbled ground tarnished by years of neglect, populated by abandoned boxes and rusting drains. Perhaps the saddest part of the alleway was a car, long since abandoned. It sat perpendicular to the wall, its wheels long since stolen.

'You're talking nonsense. It's perfect.' Bryan countered.

'Sight lines are too long, and you can't see what's coming around that corner.'

'Not at all. We stand here.' Bryan pointed at the ground where they were standing. 'We get a look down the main drag and can see that way too.' He then gestured back towards where their car was parked, forming a right angle with his arms. 'Easy access and can be used to make a quick getaway if needs be.'

'Which it shouldn't be.'

'Well, no, obviously. But it's good to know your options.'

'And what about these doorways and porches?' Tamzen pointed over to the left hand side of the main drag, where a warehouse of darkened brick presented a shadowed doorway. Not exactly large or dark enough to conceal a person, it was nonetheless something to complain about. It almost seemed to Bryan that Tamzen was looking for an excuse not to do the deal, attested to by the large amount of questions he was asking. Questions that seemed to have obvious answers. It was obvious that the door at which he was pointing was not large enough to conceal someone; it was obvious that if they stood on the corner sightlines wouldn't be an issue; and it was obvious that there would be a car positioned for a quick getaway.

It was obvious to Bryan, at least.

'If you're looking for a reason to bail, then the fact that the buyers are likely to be armed will suffice.'

'I'm not. At all.' Tamzen said, his eyes back to Bryan's own. 'I know there's money in this deal, but I'm not sure this is the place to do it. That's all.'

If his voice wasn't so gravelly and his eyes so piercing, Bryan could have mistaken it for genuine concern.

'Trust me. My contact doesn't know the place. He's the sort to spend all his time fiddling with computers and looking at smut on the internet. Scared to death of the real world. The whole deal will be on our terms.'

'That's funny, because I could have sworn that ten years ago, *that* deal was on your terms and look at what happened.'

Bryan wheeled to face him. He felt that the jab was uncalled for, and it sent a shot of anger through him. His brain searched for an appropriate response, but he managed to subdue the urge to tell Tamzen to piss off long enough to formulate a reply that dodged the issue entirely.

'Like I said, there will be three of us and two of them. If anything goes wrong, then we can quickly handle the situation and deal with it as it comes. Worst case, two dead scumbags get found by the cops and we escape with both the drugs and the money.'

Tamzen thought for a moment. Then he gestured again, though this time it was upwards.

'And what about these rooftops? Seems like a hell of a place for an ambush. What if they've sold us out already? What if they're just waiting to pounce on us?'

'Like I said, my contact is solid. He's heard hide nor hair of the buyers for years, said that they've likely spent the time getting high and slowly rotting.'

'Or they've been working for the cops.'

'Doubtful. If my contact is anything to relate to, at least.'

'Fine. I'm trusting you on this one.'

'I know, and I appreciate that you've agreed to help out. And trust me, the memory of my last deal is forever seared into my mind. There's no way I'm gonna put myself in a situation where I could get shot again. I honestly think I'd rather die than go through all that shit again.'

'Us.'

'I'm sorry?'

'You're not gonna put *us* in a situation where we could get shot.' Tamzen said flatly. Bryan responded with an apologetic nod. He hadn't meant to sound selfish.

'Yeah. You're both more useful to me alive, anyway. The deal ten years ago was organised by Tony. Didn't think anything of it.'

This much was true. The idea that anyone, least of all Tony, would dare to go against him had never even crossed his mind. It was an arrogance that had cost him dearly, and now there was no way he was going to let it happen again. Ten years ago, he had been armed with a pistol mostly for decoration and a suit to look presentable. This time, he was going to be much more prepared. All three of them would be armed and armoured with the best that they could get. He would choose the time and place to suit him, and he had dependable men by his side.

Explaining all this seemed to assuage any final issues that Tamzen had, and the last thing he asked was for a more detailed plan of exactly what was going to happen. Of course, Bryan couldn't prepare for all eventualities, but he had a solid enough gameplan to account for a great many of them. Deaglán didn't know about Tamzen, which for now was Bryan's greatest advantage. Therefore, he wanted Tamzen to remain anonymous, and only make himself known if he desperately needed to. Of course, it was entirely possible that he wouldn't be needed at all, and that Bryan would then have to pay Tamzen for doing absolutely nothing, but that was a risk he was willing to take.

The final thing they needed to do was get their supplies from Dempsey. When he had said the name, Tamzen's face had shone. They had apparently done business previously, and Tamzen was quick to explain that he once bought an old Russian assault rifle from him for twenty-five dollars. He had ended it by agreeing that despite being crazy, Dempsey was almost certainly the best to buy from for these jobs. They had agreed to visit him separately, and after dropping Tamzen off a few streets from his house, Bryan rang Deaglán from a payphone to explain where and when the deal would take place.

****

It was now the following day, mid-afternoon, with an overcast sky threatening to open the heavens upon the deal. Thus far no rain had come, and Bryan hoped that their enterprise would not be rained off. He was wearing a dark blue suit, with a black shirt, brown gloves and his usual hard-wearing shoes. He had shaved, and had arranged his hair to look as professional as possible. Normally, he wouldn't have put anywhere near as much effort into what he looked like, but he figured that impressions should be good, even if the buyers were junkies. Underneath his shirt, his ballistic vest lay, strapped to his chest atop a white t-shirt. Light despite its thickness, Dempsey had assured him that it would stop assault rifle rounds and leave him with no permanent damage. It would still hurt like hell and result in cracked ribs, but he would be alive. That was about all Bryan could ask for at this point. Deaglán had smartened up too, somewhat, though it was a far cry from Bryan's suit. Dark red chinos, canvas sneakers, and a business shirt with buttons done up to the top. He was wearing an unzipped parka, which went far to hide the holstered pistol that Bryan insisted he brought. Deaglán had not shaved, though had at least attempted to comb his hair, yet it seemed to have made it no less greasy.

They sat in the car, waiting for the scheduled time to arrive. Deaglán was wringing his hands absent-mindedly, and Bryan was alternating his view between the mirrors to make doubly sure they hadn't been followed.

'You ready?' He asked Deaglán.

'Aye. It's gonna be a little weird seeing the boys again.'

'Don't worry about it. I'll leave you to start things out with some pleasantries, but things are very quickly gonna turn to business. When that happens it'll be obvious, and I can take over. It's a fairly big alleyway, so keep your eyes on the rooftops and in the shadows. If you see anything, just cough twice like this...'

He demonstrated, a quick convulsion of the lungs that seemed like his next word had gotten caught in his throat. It was short, methodical and very obvious.

'...and I'll know something's up. I'll be doing the same. It's battlestations if that happens though, so prioritise getting out of there if so.'

'I gotcha.'

253

'Alright, we're a couple of minutes past the time we said. An old trick, depending on how jumpy the buyers seem it can give away a lot of their plans. Let's go and say hi, shall we?'

Both men stepped from the car. The sound of traffic around them was quiet, nothing that would otherwise seem out of the ordinary. From the boot of the car Bryan fetched a duffel bag, slinging it over his shoulder while Deaglán waited for him. He withdrew his pistol from its holster, checked the magazine before nodding that Deaglán should do the same. When both were convinced that they were locked and loaded, they made their way down the alleyway towards the meeting.

****

Across the city, Phil swung a foot out from his car as fiddled with the zip on his jacket. This bloody weather. Completely unpredictable: warm as summer one second, colder than a witch's tit the next. He pushed the plipper to lock the car as he walked towards the printing press. He was, truth be told, still a bit miffed about not being able to go to the deal. The Irish bloke was fine enough, but was altogether a bit too weedy for anything particularly tough. Phil was torn between whether he thought he had drawn the short straw for today. No risk, yes, but an afternoon helping Robin with menial work?

For the good of the enterprise, he told himself. It wouldn't take forever and they'd all be better for it when it was done, he told himself. He leaned a shoulder against the door to open it, his hands in his pockets since locking the car. He couldn't remember the exact details of the shipping issues they'd been having, just that he was to help Robin out as much as he can whilst also giving himself plausible deniability and a rock solid alibi about the drug deal. That way, if something went pear-shaped he wouldn't be caught in the inevitable shitshow. His mind had flashed backwards to when he was unable to help Bryan at the airport ten years previously. It had been an awful, gut-wrenching thing to live with, and he had never truly forgiven himself for it.

At least now that his best mate was out, he found it a little easier to sleep at night.

And now he had abandoned him to go and do paperwork. That thought caused a pause in Phil's step. His foot hovered above the ground for the barest second, before he continued on again.

She was waiting for him on the ground floor by the presses, fiddling with her phone whilst leaning on a spare desk. He was happily married, and H was the love of his life and nothing would ever change that, but Jesus Christ was Robin attractive. He thought that Bryan was mad for doing nothing about it, but was long past the point of trying to guide him in relation to his romantic life. There she stood in leggings, tall boots and a T-shirt, a thick beige coat with a furry hood slung over a chair nearby. She smiled at him as he approached, rubbing her hands as though they were not yet accustomed to the temperature of the building.

'Alright, Robin?' He asked her, smiling.

'The shit-bailer! Thanks for coming. I'm glad I could count on at least one of you to come and give me a had with some of this admin stuff.'

'Not a bother.' Phil replied. 'What needs doing?'

'I know Bryan's informed you about our shipping issues, but luckily enough I've managed to solve most of the issues. I just need one of you two to look over this paperwork I've thrown together, give me a countersignature, and then I can get to making the phone calls.'

'A countersignature? I thought we'd left it all in your capable hands?'

'A technicality, trust me. You aren't wrong, but for the books it needs to be done properly.'

She held out several sheets of paper, a light whistling noise as they whipped from the desk. Phil looked at them. Professionally done, headed paper featuring the updated brand and logo of the press stamped across the first page. It looked like a contract, outlining all the small details of the shipping, including times, dates and reasons. Phil flipped a few of the pages over, scanning the fine print quickly, before coming to the end where space for signatures lay. Robin had already signed it, but her signature was a lot less than intelligible. There was a capital R, that much was certain, but the rest of it trailed into a scribble too quickly to be read. To the right of it was a second dotted line for a second signature. There was no name, simply a vague description of 'Business Owner'. Phil smiled. Robin had given herself the title of 'Executive Manager.' He didn't think he knew exactly what that title meant.

'Look good?' Robin asked him.

'The three or four words that I can get my head around certainly do, yeah.' He flipped back to the first page and wagged the papers towards Robin. 'Executive Manager?'

'Well, I didn't think I could get away with *Person Who Does Everything Because the Real Owners are Career Criminals.*'

Phil glanced up at her, and they exchanged a look of amusement. 'Fairs. You got a pen?'

'Erm...' Robin looked around. 'I signed it at home earlier, but there should be one around here somewhere...' She looked around, eyes sweeping over the desk next to them. Opening the top drawer yielded nothing, but the bottom drawer did. She passed it across and Phil clicked it. As the nib drew close to the paper Robin made a slight movement with her arm, and Phil stopped.

'Don't sign your proper signature.' She told him.

'Looking at yours I was just gonna write a giant P and then do a scribble. Is that not alright?'

'I think it'll be fine, but you're a known associate of Bryan's, aren't you? So I thought you might not want your details thrown around. That's why there's no name on the paperwork.'

'I saw that. Wondering if it's not legally binding or whatever if there's no name.'

She shook her head. 'It's not a contract, it doesn't really matter. It's more like a company policy to go into a filing cabinet somewhere.'

'Right, I gotcha.' He thought for a moment about what his fake, scribbled signature should be. An amusing thought materialised that his real signature would probably be fine as it was, what with him not being a particularly well-written person. But, under scrutiny, it was obvious that his first and surname featured within it. Placing the paper onto the desk, he touched the nib of the pen to the dotted line and began to scribble a brand-new signature.

Nothing happened. No ink came from the end of the pen. He dabbed it against his tongue and tried a second time, then shook the pen and tried a third. Nothing.

'Looks like I'm not signing owt.' He said with a chuckle. 'Bloody pen's knackered.'

'Sorry.' Robin said, her eyes darting between the pen, paper and Phil's eyes. 'Go and have a look in Deaglán's office. He's got some in there. I need to make a phone call while you're doing that. Catch you shortly.'

As he moved off, Phil threw the empty pen like a dart towards a nearby cardboard box, missing it by a country mile.

All was quiet in Deaglán's office, evidence that he had rather quickly left to do the deal with Bryan and Tamzen. A cursory glance around the room brought Phil to the desk, where he opened the top drawer and began to rummage for a pen. Atop the desk, the phone's display screen blinked rapidly, showing a number of messages had been left on Deaglán's voicemail. The screen itself was a light blue, with white flashing text indicating at least seven voicemails had been left. Finding a pen that worked in the back corner of the top drawer, Phil grabbed a clean sheet of paper from nearby and scribbled in the corner, checking the ink in the pen. He thought it prudent to take a message for when Deaglán returned, hovering the pen above the page as he pressed the playback button.

'It's me. You've got the nod. You know what to do.'

Phil knew that voice. No amount of voicemail modulation could change it. A feeling of shock hit him as though flogged with it, and he stood paralysed for a moment as he pieced the jigsaw together. That was Tony. That voice was Tony's. On Deaglán's voicemail.

'Oh shit. Oh shit, shit, shit!' Phil said, voice a hoarse whisper. That message could only mean one thing: that Bryan and Tamzen were walking into a trap. He looked at the clock on the wall positioned away from the light and mocking him from the shadows. The deal was due to go down in mere minutes, and he had just learned that Deaglán worked for Tony!

And he didn't know where the deal was taking place. What had started out as shock had now changed from fear into abject terror. Phil knew where the rendezvous was, and was set to meet the three others there in an hour. But he didn't know where the deal itself was, apart from the vaguest description of 'an alleyway in the back end of town'. He had instinctively removed his car keys from his pocket, but now let them hang limply between his fingers. He couldn't go and rescue Bryan. He didn't know where he needed to go. He was going to lose his best friend again! He couldn't-

He slapped the keys onto the table and pulled out his phone. He couldn't physically save Bryan, but he could warn him. It would be close, sweet Jesus it would be close, but all he needed to do was get Bryan away from Deaglán so he could tell him to get the hell out. With trembling, shaking fingers he unlocked the phone on the third attempt. He found Bryan's number and hit the green phone.

And across the city, in an alleyway behind a coffee shop, the shattered fragments of a mobile phone sealed their owner's fate.

CHAPTER TWENTY: ORGANISED CHAOS

The buyers were waiting for them, hooded jackets of blue and green zipped up in case it rained. One, tall with a shaved head, elbowed his friend as Bryan and Deaglán approached. The other was spindly and had a full head of hair, bleached and almost as greasy as Deaglán's. They both sat on wooden crates, and their conversation died as they arose in preparation. Both men certainly looked like junkies; their gaunt, yellowed features suggesting many years of poor diet and substance abuse. The bald buyer introduced himself as Rob, which led Bryan to surmise that the other was John. Rob sported a tattoo of a spider web on his neck, which disappeared into his jacket. His lips were pale, his nose looked like it had been broken multiple times. He spoke, his accent distinctly Pennsylvanian.

'You're both late.'
Bryan eyed Deaglán to respond, who smiled warmly.
'It's good to see you too, Bobby.'
Rob snorted, folding his arms across his chest. John still hadn't spoken, though his eyes had not left Deaglán.
'Yeah, yeah. Look, we've got places to be, people to see. You got the shit or what?' As he spoke, his left hand scratched at his arm, pulling up the sleeves. Bryan could see track marks running down it. He nodded, swinging the duffel bag around.
'We wanna see first.'
'Course.' Bryan said. He took the bag from his shoulder and stepped towards the abandoned car, placing it onto the roof and sliding it across so Rob could take a look inside. Deaglán moved up to flank Bryan, standing to his right where the rear passenger door was.
'Is it there, Rob?' John asked. He looked skittish, as if he was desperate for a fix. Bryan could see that he had a rucksack on the crate next to him, which he assumed was full of money. The packages inside Bryan's own bag were still sealed shut, arranged neatly to maximise space and weight, and ensuring that no obvious bulges stuck out at inconvenient angles. Rob picked a package from inside the bag and held it between his unkempt

fingers. He lowered and raised it in minute amounts, as if testing the weight. Bryan kept a smile on his face as he did so, trying best to convey the emotion of *It's all there, honest.* Deaglán had fallen silent, looking at Rob's chewed fingernails as he brushed at the package. With a final lifting of the package to stare at it in the sunlight, Rob conceded, a smile passed across his thin lips before he placed the package back into the bag.

'Looks like we're in business.' He said, glancing at Deaglán as he spoke.

'Excellent.' Deaglán said, and as the two buyers stepped from the boxes, Bryan turned to zip the bag back up, and as his fingers traced the metal of the zip there was a quick sound of rustling leather before Deaglán aimed his pistol right between Bryan's eyes.

What the fuck are you doing? That was what Bryan wanted to ask. The question flashed in his mind in the split second that Deaglán was raising the pistol, but his instinct took over faster as his own hand went to his shoulder. A wave of nausea hit him like a punch in the gut, feelings of betrayal clashing with feelings that he should have seen this coming.

'Don't bother.' Deaglán said, his normally chilled Irish voice now the quality of steel. His brow furrowed, and he looked completely different. Gone was the bumbling, greasy IT man, replaced with a cold slab that lacked any tangible emotion. 'Put it on the ground. Slowly.'

Bryan finished removing his own pistol from its holster, allowing the trigger guard to rotate in his fingers so that the weight was on the bottom and the barrel now pointed harmlessly into the air. The safety was still on anyway, no amount of fast reflexes could have changed it. He felt betrayed, an icy feeling that sent shivers down his neck and knots into his stomach. His feet were like concrete, his mouth dry and his mind a mess. He too was scowling, unable to find words. What the hell was Deaglán doing? He must have known the dealers, after all. He had been played for a fool. He had gone along with what

Deaglán had said about losing contact with the buyers, about being unsure as to the deal, about everything. Bryan had lapped it up, so desperate to get rid of the product and get some money into his back pocket that he had danced to Deaglán's merry tune.

Bryan reached the floor, bending down to place his pistol on the ground, the barrel facing away from all four men. Deaglán kicked it away, and it slid into the corner of the alleyway, resting near a drainpipe. He turned to the buyers, gesturing with the pistol that they should move forward and grab the product.

That was when the first gunshot rang out.

Deaglán's head exploded in a shower of blood and chunks of viscera. His body hit the ground like a ragdoll, bouncing off the side of the abandoned car with such force that it left a dent in it. He made no sound; no shout for help or cry of anguish. The exit wound tore Deaglán's head almost clean in two, spraying gore across the roof of the car and pelting the buyers. The pistol that was in his hand flew a few inches into the air as he raised it to gesture at the buyers, falling back towards the earth in slow motion. The buyers and Bryan jumped backwards at the sight and sound, an involuntary noise of disgust and fear from each of the three men. Bryan's own reaction was to force a hand over his mouth and clamp his eyes shut, expecting the chunks of flesh to hit him in the face. None came. They had instead almost coated the car, and now time seemed to slow down as the gravity of the situation hit him.

The buyers had thrown themselves onto the floor, exhibiting a similar outburst of terror and revulsion at the sight of Deaglán's near-headless corpse. Behind the car they scrambled for their own weapons as Bryan's survival instinct kicked in. Battlestations. For the love of God, battlestations. He could not reach his own weapon as it had been kicked along the ground by Deaglán so instead he grabbed the Irishman's, peeling it from lifeless fingers as blood flecked the hand holding it. It was loaded, of that he could be sure. The safety was still on, but

Bryan paid it no attention as he was already running, back around the corner of the alleyway where himself and Deaglán had walked. He kept his head low as he crashed around the corner, slamming his back against the wall and aiming the pistol back in the direction of the carnage.

What the fuck had just happened? A round from a pistol hit the wall around the corner from his cover, showering pieces of mortar onto the ground. Bryan checked the gun quickly and flicked off the safety, holding it in both hands and swaying slightly. He still coughed as if choking and his heart was racing; adrenaline and blood pumping through his system causing an almost euphoric feeling of tension, fear and anger. His breathing was fast and shallow, a low thumping in his eardrums.

He knew that he was in deep shit. Not dead, but certainly in deep shit. He didn't have the drugs or the money, but moving to the corner he could see both bags - rucksack and duffel - in the same position, though the latter was splattered with deep red. The buyers had taken cover behind whatever was closest to them, and Bryan could see John behind the crate, both men mirrored in their current status. To the right, Bryan could see Deaglán's corpse, limbs splayed at horrendous angles, his chest, hands and feet the only evidence of which way he now faced. Gunfire erupted again from John, his arm sticking above the crate and firing six rapid shots towards where Bryan was sheltering. Bryan responded in kind, firing two shots towards him to suppress. He could not see Rob, which made him feel incredibly nervous. He surveyed the rooftops and windows above him, trying to work out from which direction the first shot had come.

Above the carnage of the now ruined deal, Tamzen surveyed the scene through the scope of a high-powered sniper rifle. He had seen Bryan and Deaglán arrive, the brief pleasantries and the bald buyer inspect a package. He had seen Deaglán aim his pistol at Bryan and raise it slightly above his head to gesture at his accomplices. That was when he knew he would get his one and only chance. He had been aiming at the buyers initially, scoped in at Baldie's heart in case anything went wrong. As Bryan had lowered his pistol to the ground Tamzen had mouthed a silent curse at the whole thing, before aiming squarely at Deaglán's head. He hadn't thought that Bryan would survive, but that he would instead have to kill the three buyers after the fact and make off with the drugs and money himself. But, he had a job to do. A job for which he was being paid, and so he had taken the shot when the opportunity had presented itself.

Lying down on the third floor of an abandoned office with floor-to-ceiling windows, Tamzen had arrived at the location a great deal earlier than the others. He had seen the buyers arrive next, long after his rifle was set up. His means of escape had been identified almost as soon as he had chosen the place in which to lie. He had a primary way to get out, and a secondary in case things went really wrong. Worse than that, and he had mused to himself the survival chances of jumping out of the window. The buyers had arrived three minutes early, emerging from a rusted, sorry excuse for a saloon car and walking down the alleyway. He had observed their faces, noting that no conversation took place between them from when they left the car to when Bryan and Deaglán arrived.

Tamzen pulled the bolt on his sniper, loading the next round into the chamber and sending a spent casing flying out of the side, where it clanged noisily against the leg of an office chair. Now he was scanning the crates for the two buyers, both of whom had done the wise thing and taken cover. He could see small movements from behind them, but was unable to line up a proper shot. Wattson was there, in the corner of his eye, looking up at the windows but seeming to be unaware of which one he was located at. He thought he had managed to catch the bald buyer as one of the crates wobbled, as though force was placed behind it.

He decided to test his theory.

Another gunshot cracked like thunder, followed by splintering wood. Bryan definitely saw where the shot came from that time, a tall window opened a sliver three floors up. The round tore past him as if in slow motion, and Bryan could see a trail of vapour following it as it left the barrel of the rifle. It smashed into one of the crates, tearing right through it and to the buyer hiding behind. John fell to the floor with a pained cry, his body registering shock more than pain. On the floor his head fell sideways out of cover, face screwed up and blood seeping from his mouth. As he squirmed, Bryan could see that the crate behind which he had been covering - no, *cowering* - had a gaping hole in it. The round had torn through John's stomach, gobbets of flesh tumbling from the gaping wound and seeping blood onto the hard ground. His hands opened and closed in arrhythmic motion, one attempting to hold his stomach wound and the other feebly tapping against the floor. Bryan expected another shot to finish him off, but there wasn't one. Instead, more shots came from further up the alleyway as Rob, the only remaining hostile, fired his pistol from within a secluded doorway.

Bryan swerved his body back behind the wall, looking up at the window and hoping that Tamzen would take the third shot and finish off Rob too. He waved a hand to grab Tamzen's attention, then gestured that Rob was on the same side as him, making a crescent shape with two fingers to show that he was behind cover. The shock of Deaglán's betrayal was now subsiding, replaced by determination to survive and no less adrenaline. Finally, he pointed at himself, before covering his eyes with his other hand to communicate that he couldn't see Rob. A response came from Tamzen as Bryan looked around the corner again in the form of a third shot, which slammed harmlessly into the wall thirty feet up the alleyway. Bryan thought that the shot had been made at Rob, but then could see the splintered wall and the crumbs of debris at the base. The shot had not hit its mark, but instead was intended as a guide to give Bryan eyes on the final buyer. He scooted from his cover, pistol in hand and finger hovering nanometres off the trigger, and ducked behind the car. Dodging Deaglán's body, Bryan

264

arrived at the rear quarter, glancing between smashed windows and rusted metal to see where Rob was hiding. Sure enough, there he was, planted securely behind a doorway with his own weapon.

Bryan thought he would only get a single shot at this. With very few rounds in his pistol, he didn't want to risk firing blindly anymore, but needed to close the gap somewhat to maximise his chances of hitting his target. The final buyer was shivering, a mixture of the cold weather and body shock, but was still in an awkward position. At this moment in time he had not seen Bryan, but was still hiding enough that a clear shot was not possible.

I need to get closer. Bryan thought, a gulp escaping him without meaning to. He slipped around the back end of the car, John's gurgles still not over. The wound would kill him, but it would take time. Bryan could see him, face glazed with tears, reduced to a soft mewling like a distressed animal. Long past the point of help, Bryan tried not to think about how close he had come to sharing his fate. He was still scared, but between himself and Tamzen they had all the advantages they were going to get.

He reached the destroyed crate, seeing the devastation that the sniper round had wrought. Placing a gloved hand on top of it, he felt a crackle as the wood splintered, sending his hand and forearm though it as it disintegrated. He swore aloud without meaning to, falling forward and nearly slamming his nose onto the concrete floor. Two more gunshots rang over his head, ricocheting off a drainpipe on the wall behind. A third shot tore through the crate and past his shoulder, clinking through a glass window behind him. He knew how incredibly lucky he was that the shot had missed, and knew that another, similarly placed shot would surely find its mark.

In the next instance, a impact like a mailed fist smashed into his stomach, knocking the wind from him and blackening his vision for a moment. In a lunge of desperation, he kicked out his feet, finding the side of the car, and pushed. Pain raking his stomach, eyes watering, his body slid out from the side of the crate and he levelled his pistol. He trained his sights on Rob's head, now exposed, and pulled the trigger. A single round left the barrel, smashing with wet force through Rob's upper lip. With an arc of blood and teeth, Rob's lifeless body slumped into the shadowed door.

Bryan lay for moment, wheezing and checking his stomach for damage. True to Dempsey's words, the round had not penetrated the ballistic vest covering his guts. His shirt was torn through, but the round had been stopped. Bryan could not see it, thinking that perhaps it had bounced away as he slid across the concrete.

Painfully, he arose from his side, relaxing his grip on the pistol to a single hand. His first step sent a spasm through his leg to his bruised stomach, and he swayed as he moved to check that Rob was dead, picking up the pistol and hurling it down the alleyway. Rob had died with a look of shock on his face, now a red mess without expression. As Bryan stepped back towards the abandoned car, Tamzen emerged from a nearby door, a thick bag slung over his back and a pistol in his hands.

'What the fuck happened?' Tamzen asked. He aimed down towards the exit of the alley. 'You okay?'

'I don't know! Yes. I think so, anyway.' Bryan shouted back at him, grunting with effort. 'Deaglán. Fucking Deaglán betrayed us all.'

'He got what was coming to him.'

'You blew his fucking head off!' Bryan was still shaken from it. 'Red chunks everywhere! What the hell were you thinking?! You could have hit *me*!'

'But I didn't.' Tamzen said, extra emphasis on the third word. 'I saved your damn life.'

Bryan's breaths were coming fast and loose, his heart still pounding and stomach aching like mad.

'We need to get a hold of this situation.' He said.

'Agreed. We can still be methodical about this. Everything got fucked up real bad but we can still do some stuff right.'

'Really fucking good idea to get the sniper, right?' Bryan said, a pained expression still obvious, with a nod towards the bag Tamzen was holding. Within it, the disassembled parts of the rifle.

'You're welcome. Only got three shots in with it, though.' Tamzen said, looking slightly deflated. 'I bought fifteen. And Dempsey doesn't do refunds. Did you pick up your casings?'

Tamzen held out a navy-gloved hand, in which three shell casings were placed. Bryan hadn't fired his own pistol, but retrieved it from its resting place near the drainpipe nonetheless and stuffed it back into its holster. He dropped Deaglán's pistol back on the ground near its former owner's body. Tamzen returned the shell casings to a pocket before looking towards the abandoned car.

The sound of police sirens broke the otherwise melancholic stillness of the alleyway. Bryan snapped his head up from the floor near the drainpipe and swore loudly. In the haze of gunfire he hadn't even considered that the locals would definitely have heard the gunfire and dialled 9-1-1. Immediately he was back on his feet, walking briskly over towards the abandoned car. From the other side of the alleyway, after checking Rob's body, Tamzen reached the crates. The sirens had grown steadily louder, and more consistent. Bryan dropped a hand onto the bloodstained duffel bag, and Tamzen did the same with the bag of money.

'Rendezvous?' Tamzen asked, a quickness to his words showing his desire to be very far away from this place.

'I'm not letting that money out of my sight.' Bryan said, glaring at Tamzen. 'I've worked too fucking hard to get it.'

'I will meet you there. We can't stand here and argue about it or the cops will come and take us both down. Bryan, you need to trust me.'

Sirens. Their volume was near-dizzying at this point, and Bryan felt a knot of resignation well up in his stomach, right next to the bruise.

'Fine.' He conceded. 'I'm trusting you on this one, Tamzen. You've got an hour to shake these bastards and get to the rendezvous or I'll hunt you down myself.'

'I'll be there, just try not to get killed in the meantime.'

Tamzen smiled, before scooping up the bag and running at full tilt along the length of the alleyway.

CHAPTER TWENTY-ONE: A START, AT LEAST

Bryan's hard-wearing shoes echoed as he ran down the alleyway towards his car, clapping against the concrete in unison with his muddled thoughts. The duffel bag slapped against his side in a similar fashion as he moved, strap straining and threatening to slide off. The pain in his stomach reverberated with each footfall, burning like flame. He reached the car, laying a hand on the roof as he fumbled with the keys. The lump in his throat felt like a basketball, and his eyes darted back and forth as opened the door.

The sirens were shrill and all-encompassing, drowning out all other sounds in Bryan's mind. He could no longer hear his own heartbeat in his ears, no longer hear his own footsteps clattering along. Even the pain felt like a mere shadow in the increasing noise.

Sirens. The sound was amplified, as was his fear. He needed to get the hell away from his place. No police car could be seen at this point, and as he tumbled into his car he threw the duffel bag and his gloves into the passenger seat. From a compartment under the dashboard, he pulled a tattered pair of sunglasses and flicked them on. This weather was absolutely not tailored for them, but they would at least hide his identity but for a moment. After a momentary pause for breath, wince of pain and glance in the rearview mirror, he put the car into gear and moved off.

The end of the street was where he glimpsed the first police car. A large, brutish thing with an ugly front grille, it tore past him as he reached the turning. As much a battering ram as it was a mode of transport, Bryan knew he would be hard-pressed to beat it in a drag race. The traffic lights were unkind, and as he stopped at the junction he looked into his rearview mirror. The sirens had not stopped, although he couldn't be sure if they were simply coming from within his own head. He saw two officers step from their car, one brandishing a pistol and the other a pump-action shotgun. They spoke into their radios - Bryan couldn't make out any more detail, only a hand moving towards a collar - before moving gingerly into the alleyway. The light turned green, and he pulled the car into a right turn. Luck, it seemed, was momentarily on his side, as the officers had otherwise paid him no attention as they advanced.

The right turn culminated in a police car slamming its anchors on behind him. The siren on this car changed pitch momentarily, more of a squeal than discernable noise, as if reacting to the shunting stop. Bryan's own car stopped, nearly in the centre of the road, approximately halfway through the turn before it was interrupted. His foot had slammed on the brakes instinctively, thinking that the police car was going to rear-end him. He turned in his seat, staring out of the back window. Through the lenses of his sunglasses, he could see two police officers in the car. One, a young woman in the passenger seat, was shouting at him noiselessly for nearly causing a crash. The other, an older and greying man, looked merely shocked. With a hand on the headrest of the passenger seat Bryan stared at them. His mouth was slightly open, and as he stared he saw the faces of the two officers change. They changed from anger and shock to dawning realisation. He saw the woman reach for a radio and begin to speak into it.

Oh, shit.

Bryan lurched the car forwards, moving back to stare out of the windscreen at breakneck speed. The car accelerated dramatically, the merest hiccough from wheelspin before he rocketed down the street. A moment later, the police car was on him, sirens screaming as the officers inside reported the make and number plate of the car he was driving. He tore past a bar on his left called The Traveller's Rest, moving east further towards the shopping district. In an effort to throw the pursuers off Bryan wrenched the steering wheel to the right after a short distance, now past the warehouses and with the alleyway firmly out of his mind.

This turn took Bryan into a street packed with terraced houses, awkwardly parked cars and uneven asphalt. Along each side of the road, Bryan could see that the owners of the cars paid no attention to the painted spaces, some of them parked across driveways and cut-throughs. The width of the street left much to be desired, and in some instances the distance between vehicles parked on either side was barely wide enough to accommodate Bryan's own. As he shot between two cars his passenger side wing mirror slammed inwards, a loud crunch of stressed metal accentuating it. Behind him, the police car was following at an incredibly short distance. Tentative glances in the rearview showed that the female officer had not stopped talking into her radio since the chase had begun. Her colleague had both hands on the wheel, the whiteness of his knuckles showing a worrying recklessness.

At the end of the street, after passing doors of greens, yellows and reds, a T-junction lay. Bryan turned left, and then an immediate second left onto a similar-looking street, the next one over. These houses were cut from the same cloth as the previous street, though more darkly lit and less inviting. The second sharp left turn had thrown the police chasing him off, and their car almost missed the turn, but the driver was made of stern stuff, and he threw the cruiser up onto the pavement to catch the corner by mere centimetres. The angle was far too wide upon driving up the street, however, and two vans creating a bottleneck proved their undoing. As Bryan's smaller car found space between them, the police cruiser came at them at an angle slightly too obtuse, and their front headlight caught the rear quarter of the right van. The impact sent the cruiser sprawling across the road where it impacted the second van, smashing up the front radiator and hurling the two officers forwards in their seats. From the rearview mirror, Bryan saw the male officer collide with the steering wheel, his nose surely snapping under the impact.

He had travelled in a horseshoe shape. The road he now drove on led him back to the main road he had travelled down initially.

Sure, he had thrown off one police car, but they damn sure had a description of the car and a number plate. It shouldn't be too difficult for them to put two and two together. As he approached the end of the road - which led to the original road where he had swerved left - a second police car shot past. Travelling west towards the alleyway, it tore past at such speed that Bryan barely had a chance to see the markings stamped on the car. The sirens had not abated, though he could hear that the cruiser behind him had switched its own off. The new police car did not slow, and as Bryan pulled his car into a right turn the road ahead lay dormant save for pedestrian traffic. It curved around past a petrol station, before a rectangular section of road presented itself. Bryan knew he was on the way to the rendezvous, but was unlikely to arrive there without further harassment from Sovereign City's finest. The radio, originally playing quietly to itself and largely ignored, was now playing a news bulletin, though no mention of the gunfire had yet surfaced.

Another T-junction lay ahead of him, the traffic lights changing with a speed that would only allow a few cars to go on their way at a time. A choice now for Bryan: turn right along slightly less busy streets but a longer overall journey, or move straight ahead past a recently-sold school towards a shopping district. The former option was safer, but longer; the latter more anonymous but likely to be busy. He chose the former, tailgating an SUV in a fashion that would have annoyed him greatly if the roles were reversed. The lights changed to red as his front wheels kissed the line, and he figured that explaining why he almost ran a red light would be the least of his problems should he get pulled over. A third car behind him had the same idea, following at a short distance in an attempt to get across the line before the lights turned to red. It seemed to Bryan that everyone who passed through those particular lights had the same mindset.

Behind him, two more police cruisers passed him in the opposite direction, either ignoring him or failing to make out his number plate. For once, he was glad to be part of traffic, as he would have put money on the car behind him acting as an excellent sight barrier.

At the end of this street lay a rare sight for Sovereign City - a roundabout. Indeed, it was the only one that Bryan could think of for some considerable distance, and perhaps in the entire city. Bryan hated it. He hated the fact that the bastard turning around it never seemed to indicate or look where they were going, and now his paranoia that he might get arrested or shot at from nowhere was making his anger rise. Rather than deal with the other road users, he almost threw the car around to the exit that brought him left. A blaring car horn was the reaction, and Bryan completely ignored it. He was close now, a fact that only made him more nervous. Passing bars on his left and right, long-deserted wrecks of places that were inhabited more by rot than customers, he came to the final turn that he could have to make. A church on the left-hand side, its blue sign suggesting an atmosphere of community and welcoming, loomed tall and proud as if judging him. The sirens had finally stopped. Thank God, they had stopped. Bryan's ears were no longer ringing from their incessant whining, and for the first time he could sit and think about what had just happened.

Fucking Deaglán, man.

He thumped a hand against the steering wheel, a subconscious reaction that did absolutely nothing to abate his mood. He needed to focus his thoughts, and that meant getting to the end of this street to where the rendezvous was. The road curved around to the right as Bryan passed through another set of traffic lights with ease. Designed to accommodate crossing pedestrians more than organise junctions, it was thankfully on green as he approached it. A large group of pedestrians had congregated on either side of the street, preparing to cross, though it seemed to Bryan that none of them were police. Little victories, he guessed.

The rendezvous was a car park, located behind a small cluster of houses at the end of the road. Originally intended to be a means to ease congestion within the shopping district, the park had faded into antiquity over the years, perhaps because of its awkward location away from any shop of import. That, or perhaps it was because the prices for parking were ridiculous. As a result, Bryan knew that nobody would disturb them; the only other inhabitant was a pickup truck with one wheel fitted with a parking clamp. That same truck had been there when they had cased out the rendezvous almost a week previously. Bryan had proposed that the amount of foresight that the police would need for it to be a planted vehicle was close to biblical. A glance inside had assuaged their concerns, as it looked completely abandoned, the only sign that other life had approached was an abundance of parking tickets fluttering in the afternoon breeze.

Today, though, the pickup truck was not alone in its triumphant stand against paying for parking. A second car was parked in there, seeming as if it had been driven in at some speed. As Bryan parked up properly, reversing into a space which would allow him to make a quick getaway if needed, the other car's door opened. From within the car stepped Phil, a look of thunderous ire on his otherwise jovial face. It set the character of his face plainly: *I am incredibly pissed off.*

'You stupid BASTARD!' Phil almost screamed as Bryan exited his car. He marched up to Bryan and threw a punch at him, not hard enough to cause significant damage but enough to make a point.
'What the fuck?' Bryan held up a hand to defend himself, as Phil looked like he would throw another. Bryan dropped the bag onto the floor, taking a stumbling step backwards.
'Your *PHONE.*' The voice was not a scream anymore, instead a heavy, throaty whisper said through gritted teeth.
'What about it?' Bryan said, though it was obvious from Phil's manner that he was in deep trouble with his friend. 'Did you try to get in touch with me?'

'Try to get in touch?! I tried to save your life!' Phil looked Bryan up and down, before noting that the duffel bag was the same, though smeared in one corner with what could only be blood. 'What happened? I found a message on Deaglán's answerphone from Tony. He was gonna kill you, and you didn't tell me where the bleeding meeting was taking place so I couldn't come and save you. So instead I've been sitting about like a twat for ages waiting to see if it was you or Deaglán that would come.'

'And it's me. Sorry to disappoint.'

Phil's mouth opened as if to speak, but instead his eyes narrowed. Bryan's hand had travelled instinctively to his bruised stomach, and he massaged it unconsciously with his fingers. Phil looked at him, then down at it.

'What's wrong?'

'It's nothing. I got hit.'

'You got hit?' Phil repeated. 'Are you okay?'

'Peachy. Hurts like a bitch.'

'Good.' Phil said flatly. 'Maybe it'll teach you to have your phone on.'

'Oh, yeah, a bullet wound for a forgotten phone. Perfect trade.' The words were slick with sarcasm.

'I should think you'll be getting used to them by now.'

'Well, mom always said I shouldn't get a tattoo.'

That got a chuckle. 'So Deaglán tried to pull a fast one on you then, I guess? I didn't misinterpret the very obvious message from His Lordship?'

'He did.' Bryan said, rubbing his shoulder where he had pushed himself across the floor previously. It was only now that he had slowed down that he realised how painful it was as well as his stomach. 'Bastard pulled a gun on me and was this close to blowing my head off.' He clicked his fingers as he spoke.

'And what stopped him? A supervillain monologue as you broke free from the torture device?' Phil's eyebrow was raised sceptically, as if wondering how Bryan would explain his escape and not sound clichéd.

'No. Tamzen blew his fucking head off. No frills, just splat.'

The second eyebrow shot up to meet the first in surprise. 'Crikey. Where is he now?'

'Well, that's the thing. I don't know.'

'Why not?'

'We needed to separate. The gunfire altered the cops and we thought splitting up was the best thing.'

'Ah, man, rookie mistake.' Phil said, getting a glare in response.

'No choice. I took the drugs, and he took the money. But he knows where to go. He'll be here.'

'Assuming he isn't dead.'

'Well I do apologise.' Bryan said, sarcasm creeping in once again. 'Show your usual lobotomised optimism, will you?'

This comment actually made Phil laugh. He made to wipe a tear from his eye, though one was not actually present. 'You know the best thing? If he bails on us, we're literally no better off than we were. Only thing we've got is a cleaning bill for that bloody holdall.'

'And a bruised spleen.'

Time dragged. The sun was in full retreat now, the shadows growing in length. Bryan and Phil had not said a great deal in the meantime, short of discussing the reason for Deaglán's betrayal and the deal in more explicit detail. Phil had ventured that Tony must have been paying him one hell of a lot of money, since the potential turnout from the deal was also high. Bryan had said that he didn't give a shit, and was glad the bastard was dead. And with that, the conversation had abated.

'He's not fucking coming.' Phil said, kicking at the dirt with hands in pockets.

'Don't.' Bryan warned him. The single word almost caught in his throat as he realised his friend was probably right. 'Just, don't.'

'I guess I'm just glad you're alive.' Phil said. 'Every cloud and all that.'

Bryan made a *pfft* noise. 'Alive and poor. How the fuck did I not see this coming? First Deaglán and now Tamzen. I thought you said he was trustworthy?'

'He was. I thought he was, anyway. He bailed you out of the prison, didn't he?'

Bryan didn't reply. He couldn't work out why Tamzen would go through all that trouble to then betray him later. At least in his betrayal Deaglán hadn't otherwise put himself in physical danger.

Aside from a high-powered sniper round to the head, that is.

'Unless he's dead.' Phil said grimly.

'No. No, can't be.' Bryan hadn't considered it. 'Tamzen's built like a truck, it'll take more than a few cops to take him down.'

'You say that like he isn't just human.'

'He isn't dead, alright?'

'If he is, we should prepare for it. He didn't have anything on him that would link him to us, which is a bonus.'

'I'm not gonna say it again, he *isn't* dead.'

A siren, beginning as a leaf-rustle whisper, grew in volume from the east. It killed the conversation dead. Both men swore aloud, moving with urgency back to their cars and preparing to make a quick getaway. As each second ticked agonisingly by, they expected to see flashes of red and blue reflecting off the windows of the nearby buildings. None appeared, and with a wave of relief followed shortly.

In the next moment, a car, its engine laboured and spluttering, tore around the corner and into the car park. In the low light Bryan and Phil couldn't see what it was, and reflexively grabbed their pistols to aim. The car's headlights were off, and as it came to a grinding halt Bryan could see that they were both shot out. Along its flanks, a stitching of bullet holes through the passenger door could be seen, terminating in a shot-out rear window. The car stalled as it came to a stop, the handbrake causing it to buck.

The driver door flew open, and from inside Tamzen emerged, a gritty and pained expression on his face. Beads of sweat dotted his brow, teeth bared and eyes alive with exertion. Bryan holstered his pistol, staring at Tamzen but saying nothing. Tamzen had been shot, that much he could say for certain. An ugly, bleeding wound in his shoulder was visible beneath torn fabric, Tamzen's arm hanging loosely at his side. Leaning back into the car, Tamzen produced the rucksack that had once belonged to the dealers.

Leaning it against his wounded shoulder, and with an expression that made him look close to passing out, he rummaged around inside with his good hand. Taking a stack of rolled-up bills from inside, he threw them into the footwell of his car. When he was sufficiently satisfied, he threw the rucksack onto the ground in front of Bryan.

His expression as he, Bryan and Phil stared at each other was not triumph, nor determination, pain or fear. It was simply one of conclusion, an image burned into his features that he was done with this job, unsure as to whether it was actually worth it. It evoked a feeling of never wanting to work with Phil or Bryan ever again.

'I've taken more for my arm. I'll see both of you fellas in hell.'

That was all Tamzen said. The last gravelly words from his mouth got a smile from all three men present, a nod of the head bringing their business to a close. Tamzen got back into the car with a final pained grunt before it started, and he drove out of the car park and into the waning sunlight.

Bryan and Phil looked at each other, and an eternal second passed between them. Phil was wearing a grin, Bryan looking likewise. Then they both began to laugh. They laughed as Bryan stepped forth to pick up the rucksack. It looked like whatever had been in the bag, Tamzen had taken well over half of it. They laughed at that, too. Finally, they laughed at the fact that what remained was a ridiculous amount of money. Bryan punched the air as Phil whooped in glee; the rucksack going into the boot of Phil's car to be split equally at a later date. A few moments of giddy appreciation passed, before Bryan moved to the boot of his car. Inside, a container of petrol sat patiently, and he removed the lid and splashed some of the sweet-smelling liquid around the boot and inside of the car.

'It looks like it all went swimmingly.' Phil said, a smile like a crescent moon across his weathered features.

'Well, we've certainly profited off it. Think about it. We stole the drugs from Tony, and then used them to get even more money from those dealers. Robbing one person to then rob a second. Feels almost poetic.'

'And we've got legit business ventures in the printing press. Everything is going tremendously well. I feel like we might be due a break.'

'Not likely. There's so much more that we can do.'

'That kind of big thinking will get you killed, you know. Aren't you satisfied yet?'

Bryan flicked a lighter and threw it into the car. The fire spread throughout, cleansing as much evidence as its voracious appetite would allow. As he stared into the flames, his eyes were alight with a fire of their own, burning with an ambition that would never be snuffed out.

'No. But it's a start, at least.'

EPILOGUE

The Carson Estate. Vestige Island, Sovereign City. 19:30pm.

Jason Strenger brushed at the sleeves of his coat, checked the buttons on his waistcoat and straightened his tie. He needed to make sure he looked like a million dollars. It always paid to look your best, especially given the day's events and what he now had to do.

His car was parked in the guest space. He didn't normally come here except under the direst of circumstances, though he was fairly certain that this qualified. It didn't mean he *wanted* to be here, of course. The mansion loomed above him, the near-set sun producing shadows that made the building look angry at him. No, not angry. Disappointed. Strenger supposed that he would never be able to escape people giving him those looks.

At the front door, a single guard stood. In his ill-fitting black suit and earpiece he looked more like the bouncer at one of Sovereign City's dingiest nightclubs. The guard looked at Strenger as though in the presence of an irritating younger sibling, but let him through when he explained his reason for being here.

And what a reason.

Inside, the mansion looked as it always did: ill taken care of. The years that it had been in its owner's possession had not been kind, though a decade of neglect had certainly not helped the place. Mr. Carson was a blunt and uncaring man, that much was easy to think, though it was never uttered aloud. You never did know exactly who was listening, and in this line of business it was not just the walls that had ears. It was joked that a word could not be uttered without Mr. Carson's ears burning in some way.

But allowing this once great mansion to fall to this level of disrepair? What on earth was he thinking? Did he really care so little for the place he called home?

Strenger thought about his own apartment, located across the city. A ninety minute commute in moderate traffic, he was glad that his visits to Vestige Isle were few and far between. He remembered with an irritated click of the mouth that he needed to place the recycling for collection when he got home. No doubt a takeaway box of some description would be added to it after he was finished here.

He paused outside Mr. Carson's office. There was nothing formal about it, no indication that any real business was conducted here. Instead, the door was darkened and chipped, the handle on the right door removed. Strenger didn't know why. He collected his thoughts, sucked air through his teeth and knocked on the door.

'What?' The single word barked at him from the other side, baring fangs.
'It's me, sir. Strenger.'
'Ah. Come in.'

Mr. Carson's office was huge. There was no other word for it. Rectangular in shape, Strenger was greeted by two enormous windows that ran from floor to ceiling, giving a beautiful view of the water in the distance. The view itself was slightly spoiled by the other houses on the island, but nothing that a perfect sunset could not forgive. Though Strenger didn't know it, in the far distance an apartment block stood, harbouring the one man that might one day see this whole operation in shambles.

To Strenger's right, Mr. Carson's desk sat, made of a beautiful black wood with golden feet and trim. It was one of the few things in the mansion that been worn away not through an uncaring master, but through consistent use. Mr. Carson sat in his enormous leather chair, glaring at Strenger's entrance. The glass lay empty next to him, as did the bottle of vodka in the nearby waste paper basket.

'Why are you here, Strenger? You don't normally grace us with your presence. Drink?'

Strenger could see that he wasn't the only other person in the room. To the left of the window, another guard sat in a small armchair, apparently adjusting the time on his watch. Strenger now had his back to him, arms behind his back as he did his best to look pleased to be there.

Even though that was not the case. Even though he was terrified.

He accepted the offer, and Mr. Carson produced a bottle from below the desk out of sight. A second glass followed suit, and soon Strenger had a drink, not because he was thirsty, but because he wanted something to toy with, and so that he didn't come across as ungrateful to his boss.

'It's about the deal. Something has happened, sir. I'm the one who has the job of telling you what.'
Mr. Carson's eyes darted from the notes on the desk, full attention suddenly on Strenger. It was at this moment that Strenger could see the wildness that dwelt within his boss. They were as those of a feral beast, tucked behind bags that suggested a good night's sleep had not been had for a tremendous amount of time. Strenger gulped, and immediately regretted it.
'Well, spit it out. I haven't got all day.'
'Well, sir, something went wrong. We've heard reports from our boys in the SCPD that the scene was bloody and violent. It seems like things went south for everyone.'

Mr. Carson's gaze was unwavering, pinning Strenger to the spot and making it impossible to move, no matter how much he wanted to. When he spoke, his voice was like sand across a dune.

'Tell me that Wattson is dead.'

'I... I can't, sir.'

'Why not, Strenger?'

'Because... Because...' Strenger couldn't finish the sentence. He couldn't think straight for Mr. Carson's eyes burning into his very soul. 'Gallagher is dead, sir.'

'Who?' Mr. Carson's voice still hadn't risen above very quiet.

'The Irish guy who was supposed to kill Wattson.'

'But Wattson himself is not dead.'

'That, err... That appears to be the case, sir.'

Mr. Carson's head finally lowered, and as his eyes left Strenger he felt like he was released from a vice. He felt like he could breathe again.

'Yes. That appears to be the case.' Strenger could see a smile on Mr. Carson's face, though mirth was a million miles away from his expression. He saw his boss open a drawer in the desk.

'The drugs are gone too, sir. It seems that Wattson got away with them.'

In a flash, Tony pulled a revolver from the desk and shot Strenger through the neck with it. Strenger hit the ground like a lead weight, unable to make a sound other than a gurgle in the throat. On the carpet, a crimson circle quickly formed around his neck, eyes fogging as his fingers grasped at the wound in his throat.

'Do you think I give a flying fuck about the drugs?!' Tony screamed at Strenger's body, which flailed momentarily in its death throes. He pointed a finger at the remaining guard, who had stood in fright at the gunshot. 'You. Get rid of him, and get someone to get the blood out of my carpet. If there's even a speck left in it, you'll be next.'

'Yes, boss.' The remaining guard said, before dragging the body out of the room. Tony could hear him shout some orders at other guards in the next room. He looked down at the revolver in his hand, a gun that had been unable to slake its thirst for ten years. The same weapon that had shot, but not killed, Wattson at the airport. Tony had realised that he should have killed Wattson there and then. He couldn't truthfully say why he had not done it, but it was a decision he had regretted deeply for over a decade.

He was not lying when he said he didn't care about the drugs. He had more money than he would ever be able to spend, and the police wouldn't dare touch him. He didn't need to worry about any of this being connected to him. What he needed, more than anything in this world, was to kill Wattson. Gallagher had failed him, a mere insignificant stutter. He didn't care about some grease-haired junkie anymore than he cared about the useless fucker he had just executed. He might have to reshuffle his plans slightly, but the end result would be the same.

He was going to kill Bryan Wattson. He just needed to find the right moment. He had been unsuccessful this time. But, as a smile crept across his sullen features, he had tracked Wattson down easily enough this time. And after all, he still had plenty of people working for him that could get him closer to killing his old friend.

It was simply a matter of choosing which one would cause Wattson the most amount of pain beforehand.

Printed in Great Britain
by Amazon